The Gra
Africar

ID0760337

The Granta Book of the African Short Story

Edited and with an introduction by
Helon Habila

GRANTA

Granta Publications, 12 Addison Avenue, London W11 4QR

First published in Great Britain by Granta Books 2011

A CIP catalogue record for this book
is available from the British Library.

1 3 5 7 9 10 8 6 4 2

ISBN 978 1 84708 247 3 (hardback)
ISBN 978 1 84708 413 2 (trade paperback)

Typeset by Avon DataSet Ltd, Bidford on Avon, Warwickshire

Printed and bound by ScandBook AB, Sweden

Contents

Introduction   Helon Habila   vii

The Arrangers of Marriage   Chimamanda Ngozi Adichie   1
Faeries of the Nile   Mansoura Ez-Eldin   18
Stickfighting Days   Olufemi Terry   31
Dancing to the Jazz Goblin and His Rhythm   Brian Chikwava   47

Promenade   Henrietta Rose-Innes   56
An Ex-mas Feast   Uwem Akpan   66
Ships in High Transit   Binyavanga Wainaina   92
The Moustached Man   Patrice Nganang   122
A Good Soldier   Maaza Mengiste   129
Préférence Nationale   Fatou Diome   142
Homecoming   Laila Lalami   149
Street of the House of Wonders   Rachida el-Charni   164
Bumsters   E. C. Osondu   169
Passion   Doreen Baingana   179
The Fugitive   Alain Mabanckou   200
Haywards Heath   Aminatta Forna   208
Missing Out   Leila Aboulela   215
Why Don't You Carve Other Animals   Yvonne Vera   232
The Centre of the World   George Makana Clark   236
Propaganda by Monuments   Ivan Vladislavić   252
Mme Zitta Mendès, a Last Image   Alaa Al Aswany   277
An Unexpected Death   Ungulani Ba Ka Khosa   283
The Homecoming   Milly Jafta   292
Oxford, Black Oxford   Dambudzo Marechera   295
You Can't Get Lost in Cape Town   Zoë Wicomb   301
Cages   Abdulrazak Gurnah   318
The Last Bordello   Manuel Rui   326
The Eyes of the Statue   Camara Laye   341
Slipper Satin   Alex La Guma   355

Contributors   362
Permissions   374

INTRODUCTION

I often attend lectures and conferences where some distinguished speaker will give a talk on African literature that, to my disappointment, if not surprise, begins and ends with *Things Fall Apart*, as if nothing has been written in Africa since 1958. In this collection, I want to bring things up to date and present my own generation, usually referred to as 'the third generation of African writers', who, until now, have rarely been anthologized. To put them in perspective, I have also selected a few influential and representative first- and second-generation writers to stand alongside their artistic descendants. My hope is to capture the range and complexity of African short fiction since independence, highlighting the dominant thematic and stylistic shifts over the decades.

A good description of the third generation is given by the literary critic Paul Zeleza in his essay 'Colonial Fictions: Memory and History in Yvonne Vera's Imagination':

Nowhere is the multidimensionality, multifocality, and multivocality of twentieth-century African literature more evident than in the postcolonial generation of writers born after 1960, whose creative flowering came in the 1980s and 1990s, the era of pervasive crisis for the postcolony and the triumph of postcolonial theory, both of which marked and mediated their work. This generation incorporated in their literary imaginations disdain for colonialism and distrust of nationalism that had animated earlier generations of writers who bemoaned the cultural agonies of colonialism and the aborted dreams of uhuru. The new generation had decidedly more cosmopolitan visions of the African condition, cultural production, and the subjectivities of gender, class, and sexuality.

Taking my cue from Zeleza's phrase 'distrust of nationalism', I call this generation of writers the 'post-nationalist' generation, whose inaugural sentiment can be traced back to Dambudzo Marechera's famous line 'If you are a writer for a specific nation or a specific race, then fuck you.'

My use of the term 'post-nationalist' is aspirational. I see this new generation as having the best potential to liberate itself from the often predictable, almost obligatory obsession of the African writer with the nation and with national politics, an obsession that at times has been beneficial to African writing, but more often has been restrictive and confining to the African writer's ambition. Ironically, many of the writers in this anthology are or can be post-nationalist not simply because of the reasons given by Zeleza, but also because they live and work outside their countries, mostly in the West.

This shift towards post-nationalist subject matter can be seen in recent African novels favouring the themes of travel and individual identity, like Brian Chikwava's *Harare North*, about Zimbabweans in London; Chika Unigwe's *On Black Sisters' Street*, about African prostitutes in Belgium; Dinaw Mengestu's *The Beautiful Things That Heaven Bears*, about Ethiopians in Washington, DC; E. C. Osondu's collection of stories, *Voice of America*, about Nigerians in America; Teju Cole's *Open City*, set in New York; Uwem Akpan's collection, *Say You Are One of Them*, set in different African cities; and so many more, I am sure, that I am not aware of. Perhaps it is this departure from the more obvious themes of African literature that has led some traditionally minded critics to accuse this generation of writers of not being 'ideological' enough, failing to see that this lack of ideology could be intentional and useful, an ideology in itself.

It's a sad but apparently undeniable fact that the short story has always taken second place to the novel in Africa. Some of the best African writers simply don't write short stories, which is why this anthology doesn't include some of my favourite writers: J. M. Coetzee, Wole Soyinka, Cheikh Hamidou Kane, Flora Nwapa, K. Sello Duiker, Zakes Mda, Damon Galgut, Tsitsi Dangarembga, Meja Mwangi, Boubacar Boris Diop, Chris Abani and many more. One of the best historical and critical studies of fiction in Africa covering the period from 1958 to 1970, Charles Larson's *The Emergence of African Fiction* (1971), has nothing to say about the short story. Post-colonial African writers, determined to create an alternative narrative to colonialist denigration of African culture and history, saw more possibilities with the novel than the short story. As the critic Simon Gikandi puts it in his book *Reading Chinua Achebe*, 'The novel may be the genre that is most alien to African cultures, but it is also the most amenable to representing the historical transformations and contradictions engendered by the colonial enterprise.'

This relegation of the short story to second place continued well past the immediate post-independence period. In the introduction to their excellent *The Heinemann Book of Contemporary African Short Stories* (1992), Chinua Achebe and C. L. Innes lament the sharp decline in short-story production in Africa, attributing it to the collapse of publishing companies on the African continent in the 1980s, companies like Heinemann, with its influential African Writers Series, and the disappearance of magazines like *Okike, Transition, Black Orpheus* and many more, where short stories usually make their debut before ending up in collections and anthologies. To this can be added the disappearance of a middle class in many African countries, a sector historically necessary for the survival of a short-story culture.

This appears to be the situation on the surface. On closer examination, one sees that the short story in Africa has always persisted, sometimes challenging the very assumption of its secondary status. While some magazines disappeared, others, like *Présence africaine* and Achebe's *African Commentary*, continued to publish short stories from outside the continent. Collections and anthologies also continued to be published, some of which have proved to be as enduring and as influential as any African novel; I'm thinking of, for instance, Achebe's *Girls at War*, Alex La Guma's *A Walk in the Night*, Taban Lo Liyong's *Fixions and Other Stories*, Bessie Head's *The Collector of Treasures*, Ama Ata Aidoo's *No Sweetness Here*, Ben Okri's *Stars of the New Curfew*, Can Themba's *The Will to Die*, Tayeb Salih's *The Wedding of Zein* and Nadine Gordimer's *Some Monday for Sure*.

Perhaps critics need to shoulder the blame: although short stories were being written, the critical establishment simply weren't paying them as much attention as they were to novels. Short stories were often seen as light and inconsequential. In his book *Tradition and Modernity in the African Short Story: an Introduction to a Literature in Search of Critics* (1991), which is the first book-length study of the African short story, F. Odun Balogun laments the lack of serious critical attention given to the short story, despite its widespread practice in Africa. He blames both the difficulty of publishing and 'the fact that the genre, as one observer says, is a "paradoxical form" patronized by both beginners and accomplished writers'.

Today, we are witnessing what has often been called a 'renaissance' in African literature. Writing and publishing on the continent have had their lulls, particularly in the late 1980s and much of the 1990s, but African writers have always written – it is often their only way of 'throwing' their voices into the knife-fight of their continent's socio-cultural discourse – and this tag of 'renaissance' is not at all accurate. I remember in Nigeria in the 1990s, during the darkest days of the dictatorship, when most publishing houses closed down, newspapers stepped in to fill the vacuum. The *Post Express* in particular launched a short-story and review series called Post Express Literary Series (PELS), edited by Nduka Otiono, from which grew the annual Liberty Merchant Bank Short Story Competition. PELS gave voice to numerous young writers, although not many of them managed to get any international notice because, at that time, Nigeria was cut off from the rest of the world by economic and political sanctions.

With the coming of the Internet to many parts of urban Africa in the late 1990s, a new avenue for publishing was discovered and the African short story finally began to get its long-overdue moment of recognition. The traditional publishing landscape, with its excessive restrictions, was suddenly superseded. The Internet is today doing what the newspapers and magazines did to the development of the short story in Europe and America at the start of the industrial age. It is also worth pointing out that the Internet, due to its own peculiar restrictions, seems actually to favour short stories over novels, thereby reversing the restrictions that traditional publishing had placed on African fiction.

Another factor that gave a boost to the short story in Africa, and forced critics to take it more seriously, is the Caine Prize for African Writing, which began in 2000. To demonstrate how influential it has been in the development of recent African fiction, almost half of the writers in this anthology have either been shortlisted for the Caine or have won it, from Leila Aboulela (2000) to the most recent winner, Olufemi Terry (2010).

Yet, despite its influential effect on recent African writing, the Caine Prize seems to have been founded on a common fallacy regarding the African short story. On its website, it advertised its focus 'on the short story, as reflecting the contemporary development of the African storytelling tradition'. This statement would seem to link the African short story to oral tradition in Africa and the folk tale in particular. Before you know it, the short story is declared a 'more distinctly African form'. Similarly, critics seek to find oral narrative devices in every African work of fiction.

I witnessed this rather reductionist view of African writers recently at a conference in Europe when I was invited to take part in a panel on oral literature. I had assumed that I and my fellow African writers would be asked about the influence, if any, of oral narrative devices in our writing, or to discuss the handling of it by earlier writers like Achebe and Ngugi. But no. We were simply put on stage in front of a few hundred Swedes and asked to discuss oral literature. We didn't. After a few false starts, the discussion finally found itself contemplating the literary and aesthetic values of rap music and slam poetry.

This leads to the question what exactly is the African short story? What makes a work particularly African? This is not a new query. Writers and critics have been asking exactly this since the emergence of African fiction, and I don't intend to repeat all the same arguments here. The important thing is this: we must never confuse the African short story with the folk tale. A folk tale is episodic; it often uses *deus ex machina* to extricate characters from sticky situations; it is didactic; and it mostly uses faeries and animal characters. Mastery of the folk tale doesn't necessarily make one a great short-story writer. And so most of the short stories in this collection are folkloric only in the sense that Kafka's man turning into a bug is folkloric; they use folkloric elements as Ursula Le Guin uses the archetypal myth of the scapegoat in her story 'The Ones Who Walk Away from Omelas'.

In his introduction to *The Picador Book of African Stories*, Stephen Gray quotes Congolese writer Emmanuel Dongala's description of the African short story, which I think best defines what we are working with here: 'It is indebted to the tradition of Chekhov and Maupassant, Mansfield and Hemingway; it is concentrated . . . ; its relationship to the expansive novel is that of poetry to prose; it is solely the creation of its individual author, written for experienced short-story readers, rather than any written reduction from orature.'

How can you gather together the stories of a continent that is larger than China, Europe and the United States put together? How can you 'anthologize' fifty-three countries, a billion people and over a thousand ethnic groups?

I could have organized this anthology by regions, scrupulously making sure each of the fifty-three countries, big or small, has at least one story. This is the usual logic behind the packaging of most anthologies of African writing – of, for instance, Stephen Gray's excellent *The Picador Book of African Stories* (2000); Chinua Achebe and C. L. Innes's groundbreaking *The Heinemann Book of Contemporary African Short Stories* (1992); Rob Spillman's *Gods and Soldiers* (2009); and Charles Larson's *Under African Skies* (1997). Some even have maps and diagrams explaining exactly where the stories originated, and where the originating countries are situated on the continent.

Another obvious way to arrange an anthology is by themes; Soyinka did it in *Poems of Black Africa* (1979). This plan – although I didn't use it here – appeals to me more than the geographical one because it turns the focus on the writing itself rather than the countries or regions of origin. It is instructive to note that even when anthologies are arranged by region, an unmistakable thematic pattern soon develops. Sometimes, but not always, themes are regionally determined. Achebe acknowledges this in his introduction to *The Heinemann Book* when he notes that most of the Southern African stories show 'a painful, inescapable bond to racism', while in the West African stories there's a total absence of that, an absence verging on 'complacency', and in North Africa Islam and women's place in the culture are often the dominant themes. But no region really has a monopoly on any particular theme; more often reading different writers side by side will simply show how similar we are as humans.

I eventually decided to order these stories generationally, starting with the youngest writer and ending with the oldest, the intention being to showcase the newest writing from the continent first, before moving back in time to show what came before that, as that is what these younger writers must have grown up reading.

While selecting the stories, I would sometimes write to the authors to see if they had a story they preferred to have in the anthology. I was curious to see what their choice would be and whether it would match my own. I wanted to make the selection as collaborative as possible, because I believe an anthology should also give an insight into the motives and inspirations of the writers. As an author, I am aware that often it is not my favourite story that is the readers' favourite, or the critics'. In a sense, then, this is a sort of writer's anthology of African short stories.

Alaa Al Aswany (Egypt) suggested 'Mme Zita Mendès, a Last Image', a beautiful story about childhood and romance and life's transience, a story that brings to life the old and fading expatriate community in Cairo; Leila Aboulela (Sudan/Egypt) at first suggested 'Something Old, Something New', but we finally settled on 'Missing Out'; Patrice Nganang (Cameroon) sent me the politically charged, twist-in-the-tale story of racism in pre-Second World War Germany; Mansoura Ez-Eldin (Egypt) is here with the strange and enchanting 'Faeries of the Nile'.

Regardless of the author's suggestion, before settling on a particular story, I would ask myself a simple question: ten years from now, would this story illuminate the preoccupations and concerns, literary and social, of the times in which it was written? The story of Africa, from independence to the present, is best told not in its history books and other officially constructed documents, but in its novels, short stories, poems and other artefacts.

Africa's strength is not, contrary to what most people like to think, in its homogeneity, but in its diversity of cultures and languages and religions and skin colours. It is a large place; it contains multitudes. There is so much here to celebrate, like the fall of apartheid in South Africa, the return of democracy to Nigeria and Egypt and many other African countries formerly under dictatorships, the end of the civil wars in Sierra Leone and Liberia. I hope this anthology will echo that celebratory mood, and also hint at what the future looks like. As long as people have freedom to think and discuss and travel and find fulfilment, and are not slaves to the nation and politicians, they will create art and put down their best thoughts and ideas in the form of stories.

Helon Habila

THE ARRANGERS OF MARRIAGE

Chimamanda Ngozi Adichie

My new husband carried the suitcase out of the taxi and led the way into the brownstone, up a flight of brooding stairs, down an airless hallway with frayed carpeting, and stopped at a door. The number 2B, unevenly fashioned from yellowish metal, was plastered on it.

'We're here,' he said. He had used the word 'house' when he told me about our home. I had imagined a smooth driveway snaking between cucumber-coloured lawns, a door leading into a hallway, walls with sedate paintings. A house like those of the white newlyweds in the American films that NTA showed on Saturday nights.

He turned on the light in the living room, where a beige couch sat alone in the middle, slanted, as though dropped there by accident. The room was hot; old, musty smells hung heavy in the air.

'I'll show you around,' he said.

The smaller bedroom had a bare mattress lodged in one corner. The bigger bedroom had a bed and chest of drawers, and a phone on the carpeted floor. Still, both rooms lacked a sense of space, as though the walls had become uncomfortable with each other, with so little between them.

'Now that you're here, we'll get more furniture. I didn't need that much when I was alone,' he said.

'OK,' I said. I felt light-headed. The ten-hour flight from Lagos to

New York and the interminable wait while the American customs officer raked through my suitcase had left me woozy, stuffed my head full of cotton wool. The officer had examined my foodstuffs as if they were spiders, her gloved fingers poking at the waterproof bags of ground *egusi* and dried *onugbu* leaves and *uziza* seeds, until she seized my *uziza* seeds. She feared I would grow them on American soil. It didn't matter that the seeds had been sun-dried for weeks and were as hard as a bicycle helmet.

'*Ike agwum*,' I said, placing my handbag down on the bedroom floor.

'Yes, I'm exhausted, too,' he said. 'We should get to bed.'

In the bed with sheets that felt soft, I curled up tight like Uncle Ike's fist when he is angry and hoped that no wifely duties would be required of me. I relaxed moments later when I heard my new husband's measured snoring. It started like a deep rumble in his throat, then ended on a high pitch, a sound like a lewd whistle. They did not warn you about things like this when they arranged your marriage. No mention of offensive snoring, no mention of houses that turned out to be furniture-challenged flats.

My husband woke me up by settling his heavy body on top of mine. His chest flattened my breasts.

'Good morning,' I said, opening sleep-crusted eyes. He grunted, a sound that might have been a response to my greeting or part of the ritual he was performing. He raised himself to pull my nightdress up above my waist.

'Wait—' I said, so that I could take the nightdress off, so it would not seem so hasty, but he had crushed his mouth down on mine. Another thing the arrangers of marriage failed to mention – mouths that told the story of sleep, that felt clammy like old chewing gum, that smelled like the rubbish dumps at Ogbete Market. His breathing rasped as he moved, as if his nostrils were too narrow for the air that had to be let out. When he finally stopped thrusting, he rested his entire weight on me, even the weight of his legs. I did not move until he climbed off me to go into the bathroom. I pulled my nightdress down, straightened it over my hips.

'Good morning, baby,' he said, coming back into the room. He handed me the phone. 'We have to call your uncle and aunt to tell them we arrived safely. Just for a few minutes: it costs almost a dollar a minute to Nigeria. Dial 011 and then 234 before the number.'

'*Ezi okwu?* All that?'

'Yes. International dialling code first and then Nigeria's country code.'

'Oh,' I said. I punched in the fourteen numbers. The stickiness between my legs itched.

The phone line crackled with static, reaching out across the Atlantic. I knew Uncle Ike and Aunty Ada would sound warm; they would ask what I had eaten, what the weather in America was like. But none of my responses would register; they would ask just to ask. Uncle Ike would probably smile into the phone, the same kind of smile that had loosened his face when he told me that the perfect husband had been found for me. The same smile I had last seen on him months before when the Super Eagles won the soccer gold medal at the Atlanta Olympics.

'A doctor in America,' he had said, beaming. 'What could be better? Ofodile's mother was looking for a wife for him; she was very concerned that he would marry an American. He hadn't been home in eleven years. I gave her a photo of you. I did not hear from her for a while and I thought they had found someone, but . . .' Uncle Ike let his voice trail away, let his beaming get wider.

'Yes, Uncle.'

'He will be home in early June,' Aunty Ada had said. 'You will have plenty of time to get to know each other before the wedding.'

'Yes, Aunty.'

'Plenty of time' was two weeks.

'What have we not done for you? We raise you as our own and then we find you an *ezigbo di*! A doctor in America! It is like we won a lottery for you!' Aunty Ada said. She had a few strands of hair growing on her chin and she tugged at one of them as she spoke.

I had thanked them both for everything – finding me a husband, taking me into their home, buying me a new pair of shoes every two years. It was the only way to avoid being called ungrateful. I did not remind them that I wanted to take the JAMB exam again and try for the university, that while going to secondary school I had sold more bread in Aunty Ada's bakery than all the other bakeries in Enugu sold, that the furniture and floors in the house shone because of me.

'Did you get through?' my new husband asked.

'It's engaged,' I said. I looked away so that he would not see the relief on my face.

'Busy. Americans say busy, not engaged,' he said. 'We'll try later. Let's have breakfast.'

For breakfast, he defrosted pancakes from a bright yellow bag. I watched what buttons he pressed on the white microwave, carefully memorizing them.

'Boil some water for tea,' he said.

'Is there some dried milk?' I asked, taking the kettle to the sink. Rust clung to the sides of the sink like peeling brown paint.

'Americans don't drink their tea with milk and sugar.'

'*Ezi okwu?* Don't you drink yours with milk and sugar?'

'No, I got used to the way things are done here a long time ago. You will too, baby.'

I sat before my limp pancakes – they were so much thinner than the chewy slabs I made at home – and bland tea, which I feared would not get past my throat. The doorbell rang and he got up. He walked with his hands swinging to his back; I had not really noticed that before; I had not had time to notice.

'I heard you come in last night.' The voice at the door was American; the words flowed fast, ran into each other. '*Supri-supri*', Aunty Ify called it, fast-fast. 'When you come back to visit, you will be speaking *supri-supri* like Americans,' she had said.

'Hi, Shirley. Thanks so much for keeping my mail,' he said.

'Not a problem at all. How did your wedding go? Is your wife here?'

'Yes, come and say hello.'

A woman with hair the colour of metal came into the living room. Her body was wrapped in a pink robe knotted at the waist. Judging from the lines that ran across her face, she could have been anything from six decades to eight decades old; I had not seen enough white people to correctly gauge their ages.

'I'm Shirley from 3A. Nice to meet you,' she said, shaking my hand. She had the nasal voice of someone battling a cold.

'You are welcome,' I said.

Shirley paused, as though surprised. 'Well, I'll let you get back to breakfast,' she said. 'I'll come down and visit with you when you've settled down.'

Shirley shuffled out. My new husband shut the door. One of the dining-table legs was shorter than the rest and so the table rocked, like a seesaw, when he leaned on it and said, 'You should say "Hi" to people here, not "You're welcome."'

'She's not my age mate.'

'It doesn't work that way here. Everybody says "Hi."'

'*O di mma*. OK.'

'I'm not called Ofodile here, by the way. I go by Dave,' he said, looking down at the pile of envelopes Shirley had given him. Many of them had lines of writing on the envelope itself, above the address, as though the sender had remembered to add something only after the envelope was sealed.

'Dave?' I knew he didn't have an English name. The invitation cards to our wedding had read, *Ofodile Emeka Udenwa and Chinaza Agatha Okafor*.

'The last name I use here is different too. Americans have a hard time with Udenwa, so I changed it.'

'What is it?' I was still trying to get used to Udenwa, a name I had known only a few weeks.

'It's Bell.'

'Bell!' I had heard about a Waturuocha who changed to Waturu in America, a Chikelugo who took the more American-friendly Chikel, but from Udenwa to Bell? 'That's not even close to Udenwa,' I said.

He got up. 'You don't understand how it works in this country. If you want to get anywhere, you have to be as mainstream as possible. If not, you will be left by the roadside. You have to use your English name here.'

'I never have; my English name is just something on my birth certificate. I've been Chinaza Okafor my whole life.'

'You'll get used to it, baby,' he said, reaching out to caress my cheek. 'You'll see.'

When he filled out a Social Security number application for me the next day, the name he entered in bold letters was AGATHA BELL.

Our neighbourhood was called Flatbush, my new husband told me, as we walked, hot and sweaty, to the bus stop, down a noisy street that smelled of fish left out too long before refrigeration. He wanted to show me how to do the grocery shopping and how to use the bus.

'Look around; don't lower your eyes like that. Look around. You get used to things faster that way,' he said.

I turned my head from side to side so he would see that I was following his advice. Dark restaurant windows promised the BEST CARIBBEAN AND AMERICAN FOOD in lopsided print; a car wash across the street advertised $3.50 washes on a chalkboard nestled among Coke cans and bits of paper. The pavement was chipped away at the edges, like something nibbled at by mice.

Inside the air-conditioned bus, he showed me where to pour in the coins, how to press the tape on the wall to signal my stop.

'This is not like Nigeria, where you shout out to the conductor,' he said, sneering, as though he was the one who had invented the superior American system.

Inside Key Food, we walked from aisle to aisle slowly. I was wary when he put a packet of beef in the cart. I wished I could touch the meat, to examine its redness, as I often did at Ogbete Market, where the butcher held up fresh-cut slabs buzzing with flies.

'Can we buy those biscuits?' I asked. The blue packets of Burton's Rich Tea were familiar; I did not want to eat biscuits, but I wanted something familiar in the cart.

'Cookies. Americans call them cookies,' he said.

I reached out for the biscuits (cookies).

'Get the store brand. They're cheaper, but still the same thing,' he said, pointing at a white packet.

'OK,' I said. I no longer wanted the biscuits, but I put the store brand in the cart and stared at the blue packet on the shelf, at the familiar grain-embossed Burton's logo, until we left the aisle.

'When I become an attending, we will stop buying store brands, but for now we have to; these things may seem cheap but they add up,' he said.

'When you become a consultant?'

'Yes, but it's called an attending here, an attending physician.'

The arrangers of marriage only told you that doctors made a lot of money in America. They did not add that before doctors started to make a lot of money, they had to do an internship and a residency programme, which my new husband had not completed. My new husband had told me this during our short in-flight conversation, right after we took off from Lagos, before he fell asleep.

'Interns are paid twenty-eight thousand a year but work about eighty hours a week. It's like three dollars an hour,' he had said. 'Can you believe it? Three dollars an hour!'

I did not know if three dollars an hour was very good or very bad – I was leaning towards very good – until he added that even high-school students working part-time made much more.

'Also when I become an attending, we will not live in a neighbourhood like this,' my new husband said. He stopped to let a woman with her child tucked into her shopping cart pass by. 'See how they have bars so you can't take the shopping carts out? In the good neighbourhoods, they don't have them. You can take your shopping cart all the way to your car.'

'Oh,' I said. What did it matter that you could or could not take the carts out? The point was, there *were* carts.

'Look at the people who shop here; they are the ones who im-migrate and continue to act as if they are back in their countries.' He gestured, dismissively, towards a woman and her two children, who were speaking Spanish. 'They will never move forward unless they adapt to America. They will always be doomed to supermarkets like this.'

I murmured something to show I was listening. I thought about the open market in Enugu, the traders who sweet-talked you into stopping at their zinc-covered sheds, who were prepared to bargain all day to add one single kobo to the price. They wrapped what you bought in plastic bags when they had them, and when they did not have them, they laughed and offered you worn newspapers.

My new husband took me to the mall; he wanted to show me as much as he could before he started work on Monday. His car rattled as he drove, as though there were many parts that had come loose – a sound similar to shaking a tin full of nails. It stalled at a traffic light and he turned the key a few times before it started.

'I'll buy a new car after my residency,' he said.

Inside the mall, the floors gleamed, smooth as ice cubes, and the high-as-the-sky ceiling blinked with tiny ethereal lights. I felt as though I were in a different physical world, on another planet. The people who pushed against us, even the black ones, wore the mark of foreignness, otherness, on their faces.

'We'll get pizza first,' he said. 'It's one thing you have to like in America.'

We walked up to the pizza stand, to the man wearing a nose ring and a tall white hat.

'Two pepperoni and sausage. Is your combo deal better?' my new husband asked. He sounded different when he spoke to Americans: his 'r' was overpronounced and his 't' was underpronounced. And he smiled, the eager smile of a person who wanted to be liked.

We ate the pizza sitting at a small round table in what he called a 'food court'. A sea of people sitting round circular tables, hunched over paper plates of greasy food. Uncle Ike would be horrified at the thought of eating here; he was a titled man and did not even eat at weddings unless he was served in a private room. There was something humiliatingly public, something lacking in dignity, about this place, this open space of too many tables and too much food.

'Do you like the pizza?' my new husband asked. His paper plate was empty.

'The tomatoes are not cooked well.'

'We overcook food back home and that is why we lose all the nutrients. Americans cook things right. See how healthy and chubby they all look?'

I nodded, looking around. At the next table, a black woman with a body as soft and wide as a pillow held sideways smiled at me. I smiled back and took another pizza bite, tightening my stomach so it would not eject anything.

We went into Macy's afterwards. My new husband led the way towards a sliding staircase; its movement was rubbery-smooth and I knew I would fall down the moment I stepped on it.

'*Biko*, don't they have a lift instead?' I asked. At least I had once ridden in the creaky one in the local government office, the one that quivered for a full minute before the doors rolled open.

'Speak English. There are people behind you,' he whispered, pulling me away, towards a glass counter full of twinkling jewellery. 'It's an elevator, not a lift. Americans say elevator.'

'OK.'

He led me to the lift (elevator) and we went up a section lined with rows of weighty-looking coats. He bought me a coat the colour of a gloomy day's sky, puffy with what felt like foam inside its lining. The coat looked big enough for two of me to snugly fit into it.

'Winter is coming,' he said. 'It is like being inside a freezer, so you need a warm coat.'

'Thank you.'

'Always best to shop when there is a sale. Sometimes you get the same thing for less than half the price. It's one of the wonders of America.'

'*Ezi okwu?*' I said, then hastily added, 'Really?'

'Let's take a walk around the mall. There are some other wonders of America here.'

We walked, looking at stores that sold clothes and tools and plates and books and phones, until the bottoms of my feet ached.

Before we left, he led the way to McDonald's. The restaurant was nestled near the rear of the mall; a yellow-and-red 'M' the size of a car stood at its entrance. My husband did not look at the menu board that hovered overhead as he ordered two large Number 2 meals.

'We could go home so I can cook,' I said. 'Don't let your husband eat out too much,' Aunty Ada had said, 'or it will push him into the arms of a woman who cooks. Always guard your husband like a guinea fowl's egg.'

'I like to eat this once in a while,' he said. He held the hamburger with both hands and chewed with a concentration that furrowed his eyebrows, tightened his jaw and made him look even more unfamiliar.

I made coconut rice on Monday, to make up for the eating out. I wanted to make pepper soup too, the kind Aunty Ify said softened a man's heart, but I needed the *uziza* that the customs officer had seized; pepper soup was just not pepper soup without it. I bought a coconut in the Jamaican store down the street and spent an hour cutting it into tiny bits because there was no grater and then soaked it in hot water to extract the juice. I had just finished cooking when he came home. He wore what looked like a uniform, a girlish-looking blue top tucked into a pair of blue trousers that was tied at the waist.

'*Nno,*' I said. 'Did you work well?'

'You have to speak English at home too, baby. So you can get used to it.' He brushed his lips against my cheek just as the doorbell rang. It was Shirley, her body wrapped in the same pink robe. She twirled the belt at her waist.

'That smell,' she said, in her phlegm-filled voice, 'it's everywhere, all over the building. What are you cooking?'

'Coconut rice,' I said.

'A recipe from your country?'

'Yes.'

'It smells really good. The problem with us here is we have no culture, no culture at all.' She turned to my new husband, as if she wanted him to agree with her, but he simply smiled. 'Would you come take a look at my air-conditioner, Dave?' she asked. 'It's acting up again and it's so hot today.'

'Sure,' my new husband said.

Before they left, Shirley waved at me and said, 'Smells *really* good,' and I wanted to invite her to have some rice. My new husband came back half an hour later and ate the fragrant meal I placed before him, even smacking his lips like Uncle Ike sometimes did to show Aunty Ada how pleased he was with her cooking. But the next day he came back with a *Good Housekeeping All-American Cookbook*, thick as a Bible.

'I don't want us to be known as the people who fill the building with smells of foreign food,' he said.

I took the cookbook, ran my hand over the cover, over the picture of something that looked like a flower but was probably food.

'I know you'll soon master how to cook American food,' he said, gently pulling me close.

That night I thought of the cookbook as he lay heavily on top of me, grunting and rasping. Another thing the arrangers of marriage did not tell you – the struggle to brown beef in oil and dredge skinless chicken in flour. I had always cooked beef in its own juices. Chicken I had always poached with its skin intact. In the following days I was pleased that my husband left for work at six in the morning and did not come back until eight in the evening so that I had time to throw away pieces of half-cooked, clammy chicken and start again.

The first time I saw Nia, who lived in 2D, I thought she was the kind of woman Aunty Ada would disapprove of. Aunty Ada would call her an *ashawo*, because of the see-through top she wore so that her bra, a mismatched shade, glared through. Or Aunty Ada would base her prostitute judgement on Nia's lipstick, a shimmery orange, and the eye shadow – similar to the shade of the lipstick – that clung to her heavy lids.

'Hi,' she said when I went down to get the mail. 'You're Dave's new wife. I've been meaning to come over and meet you. I'm Nia.'

'Thanks. I'm Chinaza . . . Agatha.'

Nia was watching me carefully. 'What was the first thing you said?'

'My Nigerian name.'

'It's an Igbo name, isn't it?' She pronounced it 'E-boo'.

'Yes.'

'What does it mean?'

'God answers prayers.'

'It's really pretty. You know, Nia is a Swahili name. I changed my name when I was eighteen. I spent three years in Tanzania. It was fucking amazing.'

'Oh,' I said, and shook my head; she, a black American, had chosen an African name, while my husband made me change mine to an English one.

'You must be bored to death in that apartment; I know Dave gets back pretty late,' she said. 'Come have a Coke with me.'

I hesitated, but Nia was already walking to the stairs. I followed her. Her living room had a spare elegance: a red sofa, a slender potted plant, a huge wooden mask hanging on the wall. She gave me a Diet

Coke served in a tall glass with ice, asked how I was adjusting to life in America, offered to show me around Brooklyn.

'It would have to be a Monday, though,' she said. 'I don't work Mondays.'

'What do you do?'

'I own a hair salon.'

'Your hair is beautiful,' I said, and she touched it and said, 'Oh, this,' as if she did not think anything of it. It was not just her hair, held up on top of her head in a natural Afro puff, that I found beautiful, though; it was her skin the colour of roasted groundnuts, her mysterious and heavy-lidded eyes, her curved hips. She played her music a little too loud, so we had to raise our voices as we spoke.

'You know, my sister's a manager at Macy's,' she said. 'They're hiring entry-level salespeople in the women's department, so if you're interested, I can put in a word for you and you're pretty much hired. She owes me one.'

Something leaped inside me at the thought, the sudden and new thought, of earning what would be mine. Mine. 'I don't have my work permit yet,' I said.

'But Dave has filed for you?'

'Yes.'

'It shouldn't take long; at least you should have it before winter. I have a friend from Haiti who just got hers. So let me know as soon as you do.'

'Thank you.' I wanted to hug Nia. 'Thank you.'

That evening I told my new husband about Nia. His eyes were sunken in with fatigue, after so many hours at work, and he said, 'Nia?' as though he did not know who I meant, before he added, 'She's OK, but be careful because she can be a bad influence.'

Nia began stopping by to see me after work, drinking from a can of diet soda she brought with her and watching me cook. I turned the air-conditioner off and opened the window to let in the hot air, so that she could smoke. She talked about the women at her hair salon and the men she went out with. She sprinkled her everyday conversation with words like the noun 'clitoris' and the verb 'fuck'. I liked to listen to her. I liked the way she smiled to show a tooth that was chipped neatly, a perfect triangle missing at the edge. She always left before my new husband came home.

Winter sneaked up on me. One morning I stepped out of the apartment building and gasped. It was as though God was shredding tufts of white tissue and flinging them down. I stood staring at my first snow, at the swirling flakes, for a long, long time before turning to go back inside the apartment. I scrubbed the kitchen floor again, cut out more coupons from the Key Food catalogue that came in the mail and then sat by the window, watching God's shredding become frenzied. Winter had come and I was still unemployed. When my husband came home in the evening, I placed his French fries and fried chicken before him and said, 'I thought I would have my work permit by now.'

He ate a few pieces of oily fried potatoes before responding. We spoke only English now; he did not know that I spoke Igbo to myself while I cooked, that I had taught Nia how to say 'I'm hungry' and 'See you tomorrow' in Igbo.

'The American woman I married to get a green card is making trouble,' he said, and slowly tore a piece of chicken in two. The area under his eyes was puffy. 'Our divorce was almost final, but not completely, before I married you in Nigeria. Just a minor thing, but she found out about it and now she's threatening to report me to Immigration. She wants more money.'

'You were married before?' I laced my fingers together because they had started to shake.

'Would you pass that, please?' he asked, pointing to the lemonade I had made earlier.

'The jug?'

'Pitcher. Americans say pitcher, not jug.'

I pushed the jug (pitcher) across. The pounding in my head was loud, filling my ears with a fierce liquid. 'You were married before?'

'It was just on paper. A lot of our people do that here. It's business – you pay the woman and both of you do paperwork together – but sometimes it goes wrong and either she refuses to divorce you or she decides to blackmail you.'

I pulled the pile of coupons towards me and started to rip them in two, one after the other. 'Ofodile, you should have let me know this before now.'

He shrugged. 'I was going to tell you.'

'I deserved to know before we got married.' I sank down on the chair opposite him, slowly, as if the chair would crack if I didn't.

'It wouldn't have made a difference. Your uncle and aunt had decided. Were you going to say no to people who have taken care of you since your parents died?'

I stared at him in silence, shredding the coupons into smaller and smaller bits; broken-up pictures of detergents and meat packs and paper towels fell to the floor.

'Besides, with the way things are messed up back home, what would you have done?' he asked. 'Aren't people with master's degrees roaming the streets, jobless?' His voice was flat.

'Why did you marry me?' I asked.

'I wanted a Nigerian wife and my mother said you were a good girl, quiet. She said you might even be a virgin.' He smiled. He looked even more tired when he smiled. 'I probably should tell her how wrong she was.'

I threw more coupons on the floor, clasped my hands together and dug my nails into my skin.

'I was happy when I saw your picture,' he said, smacking his lips. 'You were light-skinned. I had to think about my children's looks. Light-skinned blacks fare better in America.' I watched him eat the rest of the batter-covered chicken and I noticed that he did not finish chewing before he took a sip of water.

That evening, while he showered, I put only the clothes he hadn't bought me, two embroidered boubous and one caftan, all Aunty Ada's cast-offs, in the plastic suitcase I had brought from Nigeria and went to Nia's apartment.

Nia made me tea, with milk and sugar, and sat with me at her round dining table that had three tall stools round it.

'If you want to call your family back home, you can call them from here. Stay as long as you want; I'll get on a payment plan with Bell Atlantic.'

'There's nobody to talk to at home,' I said, staring at the pear-shaped face of the sculpture on the wooden shelf. Its hollow eyes stared back at me.

'How about your aunt?' Nia asked.

I shook my head. 'You left your husband,' Aunty Ada would shriek. 'Are you mad? Does one throw away a guinea fowl's egg? Do you know how many women would offer both eyes for a doctor in America? For any husband at all?' And Uncle Ike would bellow about my ingratitude, my stupidity, his fist and face tightening, before dropping the phone.

'He should have told you about the marriage, but it wasn't a real marriage, Chinaza,' Nia said. 'I read a book that says we don't fall in love, we climb up to love. Maybe if you gave it time—'

'It's not about that.'

'I know,' Nia said with a sigh. 'Just trying to be fucking positive here. Was there someone back home?'

'There was once, but he was too young and he had no money.'

'Sounds really fucked up.'

I stirred my tea although it did not need stirring. 'I wonder why my husband had to find a wife in Nigeria.'

'You never say his name; you never say Dave. Is that a cultural thing?'

'No.' I looked down at the tablemat made with waterproof fabric.

I wanted to say that it was because I didn't know his name, because I didn't know him.

'Did you ever meet the woman he married, or did you know any of his girlfriends?' I asked.

Nia looked away. The kind of dramatic turning of head that speaks, that intends to speak, volumes. The silence stretched out between us.

'Nia?' I asked finally.

'I fucked him, almost two years ago, when he first moved in. I fucked him and after a week it was over. We never dated. I never saw him date anybody.'

'Oh,' I said, and sipped my tea with milk and sugar.

'I had to be honest with you, get everything out.'

'Yes,' I said. I stood up to look out of the window. The world outside seemed mummified into a sheet of dead whiteness. The pavements had piles of snow the height of a six-year-old child.

'You can wait until you get your papers and then leave,' Nia said. 'You can apply for benefits while you get your shit together, and then you'll get a job and find a place and support yourself and start afresh. This is the US of fucking A, for God's sake.'

Nia came and stood beside me, by the window. She was right: I could not leave yet. I went back across the hall the next evening. I rang the doorbell and he opened the door, stood aside and let me pass.

FAERIES OF THE NILE

Mansoura Ez-Eldin

Translated from the Arabic by Raphael Cohen

It all begins at the time of Friday prayer.

The woman who lives in the stone house hugged by the Nile, next to the mooring, has been hearing mysterious sing-song voices. At the beginning she thought they were songs she knew. Then she realized that it was more like words being sung in a language she didn't understand. She comes out of the house and catches sight of what looks like white smoke swirling between the aged camphorwood trees. Not smoke exactly, but something white and cloud-like, up-right, and dancing and twisting together. When she peers hard, she sees the translucent white forms turn into phantom women, whose bodies revolve and intertwine sensuously. The voices grow distinct and become sweeter, more seductive. The phantom women sway to imperceptible rhythms that render outward existence totally silent. A silence that is listening to this music of unknown origin.

The woman in the stone house, her name is Zeenat, but every week, when this ceremony is repeated in front of her, she practically forgets her name. And her mother and father and, even, her husband, who she knows will accuse her of being mad if she tells him what she has seen.

To begin with she felt afraid, a deep primal fear possessing her since the beginning of time. She's always afraid; subsequently she starts to come up with reasons. Later her fear turned to curiosity, and from curiosity was born desire. A despairing, humiliating desire to merge with these luminous, diaphanous bodies.

She thought, They are river faeries grown tired of life underwater. She remembers how her, now dead, mother was against her son-in-law living so close to the Nile. She said that its faeries were sacred and to be respected. She has not seen a faerie before, and nobody she knows has told her they have. Yet she knows that they are beautiful, mostly, with very long black hair and burning bright eyes whose slits are vertical, and they are able to dissolve into people's bodies. She knows this as well as she knows that the sun is the sun, the moon the moon and the night the night.

She peers hard at the phantom women in front of her. As she imagines it, they transmogrify into flesh-and-blood bodies, but with silky, lustrous skin, so limpid it almost reveals what is beneath. The sing-song voice suddenly swells and the dance quickens. Then everything vanishes and silence reigns anew. At that instant she is back and can hear the rustling of the leaves and the rising voice of the Friday preacher abruptly concluding his sermon.

This was her secret, she was certain, not to be revealed to anyone. She began to wait for them in the open area in front of the house at the same time every week. She dreaded throwing anything away between the camphorwood trees. Every day she swept the ground there and sprinkled it with water. Then she decided to add drops of rosewater as well.

She thought about asking the ferryman if he had seen one of the Nile faeries before, but she feared that he would make her talk and she would be forced to say something she didn't want. She doesn't trust herself to keep a secret. As soon as someone asked her a direct question, she would reveal every detail, the significant and the peripheral.

My wife slowly finishes the housework and prepares some food for dinner.

Then she calmly sits on the bench in front of the house, taking pleasure in watching the people waiting next to the crossing point while she mends old clothes or sifts rice, and chops the vegetables to cook the next day.

Her face, submerged under wrinkles and creases, lights up when she sees the ferryman. I watch her through the window from my place on the bed where I am always laid up. In the afternoons he's not in much of a hurry. He stops to exchange a few attentive words with her. He tells her about his son who refuses to help him at work, and his old wife with her weaving skills. She gives him a drink of water or a bag full of the greens and herbs that she grows in the patch between the camphorwood trees and the giant mulberry tree.

He comes to our bank twice a day: in the morning when those who wish to cross to the other side wait for him at the mooring, and in the evening when he brings back those who went in the morning and returns with those he brought over. Often, he makes a third trip when the heat fades in the afternoon, or even around noon when the sun is high in the sky, if a group of people wish to cross the river. They stand waiting, without boredom, in the shade of the camphorwood trees, until he decides to come and fetch them.

A long time ago, before the crossing point moved next to our house, we lived in total isolation. No one came near the spot where we lived. In the early days of our marriage my wife cried a lot, at her mother's direction, in an effort to persuade me to move to another house in the same village, not on its edge like this, hugged by the Nile. I would come home late most nights, with little concern for her fear of the night and the darkness in wait for her outside the house.

Even on Fridays and days off I wouldn't stay at home. She never understood how someone like me who grew up in the city could make her move to the country, and to this isolated spot in particular. Inaam herself didn't understand it.

Once, my wife told me that when I wasn't around, she would hear voices coming from the river and its rushes. She asserted that the voices belonged to the faeries. Apparently, their frolicking in the water came with playful, ringing voices. But then she went and denied this. She was convinced that the house being so close to the river was terribly dangerous. My making fun of her didn't deter her, nor did accusing her of being mad, because her fears were too great to suppress.

That far-off day when I came home to find her unconscious among the camphorwood trees, I didn't believe her. Refusing to listen to her explanations, I even beat her up. In truth, there was no explanation. She said strange things about apparitions in the camphorwood trees. She was never the same again afterwards. I took care of her at home for a few weeks. I would see her hovering around the camphorwood trees. She would sit down with her eyes fixed on them. At the end of the day she would lie down in her bed, preoccupied, without a word.

Even her pregnancy and the birth of our son, less than a year after the episode, didn't improve her mood and restore her to her old ways. She was attached to him and made him the centre of her life, but her sadness and silent vigil continued.

She no longer left the house to go anywhere else. She didn't go to the market and never went beyond the space around the house and the camphorwood trees. It was as if she were keeping a promise she had made with herself.

She relied on the ferryman to supply her with household needs. She would give him the money in the evening to buy the fruit and meat she wanted, and he would bring it with him from the other bank in the morning. He became the umbilical cord linking her to life outside, just as Inaam would become for her afterwards.

The woman who lives in the stone house hugged by the Nile, the one called Zeenat, set off early one Friday as usual for the market in the middle of the village. Usually this trip would take no more than two hours, including half an hour to get there and the same again on the way back, but on this particular day she found that the women who had beaten her to the fruit and fresh vegetables had left nothing any good behind. She concentrated on choosing and picking until she purchased what, in part, satisfied her. When she reached the butcher's shop, however, it was closed. The owner of the coffeehouse next door told her it would open after Friday prayer, so she decided to wait. She put her shopping basket down next to her and sat on the marble platform in front of the shop. She gathered up the edges of her long black *galabeya* and covered her black plaits with her sheer chiffon headscarf and forgot, for a while, the white apparitions dancing among the camphorwood trees. If she didn't buy meat, her husband would be furious. She had grown used to his short temper, but she hated his rough voice, loudly telling her off.

As soon as prayers were over, the butcher arrived. She bought some lamb, her husband's favourite, and left in a hurry. She knew they would have gone, no doubt, but she just wanted to get there, as if they would still appreciate her desire to see them. She walked quickly on the narrow dirt track that led between the village and where her house was. The track was bordered by fields stretching away and sown with corn on the left and others, wide areas next to the Nile, planted with vegetables on the right. On the far bank there were orchards of palms, orange trees and vines. She almost tripped over the hem of her robe. It was very hot and her heavy clothing made it hotter. The track was totally deserted, as were the fields to either side that the fellahin would leave in a rush to catch Friday prayer, not returning until the end of the afternoon when it wasn't so hot.

Since childhood she has been afraid of cornfields. Her mother often warned her not to walk next to them. She asked if faeries lived in them. Her mother answered in a croaking voice, 'No, worse. Men.'

She explained to her that men hid in cornfields to lure passing girls and women and to cause them harm. At that time she didn't know the nature of this harm, but she took away the fact that men were worse than faeries.

Still tripping over her *galabeya* and carrying her heavy shopping basket, the familiar silence suddenly descended. A silence in whose presence she could almost hear her thoughts. She waited for the white smoke to swirl and for the dancing feminine bodies to appear to her. None of this happened, though. The silence intensified before a voice, not the usual one of her apparitions, carried to her. It was akin to wailing and moans of pain. She looked over to her right at a field of beans and saw that it was full of women dressed in black, their heads crowned with very long coal-black hair. They were cutting down the bean plants with their small white flowers and wailing and slapping their heads with their hands. It was a fearsome funeral rite, and despite what she was carrying, she started to run. Her heart was pounding and she tried to scream. A weak, dry voice came out. She felt the path was longer than usual. The wailing and laments grew louder and she saw that the bean plants had all been cut down and left carelessly strewn in small heaps. Having nearly reached her house, she caught sight of the ferryman landing his boat some way off. She called his name in a voice she willed would be strong and firm. To her amazement, everything stopped when she called his name: the chirping of the birds in the nearby trees came back, the distant barking of a dog, the rustle of the leaves stirred by a gentle breeze.

She headed for the mooring. Her breathing was coming in audible bursts. She asked the ferryman to help her lower the basket from her head and sat on the ground catching her breath. After a while she slowly stood up and headed for her house. She went calmly inside while the ferryman carrying the basket caught up with her. He left it in the middle of the narrow living room and headed quickly back towards the mooring. She lay down in her bed trembling. For the first time she felt relieved that her husband spent most of his time out of the house in places she didn't know and had never once cared to ask about.

Inaam arrived in the morning.

I sense her as soon as she enters the house. I heard her voice, unchanged by the years. She laughs in a loud voice when talking to my wife. She seemed happy; the words come out one after another without spaces in between. I sat up a little waiting for her to enter, but she took her time. I glimpsed her through the doorway as she embraced my wife, before touching her shoulder and adjusting her black chiffon headscarf. They went and sat down together on the divan on the other side of the living room and moved out of view.

They were talking together, but I couldn't make out the words even though their voices weren't lowered.

I woke up earlier than normal, aware that Inaam was coming today. The first Thursday of every month. Since I could no longer go to her, she has come to me on the same date. As soon as she would leave me to return to her distant village, I would live on the hope of seeing her again. My life has become bouts of anticipation, one after another, awaiting her visits. Sometimes I feel that I take greater pleasure from the waiting than from actually seeing her. In the few days before her visits I count down the hours, happy at her impending appearance. When I see her, I forget everything else. Except my joy is tinged with sadness, in the knowledge that she will leave, as usual, before evening comes.

She is still chatting away with my wife, as though she has come to visit her, not me. I think about calling her, but I hold back and continue to wait. Sometimes I feel that my wife waits for Inaam with the same yearning as me, although I can't be definite about anything to do with her. I saw her two days ago, through the ever open window, tenderly rubbing the old delivery van parked outside. She was touching it like she was touching a person she loved. Then she covered it to protect it from the rain that has been falling for two days. Yet in the past she often asked me to sell it, telling me that she couldn't bear to see it in front of the house.

In the days before Inaam's monthly visit, my wife is eager to finish all the time-consuming housework. She tidies up the house, bakes bread, does the laundry and hangs the clothes on the line stretching between the mulberry and the castor-oil bush. Then she sits down on a granite rock, calmly staring at the clothes like someone watching them as they dry and billow in response to gusts of wind. Her own clothes are soaking wet, but she pays no attention to this and remains seated in the sun until they too are dry. She never turns towards the window from which I observe her as I lie prone in my fixed place on my bed. When she gets bored, she walks with slow, decrepit steps towards the Nile and fills the green plastic bucket with water. Her body bends to the right in response to the weight of the bucket that she is holding in her right hand. She goes to water the tomato and aubergine seedlings planted in the patch between the mulberry tree and the camphorwoods next to the mooring.

Since I beat her up, all those years ago, she has barely exchanged one word with me. Even after I became ill, her heart did not soften. Many years have passed with me laid up like this. I watch her as she slowly moves around. She gazes expressionless and mumbles words I cannot make out. I ask myself, If she refuses to forget after all these years, why doesn't she leave me and spare me this pain?

I lift my eyes to the ceiling and spy the apparition of our son. He is smiling so gently it terrifies me. I turn my eyes towards the window and see the sky far, far away. This window has become my only link with the outside world. I insist that my wife keeps it open even when it's cold and wet. I expect her to object, but she dashes my hopes and remains silent. She obeys me as if castigating me with obedience. Sometimes I cast her a sudden glance and catch her stealing a look at me. When Inaam visits me, I still induce her to tell me what my wife talks about. Does she laugh with her and behave like other people or remain glowering and silent?

Finally Inaam comes in laughing. She leans over to kiss me on the forehead, then sits on the chair to the left of my bed. She tells the same stories every time. Nevertheless I perceive her as fresh and new, as though she recreates herself. But today she seems different, despite her apparent happiness. She seemed to be layering it over a certain sadness. I begged her to take me to the delivery van parked in front of the house. She smiled without comment. This is the first time I've seen her so distracted. I watched her as she was leaving. I have seen her with many kinds of eyes before. These were eyes that know they will not see you again and so flee from your eyes while she tries to speak neutrally as if washing her hands of you.

The woman who lives in the stone house, the one called Zeenat, knew that what she had been through was nothing less than a punishment for missing her weekly appointment with the dancing faeries. She was certain it was just a simple warning, a pinched ear, to be followed by more severe punishment if she did it again or made another mistake. The next week she refused to go to the market. She told her husband that she was unwell and that he would have to buy what he wanted for her to cook. He raised his voice to criticize her laziness and her non-stop complaining of a non-existent illness. As a rule, she hated his angry ranting, but she didn't acquiesce. Before the set time, she sat in the open space by the camphorwood trees waiting. When the ceremony began, she approached, not too close, but advanced towards them and stopped to watch from a few paces away. Her desire to fuse into them and with them intensified. She felt intoxicated, as though she had shed many cares that she couldn't exactly define but whose existence she could sense. Cares accumulated since time immemorial, since before she was even born. Before everything and anything.

This emboldened her to draw nearer. As soon as she was among the camphorwoods, the world she knew changed. She felt as if the world was spinning with her. She perceived the rhythms of the musical voices more clearly than at any time before. The aged trees turned ethereal and the apparitions passed through them as they danced. They formed a circle round her and embraced her gently. Little by little the circle closed in and the apparitions came closer to her. She sat on the ground overwhelmed and unable to catch her breath. The apparitions turned into what resembled a purple flame that warmed her. A purple flame tipped with a pale green light that drew closer to her and cleaved to her. The trees vanished entirely. The flame reverted into the phantom women, which fused together into one apparition with black hair that almost reached the ground, and eyes split lengthwise, milky translucent skin and an incredibly sweet voice. Zeenat was stretched out on her back trembling. She shut her eyes, unable to bear the brilliance shining forth from the eyes split lengthways. She shivered as though feverish when she felt a hand stroking her body to the beat of a mysterious song in that same sweet voice. With eyes closed and trembling, she felt the world shaking around her. She tried to cry out, but her voice was hoarse. She tried to cry but couldn't. She surrendered to the shaking, the trembling, the hand stroking her body, oblivious to everything but the moment she is living now.

Inaam hasn't visited me for two months. I don't know how her heart has led her to stay away so long. I wake up with a start sometimes, when I imagine that something bad has happened to her. I'm sure she wouldn't have stayed away so long if she could still make the journey. Troubling anxiety only overcomes me at night. The simplest idea magnifies in my head so that I can't sleep. My most disturbing fears are that something terrible has happened to Inaam, and that she's alone, there, in her far-off house.

In the past she used to say to me, 'One day you'll come and find me dead and all alone without anybody realizing.'

At every one of her visits after I fell ill, she would repeat, 'This is the last time I'm visiting you. My rheumatism is killing me!'

'I mean that little to you?' I would ask her imploringly.

She would reply seriously, 'Your wife's a blessing. She'll look after you.'

I can almost see her small house, perched alone on the fast road next to the petrol station, and enclosed by a bank of lemon and guava trees. She would know I'd arrived by the violent noise from my van as I parked it in front of the house. I'd go crashing inside, ignoring the barking of the dog outside. I'd talk to her excitedly about the goods I transported, the towns I stopped in and my friends on the road. The blue smoke of my cigarettes would fill the house and the empty beer bottles would roll around on the floor. She would pick them up and tell me off. I would laugh and take no notice.

I understand Inaam simply by looking at her face. I can easily tell whether she's angry or happy. I can even tell the reason why without her imparting it. This is the opposite of my wife, whom I don't understand at all. I've lived with her for more than forty years without figuring out what's inside her. She accepts my shouting and my temper in silence. She doesn't complain at all and doesn't know words of reproof. Long years have passed and she's still just as headstrong.

Since she started talking to Inaam, she's never once spoken about herself. She would just ask her how things were and listen attentively without comment. She always avoided talking about our son. Inaam told me that she had, more than once, tried to explain to my wife that I wasn't drunk the day of the accident, and so wasn't responsible for the death of the boy, but she changed the subject and wouldn't let Inaam broach it again.

My wife asked her to persuade me to sell the old van. She told her it had become a rusty hulk and didn't understand why I insisted on keeping it after what had happened. I remember that she pleaded with me after the accident to sell the vehicle. She couldn't bear to see it. She said something about exploiting its value, and when I answered that it had turned into scrap and wouldn't get us any money, she took refuge in silence once again. It was as though she believed that the vehicle's vanishing would bring our son back from the void. Even Inaam has confessed to me lately that she was jealous of my relationship with the van, and that she was annoyed by the mess I left behind and the empty bottles of drink that I discarded in the corners of her house.

Now my wife avoids mentioning anything about our son, but has feelings for, and an interest in, the van chassis. She may swap funny stories with Inaam, but she hasn't forgiven me. I still see her from time to time looking blankly at where the old camphorwood trees are. She becomes completely divorced from anything around her. She remains like this for a while before she drags her footsteps heavily back inside, and her lined face reveals the traces of grief and disappointment.

I look at her at times, on the verge of asking her to tell me all she saw in the camphorwood trees and what happened to her on that faraway day, but I restrain myself at the last moment. I don't know why she won't leave me. And why, despite her silence and old age, she devotes herself to serving and looking after me. Sometimes it occurs to me that she is happy at my disability. After it happened, she became calmer and more relaxed. She moves around gently and deliberately, carrying on the details of her day indifferent to my presence. While I spend the time watching her and observing that part of the outside world generously permitted me by the window, I wait, without hope, for Inaam to come. I didn't used to stay in one place for a single day. Even when things were slow and there were no goods to move, I would go out in the empty van and drive around the country, as if I were running away from something. Now it's my fate to remain a prisoner of this bed endlessly.

The woman who lives in the stone house hugged by the Nile, companion of silence and dancing faeries, the one they call Zeenat, who loves sweet, musical voices and hates shouting and uproar, this woman woke up from her trance and returned to her world and her life at the smack of a hard slap to her face. She opened her eyes to see her husband, the delivery van driver, seething with rage. He set upon her with one slap after another, and before she had noticed her nakedness and her strange position on the ground among the camphorwood trees, he had dragged her by the hair out of the camphor thicket and gathered up her clothes strewn here and there and flung them over her, expecting her to put them on. As soon as she had thrown on her robe, he resumed dragging her towards the house. He continued to shout, threatening and menacing, without listening to her tearful pleas. He didn't believe her afterwards when she told him about her faeries with their apparitions and seductive voices. He confined her to her room for weeks, and she noticed that he no longer left the house as frequently as before. He even made a point of lingering in the open space in front of the house every Friday at prayer time, as if he were waiting for the apparitions she had spoken of.

He would put the food down in front of her sullenly. When he asked her what she was doing naked in the open, she would look away without answering. She had no sensible explanation. She didn't even remember taking her clothes off. She had just stretched out in the centre of the circle formed by the apparitions drawing closer to her and shut her eyes, waiting for the world around her to become, like other days, familiar again.

Once her life had reverted to the way it had been, and her husband had returned to his life outside the home, she resumed her wait for the faeries at the same time every week. But it was in vain. They never appeared again. She even came to doubt that they had appeared before. But after many years, when she had lost her son and her husband had fallen ill and retired to bed, she started to sense a similar silence at that same time every week. An absolute silence, not followed by anything. In the camphorwood trees, she will stare in front of her, trying by means of memory to recreate the companions of the past and restore them to existence, but she does not manage. She only sees them in her mind's eye when she closes her eyes and listens to the silence surrounding her.

STICKFIGHTING DAYS

Olufemi Terry

Thwack, thwack, the two of them go at it like madmen, but the boys around them barely stir with excitement. They both use one stick and we find this swordy kind of stickfighting a bit crappy. Much better two on one or two on two – lots more skill involved and more likelihood of blood.

I turn to Lapy. 'Let's go off and practise somewhere. This is weak.' Lapy likes any stickfight, but almost always does what I say. His eyes linger ruefully on Paps and the other boy – don't know his name, but I see him a lot – and then he follows me.

I run almost full tilt into Markham and he gives me a grin, like we're best pals and he's been looking for me. Markham is my rival. We've beaten each other roughly the same number of times. Well, six to five in his favour, but one of my victories was a beauty, a flowing sequence of sticks that even I couldn't follow before I smashed his nose in nicely. Almost broke it. The satisfaction of Markham's watery-eyed submission that day makes me smile easily back at him.

'Wanna mix it up?' Markham's eyes aren't smiling any more; he won the last one and thinks he's on a roll. I know better.

'We could,' I come back smoothly, 'but it wouldn't mean much.' I hold up Mormegil. I've told no one I've named my sticks, though I'm not ashamed. I love Mormegil, but I don't think the others would understand. 'I've only got one stick with me.' I cock my head to one side enquiringly at him. To be honest, I've been leaving Orcrist, my other, so I don't have to get into any serious battles. Everyone knows I'm a two-stick man. But I'm not ready to go up against Markham again just yet. Or any of the other top stickfighters. I've been trying some new moves. I feel close to a breakthrough in terms of technique, but it's not quite there and until it is I only carry Mormegil. Mormegil is as long as our regulations allow, a lovely willow poke, dark willow – that's why I chose the name. It means 'black sword' in Tolkien's language. A sword with a mind of sorts. Turin wielded it, and it would cut anything, anyone eagerly. In the end it took his own life to avenge those he killed. My Mormegil has little knobs at the joint, and one tip is nicely pointed – we're not allowed to sharpen sticks – but this is natural. Mormegil is a killing machine, even though I've never done for anyone yet. But I will. I like Markham, but I'd like to kill him. I dream of doing it in front of a huge pack of boys. Clinically.

Markham's henchman, Tich, is a one-stick man, but he now holds up two. 'You can use this one.' He throws it to me and I catch it easily, angry at being forced to fight. I force a deep gulp of air into my lungs. Fighting angry is bad! Only Simon ever did it effectively and where's he now? I give Lapy a confident look, taking the measure of the unfamiliar stick as I do. It's rubbery, too bendy but unlikely to break. It's also too light. Much too light.

Markham's not much one for warm-ups. He bounces from one toe to another like a boxer, rolls his head, then gestures to me that he's ready. I already see a ring of boys forming round us, keen for a real spar and not that sword stuff.

He comes at me, neither quick nor slow, his arms wide. One of his sticks, an ash thing, is almost as good as Mormegil. He let me hold it once, before we were rivals. Stiff as hell and with a good weight, maybe an inch shorter than my beauty. I fend him off easily. Markham is good, but he's cautious. He knows I'll not risk much with an unknown stick. I could keep him off with Mormegil, but I feel I've got to try one of my new moves. No one'll attach too much to this particular fight so I can afford to be bold. But I'm cunning too. That's what got me to where I am. That and good reflexes.

I hold Mormegil in my left hand and the unfamiliar stick in my right, gripped in the middle – an outdated form, I know, but very good for riposting against an overeager opponent. Here he comes, Markham, his sticks a blur more from technique than power. In goes Mormegil to break that rhythm and then I bring my whippy stick in to catch the one in Markham's left. It is too bendy to give me much opening, but I am quick, and I know not to go for a body blow; the opportunity is small and he'd be able to retaliate. I bang Mormegil against the outside of his wrist, the bony bit, all the while twirling my right hand to keep him caught up. I try for his knuckles, but he is no fool, Markham. He pulls back a step, wiping his forehead with the back of his hand. I watch him change his grip to match mine. There's no sweat on me yet! He's not angry enough to make a serious error, but I feel in my gut now's the time to let him – all the boys – see what I've been working on. I drop my right grip so that I'm holding both sticks sword-like. I bang them together once and advance on him. This is me at my most fearsome: my speed frightens opponents and no one knows exactly what I've got planned, so it's now or never. Our sticks clatter against each other left to left, right to right and crosswise. I use the bendy stick to hold his every thrust and I am glad that the whippiness absorbs much of the power. Markham settles into a pattern and at the last second I drop one of my parries so that his stick whistles on, at the same time, lowering Mormegil so that my face is unprotected. Markham falls for it and doesn't try to halt his stroke, lunging at my face with gangs of force. Trust him to try and maim me – and this contest means nothing. Both his sticks are held high . . . so I fall to one knee with both of mine ready, my mind blotting out the murmured wave of anticipation from the crowd. I've thought long about this, long enough that there's no need to think now. It's not enough to go for the balls, the most vulnerable spot. No, a quick stickfighter can inflict double damage. I stab with Mormegil at his crotch, relishing its rigidness and the pain it will cause, yet pulling the stroke a little, for I am a boy, also; I know what it means to strike full strength there. Better to kill someone with a temple blow than that. At the same time, I bang the bendy stick on the ball of his knee as hard as I can and roll.

I come to my feet expecting to see Markham in the toils of agony. He feigns total indifference at first, then allows us to see he's in some pain, but only from his knee. He hobbles backward a step, kicking it out to ease it. I wait, tasting the moment but puzzled as to why he isn't clutching his balls howling.

A deep voice rolls out, that of the judge: 'Halt, boys!' Markham turns to him, a mixture of reluctance and relief on his face. I'm glad, and now every boy there turns towards the judge. He's not a stickfighter. Not even a boy, the judge. His real name is Salad, but we use both. I don't know whether he gave us the art of stickfighting, but he knows the rules and enforces them when he's around. Sometimes he's unseen for days, but his word is binding always, and not because we're afraid. The judge has a fearsome appearance; he's all muscle, like carved wood, his arms bulge, and this seems the reason for his shabby shirts – it isn't – and the strain of his thighs against his corduroys makes his hands seem normal, fragile even. But the judge, Salad, is sick. At times he can't stop coughing and, somehow, it is known among us that the muscles have surrendered their strength though they are preserved in form. The judge's voice is what commands our respect, mostly. He is very fair too.

'What's in your trousers, Markham?' The judge is quietly stern. He stands with his hands behind his back. Some of the boys are already taller than him. Markham knows he'll be forced to prove that he didn't cheat, so with little ado, he pulls out through the top of his trousers a thick sponge, much squashed, and hands it over to Salad. I grin, but joy is short-lived. The judge pronounces, 'Markham is disqualified. Match annulled.' Damn! I was certain he'd award me a victory, but now it's worked against me that the match wasn't a proper one. And everyone who matters has seen my new move too, so the element of surprise, my tactical advantage, is lost. I don't waste time trying to appeal to the judge; he's very strict, and this is why we respect him. I walk away too quickly for anybody to speak to me, Lapy at my shoulder.

In the evening I practise my forms with Lapy, who'd be a good stickfighter if he could be bothered. He never says much, but I like him for this. He's no pushover, Lapy. If he tells me something, I listen; he knows what he's about. He's got the manner of a champion stickfighter: you can never tell what's on his mind and he never seems afraid. When he feels like being scarce, even I won't see him.

Finally I light a cigarette butt I found and ask him the question that's burned on my lips for hours. 'What d'you think of the judge's decision earlier?'

He stops to glance at me in the middle of a stick manoeuvre. 'Pretty bog-standard. He cheated, but the judge didn't want to give you a total victory. Psychologically that would have demoralized Markham too much.' I watch him ponder whether to say more before he begins to weave his sticks once more. Sometimes I think of giving up this stickfighting lark altogether. I'm thirteen and getting too big to spend hours practising my sticks. The smart boys spend their days poking and scouring the dump. There's a lot of valuable stuff here – it's not just home.

The judge surprises me early the next morning; he's been watching me from behind a car wreck. Usually I'm about early, practising my sticks, snooping on what others are doing. When I notice him, I wonder how he escaped my eye for so long; it's hard to conceal such a bulky body.

He says, his voice hoarse, 'Well met, Raul.' The judge – Salad, I want to call him as the older boys do – talks like this sometimes. He moves out from behind the wreck heavily, though I know just how agile he is.

'Salad,' I say, continuing my single-stick forms. I'm not exactly angry, but it won't hurt if he thinks I am. He likes me. I feel him waiting; his silence tells me something of his mood.

'My decision yesterday was based on what I felt was fair.' I wait, hoping he'll blurt something. 'I know you and Markham are rivals. I know how evenly matched you two are. I know you feel betrayed; you think I've given him the edge because he's seen your new moves.' I'm so stunned by Salad's words that my stick hangs momentarily in the air. It's best to neither confirm nor deny, so I continue practising, keeping my face flat. My thoughts race. I now feel sheepish, angry, afraid and resentful of the judge all at once, so I push these feelings away. My concentration is so strong that when I stop to breathe a few minutes later, Salad is no longer there. At first I'm glad, and not just because my chest is heaving, but then it hits me that he wanted to tell me something and then didn't. I am hurt rather than curious. Even if it is just more stories – it is Salad after all who tells us about Mormegil, Turin and Beren – he should have said his piece.

I practise with Lapy much of that day, in a remote bit of the dump. He's a good partner, cagey. I use my new moves a couple of times but with no success. By the evening our feet blister from acid waste, and I feel like crap. My sadness has nothing to do with fighting sticks.

I feel no better the next day and decide perhaps what I need is not more practice but to trade blows with someone. I go in search of Markham, but before I find him, I come upon a group formed up in a circle round two boys, fifteen-year-olds. I know one of them, Malick; he's a brute, but I've never seen the other. They're going at it. Malick uses a lone stick, swings it like a club, although it's regulation thickness. His fights are popular because he's sly, savage. We've seen the judge pull him off people a time or two. Malick is actually not so brutish, in my opinion. I think he plays it up because he's not liked and wants to disgust us even more. The other boy uses two sticks and is very good. He blends power and finesse very well; he's strong on both hands. I wonder if he's from the dump. Malick will lose and so I stay to watch, even though I'm eager to fight this morning. His opponent seems popular; the crowd murmur his name, Peja, in a way that I detest, despite his skill. When he disarms Malick a little later, it's done without viciousness so that Malick stands empty-handed but unhurt. His eyes roll wildly in his head as he considers his options. I feel sure Malick is on the point of throwing himself at Peja to grapple him to the ground, but he doesn't. The fight is over.

Before anyone can move off, Salad pushes another boy forward by the shoulders, into the circle, and points to me. The judge only occasionally proposes fights in this way – it's not the role of a judge, really, is it? But when he does, there's excitement. This boy is a little shorter than me, sandy-haired, compact. His face is bland and I know with a jolt in my belly that he'll be good, probably better than Markham. Salad has put me on the spot, but happily I'm spoiling for a fight. I step forward with a readiness that's very like a thrill for blood. I don't know him, I may never see him again, but I want badly to hurt him in unusual ways with my sticks. Break his wrist or knock out his front teeth. Around us, as we prepare, lots of younger boys, tens and elevens. A trio of Malick's friends hang about too.

We both take time to limber up. For me, it's a chance to study my opponent. With a signal, the judge gets us going. Sandy Hair comes right in, quick as mercury, and hits my knuckles, surprisingly hard. He does not dance back and we spar up close so my longer reach is a disadvantage. He manages to catch my other knuckles. He's done something to his sticks, this one; they are somehow very hard. Being hit twice so quickly calms me. I'm sweating already and my mind is blank save for a desire to humble this boy. His quickness is at least equal to mine, I think, without dismay. I don't know that he'll tire before me either; my stomach is a pit and my vision blurs round the edges. I should've eaten something, but that's not a thought for the present. The next time he launches an attack I go back at him equally hard. His right hand is a little weaker, his ripostes less certain on that side, so I force him to retreat with Orcrist, trying to double his wrist back on itself. He sidles away, but I follow, banging his elbow. He tries to reply and succeeds in getting his right hand free. The crowd has been quiet and as we take a moment to breathe, it feels like we all take in air together. This time when he closes with me, Mormegil keeps him away, but I cannot do this for long and I only want him to think I'm tired. He is cautious too – his elbow is likely giving him pain and he teases me with his left hand, batting at Mormegil. I launch myself at him once more, feeling like I did against Markham, that it is now or never. I'm not sure what I'll do, but I feel confident enough to respond to anything. He's quick as lightning and rash – going for the eyes when he could have thumped my knuckles again. But he's in close once more and we trade blow and parry until my arms feel they might fall from my shoulders and my breathing fills my ears. I force him to aim a blow at my ribs, leaving my left side open, knowing he'll take the opening. It stings – I feel the skin redden almost instantly – and I drop to one knee, reeling a little bit. He pauses – he lacks the killer instinct – one stick above his shoulder; the other is pointed at me to ward off any blow that may come. But my stroke is aimed once again at the knee, too low for his block, and I lunge rather than swing, to jab him full on the ball of his kneecap, twisting Orcrist – not Mormegil – to cause more pain. He stumbles back, almost dropping a stick as he hops to clasp his injured knee. Mormegil comes up as I shoot up off my own knee like it's a launch pad, though it hurts like hell to do that. I pull my stroke at the last second, grudgingly.

There's something in his eyes – he's not afraid – but I see recognition beyond fear – and acceptance of what I'm about to do, of what I am. Killer. I pull the blow, or push it rather so I miss his temple – the thought flashes through me, through my entire body like a lash, that I don't know this boy and can't kill him. Mormegil lacerates his ear instead. And having changed the stroke, I drop my stick. My knuckles sear again as if in sympathy with him. And I breathe once more, like a bellows, exhausted and desperate suddenly to sit. Sandy Hair still clutches his knee, ignoring his torn ear. He's on the ground now in agony and my sorrow is complete. Salad eyes me gravely, but I can't abide his eyes on mine; there's only shame in this win. It takes all my willpower not to leave Orcrist and Mormegil as I walk off. Part of me notices – and is bitter – that no one chooses to follow me, to ask what's wrong.

I feel shunned, but the dump is actually a big place and boys here have enough of a struggle to survive not to worry over someone feeling down. I cannot find Lapy and even the lazy search of a day does not turn him up. Hunger attacks my insides suddenly and I hunt for food for hours. I even leave the dump to see what can be scavenged outside. I take Mormegil, tucked under my clothes – for protection. The fearful looks, the clutched purses of the outside are somehow welcome, an escape from loneliness. At least I'm noticed. People on the outside are scared of me but not because I fight sticks. I'm an urchin, a snot-faced, scuffed boy in rags that they want to pity but can't. I stuff my head with stale old chicken and bacon cadged from a greasy restaurant and go back to the dump, hating and enjoying the nervous looks.

When I can't take any more loneliness, I decide to go and find him, the one I nearly killed. That's how I think of him, and I can't shut him out of my thoughts. I'm resolved to go and see how he is. To explain myself. Perhaps to even say sorry, though I don't know what for. The thing is, I don't know where he stays; perhaps he's not even a dump kid. I ask boys I know and even boys I don't, describing him, hoping they saw the fight. I get a jumble of answers; short sandy-haired boys are ten a penny anywhere, I suppose. I give up, then bump into him as I go in search of Lapy once more, just to keep active. He's practising with some mates. They stop as I draw near. He gives me an almost friendly nod, though I notice his eyes are guarded, like when a madman's in the room. Talking is an effort, my tongue feels thick and ashy, and I have to ask him for a word twice before he understands. We go some way away and he makes a show of dropping his sticks, to impress his friends, I suspect. I conceal my smile.

I say it all at once, afraid to stop even for breath: 'Look, I don't know your name, and I'm not sure this will come out the right way, but I just wanted to say sorry. It was a good fight; you're a good fighter. I know what I did wasn't technically illegal, but I feel an apology is needed.' I wrestle down the urge to go on. Laconic Lapy. I must be like him. Like the Spartans too. Sandy Hair thrusts his hand at me like we've just played tennis or some other cruddy gentlemanly sport. There are no bruises on him; the ear looks whole. For an instant I think I imagined the whole thing.

'Tuor,' he introduces himself. I smile again but not with relief, with real amusement. He's no Tuor. Salad's stories! 'It was even steven,' he continues. 'A good fight like you said, and I would've done the same in your place.' And abruptly as that there's nothing left to say for either of us. I try to give him a smile that's not so grateful, friendlier, before I swivel and make off. The clacking of sticks starts up again immediately and I feel less guilty.

Days pass before I pick up my sticks again. When I do, I have a strange sense that it's not me who swings Mormegil or stabs with Orcrist, but some unseen beast that slips into me. The feeling leaves me quite numb. I try to explain it to Lapy, but he looks at me as if I've lost my marbles. He's not afraid to practise with me, though; our friendship is the same. I neither avoid Markham nor seek him out, but he's in my thoughts. Concede to Markham, give up this whole racket, my ambitions as a stickfighter, pass Mormegil on to some eight-year-old coming up, and do something less deadly, less emotionally sapping. That's what part of me feels. I too could lose an eye, or be killed.

It rains for what feels like a week and the dump is in wretched mood. There's nothing to do all day but take shelter. I experience strange exhilarations, tire myself with mad quests that keep me out in the rain. Lapy doesn't try to settle me down; he's known me too long. The morning of the third day I wake shivering, still muddy and wet from the evening before, and with both sticks clenched in my left fist like a lifeline. Lapy gives me water, tries to swaddle me, but I'm already too hot. I'm also too weak to push off the stinking kerosene-smelling blanket that suffocates me. I wake from dreams in which the sandy-haired Tuor sets me alight with a burning stick. Other boys I have fought look on, bored rather than excited.

When I wake properly, the sun peers thinly through high clouds. I smell smoke somewhere not far off, but the sight and warmth of the sun is rousing enough. Lapy has left me, likely in disgust at my screams and moans. I'm surprised at how steady I feel on my feet. Awake, I remember that Salad was also in my fever dreams and I'm suddenly dying to know what he wanted to tell me when he came to watch me practise. But first I wander aimlessly, hoping for water and perhaps a bite. I know where I can sometimes get food from someone. Not a stickfighter, but he's so good at scavenging he doesn't care if we steal from him. Sometimes.

I'm ravenous and tear at some bread so fresh it must be from yesterday, and not crust either. I've seen virtually no one, but a radio is playing nearby, a warbly song I recognize but can't put a name to. I sit next to the scavenger's sleeping den long after I've wolfed his food, somehow more wobbly from having eaten. I stand, and there he is. Tauzin – I think, watching me smugly. He's a lanky, knobbly thing, all bony knees and thrust-out elbows, not at all tough, so I don't expect him to try anything.

He speaks before I can thank him. 'That bread was poisoned. I left it as bait for whoever's been stealing my stuff. Rat poison,' he adds unnecessarily. 'Bet you didn't know I was a master poisoner. Had no idea it was you, but I don't care really. You might not even die.' He's talking too much, yabbering on as though we're in a classroom somewhere, or mates, and what he says really matters. I stick my hand down my craw, squeezing my fingers into a point and forcing them as hard as I can past my gullet. He stops, stunned, and I aim the flood of mush that comes spurting out at him; even though he's not stupid, he stopped and stood about ten feet away. A second smaller gush of puke rises and now I'm sure it's all out. I smile.

'Too late,' he tells me, but he's no longer so cool, and not just because I took him by surprise emptying my stomach. No, he's shitless now 'cause I'm advancing on him, both sticks suddenly, magically, in my left hand, a trick I've practised loads to get really good at. He backs up a couple of steps, shuffling as though he'll wet himself if he lifts his feet.

'The poison's already working on your system.'

'I've plenty of time to kill you, though.' I don't mean the words; I just want to scare him. I've no idea if he's actually poisoned me, but as I utter the threat, I know with certainty I'll carry it through. No one's around and this snivelling rat of a poisoner doesn't deserve such a quick end as he'll get. If I am poisoned, I'll be too weak later, too doubled over in pain to kill him.

It's done almost quicker than thought. He turns to run, but his long legs are more hindrance than use and I trip him easily, kicking one foot against the other. He falls like a rag doll, making no effort to keep on his feet, and it's contempt at this weakness that sets my arm in motion. Standing bent over him, I swing the two sticks in my left hand easily, a bit like a golfer, I think, and hard enough that wind whistles through the tiny space between Orcrist and Mormegil. The strike is precise enough to kill; I feel the rubbery give of his temple beneath the tip of my sticks. But once more shame comes on me, so suddenly I taste it mingling with the acid of vomit. I walk away without checking that he's dead. I feel weak again, the return of a fever.

A strange wind comes up that doesn't stir the bushes but pulls at my shorts, keens to me like a dead baby. I stand, clutching my head, afraid I'll fall if I try to walk. The dump suddenly doesn't seem empty after all. Boys are skulking all about, may even have seen me kill Tauzin, and they're just waiting for the right moment to ambush me. I would take one or two of them with me, and the certainty steadies me slightly. After some minutes I begin walking again, with purpose. To find someone who never moves from his spot.

Aias is awake but looks like he's about to die; his eyes are gummy and he holds as ever the telltale plastic bottle in his dainty fingers. Aias looks like shit, but his smile is that of a boy who loves the world. He used to be one of the very best stickfighters. One of only two legends we have in the dump. There are almost as many stories about him as about Turin. A champion with two sticks or with a single one. You were lucky if Aias fought you with a single stick; very good if he used two. It was before my time, though Aias cannot be older than seventeen. His smile is jolly, but only if you don't look too closely. He has all his teeth, but they are very nearly black, the gums too.

'Aias,' I whisper. It seems rude to speak normally around him, to disturb the sleepy peace of glue life. 'Aias, got any glue?' It takes him an aeon to look at me, to turn one muddy and one clear eye towards me. He's got the trembles. I wish I had food to offer him. The hand he extends shakes uncontrollably. He's never selfish with his glue. Involuntarily, I wipe the bottle mouth with my shirt, suck on it hard. There's not much left, barely any in fact. I suck a minute, taking small breaths through my nose and watching Aias turn his head as though it's buried in a slurry of mud. I feel a mixture of pity and stomping contempt before the warmth invades my mouth and throat. It would be easy to kill him, end his half-life, easier even than with Tauzin. I wouldn't even have to use my sticks, he's like a twig. One wrench would snap his neck. Up close his happy smile seems more a grin of pain. Glue's supposed to be a happy drug. It warms you, it's true – it's a help on cold nights – but it makes me think of blood. I get a bit twitchy on glue; my mind's full of gore. The longer you do it, the more it kills the brain, rots it, or those bits of the brain that make you fight. I suck so hard I get a headache with my warm feeling. I hand the bottle back to him, trying not to gag at his stink. His feet are dotted with yellow shit specks. I walk away with a muzzy head, concentrating on putting one foot in front of the other and clutching at the warmth spreading all the way to my fingertips. It feels like a layer on my skin and yet it's got beneath the surface at the same time, sending rays into my bones.

I almost bump heads with Markham. He steps back a pace as if to get a good look, says, 'You have your sticks – good. Salad thinks we should do a rematch.' I think my answering nod is calm, but he has a bad habit of catching me off guard. He spins and walks ahead. I follow, his two friends moving in to flank me so it feels like I have an honour guard. I clutch my sticks in anticipation. Markham's own sticks hang from the loops of his shorts; he looks ridiculous.

If anything, I start to feel warmer as I walk. When we find Salad, my headache is gone. I'm swollen with energy, and even more eager than usual. More boys draw up. Salad has a few words with us, in a stern tone. He's more tired than ever, and coughs hoarsely. His voice is normal, and his muscles have the same hard, rubbery look they always do. For the first time I notice he and I are almost the same height. His words bleed out of his mouth, I think because of the glue, and I hear nothing of what he says. I need to release the force building inside me. I can't let it escape before I finish Markham, and I know I will. Snarls echo in my head. Markham will never again challenge me.

I don't limber up; Markham eyes me, perhaps taking note of my confidence. I stand still to avoid wasting the killing essence in me; I don't want it to escape.

So that when Salad gives the signal, I go for Markham harder, I think, than I've ever gone for anyone. He's ready, though, and our sticks swirl faster and more intricately than I've seen in some time. A trick of the glue makes them catch alight. My limbs are weightless and Mormegil, like its namesake, is keen to drink. No wrist blows, no knuckle raps. I go for his throat and he aims for my head. He'll tire before my supercharged arms, so I swing and swing, using a good deal of my strength in each stroke. He sweats, I am dry, and I watch his eyes dart about trying to follow my sticks.

He doesn't give ground; I admire that. I'm pressed up almost against him and not once does he hunt for space. But I have cunning too, and when the glue in my veins gives me the signal, I switch tactics. I swing with Orcrist a second too slowly and he rises to the bait. His parry becomes harder, faster; he drives at my neck. I slip the blow, stepping back and aside, tilting my head ever so slightly so that it misses me. He tries to recover – he's almost as quick as I am – but there's time for me to smash the top of his earlobe, to parry his own return stroke and aim Mormegil's tip at his throat. Let the beast slake its thirst. He dives backward to escape, almost as though he's been hit. He thinks I'll give him time to regain his footing, but I don't. Instead I'm on him, and on his back he tries to sweep my leg with his foot just as I stab again, for his groin. Mormegil catches the inside of his thigh – the twisty fucker – and before I can strike again, with perfect accuracy this time, Salad's arm is in front of me, a barrier of muscle the size of my head. 'Fight over,' he announces, his voice coming from a long way off. 'Raul wins.' My skin tingles with the remains of the glue's warmth. My arms, my body still hum with unused force. I close my eyes a second for calm, but I cannot turn away. What happens must. I start to swing before my eyes open; I feel bold, so ready. The judge blocks with his forearm, as if he expects this. It must sting like hell even wrapped in muscle like that. His eyes are on mine without expression, but the watching boys release a gasp of shock. I smile. They do not know it, but I'm freeing them from the tyranny of authority. My next blow follows so hard on the heels of the first that Salad cannot possibly counter, and he doesn't. To his credit he only falls to one knee; I expected a hit on the temple would end him. Stunned, he's at the right height now for me to use maximum power and I hit him again cleanly across the nose. He keels forward, not even putting out his hands to catch himself. I give him a chance to roll onto his back, but before I can pick my next spot, another blow lands. Markham's. He hits the judge's knee, a downward chop like an axe stroke, and then pokes at his crotch with the other stick.

A spasm crosses Salad's face, the first one. He pulls himself into a ball, his knees up as I stab for his eyes. Markham is circling, looking for an opening, and it's like we're the only two alive in that place; the other boys are all frozen, so still as to be almost empty shells. Markham thrusts into his other eye and Salad's face splashes blood. He still makes no sound.

I'd dreamed of a killing blow, the single cut that cleanly ends life, but I've done that already, with Tauzin earlier. It was sweet. But now's not the time for precision. I swing and thrust, mindlessly raining blows, and Markham is with me, shares my aim for we club at the judge's head with no thought for accuracy. Even when he no longer moves, Markham and I swing for some minutes. Then I stop.

DANCING TO THE JAZZ GOBLIN AND HIS RHYTHM

Brian Chikwava

Independence Day, Wednesday, 18 April 2001. I still remember the morning clearly enough. Save for my suitcase and sax, the bulk of the grubby belongings were still scattered in the open courtyard. Over the city of Harare, a dirty grey sky sagged like a vagrant's winter rag, but I couldn't care less. I had just moved into my new bedsit flat. One I didn't have to share with anyone. Not with pimping goblins again. Never!

The bedsit was in a state, with paint peeling off the walls, a quarter of the parquet floor tiling coming off, and a broken geyser. Still, I did not mind. The squalid loneliness of my new home was a welcome relief. While I felt I now understood Harare and its people, I also felt that there was something that I had completely misunderstood about the city. Perhaps nine months is not long enough to fully understand a city. Before he died, my grandfather always said you can never really know a place until you have:

1. fallen in love with its music,
2. fallen in love with its women and
3. tried the *mbanje* that grows out of its soil.

I had done all but fall in love with Harare women, and my faith in my grandfather had deserted me.

I thrust my hand into my junk-filled pocket and excavated a sachet of *mbanje*. I rolled it with care. Malawi gold. The best that you could get in Harare at the time. With hindsight, I think this may be where I went wrong, because Malawi gold was smuggled in from Malawi. I avoided Harare-grown *mbanje* because I imagined there was not much difference between smoking it and smoking my grandfather's white beard.

'See where you got it wrong? You didn't smoke *mbanje* from Harare,' I can imagine him croaking.

As I puffed away, I could hear the wailing of sirens from a distance. Being Independence Day, I knew it could only be Uncle Bob's motorcade on its way to the National Sports Stadium, where he would be addressing the nation – reminding it again why it should never forget the liberation struggle. I admire Bob, though, but for reasons that are completely different to those held by his ministers, who dread plopping out of his rear. I just like confidence tricksters.

Sitting on the dusty floor, I lit my Malawi gold and started to reflect. It had been nine months since I left Bulawayo for Harare. My mother had thrown me out of the family home.

She had said, 'I'm not disowning you, my child, but it brings bad luck for a woman to keep on looking after a child who has grown a beard.'

I didn't have much of a beard, but I didn't want to start another quarrel. When I got off the bus in Harare, I flung my bag over my shoulder and headed straight to the Terreskane Beer Garden. I didn't want to go to my cousin's house straightaway because I wanted to defer expending her hospitality as long as I could; also I wasn't quite ready to immerse myself in her heroic domesticity. She had a couple of toddlers and had just had twins who cried all the time and stuck to her breasts like ticks. It made conversation with her a bit like shovelling coal onto a truck with a teaspoon. And the arrival of her husband from work did not change much either. After walking into the house, he would come to stand in the kitchen doorway in his grey suit. Looking startled, either by my presence or by what had become of his life, he would remove his heavy-rimmed glasses and rub his eyes, before saying, 'Hello, Jabu.' Then he would disappear to change clothes. After that, I would only see him pottering around in flip-flops like a caged animal, never saying much, never listening to much, just waiting for an opportunity to give my cousin another baby.

I remember stopping to buy a cigarette from a street vendor at the corner of Herbert Chitepo Avenue and Second Street, not far from the Terreskane, or 'TK' as everyone called it. I put my bag down, stretched my shoulders and yawned. My bag was fat with a pumpkin that my mother had asked me to take to my cousin, two pairs of jeans, a couple of T-shirts and an African shirt that was Made in Malaysia.

'*Une* Madson?' I asked.

The vendor nodded, opened a box of Madison Red and shoved it into my face. I took one cigarette and lit it.

'I've got a pumpkin. You can have it for a good price,' I said to him after my first puff.

He smiled knowingly, shook his head politely and stared straight ahead as if I wasn't there at all. I picked up my bag and left him alone.

I contemplated first dropping the constipated bag at my cousin's, but I knew it would be an involved process, requiring excuses, a bunch of lies and a host of other forms of deceit that would leave me carrying a skipload of guilt. Where would I dump such a load? I had been to Harare several times, but not enough to know where its emotional rubbish-dump sites were. In the end I just went to the TK and got drunk.

The TK is a place that writhes with sleep-starved civil servants, labourers, prostitutes, musicians, thieves and daring tourists – all after foul sex and disease. That's what I think anyway. Still I had not counted on coming across Tafi, the Jazz Goblin. I met him at the TK two weeks after my arrival. People called him the Jazz Goblin because his band was called the Jazz Goblin and His Rhythm. He was their frontman, ripping it out on vocals and guitar, accompanied by two absent-minded musicians: Zuze, on pennywhistle, and Costa, on percussion. This meant that Tafi had to be the goblin, propping up the performance with mad showmanship.

'You drop and die on the dance floor, you on your own. You wan stop us having fun?' he would bark into his mic every so often. Predictably, he had a colourful following: hard-drinking clerks; *mbanje* vendors; Figo, a football-crazy security guard who also sold *mbanje*; and nearly always, a troupe of girls who lived by a motto they never uttered: 'Wherever I lay my *punani* that's my home.' I liked the set-up. I also had a desire to join the Jazz Goblin and His Rhythm, even though I knew they were rubbish. I thought of it as an interesting entry into Harare's live-music scene.

Joining the trio was easier than I expected. Tafi seemed pleased by my desire to join his band. I thought he was a useful idiot – the kind of creature who feels compelled to befriend people he feels intimidated by. Tafi thought I was cool, I could tell, but didn't know why. Maybe it was because I had approached him with a fist-on-fist greeting and he had fumbled with an open hand before folding it and reciprocating in salutation. Then, I knew I had the upper hand. I was more streetwise; I had dictated the way someone ten years older greeted me. I felt cool.

The downside of this is always that coolness comes with a grossly magnified awareness of self-invention in other people. Because you are all too aware of your own self-invention, you see it in other people and lose your nerve when you see someone being cool with satanic deftness. That happened to me when I asked Tafi what days the band rehearsed. He threw his head back on his chair, lit a cigarette, blew smoke up into the air and shrugged his shoulders with a dab of detached swagger.

'Just bring your sax when we have a gig. You can play what you want, no problem.'

My heart leaped. He looked cool. Really cool. For a moment I worried that I would be rumbled in that psychological hide-and-seek. That was the first time I remember being overawed by his presence.

Over the coming weeks new things about Tafi began to emerge, but they did little to diminish the effect he had on me. For instance, he carried his guitar everywhere. I learned that this had nothing to do with his dedication to his craft and everything to do with his housing issue. I had also heard that he spent his afternoons with a gang of touts and pickpockets at Market Square who were hired to unleash violence on intransigent members of the public. But by the time all this came to my realization it was too late. I was already caught up in the affairs of the Jazz Goblin and His Rhythm.

I had just got a job as a mechanic's apprentice and was moving out of my cousin's place into a two-bed flat some ten minutes' walk from the TK. I was looking for someone to take the other room. That's when the Jazz Goblin came to me to say, 'I can take the other room and can look after the flat during the day when you are at work.'

I sensed an implicit threat of malicious burglary, yet I wasn't ready to live with Tafi so that he could guard the flat against himself. After an awkward silence I answered, 'As long as you're happy with the rent. It's Z$10,000 a month.'

He was quiet. He threw his half-finished cigarette onto the floor and took his time to put it out by grinding it with the sole of his shoe. I knew him well enough to know that he could not afford to throw away half a cigarette, but I did not want to let it bother me even though I sensed something lurking beneath his calm exterior.

A couple of days later, after a gig, he asked me if he could spend a night at my flat.

'Just tonight. I won't bring the girls,' he said.

'Yeah, no problem,' I said, trying not to sound thrown off. You don't want someone thinking that you are sensing their threats: it gives them the upper hand. Inside, I was praying that it would be just one night.

When I came from work the following day, I found him still in the flat. I didn't say anything because I didn't want it to look like I was kicking him out. That would ruin the dynamics within the band, I reasoned. But he had eaten all my bread. I locked myself up in the bathroom for an hour while he strummed his guitar and smoked *mbanje* in the lounge. For the first time I hated the smell of *mbanje*. Tafi looked too comfortable in the flat. I consoled myself with the fact that he could not possibly hijack the other room, because a colleague from work was going to be moving in over the weekend. Half an hour later I was back in the bathroom kicking myself for having just told Tafi he could stay until Saturday. He had just gazed at me vacantly and continued strumming his guitar when I expected gratitude. My insignificance weighed down on me.

I know it may look as if I didn't like Tafi, was scared of him or something like that. That may be true, but I also had other plans for the flat. After thinking about it for the previous month, I had decided that, this being the first time I had lived independently, I would turn the flat into an environment with which I would be able to make an emotional connection. I had read from an interior-decoration magazine that 'emotional connection' was the 'in thing'. But I doubted I would be able to create such a place while living with a jazz goblin. I figured out that for me, 'emotional connection' meant sticking photos of my family all over the flat – a kind of shrine to my family: my mother, sister, my grandfather, my disappeared father and my late younger brother, who was run over by a truck at the age of nine. Looking at his photos, I remembered him for his grasp of the concept of 'intention'. One day he bawled after I threw a lemon at him because he kept following me around in the house, stopping me from stealing my mother's condensed milk. When my mother asked him what was wrong, my brother had said I had narrowly missed hitting him with a lemon. My mother thought it was ridiculous. So did I. But that was because I failed to appreciate that what he was querying was my intention to hurt him. This may explain my unwillingness to appreciate Tafi's intentions when he asked to spend just one night at my flat.

When, on Saturday, my workmate Andrew moved in, Tafi simply dragged the reed mat I had lent him to the lounge. Save for a

Tonga stool, the lounge was raving empty anyway, so I didn't say anything. I wanted to preserve my street cred. A month later Tafi had successfully drilled himself to eat Andrew's food during the day and remained impervious to any protests. Andrew promptly moved out of the flat, sneezing distress. Unlike him, I was not affected by Tafi's eating habits as I had quickly stopped buying any food and only ate out. With Andrew gone, Tafi quickly hauled a horse-sized prostitute into the vacant room He called her Bhiza Ramambo – the Emperor's Horse.

Another month down the line, my 'emotional connection' project looked like a preposterous endeavour and if I had died pursuing it, my epitaph would probably have read, 'Died of misadventure.' Tafi owned both the flat and myself: the band rehearsed at the flat and Tafi told me when to come in on a song. He even told me who to buy *mbanje* from, which meant *mbanje* vendors he had not yet fallen out with for abusing the credit they gave him. He bought fish on credit from a fishmonger who regularly came to our block of flats and expected me to pay.

'The fish was for the family,' he would remind me, and I would nod sheepishly, knowing that 'family' meant Tafi since I never even once tasted the fish. But there were times when my resentments congealed and I felt pushed to challenge the inequity of our silent agreement. Then I would try to bring up the rent issue, and Tafi would simply slither into his unfathomable persona.

'You know why I sometimes write poetry, Jabu?' he would ask.

'Why?'

'It's a better substitute for things that I sometimes feel like doing,' he would say, rolling some *mbanje*.

Not knowing if this was meant to be a threat or performance poetry, I asked, 'What do you sometimes feel like doing?'

But he would not answer. Instead he would start strumming his guitar, his guttural voice softly singing:

I found it
A snake under my blankets
Cold and clammy
Tonight I will kill a snake
Tonight I will kill a snake.

I ignored him, and we left it there.

By the beginning of April 2001 Tafi was demanding that I make him tea and bring it into his room because he was the band leader. By then, the Emperor's Horse had bolted out of the stable with the Goblin's guitar. It turned out she had been servicing the Goblin on credit, and in the end had told him that if he was not paying up, next time he should buy himself a rubber *punani*.

'There are plenty available for sale now!' she had screamed from the front door.

I kept well out of it because I didn't want what Tafi owed her to end up as another family expense. That was not so hard, given that I had paid every time I delivered myself into her legs. In return, though, she had been generous with genital lice, which I began to suspect originated from Tafi; I anticipated nightmares in which armies of lice were marching into my room, instructed by Tafi to seize control of my body.

Meanwhile I owed workmates nearly Z$120,000. That's six months' wages. From a wall in the lounge, my grandfather stared with ever increasing incredulity, my brother chuckled, my father disconnected, while my mother glared.

Then one Friday evening I came back from work to find that Tafi had moved a pair of prostitutes into the flat. One, Maria, had lost her front teeth but said that it made it easier for her to suck it, and the other, Ranga, said for Z$3,000 she could make me cry. 'Five thousand dollars for both of us?' Maria offered. Sitting on my reed mat, his eyes more slits, Tafi was puffing *mbanjo* from the corner of his mouth and likely calculating his cut. Without a word, I scurried into my room and found myself taking stock: a pimp in his vice shack with his vice girls? That was it for me. I spent the following week quietly plotting a stealthy exit. On 18 April, when Tafi, Maria and Ranga left the flat for free food and a free football match at the independence celebrations, I made my move.

I'm not going to go into the boring details of it except that, for a loaf of bread each, I hired a ragtag platoon of street kids to carry my belongings. In just under an hour and a half my independence had been won. That's why I still remember the morning clearly. From the cold floor of my new flat, the rhythm of the Jazz Goblin was distant. All I could hear coming in through the broken window was the wailing sound of sirens; a creature of folklore was strutting its stuff, on its way to address the nation about independence. I had just won mine, so I took another drag of my Malawi gold and opened my lips to let out a lariat of smoke that caught my bolting thoughts by the neck and brought them crashing down. They accumulated and multiplied in the far corner of the cold floor, like my mother's beads. For the first time, my thoughts were collected. It felt like home.

PROMENADE

Henrietta Rose-Innes

I haven't changed much, over the years. When I look in the mirror, the experience is much the same as it was when I was a younger man. My teeth have not yellowed and my eyesight is remarkably good. Even my finger- and toenails, I suspect, do not edge out from my extremities as rapidly as other people's do. Everyone assumes that I'm in my early forties, when in fact I'm fifty-four – a long way from retirement, but still significantly older than my colleagues at the ad agency. Of course I'm balding now, but even this has helped to freeze me in time. I used to style my hair differently, part it this way and that, grow it and trim it; but I am stuck now with this look, this length: a conservative short cut around the bald spot at the crown. Anything else looks foolish.

It is partially the adipose layer beneath the skin, I believe, that helps to preserve my looks. Slightly plump people, I've often noticed, seem to age better than the bony ones: the skin stays taut for longer, the skeletons submerged. Yes, I am a little overweight, as I have been since my early thirties. I've tried to lose the excess, but my body remains impervious. A few years back I put myself through a stern fitness regime – low-fat foods, the gym. There was no observable impact on my weight or muscle tone. I have a metabolism in perfect equilibrium, it seems. Still, I exercise, frequently if moderately. Because what would happen if I stopped?

So it is that every evening after work, at six sharp, I take my promenade along the sea wall near my flat. I clip along at a steady pace: a little more than a walk, a little less than a jog. My fists are bunched before my chest; I thrust them forward and back, kicking my feet one-two, one-two, my elbows winging to the sides. Yes, I am one of those speed-walkers. I know it's undignified, but it's the only way to get up any kind of sweat without actually running. I have the gear: special lightweight jogging shorts, athletic socks, sweat-wicking tops in the latest high-tech fabrics. (No vests; I really am too old for that.) Once a year I buy a new pair of Nikes or New Balances, a virtuous treat.

On my outward journey, the sea lies to my left, grey or blue or silver. Fifteen minutes at a swift stride from my flat down the steep street, to the sea wall and along the path to the traffic lights opposite the garage and café. Here I pause to stretch on the strip of lawn, before continuing for another fifteen minutes along the promenade as far as the public telephones. Then I wheel round and go back in the other direction, one-two, one-two, with the sea on my right, half an hour, pausing only to cross at the lights to the café for the day's *Argus*. I roll the newspaper tightly and hold it baton-like in one hand for the rest of the route home (only unsatisfactory on the weekends, when the editions are too fat for comfort). I always take with me just enough change in the special zip-up pocket in my top – plus twenty cents, because sometimes they put up the price without warning – and my house key. No wallet or mobile phone; although the promenade is busy and safe at that time, you can never be too careful. And I like to stay light.

The thing about walking along a sea wall is that your options are limited: you can only go forward or back. You can't head off to the side without falling into the sea, or ploughing across the lawn through the children's swings and roundabouts and into the traffic. The lack of choice is soothing, and I'm quite content to follow my established route, each time the same. It is a beautiful walk, especially on still evenings when the sea is flat and the sky clear, or lightly flecked with peachy clouds. The water glows and swirls like cognac. Everyone I meet, coming or going, is gilded on either the left or right sides of their faces with pink or saffron, and they all seem serene and calm and somehow meditative in the generous light. I know I do.

People comment on that: my serenity. But often I am not calm inside, not at all, especially not in the boiling light of those late evenings. It is a dramatic coastline, and there are often grand effects: towering clouds, beating waves, gleams on the rocks where Darwin, they say, once stood and pondered geological time and the ancient congress of molten stone.

But it is not these that affect me so. It is purely the light coming over the sea, a brilliant luminosity not encountered from any other vantage point in the city. It cuts me with a kind of ecstasy – as if I'm on the verge of revelation, one I'm powerless to halt. I have been brought almost to tears, some evenings on the promenade.

There is a particular moment, when the sky goes coral pink and the breaking surf is chalk-blue, almost fluorescent in the fading light. And then each incoming swell feels as if it is rolling through my body, just under the skin, from the soles of my feet all the way to my fingernails, rolling out over the quick, making me want to reach out my fingers and touch. Although I am a controlled man, I am not immune to these things.

Controlled, that's another word I've heard people – my workmates – use to describe me. I'm a senior copywriter, moderately good at my job; good at controlling words, certainly. Words for pictures of sunsets, often with cars or couples in front of them. But I grope after language to describe the feelings I experience on my evening walks, the light in the air and on the sea. This pleases me: that some things remain beyond my grasp. That they cannot be rendered down.

Perhaps this is why I have no ambition. I've held the same position at the same agency for fifteen years and have no desire for anything greater, for a managerial position, even as the new hires are promoted around me. Such things, I know, could never fulfil my more obscure longings. I'm happy to run in place.

There are always a lot of people moving up and down the promenade: smooth-skinned models looping along in Rollerblades too heavy for their frail ankles; the old woman who sits on the same bench every evening to feed the pigeons; cheerful ladies in tracksuits, trying to shift a kilogramme or two; resolute athletes with corded thighs. Dog walkers and drug dealers and beggars, and lovers in each other's arms as they watch the sun go down. Some of them I have seen every other evening for the past three years, which is how long I've been taking my promenade now. Others are new. Recently I've started to feel I recognize individual seagulls along the route, although this is surely my imagination.

One evening a young man comes past me, sweating and steaming in a cloud of musk. Although covered up in a tracksuit, his body is obviously muscular; not the smooth, inflated-looking muscles that you see on some of the gym boys, not well-fed recreational beef, but the hard, functional build of someone who works with his body for a living. Shorter than me, but strong. He jogs fast and purposefully.

I notice him again a few days later, and from then on he intersects regularly with my evening promenade, three times a week: Mondays, Wednesdays, Saturdays. I see him going only the one way. He must loop back, as I do; but his circuit is clearly far more expansive and demanding than my own. Time-wise, he is rigid. I always pass him on my outbound trip, and always, it seems, at exactly the same place: just opposite the traffic lights where I pause to do my stretches. He waits to cross the road there, bouncing on his toes, swivelling his torso aggressively left and right. Perhaps he's heading for the gym.

Always dressed in bright, deep colours, I notice; he must have half a dozen different tracksuits, in pillar-box red, racing green, midnight blue. (These phrases come to me involuntarily.) He always wears the complete assemblage, matched top and bottom, which is quite formal – never casual in a T-shirt. A white towel is looped round his neck and sometimes he grasps its ends as he waits at the traffic lights, pulling it against the back of his dark neck. A strong, almost cuboidal block of a jaw. I think he must be a boxer. Something in the way he moves, in the build. Or maybe it's just the way he holds his fists, loosely clenched, that gives me this idea.

My certainty about his occupation grows. Who but a professional athlete would need to train so often and so hard, swathed in towel and sweat-dark tracksuit? His arms are bulkier than a long-distance runner's would need to be, he is light on his feet with a dancing stride, and there's a kind of sprightly aggression in his movements. Enormous hands, for his height. They make me self-conscious about my own flushed fists.

Two men, changeless, beating the same if opposite route; it is comforting. I've read about boxers' battles to keep their weight at certain limits, and I imagine that we are caught in a similar stasis. Like me, he is fighting to keep his body where it is.

After a while we start to nod to each other, cautiously. To test my boxing theory, one day I put up my fists – not sure, really, what I intend. He balls his and twitches them towards his chin. No smile, though. It feels tenuous, the moment: me with fists raised, unsure if this is a playful act.

Up close, I see the imperfections – the damaged skin of his brows, the way the scarring seems to have resulted in the loss of eyebrows. I notice that his nose looks broken, his earlobes thick. (Are those cauliflower ears?) Despite this coarsening of the features, he has an appealing face, set in an expression of youthful resolution, lit on one side by the setting sun.

It becomes a jokey ritual, a greeting every time we pass. The lifted hands in imaginary gloves. At least, I think it's a joke. It grows from there.

One evening, when we come face to face, he and I do that little step-step dance that happens when two people are walking straight into each other: both to the same side and then both back again.

I smile. His fists come up and this time he pauses to spar with me. Now, flinching, I know I'm right: only a pro could direct such a sparkling combination of quick almost-touches to my ribs, my jaw, my nose. The huge fists lunge at me, snap back; so close, I feel a tickle of warm air on my face and smell his sweat. I raise my hands to parry.

And after that it happens every time: each evening we do the two-step dance and spend a few moments trading phantom blows. A smile never crosses his face, as if the scars prevent it. But at the end, just before he skips to the side and jogs on, he'll give me a look and tip up his chin in brief and surely humorous acknowledgement.

A month passes, two. The woman who feeds the birds looks increasingly fragile, until I start to worry that she'll be overpowered by the sturdy pigeons bickering around her; then one day she is gone. Shortly thereafter I see the pigeons have constructed another old woman in their midst. The couples part and reconfigure, but the boxer and I remain the same, locked in our pattern, running and standing still.

Other people loop in other cycles round us, stitching up their days with a quick up-and-down along the water's edge. I think of ants, crawling in opposing circles. Clockwise ants every now and then touching mouthparts with their anticlockwise comrades, passing cryptic messages. Some promenaders I will doubtless never meet, caught as we are in orbits that never intersect; but the boxer and I are in sync.

My days pass mildly; I have other routines. The promenade is not my only circular occupation. I sit on Sunday afternoons in the flat and read the newspaper. I go out to buy myself coffee and croissants. I go to work, where I produce copy about faster, stronger, younger. When I hear my own words on TV, I don't remember ever writing them.

Sitting in my padded swivel chair before my computer station, hands poised to tap the keys, I am trapped in stillness. There is a strong desire to jump up and swing my arms, to dispel this immobility, but I stay where I am and the spasm passes. My colleagues at the other workstations do not notice this fleeting turmoil, do not see that I have paused in my typing to contemplate for a moment some grand gesture. I flex my hands, let them drop mildly back to the keyboard. My fingers renew their automatic labour.

Mondays, Wednesday, Saturdays. We never speak, but our greetings are progressively more familiar. In our small, intense interactions I notice things in great detail: the fact that his irises are black, fading to amber rims. A chipped tooth in his slightly open mouth.

Our sparring becomes elaborate. I think he might be teaching me to box. It's all very controlled, but of course there is also a tremor of fear. Huge fists in your face, what can you do but imagine those hands rubbing out your features, smearing your nose, forcing your teeth into your mouth? That's never happened to me, of course, but I can imagine the very specific sensations: nose-break pain, tooth-shatter pain, taste of blood. I do not know exactly what the mock-blows signify – violence or camaraderie. Each thrust has the potential to explode, is centimetres from rocketing into my face, from crushing my chest. I can far more easily imagine receiving such blows than delivering them. I try to picture pushing my hand all the way, sticking it between the big fists to press against that jaw. Impossible.

Sometimes, trotting on after our shadow-play, I am trembling slightly, feeling the sting of invisible gloves on my body, the smack of fists. I think of the phrase 'glass jaw'. Compared to his stony features, I am all crystal.

One Wednesday afternoon, I stay home from work with a cold. I switch on the TV at some unusual hour to catch the afternoon news: SABC2 or 3, which I would not normally watch. And I see him, I'm sure it's him, in red shorts shiny under the bright lights of the ring, his knuckles encased in bulbous mitts like cartoon hands. His lips are distended by a gum guard and he looks smaller with his top off, but I know him by his movements: the sideways skip and jump, fists flung out in that dancing rhythm. He and his opponent in blue are both compact men – is it featherweight? – but their bodies are pure wire-hard muscle, shiny brown with sweat. I don't catch his name over the dinging bell, the shouts of the crowd; and anyway, the commentary is in another language.

I lean forward, face close to the screen. It only lasts a couple of rounds. The one small, hard man drills the other to the floor with sweat-spraying strokes. I feel each blow as a twitch in my upper arms. And then it is over: blue lies flat on his back, toes up and out. My boxer's hands are raised above his head in victory, blood streaming from his brow.

Only after the ads come on do I relax my hands and let myself lean back on the couch.

He is absent from the promenade for a week. When he reappears, I am warier of him, almost ducking away from his shadow-strokes, but he is too skilful to touch me. Often I think about speaking to him, but my mouth is dry, and he is exercising so hard, so earnestly. I don't want to break his concentration.

I am not eloquent here, in this conversation of bodies. Still, I have come to depend on these playful altercations, these little knockabouts in which neither one of us falls to the ground.

Today, for the first time in months, my routine is broken. What is it that delays me? A foolish thing. A flutter of wings in my chest as I'm putting on my shoes, a kind of rushing. Something to startle a man of my age. I have to sit for a few moments, gathering myself. Only fifty-four. I have had no trouble before now. I eat well; my life does not have unusual stresses. I exercise.

As a result, I am ten minutes late in getting away. Maybe twelve. I don't check the exact time of my leaving, nor do I feel the need to hurry especially, to catch up. I am rigid in my habits, but not to that degree. The heart flutter has upset me and I'm not thinking of anything else. I set out cautiously.

I do not think of the boxer, of how I have disrupted the pattern of our meetings. I do not consider that my delay will in turn mean that he is not delayed. His circuit from unknown origin to unknown destination will not, now, be paused for our customary sparring. He will not lose that five or ten seconds, and thus will cross the road five or ten seconds sooner. I do not think of these things, and if I did, I would not see the significance.

I feel old and tired and a little sick; for once I am not in the mood for the bracing sea air, the spray, the demanding sunset light. I do not feel like meeting the radiant, youthful figure of the boxer, holding up his hands.

Ten minutes, maybe twelve. Long enough for it all to be over by the time I reach the stretch beyond the children's swings, coming up to the traffic lights. I see the small crowd ahead. A car is slewed at a shocked angle in the road, windscreen spiderwebbed. People stand with their heads down, rapt, staring at something at their centre. An ambulance pulls up. I lengthen my stride.

As I come alongside I see only people's backs. I push my way through joggers and walkers. Cooling flesh slicked with sunscreen and sweat. A couple of dogs twisting their leads round their owners' legs, weaving a mesh between me and what lies on the pavement. I step over crossed leads, squeeze between shoulders.

The boxer is lying on his back, hands at his sides, legs spread, toes pointed up and away from each other. A dachshund sniffs at his bright white trainers. There is blood. My hands, the backs of my hands, tingle as if they have just been slapped. My knuckles tingle. My face aches. I back away.

I walk on. The ambulance drives past me, but it goes slowly with no siren or lights flashing. I walk and walk. Something has reset my clock and I no longer know when to turn round. On beyond the café, on along the sea wall, beyond the phones, on until the path ends at the wall of the marina and I can go no more; otherwise I might walk for ever. Stepping up to the wall that blocks my path, I punch it with my left hand. Not hard, only enough to hurt my knuckles, not to bloody them. I wouldn't know how to hit that hard. I do it just once, then stand staring at the concrete for a moment before turning away.

I don't go back along the promenade. Instead I cross the road to the other side, towards the shops and hotels and away from the sea. The ocean is gentle and tired this evening. The incoming and outgoing waves seem to be confirming something, some truth about tides turning, time passing. Such flat phrases for that eternal suffering rhythm, but this is the best I can do.

I walk home a different way, through backstreets. It takes me a long time. I stop halfway at a random bistro and order coffee, decaf for the heart, and pick up the newspaper I failed to buy earlier. I don't know where I am in the day. I read the newspaper front to back, the sports pages and the classifieds and the obituaries. Then at last I continue home along an unfamiliar route. Down the steep roads, I can't avoid glimpsing the band of soft radiance generated by the sea. I can feel that brightness in the corner of my eye, but here where I am walking the world is darker. I'm cold in my T-shirt.

As I pass the window of the Woolworths on the corner, it is old, vain habit that makes me glance into the silvered glass. And I see clearly that age has come to me at last: decades, it seems, since this morning. The expensive walking clothes hang loose. And I know that from now on the years, which never burdened me before, will gather on my body, heavier and heavier in the life that remains. Time has started up again, speeding me down.

I step away from the glass and close my eyes. I raise up the boxer in my mind. Lifting my hands to my chest, I pick up the pace, one-two, one-two, elbows out. Through the evening streets I complete my promenade.

AN EX-MAS FEAST

Uwem Akpan

Now that my eldest sister, Maisha, was twelve, none of us knew how to relate to her any more. She had never forgiven our parents for not being rich enough to send her to school. She had been behaving like a cat that was going feral: she came home less and less frequently, staying only to change her clothes and give me some money to pass on to our parents. When home, she avoided them as best she could, as if their presence reminded her of too many things in our lives that needed money. Though she would snap at Baba occasionally, she never said anything to Mama. Sometimes Mama went out of her way to provoke her. '*Malaya!* Whore! You don't even have breasts yet!' she'd say. Maisha would ignore her.

Maisha shared her thoughts with Naema, our ten-year-old sister, more than she did with the rest of us combined, mostly talking about the dos and don'ts of a street girl. Maisha let Naema try on her high heels, showed her how to doll up her face, how to use toothpaste and a brush. She told her to run away from any man who beat her, no matter how much money he offered her, and that she would treat Naema like Mama if she grew up to have too many children. She told Naema that it was better to starve to death than go out with any man without a condom.

When she was at work, though, she ignored Naema, perhaps

because Naema reminded her of home or because she didn't want Naema to see that her big sister wasn't as cool and chic as she made herself out to be. She tolerated me more outside than inside. I could chat her up on the pavement no matter what rags I was wearing. An eight-year-old boy wouldn't get in the way when she was waiting for a customer. We knew how to pretend we were strangers – just a street kid and a prostitute talking.

Yet our *machokosh* family was lucky. Unlike most, our street family had stayed together – at least until that Ex-mas season.

The sun had gone down on Ex-mas evening. Bad weather had stormed the seasons out of order and Nairobi sat in a low flood, the light December rain droning on our tarpaulin roof. I was sitting on the floor of our shack, which stood on a cement slab at the end of an alley, leaning against the back of an old brick shop. Occasional winds swelled the brown polythene walls. The floor was nested with cushions that I had scavenged from a dump on Biashara Street. At night we rolled up the edge of the tarpaulin to let in the glow of the shop's security lights. A board, which served as our door, lay by the shop wall.

A clap of thunder woke Mama. She got up sluggishly, pulling her hands away from Maisha's trunk, which she had held on to while she slept. It was navy blue, with brass linings and rollers, and it took up a good part of our living space. Panicking, Mama, groped her way from wall to wall, frisking my two-year-old twin brother and sister, Otieno and Atieno, and Baba; all three were sleeping, tangled together like puppies. She was looking for Baby. Mama's white T-shirt, which she had been given three months back, when she delivered Baby, had a pair of milk stains on the front. Then she must have remembered that he was with Maisha and Naema. She relaxed and stretched in a yawn, hitting a rafter of cork. One of the stones that weighted our roof fell down outside.

Now Mama put her hands under her *shuka* and retied the strings of the money purse round her waist; sleep and alcohol had swung it out of place. She dug through our family carton, scooping out clothes, shoes and my new school uniform, wrapped in useless documents that Baba had picked from people's pockets. Mama dug on and the contents of the carton piled up on Baba and the twins. Then she unearthed a tin of New Suntan shoe glue. The glue was our Ex-mas gift from the children of a *machokosh* that lived nearby.

Mama smiled at the glue and winked at me, pushing her tongue through the holes left by her missing teeth. She snapped the tin's top expertly and the shack swelled with the smell of a shoemaker's stall. I watched her decant the *kabire* into my plastic 'feeding bottle'. It glowed warm and yellow in the dull light. Though she still appeared drunk from last night's party, her hands were so steady that her large tinsel Ex-mas bangles, a gift from a church Ex-mas party, did not even sway. When she had poured enough, she cut the flow of the glue by tilting the tin up. The last stream of the gum entering the bottle weakened and braided itself before tapering in mid-air like an icicle. She covered the plastic with her palm, to retain the glue's power. Sniffing it would kill my hunger in case Maisha did not return with an Ex-mas feast for us.

Mama turned to Baba, shoving his body with her foot. 'Wake up – you never work for days!' Baba turned and groaned. His feet were poking outside the shack, under the waterproof wall. His toes had broken free of his wet tennis shoes. Mama shoved him again and he began to wriggle his legs as if he were walking in his sleep.

Our dog growled outside. Mama snapped her fingers and the dog came in, her ripe pregnancy swaying like heavy wash in the wind. For a month and a half Mama, who was good at spotting dog pregnancies, had baited her with tenderness and food until she became ours; Mama hoped to sell the puppies to raise money for my textbooks. Now the dog licked Atieno's face. Mama probed the dog's stomach with crooked fingers, like a native midwife. 'Oh, Simba, childbirth is chasing you,' she whispered into her ears. 'Like school is chasing my son.' She pushed the dog outside. Simba lay down, covering Baba's feet with her warmth. Occasionally, she barked to keep the other dogs from tampering with our mobile kitchen, which was leaning against the wall of the store.

'Jigana, did you do well last night with Baby?' Mama asked me suddenly.

'I made a bit,' I assured her, and passed her a handful of coins and notes. She pushed the money under her *shuka*; the zip of the purse released two crisp farts.

Though people were more generous to beggars at Ex-mas, our real bait was Baby. We took turns pushing him in the faces of passersby.

'*Aii!* Son, you never see Ex-mas like this year.' Her face widened in a grin. 'We shall pay school fees next year. No more *randa*-meandering around. No more *chomaring* your brain with glue, boy. You going back to school! Did the rain beat you and Baby?'

'Rain caught me here,' I said.

'And Baby? Who is carrying him?'

'Naema,' I said.

'And Maisha? Where is she to do her time with the child?'

'Mama, she is very angry.'

'That gal is beat-beating my head. Three months now she is not greeting me. What insects are eating her brain?' Sometimes Mama's words came out like a yawn because the holes between her teeth were wide. 'Eh, now that she shakes-shakes her body to moneymen, she thinks she has passed me? Tell me, why did she refuse to stay with Baby?'

'She says it's child abuse.'

'Child abuse? Is she now NGO worker? She likes being a prostitute better than begging with Baby?'

'Me, I don't know. She just went with the *ma*-men tourists. Today, real white people, *musungu*. With monkey.'

Mama spat through the doorway. '*Puu*, those ones are useless. I know them. They don't ever pay the Ex-mas rate – and then they even let their *ma*-monkey fuck her. Jigana, talk with that gal. Or don't you want to complete school? She can't just give you uniform only.'

I nodded. I had already tried on the uniform eight times in two days, anxious to resume school. The green-and-white-checked shirt and olive-green shorts had become wrinkled. Now I reached into the carton and stroked a piece of the uniform that stuck out of the jumble.

'Why are you messing with this beautiful uniform?' Mama said. 'Patience, boy. School is just around the corner.' She dug to the bottom of the carton and buried the package. 'Maisha likes your face,' she whispered. 'Please, Jigana, tell her you need more – shoes, PTA fee, prep fee. We must to save all Ex-mas rate to educate you, first son. Tell her she must stop buying those *fuunny-fuunny* designer clothes, those clothes smelling of dead white people, and give us the money.'

As she said this, she started to pound angrily on the trunk. The trunk was a big obstruction. It was the only piece of furniture we had with a solid and definite shape. Maisha had brought it home a year ago and always ordered us to leave the shack before she would open it. None of us knew what its secret contents were, except for a lingering perfume. It held for us both suspense and consolation, and these feelings grew each time Maisha came back with new things. Sometimes, when Maisha did not come back for a long time, our anxiety turned the trunk into an assurance of her return.

'*Malaya!* Prostitute! She doesn't come and I break the box tonight,' Mama hissed, spitting on the combination lock and shaking the trunk until we could hear its contents knocking about. She always took her anger out on the trunk in Maisha's absence. I reached out to grab her hands.

'You pimp!' she growled. 'You support the *malaya*.'

'It's not her fault. It's *musungu* tourists.'

'You better begin school before she runs away.'

'I must to report you to her.'

'I must to bury you and your motormouth in this box.'

We struggled. Her long nails slashed my forehead and blood

trickled down. But she was still shaking the trunk. Turning round, I charged at her and bit her right thigh. I could not draw blood because I had lost my front milk teeth. She let go and reeled into the bodies of our sleeping family. Atieno let out one short, eerie scream, as if in a nightmare, then went back to sleep. Baba groaned and said he did not like his family members fighting during Ex-mas. 'You bite my wife because of that whore?' he groaned. 'The cane will discipline you in the morning. I must to personally ask your headmaster to get a big cane for you.'

A welt had fruited up on Mama's thigh. She rolled up her dress and started massaging it, her lips moving in silent curses. Then, to punish me, she took the *kabire* she had poured for me and applied it to the swelling. She pushed the mouth of the bottle against it, expecting the fumes to ease the hurt.

When Mama had finished nursing herself, she returned the bottle to me. Since it was still potent *kabire*, I did not sniff it straight but put my lips round the mouth of the bottle and smoked slowly, as if it were an oversized joint of bhang, Indian hemp. First it felt as if I had no saliva in my mouth, and then the fumes began to numb my tongue. The heat climbed steadily into my throat, tickling my nostrils like an aborted sneeze. I cooled off a bit and blew away the vapour. Then I sucked at it again and swallowed. My eyes watered, my head began to spin, and I dropped the bottle.

When I looked up, Mama had poured some *kabire* for herself and was sniffing it. She and Baba hardly ever took *kabire*. '*Kabire* is for children only,' Baba's late father used to admonish them whenever he caught them eyeing our glue. This Ex-mas we were not too desperate for food. In addition to the money that begging with Baby had brought us, Baba had managed to steal some wrapped gifts from a party given for *machokosh* families by an NGO whose organizers were so stingy that they served fruit juice like shots of hard liquor. He had dashed to another charity party and traded in the useless gifts – plastic cutlery, picture frames, paperweights, insecticide – for three cups of rice and zebra intestines, which a tourist hotel had donated. We'd had these for dinner on Ex-mas Eve.

'Happee, happee Ex-mas, tarling!' Mama toasted me after a while, rubbing my head.

'You too, Mama.'

'Now, where are these daughters? Don't they want to do Ex-mas prayer?' She sniffed the bottle until her eyes receded, her face pinched like the face of a mad cow. 'And the govament banned this sweet thing. Say thanks to the neighbours, boy. Where did they find this hunger killer?' Sometimes she released her lips from the bottle with a smacking sound. As the night thickened, her face began to swell, and she kept pouting and biting her lips to check the numbness. They turned red – they looked like Maisha's when she had on lipstick – and puffed up.

'Mama? So, what can we give the neighbours for Ex-mas?' I asked, remembering that we had not bought anything for our friends.

My question jerked her back. 'Petrol . . . we will buy them a half-litre of petrol,' she said, and belched. Her breath smelled of carbide, then of sour wine. When she looked up again, our eyes met and I lowered mine in embarrassment. In our *machokosh* culture, petrol was not as valuable as glue. Any self-respecting street kid should always have his own stock of *kabire*. 'OK, son, next year . . . we get better things. I don't want police business this year, so don't start having ideas.'

We heard two drunks stumbling towards our home. Mama hid the bottle. They stood outside announcing that they had come to wish us a merry Ex-mas. 'My husband is not here!' Mama lied. I recognized the voices. It was Bwana Marcos Wako and his wife, Cecilia. Baba had owed them money for four years. They came whenever they smelled money; then Baba had to take off for a few days. When Baby was born, we pawned three-quarters of his clothing to defray the debts. A week before Ex-mas the couple had raided us, confiscating Baba's work clothes in the name of debt servicing.

I quickly covered the trunk with rags and reached into my pocket, tightening my grip round the rusty penknife I carried about.

Mama and I stood by the door. Bwana Wako wore his trousers belted across his forehead; the legs, flailing behind him, were tied in knots and stuffed with *ugali* flour, which he must have got from a street party. Cecilia wore only her jacket and her rain boots.

'Ah, Mama Jigana-*ni* Ex-mas!' the husband said. 'Forget the money. Happee Ex-mas!'

'We hear Jigana is going to school,' the wife said.

'Who told you?' Mama said warily. 'Me, I don't like rumours.'

They turned to me. 'Happee to resume school, boy?'

'Me am not going to school,' I lied, to spare my tuition money.

'*Kai*, like mama like son!' the wife said. 'You must to know you are the hope of your family.'

'Mama Jigana, listen,' the man said. 'Maisha came to us last week. Good, responsible gal. She begged us to let bygone be bygone so Jigana can go to school. We say forget the money – our Ex-mas gift to your family.'

'You must to go far with education, Jigana,' the wife said, handing me a new pen and pencil. '*Mpaka* university!'

Mama laughed, jumping into the flooded alley. She hugged them and allowed them to come closer to our shack. They staggered to our door, swaying like masqueraders on stilts.

'*Asante sana!*' I thanked them. I uncorked the pen and wrote all over my palms and smelled the tart scent of the Hero HB pencil. Mama wedged herself between them and the shack to ensure that they did not pull it down. Baba whispered to us from inside, ready to slip away, 'Ha, they told me the same thing last year. You watch and see, tomorrow they come looking for me. Make them sign paper this time.' Mama quickly got them some paper and they signed, using my back as a table. Then they staggered away, the stuffed trousers bouncing along behind them.

Mama began to sing Maisha's praises and promised never to

pound on her trunk again. Recently, Maisha had taken the twins to
the barber, and Baby to Kenyatta National Hospital for a check-up.
Now she had got our debt cancelled. I felt like running out to search
for her in the streets. I wanted to hug her and laugh until the moon
dissolved. I wanted to buy her Coke and chapatti, for sometimes she
forgot to eat. But when Mama saw me combing my hair, she said
nobody was allowed to leave until we had finished saying the Ex-mas
prayer.

I hung out with Maisha some nights on the street, and we talked about
fine cars and lovely Nairobi suburbs. We'd imagine what it would be
like to visit the Masai Mara Game Reserve or to eat roasted ostrich or
crocodile at the Carnivore, like tourists.

'You beautiful!' I had told Maisha one night on Koinange Street,
months before that fateful Ex-mas.

'Ah, no, me am not.' She laughed, straightening her jean miniskirt.
'Stop lying.'

'See your face?'

'*Kai*, who sent you?'

'And you bounce like models.'

'Yah, yah, yah. Not tall. Nose? Too short and big. No lean face or
full lips. No first-hand designer clothes. Not daring or beautiful like
Naema. Perfume and mascara are not everything.'

'*Haki*, you? Beautiful woman,' I said, snapping my fingers. 'You
will be tall tomorrow.'

'You are asking me out?' she said in jest, and struck a pose. She
made faces as if she were playing with the twins and said, 'Be a man,
do it the right way.'

I shrugged and laughed.

'Me, I have no shilling, big gal.'

'I will discount you, guy.'

'Stop it.'

'Oh, come on,' she said, and pulled me into a hug.

Giggling, we began walking, our strides softened by laughter. Everything became funny. We couldn't stop laughing at ourselves, at the people around us. When my sides began to ache and I stopped, she tickled my ribs.

We laughed at the gangs of street kids massed together in sound sleep. Some gangs slept in graded symmetry. Others slept freestyle. Some had a huge tarp above their piles to protect them from the elements. Others had nothing. We laughed at a group of city taxi drivers huddled together, warming themselves with cups of *chai* and fiery political banter while waiting for the Akamba buses to arrive with passengers from Tanzania and Uganda. Occasionally we'd see the anxious faces of these visitors in the old taxis, bracing for what would be the most dangerous twenty minutes of their twelve-hour journeys, fearful of being robbed whenever the taxis slowed down.

We were not afraid of the city at night. It was our playground. At times like this, it was as if Maisha had forgotten her job, and all she wanted to do was laugh and play-act. 'You? Nice guy,' Maisha said.

'Lie.'

I pulled at her handbag.

'You will be a big man tomorrow . . .'

She dashed past me suddenly to wave down a chauffeured Volvo. It stopped right in front of her, the window rolling down. A man in the back seat inspected her and shook his bald head. He beckoned a taller girl from the cluster jostling behind her, trying to fit their faces in the window. Maisha ran to a silver Mercedes-Benz wagon, but the owner picked a shorter girl.

'Someday I must to find a real job,' Maisha said, sighing, when she came back.

'What job, gal?'

'I want to try full time.'

'*Wapi?*'

She shrugged. 'Mombasa? Dar?'

I shook my head. 'Bad news, big gal. How long?'

'I don't know. *Ni maisha yangu*, guy, it's my life. I'm thinking, full-time will allow me to pay your fees and also save for myself. I will send money through the church for you. I'll quit the brothel when I save a bit. I don't want to stand on the road for ever. Me myself must to go to school one day . . .'

The words died in her throat. She pursed her lips, folded her hands across her chest and rocked from side to side. She did not rush to any more cars.

'We won't see you again?' I said. 'No, thanks. If you enter brothel, me I won't go to school.'

'Then I get to keep my money, ha-ha. Without you, they won't see my shilling in that house. Never.' She saw my face, stopped suddenly, then burst into giggles. 'I was kidding you, guy, about the brothel. Just kidding, OK?'

She tickled me, pulling me towards Moi Avenue. I held her hand tightly. Prostitutes fluttered about under streetlights, dressed like winged termites.

'Maisha, our parents—'

She turned sharply, her fists balled. 'Shut up! You shame me, you rat. Leave me alone. Me am not your mate. You can't afford me!'

Other girls turned and stared at us, giggling. Maisha strode away. It had been a mistake to mention our parents in front of the other girls, to let them know that we were related. And I shouldn't have called her by her real name. I cried all the way home because I had hurt her. She ignored me for weeks.

After Mama stopped celebrating the end of our debt, she fished out two little waterproof Uchumi Supermarket bags from the carton and smoothed them out as if they were rumpled socks. She put them over her canvas shoes, tying the handles round her ankles in little bows. Then she walked out into the flood, her winged galoshes scooping the water like a duck's feet. She started to untie our bag of utensils and food, which was leaning against the shop, her eyes searching for a dry spot to set up the stove, to warm some food for the twins. But the rain was coming down too heavily now and after a while she gave up.

'Jigana, so did you see those Maisha's *ma*-men?' she asked.

'There were three white men, plus driver. Tall, old men in knickers and tennis shoes. I shook hands with them. Beautiful-beautiful motorcar . . . I even pinched that monkey.'

'Motorcar? They had a motorcar? *Imachine* a motorcar to pick up my daughter.' She stretched forward and held my arms, smiling. 'You mean my daughter is big like that?'

Otieno woke up with a start. He stood groggily on the cushions; then he climbed over Mama's legs, levered himself over me with his hand on my head and landed in the flood outside the shack in a crouch. He began to lower thin spools of shit into the water, whiffs of heat unwrapping into the night, the cheeks of his buttocks rouged by the cold.

When Otieno returned to the shack, he sat on Mama's legs and brought out her breast and sucked noisily. With one hand, he grabbed a toy Maisha had bought for him, rattling its maracas on Mama's bony face. She was still looking ragged and underweight, even though she'd stayed in the hospital to have her diet monitored after Baby graduated from the incubator.

Mama took out our family Bible, which we had inherited from Baba's father, to begin our Ex-mas worship. The front cover had peeled off, leaving a dirty page full of our relatives' names, dead and living. She read them out. Baba's late father had insisted that all the names of our family be included, in recognition of the instability of street life. She began with her father, who had been killed by cattle rustlers, before she ran away to Nairobi and started living with Baba. She called out Baba's mother, who came to Nairobi when her village was razed because some politicians wanted to redraw tribal boundaries. One day she disappeared for ever into the city with her walking stick. Mama invoked the names of our cousins Jackie and Solo, who settled in another village and wrote to us through our church, asking our parents to send them school fees. I looked forward to telling them about the lit parks and the beautiful cars of Nairobi as soon as my teachers taught me how to write letters. She called out her brother, Uncle Peter, who had shown me how to shower in the city fountains without being whipped by the officials. He was shot by the police in a case of mistaken identity; the mortuary gave his corpse to a medical school because we could not pay the bill. She called Baba's second cousin Mercy, the only secondary-school graduate among our folks. She had not written to us since she fell in love with a Honolulu tourist and eloped with him. Mama called Baba's sister, Aunty Mama, who, until she died two years ago of a heart attack, had told us stories and taught us songs about our ancestral lands every evening, in a sweet, nostalgic voice.

The sky rumbled.

'*Bwana*, I hope Naema put clothes on Baby before she left,' Mama said to me, the middle of her sentence wobbling because Otieno had bitten her.

'She put Baby in waterproof paper bags. Then sweater.'

Otieno, having satisfied himself, woke up Atieno, who took over the other breast, for they had divided things up evenly between them. Atieno sucked until she slept again, and Mama placed her gently near Otieno and began to shake Baba until he opened one eye. His weak voice vibrated because his face was jammed into the wall: 'Food.'

'No food, tarling,' Mama told him. 'We must to finish to call the names of our people.'

'You'll be calling my name if I don't eat.'

'Here is food – New Suntan shoe *kabire*.' She reached out and collected the plastic bottle from me. 'It can kill your stomach till next week.'

'All the children are here?'

'Baby and Naema still out. Last shift . . . and Maisha.'

'Ah, there is hope. Maisha will bring Ex-mas feast for us.'

'Ex-mas is school fees, remember?'

Mama groped inside the carton again. She unearthed a dirty candle, pocked by grains of sand. She lit the candle and cemented it to the trunk with its wax. Taking the Bible, she began to read a psalm in Kiswahili, thanking God for the gift of Baby and the twins after two miscarriages. She praised God for blessing Maisha with white clients at Ex-mas. Then she prayed for Fuunny Eyes, the name we had given to the young Japanese volunteer who unfailingly dropped shillings in our begging plate. She wore Masai tyre sandals and *ekarawa* necklaces that held her neck like a noose, and never replied to our greetings or let her eyes meet ours. Mama prayed for our former landlord in the Kibera slums, who evicted us but hadn't seized anything when we could not pay the rent. Now she asked God to bless Simba with many puppies. 'Christ, you Ex-mas son, give Jigana a big, intelligent head in school!' she concluded.

'Have mercy on us,' I said.

'Holy Mary, Mama Ex-mas . . .'

'Pray for us.'

It was drizzling again when Naema returned with Baby. He was asleep. Naema's jeans, *mutumba* loafers and braided hair dribbled water, her big eyes red from crying. Usually she sauntered in singing a Brenda Fassie song, but tonight she plodded in deflated.

She handed the money over to Mama, who quickly banked it in her purse. She also gave Mama a packet of pasteurized milk. It was half full, and Naema explained that she'd had to buy it to keep Baby from crying. Mama nodded. The milk pack was soggy and looked as if it would disintegrate. Mama took it carefully in her hands, like one receiving a diploma. When Naema brought out a half-eaten turkey drumstick, Mama grabbed her ears, thinking that she had bought it with the money she'd earned begging. Naema quickly explained that her new boyfriend had given it to her. This boy was a big shot in the street gang that controlled our area, a dreaded figure. Maisha and I detested him, but he loved Naema like his own tongue.

Now Naema wriggled and fitted her lithe frame into the tangle on the floor and began to weep silently. Mama pulled the blanket from the others and covered the girl's feet, which had become wrinkled in the rain.

'Maisha is moving out tomorrow,' Naema said. 'Full-time.'

Mama's face froze. No matter how rootless and cheap street life might be, you could still be broken by departures. I went outside and lay on the row of empty paint containers we had lined up along the shop's wall, hiding my face in the crook of my arm.

Guilt began to build in my gut. Maybe if I had joined a street gang, Maisha would not have wanted to leave. I wouldn't have needed money for school fees, and perhaps there would have been peace between Maisha and my parents. But my anger was directed at the *musungu* men, for they were the visible faces of my sister's temptation. I wished I were as powerful as Naema's boyfriend or that I could recruit him. We could burn their Jaguar. We could tie them up and give them the beating of their lives and take away all their papers. We could strip those *musungu* naked, as I had seen Naema's friend do to someone who had hurt a member of his gang. Or we could at least kill and eat that monkey or just cut off his *mboro* so he could never fuck anybody's sister again. I removed my knife from my pocket and examined the blade carefully. The fact that it was very blunt and had dents did not worry me. I knew that if I stabbed with all my energy, I would draw blood.

After a while my plans began to unravel. I realized that I would never be able to enlist Naema's boyfriend. Naema herself would block the plan. In fact, until that night she had been taunting Maisha to move out, saying that if she were as old as Maisha, she would have left home long ago. Besides, even if I fled to the Kibera slums, as soon as we touched the tourists, the police would come and arrest my parents and dismantle our shack. They would take away Maisha's trunk and steal her treasures

Baba started awake, as if a loud noise had hit him.

'Is that Maisha?' he asked, closing his eyes again.

'No, Maisha is working,' Mama said. 'My Maisha commands *musungu* and motorcars!' she said, her good mood returning.

'What? What *musungu*, tarling?' Baba asked, sitting up immediately, rubbing sleep and hunger from his eyes with the base of his palms.

'White tourists,' Mama said.

'Uh? They must to pay *ma*-dollar or euros. Me am family head. You hear me, woman?'

'Yes.'

'And no Honolulu business. What kind of motorcar were they driving?'

'Jaguar,' I answered. 'With driver. Baba, we should not allow Maisha to leave—'

'Nobody is leaving, nobody. And shut up your animal mouth! You have wounded my wife! Until I break your teeth tomorrow, no opinion from you. No nothing. Did you thank the *ma*-men for me?'

'No,' I said.

'*Aiiee!* Jigana, where are your manners? Did you ask where they were going? Motorcar number?'

'No, Baba.'

'So if they take her to Honolulu, what do I do? Maybe we should send you to a street gang. Boy, have you not learned to grab opportunities? Is this how you will waste school fees in January? Poor Maisha.'

He squinted incredulously, and lines of doubt kinked up his massive forehead. He pursed his lips, and anger quickened his breath. But that night I stood my ground.

'I don't want school any more, Baba,' I said.

'Coward, shut up. That one is a finished matter.'

'No.'

'What do you mean by no? You want to be a pocket thief like me . . . my son? My first son? You can't be useless as the gals. *Wallai!*'

'Me, I don't want school.'

'Your mind is too young to think. As we say, "The teeth that come first are not used in chewing." As long as you live here, your baba says school.'

'*La hasha.*'

'You telling me *never*? Jigana!' He looked at Mama. 'He doesn't want school? St Jude Thaddaeus!'

'*Bwana*, this boy has grown strong-head,' Mama said. 'See how he is looking at our eyes. Insult!'

Baba stood up suddenly, his hands shaking. I didn't cover my cheeks with my hands to protect myself from his slap or spittle, as I usually did when he was angry. I was ready for him to kill me. My family was breaking up because of me. He stood there, trembling with anger, confused.

Mama patted his shoulders to calm him down. He brushed her aside and went out to cool off. I monitored him through a hole in the wall. Soon he was cursing himself aloud for drinking too much and sleeping through Ex-mas Day and missing the chance to meet the tourists. As his mind turned to Maisha's good fortune, he began to sing 'A Jaguar Is a Jaguar Is a Jaguar' to the night, leaping from stone to stone, tracing the loose cobbles that studded the floodwater like the heads of stalking crocodiles in a river. In the sky, some of the tall city buildings were branded by lights left on by forgetful employees, and a few shopping centres wore the glitter of Ex-mas; flashing lights ascended and descended like angels on Jacob's dream ladder. The long city buses, Baba's hunting grounds, had stopped for the night. As the streets became emptier, cars drove faster through the floods, kicking up walls of water, which collapsed on our shack.

Back inside, Baba plucked his half-used *miraa* stick from the rafter and started chewing. He fixed his eyes on the trunk. A mysterious smile dribbled out of the corners of his mouth. Eventually the long stick *of miraa* subsided into a formless sponge. His spitting was sharp and arced across the room and out through the door. Suddenly his face brightened. '*Hakuna matata!*' he said. Then he dipped into the carton and came up with a roll of wire and started lashing the wheels of the trunk to the props of our shack. For a moment it seemed he might be able to stop Maisha from going away.

Mama tried to discourage him from tying down the trunk. '*Bwanaaa* . . . stop it! She will leave if she finds you *manga-mangaring* with her things.'

'Woman, leave this business to me,' he said, rebuking her. 'I'm not going to sit here and let any Honolulus run away with our daughter. They must marry her properly.'

'You should talk,' Mama said. 'Did you come to my father's house for my hand?'

'Nobody pays for trouble,' Baba said. 'You're trouble. If I just touch you, you get pregnant. If I even look at you – twins, just like that. Too, too ripe.'

'Me am always the problem,' Mama said, her voice rising.

'All me am saying is we must to treat the tourist well.'

Atieno was shivering; her hand was poking out of the shack. Baba yanked it back in and stuck her head through the biggest hole in the middle of our blanket. That was our way of ensuring that the family member who most needed warmth maintained his place in the centre of the blanket. Baba grabbed Otieno's legs and pushed them through two holes on the fringe. 'Children of Jaguar,' he whispered into their ears. 'Ex-mas *ya* Jag-uar.' He tried to tuck Atieno and Otiento properly into the blanket, turning them this way and that, without success. Then he became impatient and rolled them towards each other like a badly wrapped meat roll, their feet in each other's face, their knees folded and tucked into each other's body – a blanket womb.

Mama reminded him to wedge the door, but he refused. He wanted us to wait for Maisha. He winked at me as if I were the cosentry of our fortune. Mama handed Baby to me and lay down. I sat there sniffing *kabire* until I became drunk. My head swelled, and the roof relaxed and shook, then melted into the sky.

I was floating. My bones were inflammable. My thoughts went out like electric currents into the night, their counter-currents running into each other, and, in a flash of sparks, I was hanging on the door of the city bus, going to school. I hid my uniform in my bag so that I could ride free, like other street children. Numbers and letters of the alphabet jumped at me, scurrying across the page as if they had something to say. The flares came faster and faster; blackboards burned brighter and brighter. In the beams of sunlight leaking through the holes in the school roof, I saw the teacher writing around the cracks and patches on the blackboard like a skilful *matatu* driver threading his way through our pothole-ridden roads. Then I raced down our bald, lopsided field with an orange for a rugby ball, jumping the gullies and breaking tackles. I was already the oldest kid in my class.

Mama touched my shoulders and relieved me of the infant. She stripped Baby of the plastic rompers, cleaned him up and put him in a nappy for the night. With a cushion wrested from Naema, who was sleeping, Mama padded the top of the carton into a cot. After placing Baby in it, she straightened the four corners of the carton and then folded up our mosquito net and hung it over them. It had been donated by an NGO, and Baba had not had a chance to pawn it yet. Then Mama wrapped her frame around the carton and slept.

I woke up Baba when Maisha returned, before dawn. He had been stroking his rosary beads, dozing and tilting until his head upset the mosquito netting. Mama had to continually elbow or kick him off. And each time, he opened his eyes with a practised smile, thinking the Jaguar hour had arrived. The rain had stopped, but clouds kept the night dark. The city had gorged itself on the floods, and its skin had swelled and burst in places. The makeshift tables and stalls of street markets littered the landscape, torn and broken, as if there had been a bar fight. Litter had spread all over the road: dried fish, stationery, trinkets, wilted green vegetables, plastic plates, wood carvings, underwear. Without the usual press of people, the ill-lit streets sounded hollow, amplifying the smallest of sounds. Long after a police car had passed, it could be heard negotiating potholes, the officers extorting their bribes – their Ex-mas *kitu kidogo* – from the people who could not afford to go to their up-country villages for the holidays.

Maisha returned in an old Renault 16 taxi. She slouched in the back while the driver got out. Kneeling and applying pliers to open the back door, the driver let her out of the car. Baba's sighs of disappointment were as loud as the muezzin who had begun to call Nairobi to prayer. My sister stepped out, then leaned on the car, exhausted. There were bags of food on the seat.

She gestured at Baba to go away. He ignored her.

'So where is *our* Jaguar and *musungu*?' Baba asked the taxi driver, peering into the shabby car as if it might be transformed at any moment.

'What Jaguar? What *musungu*?' the driver asked, monitoring Maisha's movements.

'The *nini* Jaguar . . . Where is my daughter coming from?' Baba asked him.

'Me, I can't answer you that question,' he told Baba, and pointed to his passenger.

She bent in front of the only functioning headlamp to count out the fare. Her trousers were so tight that they had crinkled on her thighs and pockets; she struggled to get to the notes without breaking her artificial nails, which curved inward like talons. Yesterday, her hair had been low cut, gold, wavy and crisp from a fresh perm. Now it stood up in places and lay flat in others, revealing patches of her scalp, which was bruised from the chemicals. It was hard to distinguish peeling face powder from damaged skin. To rid herself of an early outbreak of adolescent pimples, she had bleached her face into an uneven lightness. Her eyelids and the skin under her eyes had reacted the worst to the assorted creams she was applying, and tonight her fatigue seemed to have seeped under the burns, swelling her eyes.

The driver could not easily roll up the window. He extended his arm to guard the food bags, his collateral. Baba brought out a six-inch nail and went for the worn tyres. 'What *dawa* have you given my daughter? She always comes home strong.'

The driver crumpled immediately, his pleas laden with fright. '*Mzee*, my name is Karume. Paul Kinyanjui wa Karume . . . Me, I be an upright Kenyan. I fear God.'

'And you want to steal my daughter's bags?'

'No. Please, take the bags. Please,' the man begged, trying to restrain Baba from bursting his tyres.

'*Aiie*, Baba. You shame me. Shut up,' Maisha said weakly, pushing the money towards the driver.

Baba collected the bags and strolled from the road, his nose full of good smells, until he suddenly broke into a run, to untie the trunk before Maisha reached the shack.

The driver got into his car and was about to put the money into his breast pocket when he started frisking himself. Baba stood watching from the door of the shack. Soon it was as if the driver had soldier ants in his clothes. He unzipped his pockets, then zipped them again quickly, as if the thief were still lurking. He removed his coat, then his shirt, and searched them. He recounted his itinerary to the skies with eyes closed, his index finger wagging at invisible stars. He searched his socks; then he got down on all fours, scouring the wet ground. He dabbed at the sweat, or tears, running down his face. 'Where is my money?' he said to Maisha, finally finding his voice. '*Haki*, it was in my pocket now, now.'

Maisha charged forwards and screeched at Baba until his stern face crumbled into a sheepish grin. He returned the fat wad of notes, giggling like the twins. The driver thanked her curtly, brushing his clothes with trembling hands. As soon as he'd reconnected the ignition wires to start the car, he creaked off, his horn blaring, his headlamp pointing up and to the left like an unblinking eye.

Maisha staggered into the shack, holding her perilously high heels over her shoulders. Mama had made room for her and the bags and had sprayed our home with insecticide to discourage mosquitoes. My siblings inside started to cough. As Maisha came in, Mama stood aside like a maid, wringing her hands. I could not look Maisha in the eye and did not know what to say.

'Good night, Maisha,' I blurted out.

She stopped, her tired body seized by shock. She searched my parents' faces before tracing the voice to me.

'Who told you to talk?' she said.

'You leave full time, I run away. No school.'

'You are going to school,' Maisha said. 'Tuition is ready.'

'Run away? Jigana, shut up,' Baba said. 'You think you are family head now? "All are leaders" causes riots. Stupid, *mtu dufu*! Nobody is leaving.'

Maisha glared at us, and we all turned our backs to her as she opened the trunk to take out a blanket. The sweet smell of her Jaguar adventures filled the shack, overpowering the heavy scent of insecticide. Though her arrivals always reminded us that life could be better, tonight I hated the perfume.

'Me and your mama don't want full time, Maisha,' Baba said, picking his nails. 'We refuse.'

'Our daughter, things will get better,' Mama said. 'Thanks for cancelling our debt!'

'You are welcome, Mama,' Maisha said.

Mama's face lit up with surprise; she was so used to being ignored. She opened her mouth to say something, but nothing came out. Finally she sobbed the words '*Asante*, Maisha, *asante* for everything!' and bowed repeatedly, her hands held before her, as if in prayer. The women looked into each other's eyes in a way I had never seen before.

They hugged and held on as if their hands were ropes that tied their two bodies together. In spite of the cold, beads of sweat broke out on Mama's forehead, and her fingers trembled as she helped Maisha undo her earrings and necklace. Mama gently laid her down.

I believed that Mama might have been able to persuade her to stay, but then Baba signalled to Mama to keep quiet so that he could be the negotiator.

'Our daughter,' Baba said, 'you need to rest and think carefully. As our people say, north *ama* south, east *ama* west, home the best . . .'

'Maisha, no school for me!' I said. 'I told Mama and Baba. They will return fee to you.'

'Jigana, please, please, don't argue,' Maisha said. 'Even you. You cannot even pity me this night? Just for a few hours?'

My parents sat outside, on the paint containers. I stood by the wall, away from them. I wanted to see Maisha one more time before she disappeared.

Fog brought the dew down, thickening the darkness and turning the security lights into distant halos. We could hear Maisha twist and turn on the floor, cursing the limbs of her siblings and swatting at the mosquitoes. It was as if we were keeping a vigil of her last night with us. We were restless, the silence too heavy for us. Baba mumbled, blaming himself for not going more often to sweep the church premises. He agreed with Mama that if he had swept daily, instead of every other day, St Joseph the Worker would have bettered our lot. Mama snapped at him, because Baba had always told her that he was not interested in St Joseph's favour but in a clean place for people to worship. Then Baba blamed her for no longer attending the KANU slum rallies to earn a few shillings.

The night degenerated into growls and hisses. I preferred the distraction of the quarrel to the sound of Maisha's uneasy breathing. When Maisha clapped one more time and turned over, Mama couldn't stand it any more. She rushed inside, took the mosquito net off the carton and tied it to the rafters so that my sister was inside it. She sprayed the place again and brought Baby out to breastfeed. The coughing got worse. Baba tore down some of the walls to let in air, but since the wind had subsided, it was of no use. He picked up the door and used it as a big fan to whip air into the shack.

In the morning Atieno and Otieno came out first. They looked tired and were sniffling from the insecticide. They stood before us, spraying the morning with yellow urine, sneezing and whimpering.

The streets began to fill. The street kids were up and had scattered into the day, like chickens feeding. Some moved about groggily, already drunk on *kabire*. One recounted his dreams to others at the top of his voice, gesticulating maniacally. Another was kneeling and trembling with prayer, his eyes shut as if he would never open them again. One man screamed and pointed at two kids, who were holding his wallet. No one was interested. His pocket was ripped to the zipper, leaving a square hole in the front of his trousers. He pulled out his shirt to hide his nakedness, then hurried away, an awkward smile straining his face. There was no sun, only a slow ripening of the sky.

The twins started to wail and to attack Mama's breasts. Baba spanked them hard. They sat on the ground with pent-up tears they were afraid to shed. Naema broke the spell. She came out and sat with me on the containers, grabbed my hands and tried to cheer me up. 'You are too sad, Jigana,' she said. 'You want to marry the gal? Remember, it's your turn to take Baby out.'

'Leave me alone.'

'Marry me, then – me am still here.' She stuck out her tongue at me. 'I'm your sister too – more beautiful. Guy, do me photo trick . . . smile.' She was well rested and had slept off her initial shock at Maisha's departure. Now she was herself again, taunting and talkative, her dimples deep and perfect. 'You all must to let Maisha go.'

'And you?' I said. 'You only listen to Maisha.'

'I'm big gal now, guy. Breadwinner. If you want school, I pay for you!'

She blew me a kiss in the wind. Maisha's creams were already lightening her ebony face.

Before I could say anything, Naema erupted with mad laughter and ran into the shack. She almost knocked Baba down as she burst out with the bags of food we had forgotten. She placed them on the ground and tore into them, filling the morning with hope, beckoning all of us on. Baba bit into a chicken wing. Mama took a leg. The rest of us dug into the sour rice, mashed potatoes, salad, hamburgers, pizza, spaghetti and sausages. We drank dead Coke and melted ice cream all mixed up. With her teeth, Naema opened bottles of Tusker and Castle beer. At first we feasted in silence, on our knees, looking up frequently, like squirrels, to monitor one another's intake. None of us thought to inflate the balloons or open the cards that Maisha had brought.

Then the twins fell over on their backs, laughing and vomiting. As soon as they were done, they went straight back to eating, their mouths pink and white and green from ice cream and beer. We could not get them to keep quiet. A taxi pulled up and Maisha came out of the shack, dragging her trunk behind her. Our parents paused as the driver helped her put it into the car. My mother began to cry. Baba shouted at the streets.

I sneaked inside and poured myself some fresh *kabire* and sniffed. I got my exercise book from the carton and ripped it into shreds. I brought my pen and pencil together and snapped them, the ink spurting into my palms like blue blood. I got out my only pair of trousers and two shirts and put them on, over my clothes.

I avoided the uniform package. Sitting where the trunk had been, I wept. It was like a newly dug grave. I sniffed hastily, tilting the bottle up and down until the *kabire* came close to my nostrils.

As the car pulled away with Maisha, our mourning attracted kids from the gangs. They circled the food, and I threw away the bottle and joined my family again. We struggled to stuff the food into our mouths, to stuff the bags back inside the shack, but the kids made off with the balloons and the cards.

I hid among a group of retreating kids and slipped away. I ran through traffic, scaled the road divider and disappeared into Nairobi. My last memory of my family was of the twins burping and giggling.

SHIPS IN HIGH TRANSIT

Binyavanga Wainaina

Stupid Japanese tourist. During breakfast, on the open-air patio that faced the plains of Lake Nakuru National Park, he saw the gang of baboons, saw the two large males, fulfilling with every grunt and chest bang every human cliché about male brutality. Here is an aspect of reality as consensus: the man has spent his entire life watching nature documentaries. He said this to Matano, with much excitement, over and over again, on the van to Nakuru last week. How can he remind his adrenaline that these beasts can kill, when he knows them only as television actors?

So, he hid a crust of bread and, when everybody was done with breakfast, threw it at the group of baboons outside and aimed his camera at them. The larger male came for the bread and then attacked the man, leaving with a chunk of his finger and decapitating the green crocodile on his shirt. The baboon was shot that afternoon. A second green crocodile replaced the first.

That was last month.

Then there is Matano's boss/business partner, Armitage Shanks, of the Ceramic Toilet Shanks, or maybe the Water Closet Shanks, or the Flush Unit Shanks. Or maybe a Faux Shanks: it is possible he borrowed the name. Matano had never asked. He knew that Shanks carried a sort of hushed-whisper weight in Karen and Nyali and

Laikipia, together with names like Kuki and Blixen. Matano also knew that somewhere in the Commonwealth, some civil servant shat regularly in an Armitage Shanks toilet.

Shanks lives in Kenya, running a small tour firm, hardly heroic for a man whose family managed to ship heavy ceramic water closets around the world, but he hit on a winning idea.

Some dizzy photographer woman, Diana Tilten-Hamilton, had been telling him about the astrological history of the Maa people, told him about her theory that they were the true ancient Egyptians, showed him her collection of photographs, just days before they were shipped to the publisher of coffee-table books: photos packed with pictures of semi-naked Maa astrologers, gazing at the night sky, pointing at the stars, loincloths lifted to reveal lean, scooped-out copper-coloured buttocks.

He found his great idea.

Heirlooms.

So he hired ten of the best woodcarvers from the Mombasa Akamba Cooperative, hid them out in a small farm in Laikipia and started a cottage industry. Masai heirlooms. The spin: thousands of years ago, in the great Maa Empire, Maa-saa-i-a, a great carver, lived. It was said he could carve the spirit of a moran warrior from olivewood. At night he occupied the spirit of the bull. During the day he spun winds that carve totem spirits out of stray olivewood.

When the Maa-saa-i-a Empire fell apart, after a great war with the Phoenicians over trade in frankincense and myrrh, the remaining Maa scattered to the winds. Some left for the south and formed the great Zulu Nation; others remained in East Africa, impoverished but noble; others fought with Prester John; and others became gladiators in Rome.

The great carver, um-Shambalaa, vanished one night in the Ngong Hills, betrayed by evil spirits who had overwhelmed the ancestors. He waits for the Maa to rise again.

Until last year nobody knew the secret of Maa-saa-i-a, until

Armitage Shanks went to live among the (rare) highland Samburu. He killed his first lion at seventeen, with his bare hands (witnessed by his circumcision brother, Ole Lenana), and saved the highland Samburu with his MTV song, 'Feed the Maa' (sung with his former rock band, the Faecal Martyrs). Shanks was asked by the Shamanic elder of the Greater Maa to be an elder. His name was changed. He is now called Ole um-Shambalaa, 'the Brother Not Born Among Us'. The elders pleaded with Ole um-Shambalaa to help them recover their lost glory. They gave him all 300 of their ancient olivewood heirlooms to auction, to raise money to make the Maa rise again . . .

This was how Matano came to manage WylDe AFreaKa tours. Shanks was now a noble savage and could not be bothered with tax forms . . .

Or airport welcoming procedures . . .

Dancing girls in grass skirts singing, 'A-wimbowe, a-wimbowe . . .'

Dancing men singing, 'A-wimbowe, a-wimbowe . . .'

Giant warrior with lion whiskers and shiny black make-up walks on all fours towards clapping German tourists, flexing his muscles and growling, 'A-wimbowe, a-wimbowe . . .'

In the jungle . . .

Actually, Shanks lost interest in WylDe AFreaKa right from the start. Apart from an annual six-month trip to wherever Eurotrash were camping out, to 'market' (where he avoided all the Scandinavian snowplough drivers and Belgian paper-clip packers and Swiss cheese-hole pokers who were his real clientele and spent time in Provence and Tuscany and the South of France), he generally worked on other projects. First there was the constructed wetland toilets (it is hard for a Shanks to keep off the subject), then the Faecal Martyrs, who got to number eight in the charts on the Isle of Man and toured Vladivostok ('Feed the Maa-aaa-aah. Let them know it's Easter time . . .'); then the Nuba Tattoo Bar he started in London, opened by a cousin of Leni Riefenstahl. The tattoo bar had naked Nuba refugees operating the tills, before the SPLA threatened to bomb him (Shanks claimed

in a BBC interview). Then there was the spectacular disaster Foreign
Correspondent, the Nairobi coffee shop that failed because people
complained that they kept losing their appetites in a place decorated
with grainy black-and-white pictures of whichever Africans happened
to be starving at the time. In between all these ventures, Shanks was
learning tantric sex, polishing off a bottle of Stoli every night and
keeping away from Mr Kamau Delivery, his coke dealer, whom he
always owes money. Lately, though, he has been more scarce than
usual. Sombre. Matano knows this is a phase, a new project, which
always means a short season where more money will not be available.
He paid out salaries three days early, before Shanks could get to the
account.

The van leans forward to the ramp as Matano prepares to board the
ferry. He looks at the rear-view mirror. The couple he has just picked
up at the airport stop gesticulating excitedly; their faces freeze for a
second; they look at each other; the man's eyes catch Matano's.

   Jean-Paul turns away guiltily and says to his wife/lover/colleague,
'Isn't this great? What a tub! Wonder when they built it – must be
before the war.'

   'Is it safe, do you think?'

   Matano smiles to himself. He looks out at the ferry and allows
himself to see it through their eyes.

   Stomach plummets: fear, thrill. Trippy. So *real*. Smell of old oil,
sweat and spices. So exotic.

   Colour: women in their robes, eyes covered, rimmed with kohl;
other women dark and dressed in skirts and blouses looking drab;
other women sort of in-between cultures, a chiffon blouse and a wrap-
around sarong with bright yellow, green and blue designs. Many
people are barefoot. An old Arab man, with an emaciated face and a
hooked nose, in a white robe, sitting on a platform above, one deformed
toenail sweeping up like an Ali Baba shoe. A foot like varnished old
wood, full of cracks. He is stripping some stems and chewing the flesh

inside. There is a bulge on one cheek, and he spits and spits and spits all the way to the mainland. Brownish spit lands on some rusty metal, pools and trickles, slips off the side onto some rope that lies coiled on the floor.

The tourists' eyes are transfixed, somewhere between horror and excitement. How *real*! Must send a piece to *Granta*.

Same scene through Matano's eyes: Abdullahi is chewing miraa again, a son of Old Town society; banished son of one of the coast's oldest Swahili families, who abandoned the trucking business for the excitement of sex, drugs and Europop (had a band that did Abba covers in hotels, in Swahili, dressed in kanzus: 'Waterloo, *niliamua kukupenda milele . . .*'). Now he is too old to appeal to the German blondes looking for excitement in a hooked nose and cruel desert eyes. To the Euro-wielding market, there are no savage (yet tender) Arab sheiks in Mills & Boon romance books any more; Arabs are now gun-toting losers, or compilers of mezze platters, or servers of hummus, or soft-palmed mummy's boys in European private schools. There are no Abba fans under sixty, now that everyone listens to Eminem and Tupac. Now Abdullahi has become a backdrop, hardly visible in the decay and mouldy walls of Old Town, where he has gone back to live . . .

Matano's mobile phone rings, jerks him out of his daze.

'Ndugu!'

It is Abdullahi, and he turns to look at him. Abdullahi smiles, the edges of his mouth crusted with curd from the khat. He lifts his hand in an ironic salute. Matano smiles.

'Ah,' says Abdullahi. 'Your eyes are lost in the middle of white thighs again, bro. You're lost, *bwana*.'

'It's work, *bwana*, work. So, you know how it is when the *mzungu* is on his missions?'

'So, did you think about the idea? I have everything ready. The guy can come into Shanks's house tonight.'

'Ah, brother, when are you going to see that I am never going to play that game?'

'*Sawa*. Don't say I didn't warn you when you see my Porsche, and my house in Nyali, and my collection of plump Giriama sweetmeats. You swim too much in their waters, brother. I swam too, and look what happened. Get your insurance now, bro. They will spit you out. Dooo do . . . brother! This deal is sweeeet, and the marines are arriving tonight, *bwana*.'

Abdullahi sends a projectile of brown spit out into the sea and laughs.

Matano shakes his head, laughing to himself.

Poor Abdullahi. Ethnic hip-hop rules the beaches: black abdominal muscles and anger. The darkest boys work the beaches, in three European languages, flaunting thick charcoal-coloured lips, cheekbones that stand like a mountain denuded of all except peaks, dreadlocks and gleaming, sweaty muscles.

Abdullahi makes a living on the ferry, selling grass and khat, chewing the whole day, till his eyes look watery. These days he isn't fussy about how he disposes of his saliva. They used to hunt white women together. Once in a while Abdullahi comes to Matano with some wild idea – first it was the porn-video plan, then the credit-card scam, always something proposed by his new Nigerian friends.

Abdullahi forgot the cardinal rule: this is a game, for money, not to seek an edge. Never let the edge control you. The players from the other team may be frivolous; they may be able to afford to leave the anchor of Earth, to explore places where parachutes are needed. This is why they are in Mombasa. The Nigerians would discard him as soon as he became useless, like everybody else.

Matano once got a thrill out of helping Abdullahi, giving him money, directing some Scandinavian women to him, the occasional man. Being Giriama, Matano resents the Swahili, especially those from families like Abdullahi's, who held vast lands on the mainland and treated Giriama squatters like slaves, but Abdullahi was a victim of his own cultural success. How are you able to pole-vault your way to the top of the global village if you come from three thousand

years of Muslim refinement? You are held prisoner by your own
historical success, by the weight of nostalgia, by the very National
Monumenting of Old Town, freezing the narrow streets and turning a
once-evolving place into a pedestal upon which the past rests.

Matano, the young boy in a mission school, from a Giriama
squatter family has not got this sort of baggage (the our-civilization-
has-better-buildings, more-conquests-than-yours baggage). Every
way directs him upwards. He hates the ferry. As a child, on his way to
school, sitting on his father's bike, he would get a thrill whenever they
climbed aboard. These days, he hates it: hates the deference people
show him, their eyes veiling, showing him nothing. They know he
carries walking, breathing dollars in the back seat. Once, a schoolboy,
barefoot like he used to be, sat on one of the railings the whole way
and stared at him – stared at him without blinking. He could taste the
kid's hunger for what he was. Sometimes he sees shame in people's
eyes, people carrying cardboard briefcases and shiny nylon suits,
shoes worn to nothing. They look at him and look away; he makes
their attempt to look modern humiliating.

Then there is the accent business. Speaking with the white people
with so many people watching, he always feels self-conscious about
the way he adjusts his syllables, whistles words through his nose and
speaks in steady, modulated stills. He knows that, though their faces
are uncertain here, on this floating thing carrying people to work for
people who despise them, he will be the source of mirth back in the
narrow, muddy streets of the suburbs, where his people live. They
will whistle his fake *mzungu* accent through their noses and laugh.

In a town like Mombasa, his tour-guide uniform is power. He has
two options to deal with people. One: to imagine this gap does not
exist, and be embarrassed by the affection people will return. Behind
his back they will say, 'Such a nice man, so generous, so good.' It
shames him, to meet wide smiles on the ferry every day, to receive a
sort of worship for simply being himself. The other way is to stone-
face. Away from his home and his neighbours, to reveal nothing: to

greet with absence, to assist impersonally, to remain aloof. This is what is expected. This is what he does most of the time, in public places, where everybody has to translate themselves to an agenda that is set far away, with rules that favour the fluent.

Of course, he can be different at home, in Bamburi Village, where people find themselves again, after a day working for some Gikuyu tycoon or Gujarati businessman or Swahili gem dealer or German dhow operator. Here, people shed uncertainty like a skin; his cynicism causes mirth. He is awkward and clumsy in his ways; his fluency falters. His peers, uneducated and poor, are cannier than him in ways that matter more here: drumming, finding the best palm wine at any time of night, sourcing the freshest fish, playing bao or draughts with bottletops, or simply filling the voided nights with talk, following the sound of drums when the imam is asleep and paying homage to ancestors who refuse to disappear after a thousand years of Muslim influence.

What talk!

Populated with characters that defy time, Portuguese sailors, and randy German women, and witches resident in black cats, and penises that are able to tap, tap a clitoris to frenzy, and a padlocked Mombasa City Council telephone tweaked to call Germany and tell your SugarOhHoneyHoneyMummy, 'Oh, baby, I come from the totem of the Nine Villages. Warriors' – growl – 'no woman can resist us. How can I leave you, baby, so weak and frail and pale you are? My muscles will crush you; my cock will tear you open; we cannot be together; you cannot handle me in bed' – sorrowfully – 'I am a savage who understands only blood and strength. Will you save me with your tenderness? Send me money to keep my totem alive: if my totem dies, my sex power dies, baby. Did you send the invitation letter to immigrations? I am hard, baby, so hard I will dance and dance all night, and fuck the air until I come in the ground and make my ancestors strong. My magic is real, baby. Have you heard about the Tingisha dance, baby, taught by my grandmother? It teaches my hips to grind round and round to please you. Will you manage me? A whole night, baby? I worry you may be sore.'

You must be entertained. Material is mined from everywhere, to entertain millions of residents in whitewashed houses and coconut-thatch roofs, who will sit under coconut trees, under baobab trees, under Coca-Cola umbrellas in corrugated-iron bars. Every crusted sperm is gathered into this narrative by chambermaids, every betrayed promise, every rude madam whose husband is screwing prostitutes at Mamba Village, every leather breast, curing on the beach, every sexcapade of every dark village boy who spends his day fuck-seeking and holding his breath to keep away the smell of suntan lotion and sunscreen and roll-on deodorant and stale flesh stuck for twelve months of the year in some air-conditioned industrial plant.

The village is twelve huts living in a vanishing idyll. From the top of the murram road, where Bamburi Cement Factory is situated, there is a different territory: the future. Beyond the cement factory, Haller Park, an enormous constructed ecology in a park, incredible to all, but not yet larger than the sum of its parts: it still needs a team of experts to tweak its rhythms. There are also enormous ice-cream cake hotels, crammed rooms in hundreds of five-shilling video halls, showing One Man, One Man, who can demolish an entire thatched village in Naam, with a mastery over machinery full of clips and attachments and ammo and abdominals. Even the movements are mastered and brought home, the military-fatigue muscle tops bought in second-hand markets, the bandana, the macho strut, the slender back, missile launcher carved from wood, lean back and spray; the sound of the gun spitting out of your mouth.

'Mi ni Rambo, bwana.'

'Eddy Maafi.'

Video parlours rule. With Chinese subtitles.

The couple at the back of the van are still talking. He is lean and wiry and tanned and blond and has a sort of intense, compassionate

Swedish face, a Nordic nature-lover. He has the upright American accent continental Europeans like to adopt. He is wearing glasses. She is definitely an American and looks like she presents something on TV, something hard-hitting, like *Sixty Minutes*. She has a face so crisp it seems to have been cut and planed and sanded by a carpenter, and her hair is glossy and short and black. She is also wearing glasses. They are the producers of some American TV programme . . . Shanks told him to give them the fat-sultan treatment, which he defines as 'Grapes, recliners over a sunset, hard but honest barbarian boys, or voluptuous barbarian girls and Anusol suppositories always in the glove compartment.'

'The place is a bit cheesy, but the food's great, and anyway, we'll be roughing it in Somalia for a while. Jan said he hasn't found anywhere with running water yet. We mustn't forget to buy booze – Mogadishu is dry, apparently.'

'Shit. How many bottles can we take in?'

'Oh, no restrictions – there's no customs and they never bother foreigners.'

'Do you think we'll get to meet Shanks? He sounded great on the phone.'

'He'll come across brilliantly on camera. He does actually look Maasai – you know, lean and intense sort of . . .'

'The red shawl won't work, though. It's too strong for white skin.'

'It's amazing, isn't it. How real he is? I could tell, over the telephone, he has heart.'

'Do you think he's a fraud?'

'A sexy fraud if he is one. He hangs out with Peter Beard at his ranch in Nairobi. I saw it in *Vogue*. He drinks with Kapuściński.'

There was a brief and reverential silence as they digested this miracle.

'Should we call him Shanks or um-Shambalaa?'

They both giggle.

When they met Matano at the airport, they said they were thinking about doing a film here, although wildlife wasn't their thing. They say they like human-interest stories, but this is all sooo gorgeous, so empowering. 'We must meet um-Shambalaa. Isn't he positively Shamanic?'

There is something about them that Matano dislikes. A closed-in completeness he has noticed in many liberals. So sure they are right, they have the moral force. So ignorant of their power, how their angst-ridden treatments and exposés are always such clear pictures of the badness of other men: bold, ugly colours on their silent white background. Neutral. They never see this, that they have turned themselves into the world's *ceteris paribus*, the invisible objectivity.

He puts on a tape. Tina Turner: 'Burn, baby, burn . . .'

'Looking for something real,' they keep saying.

Twenty years he has been in this job, ever since he took it on as a young philosophy graduate, dreaming of earning enough to do a master's and teach somewhere where people fly on the wings of ideas, but it proved impossible: he was seduced by the tips, by the endless ways that dollars found their way into his pockets, and out again.

He has seen them all. He has driven feminist female genital mutilation crusaders, cow-eyed nature freaks, cutting-edge correspondents, root-seeking African Americans, Peace Corps workers and hordes of NGO folk: foreigners who speak African languages and wear hemp or khaki. Dadaab chic.

Not one of them has ever been able to see him for what is presented before them. He is, to them, a symbol of something. One or two have even made it to his house, and eaten everything before them politely, then turned and started to probe: so is this a cultural thing or what? What do you think about democracy? And homosexual rights? And equal rights?

Trying to Understand Your Culture, as if your culture is a thing hidden beneath your skin, and what you are, what you present, is not authentic. Often he has felt such a force from them to separate and break him apart – to move away the ordinary things that make him human – and then they zero in on the exotic, the things that make him separate from them. Then they are free to like him: he is no longer a threat. They can say, 'Oh, I envy you having such a strong culture,' or, 'We in the West, we aren't grounded like you . . . Such good energy . . . This is so real.' Da-ra-ra-ra.

Ai!

All those years, the one person who saw through him was a fat Texan accountant in a Stetson, who came to Kenya because he had sworn to stop hunting and start takin' pictures. After the game drive they had a beer together and the guy laughed at him and said, 'I reckon me and you we're like the same, huh? Me, I'm jus' this accountant, with a dooplex in Hooston and two ex-wives and three brats and I don' say boo to no one. I come to Africa an' I'm Ernest Hemingway, huh? I wouldn't be seen dead in a J.R. hat back home. Now you, what kinda guy are you behind all that hoss-sheet?'

The van lurches out of the ferry and drives into Likoni. What is a town in Kenya these days? Not buildings: a town like this is nothing but ten thousand moving shops, people milling around the streets, carrying all they can sell on their person. The ingredients of your supper will make their way to your car window, to your bicycle, to your arms, if you are on foot. If you need it, it will materialize in front of you: your suit and tie for the interview tomorrow; your second-hand designer swimsuit; your bra; your nail-clippers; your cocaine; your Dubai clock radio; your heroin; your Bible; your pre-fried pili-pili prawns; your pirated gospel-music cassette; your stand-up comedy video; your little piece of Taiwan; your Big Apple, complete with snow falling, and streets so pure that Giuliani himself must have installed them in the glass bubble.

The hawker's new sensation is videotapes. Reality TV Nigerian style has hit the streets of Mombasa. Every fortnight, a new tape is released countrywide. Secret cameras are set up, for days sometimes, in different places. The first video showed a well-known councillor visiting a brothel; the next one showed clerks in the Ministry of Lands sharing their spoils after a busy day at the deed market (title for the highest bidder, cashier resident in a dark staircase). Matano hasn't watched any of them yet. He hasn't had the time this tourist season.

The Swedish nature-lover, Jean-Paul, looks out at produce knocking on the van window. His face seals shut, and he takes a book out of his bag: *Jambalaya, the Water-Hungry Sprite.* Matano has read about it in a New York magazine that one of his clients left behind. A book written by a voodoo priestess (and former talk-show host) who lives in Louisiana, which had the critics in raptures. The Next Big Thing. The movie will star Angelina Jolie.

Matano's blind spot. Extract of a conversation that Matano had with one of his annual Swedish lovers, Brida, who adores Marquez:

'What is it with you white people and magic realism?'

Brida runs her nails down his chest and turns the page in her book. Matano jerks away.

'Don't you find it a bit too convenient? Too guilt-free? So you can mine the ashrams of India, or the manyattas of Upper Matasia, or Dreamland Down Under, with a didgeridoo playing in the background, without having to bump into memories of imperialism, mad doctors measuring the Bantu threshold of pain, Mau Mau concentration camps, expatriates milking donors for funding for annual trips to the coast to test, personally, how pristine the beaches aren't any more . . .'

'Don't be so oppressed, darlink! I'm Swedish! Can we talk about this in the morning? I promise to be very guilty. I'll be a German aid worker, or maybe an English settler's daughter, and you can be the angry African. I will let your tear off my clothes and—'

'Why should it bother you? You come every December, get your multicultural orgasm and leave me behind churning out magic realism for all those fools. Don't you see there is no difference between your interest in Marquez and those thick red-faced plumbers who beg for stories about cats that turn into jinnis, flesh-eating ghost dogs that patrol the streets at night, the flesh-eating Zimba reincarnated? I mean, every fucking curio dealer in Mombasa sells that bullshit: "It is my totem, ma'am, the magic of my family. I am to be selling this antique for food for family. She is for to bring many children, many love. She is buried with herbs of love for ancestors to bring money. She was gift for great-grandmother, who was stolen by the ghosts of Shimo La Tewa . . ."'

Brida laughs and puts her book down for a moment.

'It is life, eh? Much better way to make money than saying, "Oh, I be sell here because I be poor. My land, she taken by colonizer/ multinational beach-buying corporation/German dog-catcher investing his pension/ex-backpacker who works for aid agency . . ."'

Brida runs her fingers across his forehead, clearing the frown. 'Don't spoil my book, darlink. I'm in a good part. In the morning we talk, no?'

'Why should I make it easy for you? Why don't you read your own magic realism? At least you are able to see it in context. You nice, liberal, overeducated Europeans will look down on trolls and green-eyed witches and pixies, though these represent your pre-Christian realities, but you will have literary orgasms when presented with a Jamaican spirit-child, or a talking water closet in Zululand.'

'You think too much, Matanuuu. I shall roll you a joint, eh? Maybe we fuck, and then you can present your paper at the Pan-African Literature Conference, while I finish my book in peace.'

Matano laughs.

Jean-Paul turns to the *Sixty Minute* woman and says, 'God, her prose sings. Such a hallucinogenic quality to it.'

She looks dismissive. 'I prefer Allende.'

She leans forward towards Matano and slows her drawl down, presenting her words in baby-bite-sized syllables: 'So, which Kenyan writers do you recommend, Matanuuu?'

'Karen Blixen,' he says, his face deadpan. 'And Kuki Gallmann . . .'

Ngugi is only recommended to those who come to Kenya to self-flagellate, those who would embrace your cause with more enthusiasm than you could, because their cause and their self-esteem are one creature. They also tend to tip well, especially after reading *Petals of Blood*.

When he is alone. When he is alone, he reads Dambudzo Marechera, who understood the chaos, understood how no narrative gets this continent, who ends one, 'And the mirror reveals me, a naked and vulnerable fact.'

He remembers the name of the *Sixty Minute* woman: Prescott Sinclair.

There is nowhere Prescott has been where the sea smells so strong, and she opens the in-flight magazine one more time just to look at the piles of tiger prawns being grilled on the beach, and the fruit cut into fancy shapes.

She is irritated with Jean-Paul again. She likes to work with him outside America – he makes a good and harmless chaperone – but she finds his matter-of-factness annoying. He motors through everywhere and everything at the same pace, disinterested in difference. He reads the right books, is perfectly accommodating to her moods, is never macho, bossy or self-serving. He is apologetic about his fastidiousness. She has tried, many times, to goad him to reveal himself, to crack. She is starting to think the person he presents is all he is.

Brynt, her boss: the work maniac, sex maniac and ulcer-ridden, seeker-of-mother-figure (who must come) wrapped in pert breasts, fat-free. He is exactly the man she has constructed herself not to have to want. She cannot resist him. He wears her out, demanding she leaves her skin behind with every new job, becomes somebody else, able to do what she never would. In bed, she must be the tigress, the woman able to walk away purring while he lies in bed, decimated. Sex for him is release: he carries electricity with him everywhere, but can't convert it into a memorable experience. She has in her mind, whenever she thinks of him, the image of a loose electric cable, writhing around aimlessly on concrete, throwing sparks everywhere. She can't leave him alone – his electricity continues to promise but always fails to deliver, and often it feels as if it is her fault: she isn't being for him what he needs to convert his electricity into light.

She broke up with him a month ago. Has avoided his calls. Taken her work home. Volunteered for jobs abroad. Jean-Paul must know, but hasn't ever said a word. Why is he such a coward?

The driver, who has been quiet since she tried to make conversation with him, turns to them, smiles and says, 'Welcome to Diani! We are now turning into Makuti Beach Resort. *Karibu!*'

Does the person define their face, or does one's face define their person? Matano often wonders. Why it is that people so often become what their face promises? Shifty-eyed people will defy Sartre, become subject to a fate designed carelessly. How many billions of sperm inhabit gay bars and spill on dark streets in Mombasa? How does it happen that the shifty-eyed one finds its way to an egg?

Trust can have wide eyes, deep-set; mistrust is shifty, eyes too close together. Or is it? Among the Swahili on the coast, it is rude to look someone directly in the eye; one must always be hospitable, hide one's true feelings for the sake of lubricated relationships, communal harmony. Smarmy, an English person may call this, especially when it is accompanied by the smell of coconut oil and incense.

Armitage Shanks, by the born-with-a-face-personality theory, is a martyr. Eyes that hold you: sea-green, with mobile flecks that keep your eyes on them whenever he says anything. Spiritual eyes: installed deeper in the sockets than usual, little wings on the edges of the eyelids lift them to humour, and lines of character. He would be a spiritual leader, a man whose peers would seek out for quiet advice. If he were a Muslim, he would be interrogated at every airport in the West.

What sorts of mechanics define these tiny things that mean so much to us? What is done to the surface of the eye to make light gleam on it in such a liquid manner? Are there muscles that are shorter than most people's, attaching the eye to the face, or sinking the eyeball deeper into the skull? What child was born, a million years ago, with the eyes of an old and humorous man? What words were whispered around the village? About this child's wisdom, his power to invoke ancestors, so women threw themselves into his bed as soon as his penis woke up and said hello to the world.

Ole um-Shambalaa's face is lean, ascetic, lined and dark, nearly as dark as Abdullahi's. The hair is blond, closely cropped. Ole um-Shambalaa is not supposed to be frivolous. Any more.

He leans forward to open the door of the van and smiles. Prescott and Jean-Paul make their way out, both flustered by the heat and by the fact that they are not sure what rules he plays by. Will he bow down to greet them? Or kiss their noses? Would shaking hands seem terribly imperialist? Shanks does not guide them; he stands there, still, in a way only Eastern religious people in films or certain animals can be: muscles held tense, smiling with enough benevolence to awaken the belly. Wings of warmth will flutter in the stomachs of these two guests.

A millisecond before Prescott blurts out her learned Maasai greeting, he reaches both his hands to her and takes her hand. He does the same with Jean-Paul, looking shyly at the ground, as if humbled by their spiritual energy.

He turns, without greeting Matano, and heads for the lobby, tight, lean buttocks clenching as he walks. Prescott is shocked at her thoughts. It seems sacrilegious to think of sex with this man, but she wonders, despite herself, whether he practises tantra or some exotic Maasai form of spiritual orgasmism. Oh shit, don't they practise female genital mutilation?

Matano makes his way to the staff quarters. He always has a room at the hotel, but he uses this only for what Shanks calls 'Vagina Dialogues'.

The staff houses are all one-roomed: cheap concrete and corrugated-iron structures, arranged in an unbroken square. Matano finds his colleagues seated on three-legged stools in the inner courtyard, playing bao.

'Dooo . . . do. *Matano mwenyewe amefika. Umepotea ndugu.*'

'You've been scarce, brother.'

Outside this courtyard, Otieno is known as Ole Lenana. Every day, shining like a bronze statue, dressed in a red loincloth, with red shoulder-length braids, he heads off to the beaches to get his picture taken by tourists, a pretend Maasai. He used to be a clerk at Mombasa County Council. He receives a small pension from Frau Hoss, a fifty-year-old German lady who comes to Mombasa for two weeks every year, to paint her wrinkles tan and to sleep with a darker tan.

Otieno swears by *vunja kitanda* – Break the Bed – a combination of herbs he insists gives him stamina, even with old, gunny-bag breasts. Matano has something to tell him, about Frau Hoss.

Matano says his hellos, then goes into Otieno's room. Inside, it is partitioned with various kangas. The bedroom is a curtain stretched across the side of the bed; in the living room is a money plant in a cowboy cooking-fat tin, three cramped chairs, covered in crocheted doilies, and a small black-and-white TV. There are photo albums on the coffee table. In a trunk under the table are Matano's books, most given to him by tourists, maybe half of them in German. He picks out one that he received a week ago. He has been waiting since to see Otieno, to show him Frau Hoss's book.

He strips, puts on his black swimming trunks, wraps his waist in a blue kikoi. He joins the rest, sits on a stool, legs left higher than his shoulders, kikoi curled into his groin for modesty. He can smell coconut milk and spices. Women are cooking at the other end of the courtyard, chatting away, as they peel, crush, grind and plait each other's hair.

'So, did you see um-Shambalaa?'

The group of four burst out singing, 'Um-Shambalaa, let's go dancing. Ole um-Shambalaa, disco dancing . . .'

Matano laughs. 'He has lasted till lunch without coke? He is serious about this *maa-neno*?'

Otieno turns to Matano. 'He is paying me, *bwana*, to be Ole Kaputo, the Maa chief's son.'

'Nooo! Ai! This deal must be of much money! That is why he was afraid to talk to me. There'll be bumper harvests this time. I think these ones are television people. From America.'

There is silence as the rest digest the implications of this. America. The bao game proceeds, and conversation weaves languidly around them.

Matano passes the book round. Kamande, the chef, takes one look at the cover and hoots with laughter. Otieno is on the cover, body silvery, courtesy of PhotoShop, kneeling naked facing the mud wall of a manyatta. Everything in the shot is variations of this silvery black, his red Maasai shawl, the only colour, spread on the ground. Two old white hands run along his buttocks, their owner invisible. It must be near sunset: his shadow is long and watery, a long, wobbly shadow of cock reaches out to touch his red shuka.

Otieno looks bewildered, then grabs the book. His eyes frown, confused: who is this person? Recognition. Gasp. The book changes hands, all round the circle, and everybody falls over themselves laughing. The women come to investigate. Fatima, Kamande's wife, looks at it, looks at Otieno, looks back at the book.

'Ai! Why didn't you tell me you had a beer bottle in your trousers? I will find somebody for you if you learn to use it properly! Not on these white women – what can they show you?'

The women laugh and carry the book away to pore over it.

Otieno turns to Matano. 'Where did you get it?'

'A tourist left it in the van last week. Frau Hoss said she taught you – tantric love.'

'I will sue!'

'Don't be stupid,' says Matano. 'Write your own book. Let's write it, *bwana*! The publishers will eat it up! African sex is hot in Germany

. . . You will make a killing! Call it *My Body Defiled*. Then make sure you sit without your shirt on the cover looking sad and oppressed.'

They laugh.

Prescott sits with Jean-Paul at the pool bar next to the beach, watching the sunset, having a drink and waiting for Shanks.

There is no barrier from here to India. There are scores of short, muscular boys silhouetted against the dusk, covered in and surrounded by curios, doing headstands and high jumps and high fives and gathering together every few minutes to confer. Sometimes they look at Prescott. One winks; another bounces his eyebrows up and down. Then she is relieved as they spot a tourist, gather up their wares and go to harass someone else. There is music playing at the bar: some sort of world music for Europop fans. '*Jambo, jambo, bwana. Habari gani? Mzuri sana . . .*'

From a well-known guidebook: 'The Kenyan's smile is the friendliest in the world. He will tell you, "*Jambo*", and serve you *dawa* cocktails.'

The beach boys cannot come to the hotel, but Prescott has been told that they will be all over her in six international languages if she crosses the line of the coconut trees.

One of the boys walks towards her, managing to bounce off the balls of his feet with every stride, even in the sand. He has a brief chat with the security guard and walks up to their table. She looks at his lean face, eyes like a startled giraffe, with thick, stiff strands of eyelash.

'*Jambo!*'

'*Jambo.* I'm afraid I'm not buying anything today. No money.'

Jean-Paul is shut away, among characters that talk like blackened fish, and look like bayous, and make love like jambalaya. Somebody with a banjo is searching for a lost gris-gris bag.

Beach Boy frowns and slaps at his chest, puffed up. 'Us, you know, *Beach Bwuoys*, it is only money! We want to sell you Bootiful Hand-u-craft of the Finest T-u-raditional Africa. Eh! A man like me, how it feels to run and chase white *mzungu* every day: buy this, buy this? I dig to get cool job, any cool job: garden, office or bouncer in Mamba Village Disco, even navy offisaa. I have diploma, marine engineering, but Kenya? Ai! So now t'fuzz, the pow-lice, they chase homebwuoys. And the hotel, they chase homebwuoys. But this beach, this is our hood. Dig? So you want special elephant-hair bracelet? Is phat! Very phat!'

He isn't smiling. He is looking out to sea, tapping his foot on the ground like a glass vase of testosterone, just waiting to be shattered. In Philadelphia, she would have been terrified of him. She would walk past, her tongue cotton wool, a non-racial smile tearing her reluctant face open. Now she wants to pinch his cheeks and watch him squirm as his friends look on.

'I want a necklace, a Maasai necklace. Can you get me one?'

He looks at her with seamless cool and raises one eyebrow, then frowns. *Tsk, tsk,* he seems to say, *that is a hard one.* The silence lasts a while,; then he looks at her and says, 'For you, Mama, because you so bootiful, I will try.' And he bounces back to his mates, one arm swinging with rhythm round his back like a rap artist walking to his Jeep.

She laughs.

Jean-Paul says, 'God, look at that sunset.'

Prescott says, 'It's never as good as the postcards, is it? Fuck, poets have a lot to account for. They've killed the idea of sunsets, made meadows boring and completely exterminated starry nights. Sometimes I think they're just as bad as Polluting Industrial Conglomerates Run by Men.'

Jean-Paul smiles patiently and looks across at her, compassion in his eyes. She wants to slap him. Brynt hasn't phoned. Though she isn't taking his calls, it's important that he calls, so she can get the satisfaction of not taking his calls.

Shanks appears from the glass doors on the other side of the pool.

He has tucked his red Maasai cloth into his shorts, his torso is bare, and his arms are draped over an ivory walking stick that lies on the back of his neck. His silhouette is framed by the last vague rays of the sun, the postcard silhouette of the Maasai man whom the Discovery Channel will introduce, deep-voiced, as 'an ancient noble, thriving in a vast, wild universe'.

He squats on his haunches next to them and glides his eyes around them both. Smiles.

'Peace.'

Prescott smiles vaguely. Jean-Paul has cracked already: his mouth is wide open.

'You have eaten?'

They nod.

'Come.'

They follow him. His walk is not graceful, like Prescott expected. Rather, it is springy: he bounces to one side on one leg, then does the same on the other. It is a distantly familiar movement, again, something from *The World of Survival* or Discovery. Some walk some ethnic peoples do somewhere in the world, and they are noble.

They leave the residents' area of the hotel and cross through a gate; before them, sitting under a vast baobab tree, is a huge whitewashed mud-and-wattle hut, with a beach-facing patio constructed of rugged acacia branches, stained pine-coloured. There is an enormous apple-green couch shaped like a toilet, with large sewn lettering that reads, 'Armitage Shanks.'

Shanks points to it. 'My great-grandfather had a tremendous sense of humour. He furnished his drawing rooms with seats that looked like toilets.'

They sit on the cushions on the floor. Shanks crosses his legs as he stands and lowers himself straight down into a cross-legged sitting position.

A very tall man walks out of the hut, carrying a tray. He is introduced as Ole Lenana. It is Otieno.

'My circumcision brother.'

Shanks and Ole Lenana chat away in a strange language. Ole Lenana joins them, unplugs the beaded tobacco pouch hanging from his neck and starts to roll a cigarette.

'Did you know' – his voice startles them, suddenly the voice of Shanks, not um-Shambalaa – 'in the sixteenthth and seventeenth centuries, before commercial fertilizer was invented, manure was transported by ship, dry bundles of manure. Once at sea, it started to get heavy, started to ferment, and methane would build up below deck. Any spark could blow up a ship – many ships were lost that way. Eventually people began stamping the bundles "Ships in High Transit" so the sailors would know to treat the cargo with respect. This is where the term "shit" comes from: Ships in High Transit. Many of those around these days . . .'

Prescott is wondering whether this is how the Shanks family sanitizes their history: faecal anecdotes that have acquired the dignity of a bygone age, presented in a dry, ironical tone.

'The Maasai build their houses out of shit. This is a house built from the shit of cattle, mixed with dung and wattle, and whitewashed with lime. You know, forget the bullshit in the brochure. That was for *Vogue*. I can see you two are not from the fluff press. I don't really believe this Maa-saa-i-a mythology stuff, because it makes no sense to me. I make myself believe it because I need to. Maybe, being a Shanks, it is the shit that attracted me. Maybe it was to do something that would give me a name and a life different from something branded in toilets around the world. Maybe I was tired of being a name that flushes itself clean with money every new generation. Maybe I like the idea of having the power to save an entire nation. Or maybe it was just for the money. All I can tell you is that I want to help save these people, that these heirlooms you will see tomorrow are the most exquisite creations I have ever seen. The world must see them.'

Prescott says, 'But don't you think there's something wrong with that? Isn't it like taking ownership of something that isn't ours?'

She is thinking, Houses of bullshit, my God . . .

Shanks says, 'I earned my membership, like any Maa. They trust me. I am one of them.' He was um-Shambalaa again and stood, and he and Ole Lenana gripped forehands and looked deep into each other's eyes, and Ole Lenana fell to his knees and muttered something guttural, emotional and grateful.

The cigarette is being passed round: Jean-Paul, Prescott, um-Shambalaa. Dope. She looks up, starled by a shadow. It is the tour guide, Matano, his torso bare, muscles gleaming. He is drinking beer.

'The sisters are here to sing.'

They walk in, women shrouded in red cloaks, singing. Voices, mined from a gurgly place deep down in the throat, oddly like percussion instruments. This is a society that lives laterally, Prescott thinks, not seeking to climb up octaves, find a crescendo, no peaks and troughs: ecstacy sought from repetition, as the music grabs hold of all atmosphere, the women begin to bleat, doing a jump every few moments, a jump that thumps a beat to the music and lifts their piles of necklaces up and down. Up and down. Ole um-Shambalaa stands up; Ole Lenana joins him. They head out to the garden and start to jump with every bleat. Prescott has an image in her mind of the stomach as a musical instrument, bagpipes squeezed to produce the most visceral sounds the body can. She finds herself jerking her neck forward and back, to the beat. The tide must have risen, for the waves seem to be crashing on the beach with more fervour than she can remember. Damn him, damn Brynt. She will not cry.

The women have gathered round Jean-Paul's cushion. There is an expression of mild panic on his face, which he can't shut out. They grab his arms, stand him up. He starts to jog himself up and down, a tight smile on his face, his eyes wild, looking for a way to bolt.

None of the women singing know a word of what they are singing. Not three hours ago, they were chattering away in Kiswahili while cooking supper. After dark, they don beads and kangas and practise in the servants' courtyard, heaving and gurgling and making all kinds of pretend Maa sounds. This is why the hotel allows them to stay in the quarters with their husbands.

Matano is watching Prescott. She is just about to allow herself to be reckless. He slowly makes his way towards her, stands behind her chair, allowing his presence to occupy her space.

At the airport he caught her standing alone, looking bewildered about this new place. Those eyes, her skin so white, made him shiver. He has in his mind the constant idea that white women are naked, people with skin peeled like baby rabbits, squirming with pain and pleasure in the heat. It is always profoundly disturbing to him that they are rarely like this in reality, so forward and insistent, interrupting his seduction with demands – 'There! There!' grabbing his face, holding on to it, making his tongue work until they are satisfied. Many of them have no faith in his abilities, feel they need to manage all his activities.

Was it Anaïs Nin who wrote the erotic story of a wild giant beast of a man, an artist, and a brash and demanding woman came on to him, and he rejected her, and she chased and chased him, learning to be demure? One day, long after she had submitted and become who he wanted, he jumped on her and they molested the bed for the whole night.

Jean-Paul has succumbed. It started with the women laughing at him, as they watched his body awkwardly trying to find a way into the rhythm. He burst out laughing at himself, and his movements became immediately more frenzied. Now he howls, and jerks faster, a string puppet out of control.

An hour later Prescott sits with Matano at the edge of the camp. Ole um-Shambalaa is sitting cross-legged in the garden, absolutely still. Matano wraps his hand round her waist and is singing a Maasai song in her ear, ever so softy. Behind him, the women's self-help group are still singing. Their eyes have become glazed; they look like they could go on for ever.

She can't seem to stop shaking. It must be the dope. And the music.

She jerks out of his embrace and says, 'I'm sorry, I'm just wiped out. I've got to go and lie down.'

He shrugs and turns her to him and smiles, looking at her, looking at her. Then his large hand reaches and pushes her hair behind her ear, his wrist leaving a smear of sweat on her cheek. She is singed by it, and immediately afraid.

She can't sleep. Her heart is thudding in her chest, and when she lies on her back, an enormous weight seems to force her down, pushing her into her bed, and she has to struggle to breathe. It must be the dope. She stands. It is quiet outside; they've all gone to sleep. She stumbles out of the tent, her legs numb, stinging like pins and needles. The feeling spreads over her body and she goes to the bathroom and looks at her face in the mirror. It looks the same, a bit wild, but not much different. She sees the Maasai necklace hanging out of her toilet bag and takes it and puts it round her neck. She looks in the mirror: on her it looks tacky. The strong colours suck up her face.

There is a message from Brynt on her phone: *Did you find Shanks? Call me.*

What reins you back in? she wonders. What makes you want to be what you were again? After this mind-bending magic, how can Chicago compete with this primal music, with bodies rubbing themselves against thick, moist air?

Maybe truth is always a consensus. Maybe it doesn't matter what kind of proof backs up your submission; maybe your submission has no power without being subscribed to by a critical mass of people. What is the truth here?

Back home, there is fear so far inside fear you don't feel it. Mortgages, a lifeline that cannot escape upward mobility: you have to be sealed shut from those who live laterally to thrive. If you cannot maintain openess to this, you can always control it. Packaging. Sell it, as a pill, a television programme, a nightclub, a bonding retreat, a book, jambalaya prose. Control it. Make the magic real. Allow it only to occupy a certain time. This is the human way – the rest is animal. But tonight it will be real; it is real. Brynt is a faraway myth. It will be different in the morning. But now, she heads back to um-Shambalaa's.

Matano finds himself thinking about Abdullahi's proposal. A week ago Abdullahi took him to meet the Nigerians, who intimidated him, strutting like nothing could govern them, buy them. Noticing his scepticism about the deal, one of them laughed at him.

'You Kenyans! You let these *oyibos* fock you around, man. Eh! Can't you see your advantage, man? You know them; they know shit about you. So here you are, still a boy, still running around running a business for a white guy. So stoopid! I saw him in the inflight magazine when I was coming from Lagos with new stock. Ha! Um-Shambalaa!'

The group of Nigerians broke into the Kool & the Gang song on cue: 'Let's go dancing. Um-Shambalaa, disco dancing . . .'

'So do you dance for um-Shambalaa? For dollars? We're offering you real money, man. Four hours, you let our guy in and you have enough money to fuck off and buy a whole disco, where you can dance for German women the whole night, brother.'

Matano wonders for a moment why this deal is worth so much, then remembers the numbers. The thousands who gather under baobabs to listen to stories of the strange hotel tribes. The closed-loop system the Nigerians have devised to reduce piracy. All the videos are released to the video parlours on the same day, at the same time. FM stations who have taken to advertising in the videos. Politicians who pay to feature in the urinal breaks. NGOs who pay to send 'Wear condom' messages between sex scenes.

Matano looks at the group on the grass now. Jean-Paul is slow-dancing with Otieno (Ole Lenana), who will argue in one of the afternoon sessions in the courtyard that the best way to get his revenge is to fuck them.

'There is nothing more satisfying than making a white man your pussy!'

The rest will laugh and call him *shoga*.

They will all make sure Fatima does not hear them speak. They value their lives. Kamande will look back nervously to see that she is otherwise engaged.

For what? Matano thinks. Fifty dollars? Maybe a watch? Why should Jean-Paul give a shit how he is judged in the laugh sessions under baobab trees? Who, in his circle of peers, in his magic-made-real characters, will care?

He calls Abdullahi and says, 'Send them in, bro. Bring in the guy. The back door is open.'

He sees Prescott walking towards him. He will perform on the sofa of um-Shambalaa's house. The drinks are laid out, the dope. Servants wander in and out and are soon invisible in the revelry.

Morning is another part of the lottery. The sun will rise. Somebody will receive a call; Chicago will roar back into her life, down a telephone line. She will wash Matano's smell off her, sit on the toilet and cry, still stuck to chasing the spewing electric cable. Jean-Paul will see a pile of tacky plasic beads on the floor, red hair dye on his pillow, will smell stale nakedness on his sheets. That Lenana is no other reality in the morning. He wants money, is listening to Kiss FM, has spashed himself with Jean-Paul's cologne, before examining the shadow of his penis with some satisfaction. He must spend the next few weeks practising his German. He will be on German TV soon, if all goes according to plan. Jean-Paul is itching for him to leave, for the chambermaid to come in and clean last night away. He will sit on the beach and escape to the bayous. Tonight, he will only see um-Shambalaa's reality through a camera, for their programme *A World of Cultures*.

Fatima and her troop of women share the spoils in the morning. Ole um-Shambalaa paid them an extra bonus, just to make sure there was no mischief. Fatima cannot stand um-Shambalaa and is not afraid to hide it: he cannot do without her. She is the most plausible gurgler and Kamande is the best chef this side of the island and, because he has the same name as Blixen's badly spelled 'Kamanti', is worth more in drinks-before-dinner anecdotes. Fatima managed to get thirty dollars from Jean-Paul, by threatening to take his shirt off while they danced last night. About three dollars of this money will be offically declared to husbands; the rest will go to their communal slush fund. Things will appear in the household, conveniences explained away. School fees will be mysteriously paid.

'Ai! Don't you remember? It was a gift from Mama So-and-so, after I helped her cooking when her relatives went away.'

The nest egg is growing. Every three months each gets a lump sum. Khadija is planning to leave her husband soon. She works as a chambermaid and will return, after the morning shift, with a collection of forensic stories: red hair dye on a pillow, how Otieno smells just like Jean-Paul's bathroom. And Matano, when will he leave those white women? It is definitely time they found him a wife . . .

Abdullahi is thirsty. The ferry smells of old oil. Last night, after the operation in um-Shambalaa's house, he took an old lover to bed and performed like never before, surrounded by Abba, incense and cocaine. Today he will buy himself a car.

The practised will thrive in the morning: both made their transitions before dawn. Matano left um-Shambalaa's room, after carefully pulling strands of Prescott's hair from his short dreadlocks. He made his way back to the courtyard, lay out on his kikoi watching dawn and counting the stars, the way he used to with his mother as she cooked in another courtyard, not five miles away. He reads Dambudzo.

Ole um-Shambalaa is in his small plane. He woke up at four in the morning. He sat on the Art Deco Shanks toilet and expelled. Sunrise will find him in Laikipia, talking to the elders, tracking an elephant, chatting to the young morans, learning new tricks. He will visit his factory, explain to the greediest of the elders how they can benefit from it, dish out wads of cash, enough to buy a goat or two. He will call his new enterprise a conservancy. The Maa Conservancy. He will return at dusk, when his colour is hidden by shadow, ready to play for Prescott's cameras. Tonight he will show them the heirlooms.

Abdullahi brings Matano the tape and his cut in the afternoon. Two hundred thousand shillings. Not enough to buy the disco, but just fine, thank you. They sit in the TV room of the hotel, with some of the staff, and laugh and laugh and laugh at the lateral gurgles and drunken sex talk. For the next few months this will be the main feature in every video hall at the coast. Sold to them, one time, and in a closed loop to limit piracy (as if anybody would risk pirating the Nigerians), for 5,000 shillings per tape. Ten bob entry, sex, imitation Maasai women and 'Um-Shambalaa, let's go dancing.'

Fock the copyright, we're Nigerian.

Someone is shouting loudly in the lobby, drunk. The first marines are checking in: ship landed today, exercises for Iraq. Matano smiles to himself and catches Abdullahi's eyes. Which one of them will call the Nigerians?

'Hey, bud, did you see them honkin' hooters hanging at the pool bar?'

'I wanna beach-view room, you stoopid fuck. Fucking Third World country. Fucking Ay-rabs everywhere.'

THE MOUSTACHED MAN

Patrice Nganang

O, you cannot spend your whole life running away from your destiny. No, no, you cannot for sure. You can hide under your bed; fate will send a serpent to bite you. You can protect yourself under a tree when it rains; it will send lightning to transform the tree and you into ashes. You can find shelter in water, between the fishes; it will send an extra-hungry crocodile for your personal entertainment! This is what shot through Ngono's head as he ran away and turned a corner into Frühlingsgasse. He thought of his parents, of his ancestors, of his life in the missionary school. He thought of his friendships, particularly of his friendship with Charles Atangana. (Actually, I can say, it was not a real friendship, but a struggle to survive, as all colonial lives were.) He thought of the kids playing on the streets of Yaoundé. He thought of the freshness of life there at night and of all the spirits people thought were living in the first streetlamps that had been installed the year before he left.

'It is the spirits of the deceased,' people said.

But also: 'Of the unborn.'

He thought about his father, who used to laugh at those stories, even though he was not a Christian. He also thought of his mother, especially his mother. He saw her face on a streetlamp. She was telling him to run and run and run. He saw his brothers and sisters, who were saying the same: run and run. They too were streetlamps. He thought about all the people, women, men, kids, who lived in his family estate in Nkomkana, in Yaoundé. All of them, uncles, aunts, nephews, grandfather, grandmother; all of them were telling him to run for his life (*Run, Ngono, run!*), to remember that he was the first of his people to go to the white man's country.

The worst thing for an intelligent black man, really, is to wait to be killed by a racist. It is simply not worth it! It is not worth it! He saw the faces of his family gathered along the Gasse. They were the spirits he had thought streetlamps could not be. But he also distinctively heard his father. This time not a streetlamp, his father was calling him a 'coward' in Ewondo.

'What are you running from, eh?' his father was asking. 'From those sons of rats?'

'Are you running away from those *mosquitoes*?'

That is what his father was saying.

'Aren't whites men too? Are you now such a coward that you run away from men like you?'

I am not a coward! Ngono thought.

He had not yet turned to look at what was still following him and forcing him to run through the night, but, more overwhelming than the prospect of facing death, it was the certainty of a life of cowardice that made him suddenly stop in his tracks and walk back towards his assailants. He even ran back towards them, so eager was he to prove to himself and to his father that he was not a coward, that an Ewondo man has never lived in cowardice, that he would not be the first to prove that proverb wrong. This is what is written in the police file about the case; then they state in unambiguous terms that it is 'the negro' who attacked first. Since there is no other source to balance this statement, let me thus assume it is true; Ngono was the attacker, not the victim.

'I am not a coward!'

This is what he shouted, but he said it in Ewondo for he was mainly addressing his father, his ancestors, even if it sounded like a call to a tribal war shouted in the depths of Berlin in 1913.

'I am not a coward!' he shouted, and smashed his head onto the mouth of the first of the men who were following him. He realized later that the man had a moustache, but for now, he just saw him fall like a tree. The suddenness of Ngono's turn, his cry ('his tribal war cry') and the madness of the whole situation made the group of men stop. One even tried to run away. The men had not expected Ngono to react with such savagery. And Ngono had never known that such violence was hidden within his head, waiting patiently, silently, calmly for the right moment to blast the mouth of a moustached German racist.

'You want to play cat and mouse?' one of the men said, showing his bare hands.

'Let's go!' said another. 'This is nonsense.'

'No, let's stay!' said the third.

'And civilize him!'

Ngono heard them speak. He knew what his father had taught him: 'Take one, only one of them-o, and make him regret the day he was born.'

He said, 'Cowards!'

But this time he was not speaking to his father any more. He said it in German and added, 'Imperialists!'

Again and again: '*Imperialistische Feiglinge!*'

His assailants understood what he said very well. The man with the smashed and now bloody moustache suddenly stood up, his hands held like fists. Another one was saying, 'You call us cowards?'

He was laughing and pointing at Ngono, as he spoke to his friends.

'Do you hear?'

'Cowards?'

'Us?'

This question may have twisted the mind of the third one, a rather small and bald man who ran towards Ngono and punched him in the belly. What followed was a frenzy Ngono did not have any words to describe in his report at the police station. He was hit with feet, with hands, with stones, with light and night. He was hit with words, with bricks from the asphalt. He was hit with all the streetlamps, which strangely turned against him. Damn German streetlamps! Were they also racist? He had thought they were his friends, his family! He was hit by the moon, which cast a beam of light in the Gasse for him to still open his eyes and see his assailants leave him for dead. He stood up. His feet were dancing. His body was shaking. His mind was full of the contradictory words of his father, who was speaking to him in Ewondo and finishing his sentences in German: 'Has my water produced such a *Feigling*?'

'IMPERIAL COWARDS!' Ngono said in German.

This time again, it was the moustached man who stopped first and turned back.

'Cowards?' he said.

He was holding his mouth and spitting blood.

'Adolf,' said his neighbour, the small, bald man, 'let him be. It is just a negro.'

'He is just a monkey,' said another man.

But the moustached Adolf could not give up. Maybe it was his smashed mouth that made his blood boil. Or maybe an evil will that was running in his body, reddening his eyes, telling him that this whole monkey business needed a final solution. Or simply because he had never before been called a 'coward' by a black person, by 'a negro'. Holding his fists up like a boxer, he walked towards Ngono, who could not stand up straight any longer.

'Coward?' he was saying. 'Are you talking to me?'

And Ngono at this moment was thinking of his father's words: 'One, just take one of them-o, my son, and make him regret that he was born by a woman.

'And make him wish his mama was a whore.

'And make him regret that his father had balls.

'And make him wish to defecate in his dreams.'

He answered his father. In fact, he asked him to leave him alone. It sounded like a magical invocation to the moustached man and to his friends. Ngono had spoken in his mother tongue. They stopped, puzzled. Ngono did not stop asking his father to leave him to 'teach that bastard'. The old man did not stop encouraging him either. He was now saying, 'And make that son of a bitch eat from his anus.'

'Yes,' Ngono said, 'COWARDS!'

His father could not be silenced.

'And make him fuck his chicken!'

The Ewondo lecturer was dancing on his feet, his ears full with the familiar and angry voice of his father, but his fingers were pointing in the air, as if showing a sign of victory.

'One by one!' he said.

And again: 'Come one by one!'

The men were laughing and looking at each other.

'One by one!'

And laughing, they all advanced together towards Ngono, in closed rank behind the moustached man. They did not laugh long. This time the lecturer had taken a stone from the street. He threw it towards the small, bald man but missed his head. He heard a cry, the cry of an animal, of a dog. The men dispersed. The stone smashed onto the asphalt.

'He is mad,' a voice said.

'*Ilang nuazut!*' screamed Ngono. 'Come one by one, one by one, and I will make you fuck your cat!'

'I said we have to finish him.'

This, Ngono heard the moustached man say, even though he was holding his bloodied mouth when cursing.

'What are you waiting for?' the lecturer was screaming in the night. 'Bring it on, *belobolobo!*'

He was dancing a dance of death.

'Come, all of you,' he said, 'and I will finish you!'

He was moving and dancing.

'And I will civilize you!'

The man he had missed with his stone was the first to hit him. His eyes were bloodshot. He had held his fist behind his back when approaching, but Ngono was not impressed. The fight that followed went down in the archives of the Sittenpolizei as one of the thousand and more altercations that occurred in Berlin in those nights before the Great War. It is not that the racists left our poor Ngono dead in the street. Their boxing match with a black man who had learned courage from streetlamps was stopped by the police, who were alerted by someone. They ran away when they heard the whistles. Ngono was the only one to be arrested. Of course, he could also have run his soul out of his legs. There was no way for him to hide in the Berlin of those years, where one could still have put all the black people into an apartment room and locked the door. He did not receive a free ship fare to go back to Cameroon, as one might have expected in such a blatant case of public disturbance by a 'drunken imperial subject'. This was due, he learned later, to the benevolence of a Professor Doctor Med. Doctor Phil, who chose to remain anonymous, but paid the bail for his release.

'You are a lucky bastard,' the police officer said, when opening Ngono's cell to let him out. 'Just go before I change my mind. *Weg damit!*'

And he added, 'Berlin is a great city, isn't it?'

In his report, there is no mention of a moustached Adolf. It is clear that such news was worthless to the police. Adolf, Rudolf or the like were very popular names back then. And the moustache was one of those things all German men before the war thought made them irresistible to girls. There is therefore no way to sort out the words Sara told me her father used to explain why he had lost two fingers in Germany. She mentioned an 'Adolf who had a moustache' being 'one of the three cowards', as the dean quoted him saying, 'who did not even have the guts to fight him one by one like men.' A late correction:

she was not 100 per cent sure if the name of her father's moustached assailant was 'Adolf' or 'Adorf' and this adds to my confusion. But maybe it is me, dear reader, who is trying to make her say things she cannot have meant and name people she did not refer to. She was not yet born herself, anyway, but sometimes, yes, sometimes, I see myself dreaming that Ngono's punch on the mouth of a moustached Adolf or Adorf (never mind) in Berlin had made the man mute. We all know that it may have saved our humanity from a savagery the Ewondo lecturer did not live to tell.

A GOOD SOLDIER

Maaza Mengiste

This was his father: 'Good soldier, what do you have to confess?'

This was him: 'I am not the one you want. I am not the one you can break.'

His father woke him with the same question every day. He'd started after they came to Los Angeles last year, after they'd spent six months in a falling-down building in Khartoum fleeing soldiers in Addis Ababa. It was 1980. His father was getting him ready to face the enemy. When he turned eleven, he'd be promoted to general and his real strength would be tested. Benny was ten, too afraid to ask what he was supposed to confess and how his father's enemies could get to Los Angeles from Ethiopia.

His father didn't talk about his time in jail. He never spoke about the night the soldiers brought him back, bound, and dumped him on their doorstep, then snatched Benny's mother, Emebet, off the sofa and out of Benny's embrace. It seemed he'd forgotten about that night, about the way the soldiers seemed to fall on top of them in one downward swoop, as final and swift as a hammer's blow. Benny and his father had used his mother's crucifix necklace to pay for a midnight ride in a covered truck out of Addis Ababa. They'd walked from Debre Markos to Bahir Dar and barely made it into Sudan before checkpoints along the borders were reinforced. In all that time his father never spoke a word, never mentioned his mother's name or jail or soldiers, as if the heat had dried up his memories along with his throat.

Life for Benny before his father's arrest was a series of handclaps and foot races, marbles games and American movies. His mother laughed. Her eyes sparkled like water in the sun. Her long hair flowed down her back like a dark, soft ribbon. His father sang for a band called the Golden Sounds of Ethiopia. He had a voice that trembled like a leaf in the wind. They lived in a home near the centre of Addis Ababa with two bedrooms and one bathroom. In the rainy season, from June to September, Benny practised drumming to the sound of fat raindrops flattening onto their corrugated-tin roof. There was no shooting at night. No soldiers breaking down doors and coming back to leave fathers on verandahs. No father waking him up in a tiny Los Angeles apartment empty of his mother, asking about breakable boys.

After his mother was taken, Benny and his father waited in silence for her return for three months, listened every night for the thud of a body falling on their doorstep. They left the front door unlocked, and as one week bled into the next, they left the door ajar, then wide open. Benny's father sat on the sofa and watched the entrance from sunset to sunrise, his scars healing in stripes and circles over his arms and legs. He refused to talk, seemed to stare at the wall with his tongue clamped between his teeth, his eyes a darker black than when he'd left.

One night, after a long, hard rain in the month of July, Benny heard his father run down the hallway towards the front door. He sprang out of bed and stood behind his father as two soldiers pushed their way in.

'Where is my wife?' his father said, looking behind them outside. 'You took Emebet.'

'We're finished with her,' one said with a smirk. 'Give us more names tomorrow. We know there are others she wouldn't say. And this boy' – they pointed to Benny – 'they start working for you young, don't they?' They stared hard at his father and they nodded to each other.

His father sank to his knees and held his head in his hands. He pressed his forehead into the floor at the soldiers' feet and Benny thought his father was begging them for something, but they left and his father still stayed as he was, head to floor, begging instead an invisible god for a secret request.

When he stood up, his father was a different man. All the words he'd refused to speak since his mother was jailed seemed to spill out of him.

'Beniam, listen to me.' He grabbed him by the shoulders and shook him. 'We have to leave. There's no other choice. Pack a shirt and a jacket. Put on your shoes.'

'What about Emama?' Benny asked, already aware that a mother gone to jail for three months might never come home.

His question forced his father to kneel and hold him. 'Go pack your things. Don't tell anyone anything. Never talk about this. Now hurry!' Then his father raced into his bedroom and came out with a small sack that Benny knew held his mother's best jewellery. He was taking off his wedding ring and tucking it into the mouth of the bag. 'Are you ready?'

Benny rushed into his room and grabbed his clothes, shoved them in his small blue suitcase, then stood in the middle of the living room and stared at the sofa his mother used to sit on. His father was dialling a number, his fingers fumbling to fit in the holes of the phone. He spoke low, but the night air was so thin, sound carried as far as it wanted.

'Leul,' his father said, calling his close friend and a drummer in the band, 'they're coming for Beniam unless I give more names. Emebet . . . I need help . . .' and he seemed to break into two, double over himself, but he stood straight again and repeated the words. 'I need help.'

Leul came to pick them up, his eyes wide and alert. He shoved them into his back seat and pulled a blanket over them. 'The truck will take you as far as it can. He's my cousin. Give him something small. Save the rest for later.'

Benny kept his eyes closed like his father told him and the car seemed to dip and float over every bump, rattling in a sharp wind, hurtling them towards Nazret and Bahir Dar, then through villages without signs and names. Hot sun and dry wind.

My son. He is all I have of his mother now. I know what they've done to her because of me. I understand what else they want to do. How do you beg a god for something you can't begin to speak? There's only escape. We walked until Beniam's feet bled; then I held him until mine had no feeling. Fear kept me upright. One foot in front of the other. Don't think about that foot once held in the clutches of a monster with stones for eyes.

Emebet told Benny the story of his father. They were sitting on the sofa staring at the door, waiting for him to walk through and come home from jail after two months. 'Your father's band turned love songs into battle cries. He had the power to bring people to their feet. They loved him and a revolution always starts in the name of love. What can shake a government of butchers more than a voice that carries a thousand with it? They took your father to silence him, but once a voice is heard,' she said, 'it is free. He didn't want you to know anything, to protect you, but you must. These days are turning people inside out. You have to be ready.' Benny didn't know what to do except sit with his mother and hold her when she cried.

This was Beniam's mother: radiant with a beauty mark on her left cheek. We met when I was a student at Yared School of Music. She was studying economics at the university. She liked to hold my hand when she thought no one was looking. She had a laugh that made me smile. Her hair fell in thick waves to the middle of her back. When I was jailed, she shaved it off. Neighbours told her it was bad luck to mourn before a person was dead. She said one way of life had died for ever. Sometimes she sang with my band; other times she was the first to stand and dance *eskesta*. What I remembered of her face was from a photograph I brought out of Addis Ababa. It was for our son. For the day he asked how it was that I survived and she did not. It would replace all of his questions, force us back to the time when she still smiled with flowing hair.

He'd come to Los Angeles from Khartoum because it was where Leul had moved.

'The sun,' Leul had told him, 'it's like Addis. There are jobs, beaches and automatic car washes – you don't have to do it yourself. Can you imagine?'

Leul had left out the part about the hundreds, then thousands, of Ethiopians also fleeing repression and running to Los Angeles, bringing with them memories and extinguished lives, old loyalties and new enemies. From Fairfax to Crescent Heights and extending into streets with names like Manhattan Place and Western Avenue, the community grew and found each other and began to point out who was who, who used to be what, who was no longer one of their own. Mesfin stayed away from the community as much as he could, afraid of being recognized as the voice that gave the names of so many who were now dead. He refused Leul's offer of a meal on Fairfax or a beer on Crescent Heights; he wouldn't have attended Medhane Alem even if he'd believed in a god.

'You weren't the only one forced to say something,' Leul reminded him again and again. 'It didn't matter what names you gave – they were going to get whoever they wanted anyway. Give it time.'

But Mesfin could see that even faithful Leul looked away when he reminded him of Emebet and Marcos. 'There's not enough time for what I've done.'

He found work in the suburbs, away from Ethiopians.

Then there came a day when an Ethiopian customer walked into

the restaurant where he worked and stared at him across the room. It
was a balding man with thick features and sharp eyes. He pointed to
him and spoke to the hostess. The hostess walked the man to one of
Mesfin's tables and slid a menu towards him. Mesfin served his other
tables until there was nothing else to do but go to him. He noticed
the man was flicking a cigarette lighter repeatedly. His posture held
a military rigidity.

'Do you know what you'd like?' he asked, speaking in English.
He kept his eyes on his notepad, tried to still his own shaking hands.
He noticed again the awkward angle of his deformed fingers around
his pen. One day, he thought, he'd learn to type to ease the pain of
writing.

The man stared at him for uncomfortable minutes. 'Your name is
Mesfin Gebregiorgis?' he asked in Amharic. 'You were singing before,
in Addis?' A sly smile played on his thin lips. He wasn't asking a
question as much as reconfirming. His hands were flat on the table.

'Mike,' Mesfin said, pointing to his nametag and avoiding his face.

'I met someone in your band once,' he said. He leaned forward and
whispered the name. 'Dereje. DJ.'

Mesfin's knees buckled and he balanced himself on the empty
chair near him. DJ, his pianist, the youngest in their group, the one
with a sly smile and blossoming Afro that framed a handsome, kind
face. Dereje. How easy the name had been to say when asked in the
right way. Dereje. 'Dereje who?' the stone-eyed monster had asked,
whispering with a hand on the switch, ready to send fire and light
through his veins again. 'Good, good, who else?' The whisper like a
hiss. DJ. Brought in front of him to witness his traitorous nod, then
led out to become one of the many secrets not even Leul knew about.

'The only way we can hide is if we let each other, isn't it?' the man
asked with the same stone-eyes and hiss. 'Mesfin, husband to the
lovely Emebet.' He picked up the menu. 'Coffee, please, sugar.'

Mesfin opened his mouth and found no words. Before he could
run to the back and vomit everything out, the lieutenant took his

arm and pulled him close. He shrank from the familiar grip, from the smoker's breath asking questions that would soon be followed with a cigarette pressing intense heat into his chest, trying to burn a hole into his shrinking heart.

'Mike,' he said, speaking as if a laugh were caught in his throat, 'here's something funny: I applied for a position here after I got my green card. We could have worked together again. A pity they had enough staff.' He glanced around, taking in the decor, then leaned back and stared at Mesfin. 'Nothing you say about me will ever be as bad as the things you've already said. You buried more people than I did.' He smiled. 'Some people think being in this country means they've left the old things behind. Keep your mouth shut.' He smoothed his moustache with two fingers, then tapped the table. 'Coffee.'

Mesfin sat in his car with his head on the steering wheel, his damaged fingernails tracing the creases of his black work trousers, following the straight line until a ridge of scar tissue pushed them on a crooked path. Eyes closed, he thought of the day his wife's name was pulled out of his body, quivering like a drop of water hanging on a dead leaf. Emebet. Mesfin pushed the seat back and bent his knees to his chest. With his arms gripped tight round his legs, he hummed, then sang of a man who yearned for his love, who called to her with an untainted voice springing from a chest that held a loyal heart.

'Good soldier, what do you have to confess?'

'I am not the one you want. I am not the one you can break.'

It was just a question followed by other simple questions. He was only a soldier preparing for the enemy, not a general who'd been tested. All Benny had to do was answer the way he'd been taught.

But one night his father came home after his shift at work with a large coffee stain eating through his white shirt.

'What happened, Daddy?' Benny asked, pointing to the stain, then looking at the dark circles under his father's eyes.

'Just someone from back home,' he said. 'They wanted to sit at my table.' He walked into the kitchen and turned on a pot of tea.

Leul shook his head as if he knew what else his father was saying and emptied the ashtray into their sink. He was their roommate and his father's only friend in Los Angeles. A square-jawed drummer with thick hands who washed dishes in the same restaurant his father worked. 'This will happen,' he said.

His father and he ate from takeaway cartons of food that his father brought, while Leul sat quietly and blew rings of smoke into the air, shaking his head periodically. After dinner Benny did his homework and watched his father shuffle cards for the men's nightly game of secca. Cards dealt, each of the men waited for the other to begin a story about a good moment in Ethiopia.

His father started. 'The night at the Addis Ababa Hilton, do you remember?' His father rubbed his head with the crooked fingers of his right hand. His smile seemed to drag his eyes down, make them sadder than they looked already. He still wore the stained shirt.

'Our white tuxedos and black bow ties,' Leul said. 'We sang of Ethiopia.'

'We sang for Ethiopia,' his father said. A cigarette burned in between his swollen knuckles. A thread of smoke fanned into a haze in front of his eyes. He looked down.

'Haile Selassie was alive,' Leul said, and he drifted past the game of secca and into the Hilton Ballroom.

His father folded one leg over a knee and traced the edge of a scar creeping up his shin. 'We wanted to pretend nothing was happening, that the coup would be bloodless.'

'Marcos wanted us to sing your song first,' Leul said, a gentle smile on his face. 'He had his *krar* and he didn't want DJ's piano, just your saxophone and then your singing. They were both so stubborn.'

Mesfin closed his eyes. He tried to pull his trembling lips into a smile.

'Marcos,' Leul sighed.

The men were quiet as Benny tried to imagine the real story they left unsaid. He watched his father for hints about that night his body landed back in his life but tore his mother out of his arms. He tried to look at him with new eyes, not with the eyes of a mother-less boy.

This was his father, Mesfin: a tall man with a sloping forehead and an aristocratic nose. His lips were rounded, and his teeth were perfectly straight. His skin was smooth, golden shades under a deep brown. He walked in even, elegant strides Benny had always admired. He didn't look suited for cells half flooded with dirty water, crammed full of soiled prisoners nursing open wounds with stinking rags. This was what his mother told him it was like in prison. 'We are so lucky, Beniam,' she said, 'to be here with each other and not there. When he comes back, you must promise me to do everything you can to help him.'

After Leul went to work, his father went into his room to change his coffee-stained shirt. He told Benny to wait for him in the living room. When he came out, he was carrying a plastic bag and an old newspaper clipping from an Ethiopian newspaper. He wasn't smiling. He looked old and he hadn't shaved. He sank into the couch and stared at the clipping. It was a picture of a man with a moustache and hard eyes in a military uniform.

'I didn't know how to prepare myself for what happened to me. I thought I was safe.' His father seemed to struggle with a thought. He put the news clipping on the table and opened the plastic bag. He took out a brand-new skipping rope with bright orange handles. 'On the ground,' he said, his eyes focused on the article. 'Soldier, please.'

'Yes, Daddy,' Benny said, as he slid off the couch to the floor. 'I mean, yes, sir.' He swallowed. There was a knot forming in his stomach, making him feel like he had to throw up.

'I promised myself I'd never let that happen to you,' his father said, speaking softly. He reached for the scissors and began cutting the orange handles off the ends of the rope. 'I wanted to wait until you were older, but the enemy's here. He can attack again. We have to be ready.'

Benny stood up, frightened by the way his father's voice shook, by the way he refused to look at him, by the way he seemed to harden in front of him. 'I can skip fast, Daddy.' Benny's heart was hammering so hard he could see his shirt pulsing up and down.

'Brave soldier, sit.' His father took a deep breath. 'Tell me again why we do drills.' He spoke lovingly, but his voice was tight. 'I've taught you this much so far.'

Benny let his legs buckle under him like they wanted and sank to the floor. 'To be prepared,' he said, trying to hold back his fear.

'And why do we have to be prepared?' His father looked sad and serious at the same time.

'We have to be able to withstand enemy advances.'

'And who are the enemies, my good soldier?' His voice, thick, his words slow as if forcibly dragged out of his mouth.

'The enemies of my people come disguised as my people,' Benny said. 'They speak with forked tongues and have no scars. They make the scars, sir.' He'd memorized the answers after saying them every day for almost a year. They were automatic. It was the first time he'd paid attention to what he was actually saying.

Benny remembered the day he saw his father without his shirt on. Long, raised scars crisscrossed his back. They looked like shoelaces keeping him from splitting down the middle. His father had spun round, then dropped to his knees in a single motion when Benny asked, 'What happened?' His father had stared at him unfocused, blinking for a long time, his fists clenched.

'Benny?' he'd asked as if it was a stranger in front of him and not his only son. Then, 'My God, Beniam.' His father had got off his knees and held him tight and told him the marks were from a fight with an enemy a long time ago.

'The enemies try to turn you into one of them,' he said now. 'They do things to you so you become the enemy of your people.' His father walked round him in wide circles, the rope dangling in his hand, swinging with each step. 'To fight the enemy is an act of love, strong soldier.'

Benny was shaking. He thought of his mother and her stories about the love songs his father made into battle cries. He thought of his promise to her to help his father and be a good son. He trembled as his father knelt in front of him and kissed his forehead, but he didn't get up and run like he wanted.

'Knees up and arms out,' his father said.

Benny brought his knees to his chest and extended his arms, his sides already aching from what he knew was next. It was the same way his father had been tied when he was dropped at their door.

His father tied his wrists together. He looped the rope several times. He laced the rope round Benny's ankles and wrists so that by the time he was done Benny was bound ankle to wrist. He was shaped like a circle.

'Stay in position until I give the order,' his father said. He pushed the newspaper clipping towards Benny. 'Memorize this face. Enemies never change. We're the only ones who change.' He wiped his eyes and left the room.

'We have to be prepared. To be prepared is to be armed. I am not the one you want. I am not the one you can break. I will not tell a lie. I will not give you names. I don't know anyone but myself. I am an army of one.' Benny said the lines his father taught him again and again while he stared at the article and burned the man's rounded face into his memory.

Soon his arms and legs started hurting. 'Sir,' he said, his voice soft. 'Sir, do you hear me?' He grew louder, more desperate. 'Sir?'

There was no answer.

He scooted himself forward like a snail scraping itself across dirt. He did it again before he realized that the movement was tightening the rope round his ankles and wrists. The pain in his back was sliding over his shoulders and down his arms. His legs were cramping.

'Sir!' he cried out. Then, when nothing happened, when his father didn't come out of his bedroom, when he heard the faint traces of the saxophone his father bought months ago and had never played, he panicked. 'Daddy! Daddy!'

His father ran in, his face so twisted that Benny knew he'd heard him calling. His father dropped to his knees without a word. It wasn't until his father untied him, until he took him in his arms and kissed his cheeks and his forehead that Benny saw his father's tears were falling as fast as his.

'It'll get easier,' his father whispered as he held him close and wiped his eyes. 'You'll get used to it. I promise.'

This is the lieutenant: 'Are you ready to confess?'

Mesfin's legs are strapped to a metal chair. A pair of pliers on the table still grip his torn fingernail. His hands are broken. His thumb hangs limp. They want to cut his tongue, split it in half. 'Can the Golden Voice sing with a forked tongue?' they ask, and laugh.

Has it been only three days? It is a year of nights. Mesfin has folded himself into boxes. In here is Emebet in a long dress. In there is Beniam and his wide smile. In there his saxophone. This one holds his mother. This one his father. His voice, he puts in that one and closes the box tightly so it does not escape.

'Tell us,' they say, 'and you will sing again, you will speak your wife's name, you will call your son to you.

'Are you ready to confess?'

This is Mesfin stripped of everything but burns and broken bones: 'I am not the one you want.'

'You are the one we can break,' the lieutenant says. He smiles with crocodile teeth, small white daggers hanging in his human mouth. 'I have seen your wife. Beautiful. Here's a list of names. Tell us who else is in the resistance; we'll leave her alone.'

Mesfin is crying.

'Marcos. Seifu. Bekele. Seyoum. Nardos. Mikael. Kidane.'

'There are more, I am sure.'

'Yes.'

Night grows and swallows the day.

PRÉFÉRENCE NATIONALE

Fatou Diome

Translated from the French by Polly McLean

The law changed very quietly, thanks to Mr Borders: if you're married to a French citizen, it will now take two years' fucking for the fragrance of France, and its papers, to rub off on you. For African women married to French men, access to citizenship increases with the fecundity of their womb, though the French foetuses know nothing of *préférence nationale*. But Mr Borders is not as foolish as he may seem. By delaying the conferral of citizenship to two years after marriage, he is counting on the flighty nature of his countrymen and the racism of in-laws to destroy the couple before the fateful day. Then, as the ex-wife of a French man, the foreign woman becomes no more than an exotic ex-object. And as with any object, she has no rights, not even the right to earn an honest living. Left to her own devices, she does her best to survive. The government soothes its conscience by supplying a list of contacts, each as worthless as the last. They all say, 'Yes, but you are not entitled to that benefit because you're not a French citizen. Try this other department.'

In the end I realized that while this country has an organization dedicated to looking after abandoned animals, it provides nothing for foreign women abandoned to poverty by French men. They won't give me citizenship, but my Senegalese cat has his papers. Perhaps it's because he's ginger.

But back to *préférence nationale*. If we accept that Poseidon's chariot was pulled by seahorses, it follows that the great trunk of the baobab grows from frail roots. Laws only gather pace when ordinary people start applying them. Termites can cause the collapse of African mahogany trees, and just as the size of an anthill depends on the number of worker ants, so a royal court would be nothing without its servants. It is thus the small employers who make *préférence nationale* something to be reckoned with.

I was looking for a job in one of Strasbourg's free papers and came across this ad: *Large bakery in the city centre looking for salesgirl. Dialect desirable. Please come to the shop.*

I wrote down the address and told a French friend about it on the phone that evening.

'Are you nuts?' she protested. 'You could do better than that. I've the same qualifications as you and I'm finishing my teacher training. You'll be bored shitless selling bread and pastries all day!'

'I'd be happy to do something else,' I replied. 'My qualifications may be French, sweetie, but my brain isn't recognized as such and so is not allowed to function. And in the meantime I have to eat. At least selling bread I won't starve.'

'But this is ridiculous,' she said. 'I'm sure you can find something else. You can't have gone about it right.'

I'd heard that comment a hundred times. My French friends having no awareness of what life here was like for me, often thought I was being paranoid. I didn't resent them for it. When you have Cleopatra's nose and the complexion of Anne of Austria, you don't feel French racism like someone with Mamadou's skin.

The next morning I went to the bakery. Apart from the chocolate cakes and a few overcooked baguettes, everything was white. The men were called Pierre, Paul, Joseph and Martin; the female sex was represented by Gertrude, Josiane and Jacqueline. No sign of Aisha, or Mamadou.

The boss welcomed me with a German moustache, an Alsace accent and a hat in the colours of the French flag. From the way he stared at me, I could tell I hadn't made it through the qualifying round. This man didn't like chocolate in the flesh. I forced myself to smile, and said, 'Hello, sir. I've come about the job you advertised.'

He shook his head, as if to say, *Another one who wants the coats off our kids' backs*. But he came at it more shrewdly than that: 'Oh, speak a little Al-sat-ian, do you?'

It's true that the advert had said, *Dialect desirable*, but I'd come with mine, rather than his. I thought all French people spoke French at least as well as those they had colonized. Now, though, I was linguistically more French than one of Victor Hugo's compatriots, and what's more he was asking me to connect with his clients in Alsatian. So I gave him the reply he was expecting and hoping for: 'No, sir.'

I thought, I've only been eating *kouglof* for two years and already he wants me to adopt his language. I could see the refusal in his muddy-coloured eyes. As if to both justify that refusal and humiliate me, he said, 'Why don't you go and work in your own country?'

He used the '*vous*' form, but it wasn't politeness – he'd used '*tu*' before. It was a hold-all – yes, a vast bin bag for all the foreigners he would have liked to throw in the Rhine.

It gave me the right and the duty to be rude. Internally, I let loose: You ought to be asking me why I even want your stinking job. For two long years my vagina kowtowed to a dick like yours, a plastic-wrapped French dick that gave me nothing but crabs. If a single one of his sperm had gone astray, the state would have given me just about enough to live on – or rather to feed the little French baby and survive on the crumbs. But that didn't happen: my feelings dispossessed me and the national preference of my in-laws got the better of my dreams of freedom. Goodbye, sir. You have impoverished our African soils by making us grow sugar cane and peanuts for your people, you've plundered our reserves of phosphate, aluminium and gold to enrich your country at our expense, and, to top it all off, you've made my people into Senegalese *tirailleurs* and used them as cannon fodder in a war that wasn't theirs. A war in which you made them kill in the name of a freedom you refused them on their own African soil. A war on white soil, where my grandfather's eye still remains, blown out by a piece of shrapnel. And that eye is watching you, sir: it is right here, I can see the horrors of your history reflected in it, and it sees, today, how you treat his children who have come to reclaim it. I came, sir, guided by the smell of my people's blood, my people who left behind child-bearing women and, despite their courage, became fertilizer for your arrogant land. I came because I heard the war cries from the many anonymous graves in Verdun echoing all the way to orphan Africa. Most of all, sir, I came to re-establish the truth. You taught me to sing 'Nos ancêtres les Gaulois' and I realized that wasn't true. I want to teach your kids to sing 'Nos ancêtres les tirailleurs sénégalais', because France is a granary on stilts, and some of its beams come from Africa.

Still without work, I continued to believe that my grandfather's eye would light my path in Europe. After all, the African gods promised eternal protection to those who honoured them with physical sacrifice, and their descendants. Perhaps the European gods would be similarly generous. So three days later I started looking through the free paper again. A new ad caught my eye: *Student required for French lessons. Degree essential. For appt call 03 88 . . . after 7 p.m.*

I took down the number, but this time didn't mention it to my friend. She would have asked me how it had gone at the bakery and wouldn't have believed what I told her. She'd have lectured me: 'You're so bloody paranoid – I'm sure he's not racist, just a bit rude.'

At 7.10 p.m. I rang the number. A woman answered. She told me she was a cashier at one of the big Strasbourg supermarkets and was looking for someone to tutor her eleven-year-old daughter. She suggested meeting the following afternoon, in a city-centre café.

Given that the advert had specified a degree, I'd imagined the pupil would be preparing for their baccalaureate, but I agreed to meet her anyway – a person has to eat, whether Job or Jupiter is paying.

When I arrived at the café it was packed, but Madame had told me she would be wearing 'a white jersey with blue stripes'. I spotted her immediately: with her blood-red lipstick, she was a one-woman French flag. I introduced myself and showed her a part of my brain that had been lying dormant in a folder: the famous degree.

Then the waiter, aware of his duties to capitalism, approached in a friendly way and asked, 'And for you, madame?'

I ordered some kind of juice, thinking, that's funny – when it's time to cash up, national preference is nowhere to be seen. The waiter brought my glass.

The woman opposite me examined the piece of paper, then gave it back to me, saying, 'I want a European-type person.' Lifting her chin in the air, she added, 'I don't want anyone messing up my child's education.'

Madame is French, true, but hasn't even passed her baccalaureate and seems to think she could not tutor her daughter herself. She is refusing me work on account of my black lips, which can at the very least drone the niceties of French grammar better than hers. Pouring juice on top of my rage, I stand up and leave her with this parting shot: 'Goodbye, madame. If you had what I have between my ears, you wouldn't be working as a supermarket cashier.'

'Come back!' she cries. 'You haven't paid for your drink!'

'No,' I say wryly, 'the pleasure's all yours, madame. Think of it as travel expenses: being a cashier, you'll know that everything must be paid for, even the services of coloureds, as you call us.'

I was raging more at her doing Mr Borders' dirty work than at her personal ignorance, which was merely the result of cultural poverty. After all, it's the leaders' foolishness that makes the masses so mindless. When the guide is blind, everyone behind them walks in darkness. I was pondering all this when I heard the cashier yell, 'Go back to your jungle!'

Racists seem to have such a poor vocabulary; perhaps it's their chronic lack of education. My mother-in-law shouted exactly the same phrase at me, and before I had time to go home, she had clasped sonny back to her bosom.

'You should come with me, for the fresh air,' I retorted. 'It's revitalizing – and would save you a facelift.'

She shut her red mouth and sat there muttering, squashing her flabby buttocks into the chair. She was scarlet. Inside, I thanked God for not afflicting me with that particular mark of embarrassment or anger. My skin, at least, always keeps its dignity.

As I was leaving the café, an ageing man winked at me and gestured to the empty chair opposite. I gave him a little smile as I left, thinking to myself, Another lonely old man regretting the family he's never been able to build, because he's always been so busy loving himself in the rare cries of joy and frequent tears of the women he's possessed. No, I wouldn't accept his invitation; he might be one of those old fogeys who love or hate their mother too much to be able to make another woman happy. And no, again, because he might turn out like the man who was delighted to have a black woman in his bed but too ashamed to hold my hand in the street, and who asked me to shut myself away upstairs when his mother arrived unexpectedly. Good riddance, sir!

As I walked along, I found myself taking my residence permit out of my wallet. On the back, just below my arrival date and above my address, was written in capital letters: ANY WORK IN METROPOLITAN FRANCE WITHIN THE SCOPE OF THE CURRENT LEGISLATION. A lovely illusion, I thought – all it needed was OFFICIAL OR UNOFFICIAL at the end.

That evening I called a friend from college, an ash blonde, a real *appellation d'origine contrôlée* white girl. She was looking for some part-time work while she did her degree. I gave her the cashier's number. The next evening her happy voice rang out of my answering machine, 'Thanks for the tip. I started work for that lady this morning. But if you're interested, she has a neighbour who's looking for a cleaner.'

HOMECOMING

Laila Lalami

For five years Aziz had imagined the scene of his homecoming. In his carefully rehearsed fantasies, he would come home on a sunny day, dressed in a crisp white shirt and black slacks, his hair gelled back and his moustache trimmed. His new car would be stacked to the roof with gifts for everyone in the family. When he rang the doorbell, his wife and his ageing parents would greet him with smiles on their faces. He would take his wife into his arms, lift her, and they would twirl, like in the movies. Within days of his arrival he would move them from the decrepit apartment in a poor neighbourhood of Casablanca to one of those modern buildings that sprang up daily in the city.

But as the date of his return to Morocco approached, Aziz found that he had to alter the details of his daydreams. He had imagined he'd arrive in a late-model car, but now he thought that a car trip would be impractical and besides, he didn't think his beat-up Volkswagen could sustain the 800 kilometres from Madrid to Casablanca. So he had booked himself on a Royal Air Maroc flight instead. To make matters worse, the image of his family greeting him at the door of their apartment grew dimmer. His father had died during his absence, and now his mother and his wife lived alone. He also had trouble visualizing his wife's face as easily as he had in the beginning. He remembered her to be slender and distinctly shorter than he, but he couldn't quite recall the colour of her eyes, whether they were green-brown or grey-brown.

These uncertainties made for a stressful few days, culminating on the day of his departure. He arrived at Barajas Airport three hours before his flight. He made sure again and again that his passport and work visa were in order so that he could re-enter Spain after his trip. Once he got on the plane, he couldn't eat the light meal they served during the hour-long flight. He filled out his customs declaration as soon as it was handed to him, repeatedly checking to see that he had entered the correct information from his passport.

When finally the plane flew over the port of Casablanca, he looked out of the window and saw the beaches, the factories, the streets jammed with cars, the minaret of the King Hassan Mosque, but he couldn't locate the medina or the dome in the Arab League Park. He held on to the arms of his seat as the plane began its descent.

It was Aziz's first time inside the Mohammed V Airport in Casablanca. He had left the country on an inflatable boat out of Tangier, in pitch dark, with two dozen other immigrants. He had been caught right on the beach in Arzila by the Spanish Guardia Civil and sent back to Morocco on the ferry two days later. He had spent a few months in Tangier, hustling, and tried again to cross, on a balmy summer night. This time the current had helped him and he had landed on a quiet beach near Tarifa.

A few days later he was in Catalonia, ready for the farm job he had been promised by one of the smugglers he'd paid. It was tough work, but at least it was work, and he tried to keep his mind focused on the pay packet at the end. What he remembered most about that first summer was the hunched figures of his fellow workers and the smell of muscle ointment inside the van that they took to work every morning. When the long-awaited pay packet turned out to be a pittance, he was too afraid to complain. He thought of going north and crossing into France but was afraid to tempt fate again. After

all, he had already been luckier than most. The trip in the inflatable
Zodiac had been an ordeal he wanted to forget, and he didn't think
sneaking across the border in the back of a vegetable truck would
be any easier. So he travelled south instead. He arrived in Madrid in
November, with only a vague address for a friend who worked in a
restaurant and might be able to help him out.

The Casablanca airport was impressive. The marble floors, the
automatic doors, the duty-free shops – everything looked modern.
But the queue for passport control was long. After waiting an hour
for his turn, Aziz stood at the window where the officer, a man whose
purple lips attested to heavy smoking, cradled his chin, an unfriendly
look on his face.

'*Passeport*,' he said.

Aziz slid the green booklet bearing the imprint of the pentacle
under the glass window. The officer typed something on his keyboard,
then leafed through Aziz's passport.

'Where do you work?' the officer asked.

Aziz was taken aback. 'In an office,' he said. That was a lie, but he
didn't understand what his job had to do with checking his passport.
He feared that telling the truth, that he washed dishes, would make
the officer look down on him.

'Do you have your national ID card?'

'No.' Aziz stiffened. He stood with his back straight, trying to
control the surge of anxiety that was overtaking him. He didn't want
to appear nervous. The officer sighed audibly and started typing
away again at his computer. He stamped the passport and threw it
across the counter. 'Next time, have your ID with you.'

Aziz walked to the luggage area and collected his bags. The
customs officer asked him to open his suitcase, prodding the contents
with his baton. He saw a pack of ten undershirts, still in their plastic
wrapping. 'Are you planning on reselling any of these?' he asked.

Aziz knew the type. They harassed immigrants in the hope that they would get a banknote slipped to them. He didn't want to play that game. His voice was cool and disaffected when he replied no. The officer looked behind Aziz at the queue, then closed the suitcase and marked it with a tick in white chalk. Aziz was free to go.

He rode the escalator down to the train station. The shuttle train had been nicknamed Aouita, after the Olympic gold medallist, because it was fast and always on time. Aziz smiled now at the thought of it, at how his countrymen were always quick to come up with funny names for everything. He took a seat on the train, which departed right on time. Outside, the road was littered with black plastic bags. Trees, their leaves dry and yellow, swayed in the wind. In the distance an old truck lay on its side, abandoned, its wheels in the air. Soon they entered the metro area, with its factories and apartment buildings.

He got off the train at Casablanca-Port, the stop nearest to his old neighbourhood. As he stepped into the station concourse, he found himself in the middle of a crowd, of boys selling cigarettes, men offering to polish shoes, beggars asking for change. He held his suitcase and hand luggage firmly. His throat was dry. He started walking in earnest – the apartment was a short distance from the station and there was no need to take a cab. The cart that sold boiled chickpeas in paper cones was still there up the street, and the same old man in a blue lab coat and wool hat still worked at the newspaper stand. A group of teenage girls on their way to school crossed the street in Aziz's direction. Several of them had scarves on their heads, and despite himself Aziz stared at them until they had passed him.

When he arrived at the marketplace entrance, the vendors were still opening their shops, preparing their displays of fruits, vegetables and spices. A butcher was busy hanging skinned lambs and cows' feet. Aziz felt nauseous at the sight of the meat. Carts creaked behind him as the drivers rushed to make their deliveries. Shouts of 'Balak!' warned him to stand aside, and twice he had to flatten himself against a wall to avoid being run over. He felt beads of sweat collecting on his forehead, and the unbearable weight of his sweater on his chest. He wished he could take it off, but both his hands were busy and he was too nervous to stop before getting home.

Aziz turned onto a narrow alley and continued walking until finally he found himself at the entrance of the building, a rambling, turn-of-the-century riad that had been converted into small apartments. Aziz crossed the inner courtyard and knocked on the door of the apartment. The only response he received was from his own stomach, which growled as it tied a knot. He looked over towards the window and saw that the shutters were open. He knocked again. This time, he heard footsteps rushing and there she was, his wife.

'*Ala salamtek!*' Zohra cried.

'*Llah i-selmek,*' he replied. She put her arms around him and they hugged. Their embrace was loose at first but grew tighter. Aziz's mother shuffled slowly to the door, and she wrapped one arm round him, the other one holding her cane. She started crying. Aziz let go of both women, grabbed his suitcase and hand luggage, and stepped inside.

The apartment was darker than he remembered. The paint on the walls was flaking. One of the panes on the French windows was missing, and in its place was a piece of cardboard, but the divan covers were a shiny blue, and there was a new table in the centre of the room.

Aziz's mother broke into a long ululation, her tongue wagging from side to side in her toothless mouth. She wanted all the neighbours to know of the good news. Zohra joined her, her voice at a higher pitch. Aziz closed the door behind him, and now they all stood in the living room, laughing and crying and talking.

Zohra looked thin and small, and she had defined lines on her forehead. Her hair was tied in a ponytail. Her eyes – he saw now that they were grey-brown – were lined with kohl. Her lips had an orange tint to them. She must have rubbed her mouth with roots of swak to make her teeth whiter.

'Are you hungry?' Zohra asked.

'No,' Aziz said, his hand on his stomach. 'I couldn't eat.'

'At least let me make you some tea.' Aziz knew he couldn't turn it down, and besides, he longed to taste mint tea again. Zohra disappeared into the kitchen and he sat next to his mother. Her eyes scrutinized him.

'You look thinner,' his mother said. She herself seemed to have shrunk, and her shoulders stooped. Of course, he told himself, it's been a few years; it's normal. 'And your skin is lighter,' she added. Aziz didn't know what to say to this, so he just kept smiling as he held her wrinkled hand in his.

Zohra came back with the tea tray. Aziz sat up. She was still very beautiful, he thought. When she gave him his glass of hot tea, he noticed that her hands seemed to have aged a lot faster than the rest of her, the skin rough and dry. Her knuckles were swollen and red. He felt a twinge of guilt. Perhaps the money he had sent hadn't been enough and she'd had to work harder than he thought to make ends meet. But it hadn't been easy for him either. He took a sip.

'Let me show you what I brought for you,' he said. He put down his glass and went to open the suitcase. He took out the fabric he bought his mother, the dresses for Zohra, the creams, the perfumes. The two women oohed and aahed over everything.

When he took out the portable sewing machine, Zohra looked at it with surprise. 'I bought one last year,' she said. She pointed to the old Singer that lay in a corner of the room.

'This one is electric,' he said proudly. 'I'll install it for you. You'll see how much faster it is.'

Within an hour of his arrival a stream of visitors poured in to see Aziz. The tiny apartment was filled with people, and Zohra kept shuttling between the kitchen and the living room to refill the teapot and the plate of halwa.

'Tell us,' someone said, 'what's Spain like?'

'Who cooks for you?' asked another.

'Do you have a car?' asked a third.

Aziz talked about Madrid and how it could get cold in the winter, the rain licking your windows for days on end. He also talked about the Plaza Neptuno, near the Prado, where he liked to wander on summer days, watching the tourists, the vendors and the pigeons. He spoke of his job at the restaurant and how his manager liked him enough to move him from dishwashing to clearing tables. He described the apartment in Lavapies, where he lived with two other immigrants. They took turns cooking.

'Did you make friends?' someone asked.

'Some,' Aziz said. He mentioned his neighbour, who had always been kind to him, and his boss at the restaurant. But he didn't talk about the time when he was in El Corte Inglés shopping for a jacket and the guard followed him around as if he were a criminal. He didn't describe how, at the grocer's, cashiers greeted customers with hellos and thank yous, but their eyes always gazed past him as though he were invisible, nor did he mention the constant identity checks that the police had performed these last few years.

Zohra's mother, who lived down the street, had also dropped by, and she sat quietly through all the conversations. Finally she asked, 'Why would you work there while your wife is here?' She clicked her tongue disapprovingly. Aziz looked at Zohra. He wanted to talk to her about this, but they hadn't had any time to themselves yet. He cleared his throat and refilled his mother-in-law's glass.

'Where is Lahcen?' Aziz asked. 'I thought he'd be here by now.' He and Lahcen had exchanged letters in the beginning, but as time went by, they had lost touch. Aziz had received the last postcard from Lahcen two years earlier.

'He's moved to Marrakesh,' Zohra said. 'Everyone has mobile phones now, so he couldn't sell phone cards any more.'

After the guests left, Aziz's mother went to spend the night with the neighbours next door so that he and Zohra could have the apartment to themselves. Aziz stepped into the bedroom to change into a

T-shirt and jogging bottoms. He sat at the edge of the bed and looked around. There was a faded picture of him tucked in a corner of the mirror on the old armoire and a framed one, of the two of them on their wedding day, hanging on the wall by the door. Under him, the mattress felt hard. He bobbed on it and the springs responded with a loud creaking.

Zohra busied herself for a while in the kitchen before finally turning off the lights and coming into the bedroom. She had been talkative and excited during the day, but now she seemed quiet, shy, even. Aziz sat back against the pillow and crossed his legs.

'You must be tired,' Zohra said, her eyes shifting.

'I'm not sleepy yet,' Aziz said.

Zohra looked ahead of her, at the streetlights outside.

'I have something to tell you,' he said. He swallowed hard. Zohra looked at him intently. 'I have some savings, but . . .' He swallowed again. 'I don't think it's enough.'

Zohra sat on the edge of the bed. 'How much?' she asked, a look of apprehension on her face.

'Fifty thousand dirhams,' he said. 'It could have been more, but the first year was tough.'

Zohra reached over and took his hand in hers. 'I know it was.'

'There was the rent. And the lawyer's fees to get the papers. And the money I had to send every month.'

'Fifty thousand is a lot. You could use that for a start. Maybe start a business?'

Aziz shook his head. 'It's not enough.'

'Why not?'

'That would barely cover the lease for a year. Then there's inventory and maintenance.' Aziz shook his head. 'Not to mention all the papers.' He thought of the queues he had seen in government offices, people waiting to bribe an official to push their paperwork through.

'So what are we going to do?' Zohra said.

'Go back to Spain,' Aziz said, looking down. His wife had sacrificed so much already. Her parents had only agreed to let her marry him because they thought that at the age of twenty-four it was better for her to be married to someone who was jobless than to stay single. She had stood by and helped him save for the trip, waited for him, but at least now she wouldn't have to wait any longer. 'And I've started your paperwork, so you will be able to join me before long, inshallah.'

Zohra let go of his hand. She nodded. Then she stood up and turned off the light. He heard her take off her housedress and get on the bed, where she lay on her side. When he got closer, she stayed still, her knees to her chest. He moved back to his side of the bed and tried to sleep.

The next day Aziz was startled out of his slumber at five by the sound of the muezzins all over the city. He lifted his head off the pillow for a few seconds before letting it rest again and, eyes closed, listened to them. In Spain he missed the calls for prayers, which punctuated everything here. He smiled and fell back to sleep. Later the sound of cars and trucks whizzing by the industrial street a few blocks away from the apartment did not wake him, but the smell of the *rghaif* Zohra was making was too much to ignore and he finally got out of bed around nine.

When he came out, his mother was sitting on the divan in the living room, looking regal and aloof. He kissed the back of her hand, and in response she said, 'May God be pleased with you.' Zohra entered the living room and, seeing him there, went back to the kitchen to get the tray of food. She placed the communal plate in the middle of the table, pushing it a little closer to Aziz. She poured and passed the tea round. Then she brought a glass of water and a pill for Aziz's mother.

'What's the pill for?' Aziz asked.

'Blood pressure,' Zohra said. She sat down and started eating.

'I didn't know.' He struggled to think of something else to say. 'The *rghaif* are delicious.'

'To your health,' she replied.

He chewed in earnest, relieved that, with his mouth full, he couldn't say anything. Fortunately a knock on the door provided some distraction. A little girl came rushing in without waiting to be let in. She looked about six years old. Her hair was in bunches, and her blue trousers were ripped at the knees.

'Who is she?' Aziz asked his mother.

'Meriem, the neighbours' kid. She's always here.'

The child jumped into Zohra's arms and Zohra laughed and planted loud pecks on her cheeks. 'Do you want something to eat?' Zohra asked. She sat the child on her lap and handed her a rolled *rghifa*, dipped in melted butter and honey. She smoothed her hair and tightened her bunches.

Later Zohra took Meriem to the kitchen, and when they emerged, the little girl was holding a wooden tray loaded with fresh dough on her head. She was taking it to the neighbourhood public oven. 'May God be pleased with you,' Zohra said as Meriem left. Zohra sat down again. 'Isn't she sweet?' she said. Aziz nodded.

They finished breakfast. Zohra cleared the table and then announced that they had been invited to have lunch at her sister Samira's house, down in Zenata. She went to the bedroom to get her jellaba and slid it over her housedress. She stood facing him now. 'If I go to Spain with you, who will take care of your mother?' she asked.

'My sisters,' Aziz said, waving his hand. 'She can go live with them. You've done more than enough.' Aziz was the youngest in his family, and the responsibility for his mother would normally have gone to her daughters or to her firstborn, and he was neither.

Zohra nodded. Then she drew her breath and added, 'But I don't speak Spanish.'

'You'll learn. Just like I did.'

'Couldn't you just stay here?'

Aziz shook his head. His lips felt dry and he wet them with his tongue. 'We can talk about it later,' he said.

They took the bus to Samira's house. Aziz sat by a window and looked at the streets passing by. New buildings had sprung up everywhere, squat apartment houses with tiny windows that had been outlined with Mediterranean tiles, in a futile attempt to render them more appealing. Internet cafés were now interspersed with tailor shops and hairdressers. He was startled away from the window when a bus coming in the other direction passed by, only inches away. Car horns blared from everywhere, and motorcyclists barely slowed down at intersections.

They got off the bus and started walking. The smell of burnt rubber made Aziz's nose feel stuffy. 'Do you smell that?' he asked. Zohra shook her head. 'It's a strong odour,' he said. She shrugged.

They passed a school and Aziz saw children playing a game of football on the grounds. It reminded him of his own childhood and he smiled.

They arrived a little after the midday prayer. Samira answered the door and Aziz was shocked to see her hair fully covered in one of those Islamic scarves that had seemed to multiply since he left. Collecting himself, he leaned over to give her a hug, but she stepped back from him and said, 'Welcome, welcome.'

Aziz straightened up. Unfazed, Zohra stepped in and took off her jellaba. They sat down on the foam-stuffed divan, and Mounir, Samira's husband, appeared. Aziz kept looking at Samira. Finally he asked, 'When did you put on the hijab?'

'Two years ago,' she said, 'by the grace of God.'

'Why?' Aziz asked.

'Because that is the right way,' Zohra answered.

Why was Zohra defending her? Aziz sat back. 'So that means *you* are on the wrong path?' he asked her. Zohra shot him a look that said, *Stop it*. He pretended not to notice. 'Well?'

Samira tilted her head. 'May God put us all on the righteous path. Amen.' She got up and started setting the table for lunch.

'How long will you be staying?' Mounir asked.

'Only ten days,' Aziz said.

'He's going back again for a while,' Zohra said.

Samira brought the plate of couscous. 'You should go with him,' she said. 'Husbands and wives belong together.'

Aziz watched for Zohra's reaction. Perhaps her own sister could convince her better than he could.

'I don't know if that's the life for me,' Zohra said. But her tone was weak, and Aziz could see that her sister had planted a seed that he could cultivate until he convinced her.

That night Zohra came into the bedroom and turned off the light. But this time when Aziz reached for her, she didn't turn away. He took her into his arms. It felt strange to be making love to her again. He had forgotten how small she was, and while he was on top of her, he worried that his weight might be too much, so he supported himself on his forearms. Being with her brought to mind the women he had slept with while he was gone. He was ashamed to have cheated, but, he reasoned, he had been lonely and he was only human. He told himself that he had never intended to cheat on her, that the women he had slept with had meant nothing to him, just as, he was sure, he'd meant nothing to them. Now he wondered what his wife would look like in a sexy bustier, straddling him, her arms up in the air, moaning her pleasure out loud. He couldn't imagine Zohra doing it, but maybe she would, if he asked her. He came out of her and put his arm under her so he could scoop her up and place her on top of him, but she raised her head and gripped his arms in panic. Her eyes questioned him. He entered her again and resumed their lovemaking.

When it was over and he lay in the dark, he wondered what had been on her mind. He feared that it was only one thing. He had seen how she had looked at the neighbours' child and he wondered if he should have stayed away from her tonight. He told himself that he'd have to use a condom next time. He didn't want to risk having children yet, not like this, not when they had to wait for her paperwork, not until he could support a family. He lay on the bed, unable to sleep.

A few days later Aziz went to visit his father's grave. Zohra led the way, walking swiftly among the rows of white headstones gleaming in the morning light. She stopped abruptly in front of one. Aziz's father's name, Abderrahman Ammor, was carved on it, followed by the prayer of the dead: *O serene soul! Return to your Lord, joyful and pleasing in His sight. Join My followers and enter My paradise.* The date of his death followed: *27 Ramadan 1420.*

Aziz recalled one day in 2000 when a letter had arrived announcing that his father had passed away. Zohra didn't have a telephone, so he had called the grocer and asked that someone get her. He had called back fifteen minutes later, but there was oddly little to say. By then his father has already been dead a month and the event carried no urgency. He felt a great deal of shame at not being able to cry. In Madrid life went on, and his grief, having no anchor, seemed never to materialize. Now he found it hard to conjure it on demand.

'I wish I had been there in his last days,' Aziz said.

'The entire derb came to his wake,' Zohra said.

Aziz got down on his knees and took out a brush from Zohra's bag. He started clearing the dead leaves from the headstone. 'I wish I had been there,' he said again.

Zohra kneeled next to him. 'I don't want the same to happen to us. We should be together.'

Aziz took a deep breath. He had waited for her to make up her mind, and now that she seemed to agree with him, he didn't feel the sense of joy he expected. When they left the cemetery, he told Zohra that he wanted to go for a walk before dinner, so while she took the bus home, he headed downtown, to the Avenue des Forces Armées Royales. At the Café Saâda he peeked inside and saw the patrons standing at the bar or sitting in groups, huddled over their beers and gin and tonics. On the terrace, customers sat indolently over their mint tea. He chose a seat outside, in the sun, and ordered an espresso. He looked around. Something struck him as odd, but he couldn't quite put a finger on it. It wasn't until the waiter came back with his coffee that he realized there were no women at all.

Some of the men played chess; others smoked; many read the newspaper. Those who sat closest to the stream of pedestrians passed the time by watching people, whistling every now and then if they saw a pretty girl. Aziz wondered why the place was so packed in the middle of the afternoon on a Wednesday, but the serious expression on everyone's face provided an answer to his question: they were unemployed. Aziz finished his coffee and left a generous tip before walking down the avenue. The fancy shops displayed leather goods, china, silk cushions, souvenirs, expensive wares that he knew most people in his neighbourhood could never afford.

By the start of his second week in Casablanca, Aziz had seen every sibling, cousin, neighbour and friend. He had heard about the weddings, births and deaths. He had been appropriately shocked at how much his nieces and nephews had grown. But he found little else to do. The cinemas showed films he'd already seen. He'd have liked to go to a nightclub, but he couldn't imagine Zohra going with him or even letting him go. Most of the programmes on TV bored him, and unlike all their neighbours, Zohra refused to have a satellite dish. 'No need to bring filth into the house; there's enough of it on the street,' was how she put it. So he sat at home, on the divan, and waited for time to pass.

On the eve of his departure Aziz took his suitcase out of the armoire and began packing. Zohra sat on the bed, watching him. When he finished, he took out a stack of notes from the inside pocket of his suitcase. He put the money in her hand. 'This is all I have.'

Zohra didn't move. She kept looking at him.

'I'll save more,' he said, 'and then I'll come back.'

There was a sceptical look in Zohra's eyes and it made Aziz feel uncomfortable. What did she expect of him? He couldn't give up an opportunity to work just so he could be at home with her. Did she have any idea what he'd gone through to make it in Spain? He couldn't give it all up now. He *had* to go back.

The grandfather clock chimed the hour.

'When are you sending me the papers?' she asked, at last.

'I don't know,' he replied.

Zohra started crying. Aziz tapped her shoulder, in an awkward attempt at consolation. He couldn't imagine her with him in Madrid. She was used to the neighbours' kid pushing the door open and coming in. She was used to the outdoor market, where she could haggle over everything. She was used to having her relatives drop by without notice. He couldn't think of her alone in an apartment, with no one to talk to, while he was at work. And he, too, had his own habits now. He closed his suitcase and lifted it off the bed. It felt lighter than when he had arrived.

STREET OF THE HOUSE OF WONDERS

Rachida el-Charni

Translated from the Arabic by Piers Amodia

She saw him coming towards her, whistling and humming. He stopped in front of her to ask politely if she knew the way to Poppy Street. Not for a moment did she imagine that he would use the second she took to think to snatch her gold necklace and take to his heels.

He had come down the same side of the street that she had been walking on, absorbed in her thoughts. Nothing in his appearance suggested any need for doubt or caution; rather, his elegance aroused respect, peace of mind and even suggested he was well-off.

His hand struck her and she felt as if her breastbone had been shaken loose. For a moment she was paralysed, but quickly recovered from the shock and turned to him, screaming furiously, 'Stop, thief! My necklace, my necklace!'

Fuelled by rage, she started after him, all the while continuing her anguished cry. People came out from the shops, houses and workshops that lined the street. They stood there not moving, watching the scene in dismay.

She was quicker than he could have imagined and in just a few moments was able to catch up with him and hinder his way. Perhaps he had not calculated that a woman could chase a thief with such persistence.

He began to zigzag. The sun came out and blazed down on people's heads. The light cascaded over his sweating face, making the necklace wrapped round his crooked fingers glitter. It had a dangling gold plaque, with the Tower of Babel on one side and the Dome of the Rock on the other. Throughout her life she had repeatedly mislaid her jewellery without being sad for long, or even concerned about the value of what she had lost. This time. however, she felt as if her soul had suddenly been wrenched from her body.

Teeth clenched, she caught up with the thief and stretched out her hand towards him, her fingers almost managing to grab him. He turned to her, his body spiralling, but his right leg bent behind him, making him lose his balance and enabling her to grab the hem of his shirt. She seized hold of him, thwarting his movements as the shirt rode up across his dark back. He tried to escape her powerful grasp but was unable to do so.

People swarmed around them like bees, but no one made a move to help her. They stood there dazed as if they had lost their minds. She broke into another wave of anguished cries, as if imploring help: 'Thief! Let me have my necklace!'

Suddenly he drew a knife from a hidden pocket in his trousers and turned towards her, brandishing it in her face. She became aware of the scuffle of feet as people backed away. Voices raised around her, warning her what to do:

'Move back – he's armed!'

'Fool! He'll slash your face!'

'You're weaker. How do you dare?'

'Stubborn woman!'

Her face became more hard-set, as if some mighty devil dwelled in the depths of that young woman who always seemed so calm. She possessed great courage. Not for an instant did she experience real fear. Nor was she going to back down.

A youth from one of the workshops came to help her, but the men held him back, saying in a tone that revealed more violence than wisdom, 'Do you want to die? Leave her to it. She and no one else is responsible for her stubbornness.'

Their peevish voices, full of fear, insinuated their way into her heart and wounded her. Again, she became aware of them hopping around her like little birds. 'There's no point in resisting: the man has a deadly weapon!' said some, in their defeatism.

Their submissiveness only increased her stubbornness. A blind ferocity exploded inside her. She attempted to make her fingernails a force equal to the knife he was waving before her. She moved them deftly around, seeking an opening through which to get at his face, at the same time whispering determinedly under her breath, 'Had he all the weapons of the world, I would not give up my necklace!'

In that instant he turned towards her glaring, his lips drawn back with malice. She saw her tense face reflected in the pupils of his yellow eyes as he snarled through clenched white teeth, 'You stubborn little savage!'

He took her by surprise with a number of brutal punches aimed at her temples and face. She lost her balance and her body slid under his. The punches continued, causing her grip on his shirt to slacken, and finally he managed to free himself. The pig then kicked her in full view of all who stood there, terror gnawing at their faces, paralysed in their cowardice. He kicked her once more, violently, then ran off.

Immediately she gathered herself together and got up to continue the chase, her hair dishevelled, blood running from her nose and her clothes covered in dust.

With all her strength she ran, screaming, 'My necklace!' By then he had reached his companion, who was waiting on a motorbike at the street corner. He sprang on behind his mate and the bike took off, cutting its way through the crowds. At that moment she realized that everything had been planned in advance.

She fell to her knees, her strength and resolve slipping away. She began crying hot, stinging tears. A tremor of shame ran through her body, shame at being an inhabitant of that street: the submissiveness of her neighbours was a harder blow than the stranger's aggression. As her sadness reached its height, she remembered the girl who had been raped by a number of youths in a Cairo street with not a single passerby moving to help her. Their hearts were closed and they were content in following the scene as if watching some entertaining and exciting film.

Her imagination raced to times past when an attack against a she-camel had caused two Arab tribes to fight a fierce war lasting forty years. She felt the people's shame and heaved a heavy groan as something deep inside her became cold and hard. Just then, the call to noon prayer broke out in the air, the voice of the muezzin accompanying her inner grief and the purity of his voice pouring balm on her soul.

The people crowded round her, comforting her yet avoiding her gaze.

'We're sorry for what happened.'

'You shouldn't have put yourself in danger.'

'How could you seek your own destruction with such determination?'

'You warded off the danger; now live and hope for better things.'

'You should keep your possessions concealed, not put them on display.'

With her wounded pride she gazed at the people's faces and felt as if a wall stood silently between her and them. Then, as she raised herself up, still covered in the dust of battle, she heard a quiet, hateful voice say, 'Shame on you! You've made yourself a laughing stock. Wretched!'

She swung round, looking for the owner of the voice. She stared fixedly at their faces, then shouted, 'Gutless, spineless cowards! Since when has standing up for yourself ever been something to laugh about?'

The words were spoken harshly and painfully, the violence emerging from her mouth and holding a ferocious sway over everyone present.

She continued alone towards her parents' house at the end of the street, feeling as if her mind had been divested of weighty illusions. She tried to walk steadily under the sun, which, having banished the veil of clouds, had begun to blaze down, breathing its blind malice upon her.

BUMSTERS

E. C. Osondu

They were sitting under one of the raffia huts when Mallama let out a hiss. Pat had only become aware of the sound since arriving in the Gambia. The hiss was an all-purpose sound. It could signify anger, exasperation or, as she would later learn, in this instance, a sign of disgust.

'What do white women see in these bumsters? They are layabouts. Most of them have diseases, and quite a few of them are drug addicts.'

Pat looked up and noticed the reason for Mallama's anger. A much older white lady who at first glance could not have been less than at least sixty-five was walking hand in hand on the beach with a twentysomething Gambian boy. They were laughing. The lady seemed to be laughing very hard at something the boy had said. Pat took another look at the couple. They both seemed really happy and carefree. She turned to Mallama.

'Who are they?' she asked, nodding in the direction of the now departed couple, who were apparently headed towards one of the more exclusive beach huts.

'The boy is a *bumster*,' Mallama replied.

Two years later Pat returned to the Gambia. Her husband had died the year before. He had died of cancer and his illness had not been easy on either of them. She needed a break from it all. She had checked into a hotel, deciding to get in touch with Mallama at some point during her visit.

On the second day of her arrival the young man who had helped take her luggage to her room from the lobby knocked on her door. He was dressed in the red-and-black uniform of the hotel, with the garish hotel crest of a lion and a palm tree sewn onto the pocket. He smiled at her and introduced himself as Usman.

'Madam lost someone very close to her and is unhappy,' he said.

She could not tell if he was asking a question or making a statement. For some reason Pat always assumed that non-Westerners had a gift for divining. It was not something she had given much thought to; she merely assumed it. The same way one assumes the blind have an acute sense of hearing.

'Why do you say that, Usman?' she asked.

She found the name pleasant on her lips. She thought the uncomplicated nature of the name rather charming. Besides, the two syllables that made up the name were familiar – 'us' and 'man'.

'Usman can help Madam be happy again.' He smiled as he said this and bowed.

'Everyone wants to be happy, including you, Usman,' Pat said.

'I will arrange introductions. If Madam is happy, Usman would be happy,' Usman said as he smiled, bowed his head and left.

That evening Usman returned with a tall dark man who seemed to be in his thirties. Usman introduced him as 'my senior brother'. His name was Ahmed. The first thing that struck Pat about Ahmed was that he had the gracious look of a camel in repose. Usman left and returned with a tray of hot water, Lipton teabags, milk and sugar. He handed the tray to Ahmed. Ahmed sat at Pat's feet and began to brew her a cup of tea. He added a cube of sugar without asking her if she drank her tea with or without sugar. There was a certain serenity that he brought to the task. Pat had never had anybody brew her tea for her. She accepted the cup of tea thankfully. They had not exchanged many words. Ahmed made a cup for himself, took a sip and smiled.

'My small brother, Usman, say Madam travel from far and lose someone and is not happy. God bring Madam happiness soon. Usman here to help Madam be happy.' He smiled and took another sip from his teacup.

'Happiness – is that not all we want? I will be quite glad if you could show me the happiness tree and we can both sit underneath it.'

Ahmed smiled and said nothing for a while. He raised his pointy finger and said to her, 'God give happiness. Me, I fear God. You believe in God, madam?'

From her previous travels she knew that to answer in anything but the affirmative would be deemed highly offensive.

'Yes, I believe in a kind and happy God,' she said.

She went with Ahmed to the market, a large, open space with lots of colour. She would remember the Gambia as the most colourful place she had ever been to. The women had colourful cotton wrappers and head ties in dazzling green, pink, yellow and even red. They tied their babies to their backs with brightly coloured pieces of cloth. She thought the babies looked contented, even carefree as they slept against the warmth of their mothers' backs. She wondered why women in the West who didn't carry their babies in prams carried them in front, kangaroo style.

She did not particularly want to buy anything, but Ahmed steered her in the direction of some men who sold carvings. She thought the carvings grotesque and not very well done. The masks scared her, bringing to mind a movie she once saw, or probably a story she once read, in which a Western couple bought a carving from Africa that began to frighten them back home in America. She recalled that the object had brought the couple much misfortune, and when they were planning to throw it away, their house had caught fire and burned down, along with the carving. An anthropologist had somewhere in the movie or story commented that the carving must have been an

African god or goddess of some sort and belonged in a shrine.

She refused to buy anything. When Ahmed noticed her refusal, he turned to her and said, 'Maybe Madam will like to drink some *ataya* to clean her system and make blood pure.'

'What is *ataya*, Ahmed?'

'Come – we go try some *ataya*. You sure like it.'

He led her into a shed that offered coolness from the heat of the open market. On top of a large stove was a giant black pot emitting a somewhat strong but not unpleasant herbal aroma. Ahmed asked the proprietor for two cups of *ataya*. She watched as he poured first into a cup before then pouring the same aromatic liquid into a second cup and finally back into the original cup. She asked Ahmed why the man did that and Ahmed said it was to make the *ataya* cool enough to drink. She was soon handed a cup filled with the liquid. She took a cautious sip. It was not bad. It tasted good, as a matter of fact. Only it was too sugary. She drank and looked around her. She saw another patron, a young man. He was taking huge gulps of the *ataya*. The proprietor took a rumpled stick of cigarette out of his pocket and lit it, took a few puffs, pinched out the cigarette and put the quarter-smoked stick behind his ear. Pat thought the act cute and smiled to herself as she took a larger sip from her cup.

Turning to her, Ahmed said, 'You see this *ataya*, it is good for everything – fever, pain, bellyache – and it cleans the blood very well. You take *ataya* every day, before long you see changes all over your body. You become a young girl.' At this reference to her age, Pat wondered how Ahmed saw her. She had not given a thought to the age difference between Ahmed and herself. He seemed not to be that young. He had a maturity that created an impression of a wise old man. For some reason animal imagery always came to her mind when she thought of Ahmed. He reminded her of a camel, an animal she had only seen in books and on TV. It was probably the way he folded his legs under him when he sat down.

As they left the *ataya* stall, she felt spritely. The warm wind cooled her face. She felt lighter on her feet. A sense of freedom overcame her. All the faces she saw on the narrow street looked happy and satisfied. She almost wanted to hold Ahmed's hand but stopped herself. She had not seen anybody holding hands on the streets.

'You want to come back to the hotel with me?' she asked Ahmed.

'Oh, yes, if Madam want me to, I will be very happy to come,' Ahmed said.

'Let us go, then,' she said. She was feeling so good. Her intention was to walk to the hotel.

'Better to take taxi – too many people, too many eyes,' Ahmed said, and hailed a passing cab.

When they got to her room, she went to the bathroom and washed her face. Water had never felt that different. There was a certain separateness between the water and her face and then they became one. As she stepped out of the bathroom, Ahmed was holding a cup of iced water towards her.

'Cool your throat with this. Sometimes *ataya* make the throat very dry,' he said. She drank the water and a feeling of gratitude overwhelmed her. The thought that ran through her mind was, He knows exactly what I want. Nobody had ever known what I desire in this way. She gestured to Ahmed to hold her. He came towards her and held her. She could smell the aromatic herbal smell of the *ataya* on him as she led him to the bedroom.

Pat opened her door and saw Usman standing there. His face was sweating slightly and he looked gloomy.

'What can I do for you, Usman?' she asked, smiling.

'Sorry, madam, but there is small trouble.'

'Trouble? What kind of trouble?'

'Ahmed send me. There is trouble with Ahmed madam. She want to cause trouble with you and Ahmed.'

She found the talk of trouble and Ahmed's name a bit confusing. She took in a long breath and tried to be patient. She needed to get to the bottom of this and the best way was to start all over again very slowly.

'What happened to Ahmed?'

'Nothing happen to Ahmed. It is Ahmed's wife that says she wants to come and make trouble here in the hotel. She say someone saw you and Ahmed in the market walking together like husband and wife and told her. She lock the door against Ahmed and is threatening to come to this hotel and cause trouble for you. She is calling you a husband-snatcher. Ahmed say to tell you to send him money to give his wife so she stop threatening to cause trouble and not embarrass you in the hotel.'

Now she understood. So Ahmed was married and there was a poor little Mrs Ahmed.

'So what does Ahmed want me to do?'

'Ahmed is requesting two hundred dollars to give the wife so she no cause trouble. She will use the money to start a little business. Have her own stall in the market. She want to be senior wife. No problem after that.'

She went to the bureau de change in the lobby of the hotel and changed some of her traveller's cheques and handed the money to Usman. He thanked her profusely and bowed twice to her as he pocketed the money. She didn't smile. Usman wanted to say something but looked at her and kept quiet and walked away.

For the first time since she came to the Gambia, she walked to the hotel bar and ordered a stiff bourbon.

Pat had often thought about seeing her dead husband just one more time. She had toyed with the idea of consulting a medium. She recalled walking into a booth at the state fair one summer to consult a palmreader. One look at the reader and she realized she had made a mistake. The woman had the odour of stale cigarette smoke clinging to her, and her hands were sweaty. The only thing she told Pat as Pat let her put her cringing hands in hers was that Pat was unhappy. Of course she knew she was unhappy. She did not need a palmreader to tell her that. When she asked the woman if she could talk to her late husband, the woman had laughed out loud and asked, 'You mean like Whoopi in *Ghost*? Nah, only the dead can speak with the dead.'

That night in her room at the hotel, Pat dreamed about her late husband. Their conversation was almost commonplace. He asked her about her hips. Were they still giving her pain? Was the pain medication working? Had she been able to consult the doctor in Florida about non-invasive laser surgery?

She in turn asked him about his karate. He looked as fit as ever. He did not responded but changed the topic. They talked about the cat, Old Country. The cat had wandered in one day and stayed. He looked quite old and they had given him the name Old Country, a joke they shared about America not being a country for old men and women. They talked and talked; then her husband said he had to leave now. He walked away. When Pat opened her eyes, the sun was shining in through the window. Day had broken.

Ahmed came in later that day with a large Thermos filled with *ataya*. Before she could ask him any questions, he filled a cup for her and she drank it gratefully. After taking the drink, she found herself suddenly becoming talkative.

'But you never told me you had a wife, Ahmed. Were you being sneaky?'

'But you know I am not a small boy,' Ahmed replied.

'I know, but don't you think I deserve to know? She would have embarrassed me before other guests here. That wouldn't have been nice.'

'I would not have let her cause you embarrassment. She only make threats.'

'Usman told me she was going to make trouble for me.'

'She is a God-fearing woman. No cause trouble at all. Only make threaten because she need help. I tell her you are a kind woman and you fit to help us, that's all.'

He offered her another drink of *ataya*. She took it. As if reading her mind, he went to the handwash sink and got her a cold glass of water. She drank it. She felt a huge urge to laugh and did so out loud.

'Ahmed tell you that I will help you be happy. See now you are happy. See how you are laughing like a child playing in the rain.'

She found his comment even funnier and laughed aloud once more. Taking his large hands in hers, she led him to the bedroom.

'Ahmed in big, big, trouble,' Usman said, stretching out both palms in the air to indicate the size of the trouble.

'You do love to bring bad news, my dear Usman, don't you? Now tell me, what is this big, big trouble?' Pat asked.

'He was arrested by soldiers when he was leaving the hotel last night. He is not supposed to move around by that time of the night. Soldiers patrol around at night to protect and give security. Too many bad things happening nowadays. Government put soldiers to guard the streets. The soldiers take Ahmed and lock him up in guardroom. They beat him small but not too much. Ahmed manage to send message through kind army corporal.'

'Where is he being held? I want to go there and let them know he was with me. I can speak to whoever is in charge.'

Pat recalled that she had noticed during her last visit that people deferred to her here because of the colour of her skin.

'No, no, you cause more trouble for him if you go there. Moving with foreign woman make his case worse. Give Usman money, Usman go bail him out one time. He come back to Madam, no problem. He make Madam happy once again.'

'And where am I supposed to pluck this money from? From the money tree here in my room?'

'Money tree?'

'Look here, Usman, I am not rich, but that is beside the point. I want to see who is holding your brother. I can testify that he was with me last night. My word should count for something, even here in your country.'

'Ahmed in big, big trouble. Nobody to help him unless you kind, madam. He said go to her, tell her Ahmed in big, big trouble – Madam is kind woman: she help me get out of trouble.'

'You know what, Usman? You'll need to give me some time to think about this. By the way, how much are they asking for?'

'Five hundred dollars, because this is big, big trouble,' Usman said.

'I see,' was all Pat could say.

'The more he stay in detention, the bigger the trouble become. You help him, madam. Only you can help him now, because he has nobody.'

'I will think about this, OK?'

Something about Usman's manner made Pat think that there was something not quite straight about his story. Why else would he not want her to intercede in some way? She hoped they did not see her as some kind of money tree that was ripe for a shake-down.

Pat recalled that Mallama's husband, whom she and her late husband had nicknamed 'the Colonel', was a soldier, though he was originally trained as a dentist. She picked up the phone and called Mallama.

They were sitting on the beach. It was the day before Pat's departure. Mallama had suggested they go to the beach before she left. After her call that day Mallama had driven down to the hotel and taken her to their house. She had also called her husband, the Colonel, who had in turn got Usman and Ahmed arrested. He had also helped her get a refund from the hotel.

'The beach is almost empty. Where are the bumsters and their clients?' she asked Mallama.

'They have been swept off the beaches. The government launched a campaign called "Operation Keep Our Beaches Clean", which got rid of them.'

'And their patrons, have they been swept off as well?'

'We hear the economy is bad over there right now,' Mallama said, laughing. 'Seriously, though, a few still come, but they stay in the hotels and the hotel boys called "connectors" link them up. Usman must have mistaken you for one of those women and brought in his friend.'

'I'd love to drink *ataya* one more time before I leave,' Pat said.

'*Ataya*? How do you know *ataya*? We drink Tetley, PG Tips and Lipton tea. *Ataya* is for *bush people*.'

'But I loved it when Ahmed took me to an *ataya* shop in the market. He later brought some in a Thermos flask to the hotel. I found it a rather refreshing kind of tea.'

Mallama glanced at her with mouth wide open.

'No, you did not. Don't tell me you did. You did not.'

'I did and I loved it, I must confess,' Pat said.

'You know what these criminals do? They connive with the *ataya* sellers to add marijuana to the tea when they take foreign women to the stalls. So what happened after you drank it in the stall?' Mallama asked.

'I went back to the hotel and took a nap,' Pat said.

Mallama exhaled slowly. 'And that time you said he brought some for you in a Thermos flask?'

'Oh, I took the Thermos from him and thanked him. I had the drink later and went to sleep.'

'Thank goodness. You were lucky.'

'Oh, yes, I was indeed very lucky. My late husband used to call me Lucky Girl,' Pat said, smiling as they both rose to leave. Now she had a story to tell her husband when next he came to her in a dream. In all their travels to different parts of the world he had always complained that they had never been on any real adventure. She had a real adventure story for him.

PASSION

Doreen Baingana

You know how we're taught to throw superstition aside and move forward into the modern world? Or maybe you don't, but for us here at Gayaza it's a recurrent theme. Gayaza High School, Kampala, Uganda, for your information. The world's centre of boredom. We are forced to find ways to entertain ourselves; it's no wonder a rather fantastic juju experiment conjured its way into my head and took over. I was irritated by all the propaganda against 'black magic', and the way it was persistently pounded into our supposedly still-soft heads. I mean, why insist so strongly against juju if it doesn't exist? If it really has no power? I know, I know, Livingstone or someone said something declaratory against disease, superstition and backwardness in Africa. I've heard it once too often.

Anyway, I decided, after listening to yet another Sunday sermon on the topic (yes, we get lectured on it both in class and in church), that I simply would not accept this. As if I had a choice. Let's just say I did have a choice. I would, at least, first find out for myself whether juju worked or not. Logical, no? So this is my story about an exploration into our darkest heritage. The womb of knowledge, perhaps! Are you ready?

I should start with whom, what and where. Right. OK, my name is Rosa. I am seventeen years old and in senior five – that's HSC, or A

levels – at Gayaza, a girls' boarding school that used to be a missionary
school way back in the colonial days. You'd think it's still one now,
what with all the savedees – i.e. born-again Christians – running
around, and the old white British women who won't relinquish power
because they can no longer go back home after more than forty years
here. What would they do there, poor women? One winter would kill
them, and they wouldn't have anyone to lord over except carers in
nursing homes. You should see the *bazungu* here, so know-it-all and
steely-gracious before wide-eyed, frightened and secretly glowering
with anger 'natives', namely us. Really, this is *not* meant to be a tirade
against the hardy old ladies, who faced army men with guns for our
sakes during the Amin days and each coup thereafter, and are still
alive to tell the harrowing stories. Their juju must be stronger, ha, ha.

A little bit of gossip may be necessary at this point. Miss Straw, the
headmistress, is said to have lost her betrothed in the Second World
War, when she was just eighteen. This explains her vacant blue stare: it
is the faraway, dreamlike look of lost romance, her eyes as blue as the
vast ocean her young soldier drowned in. No one knows who started
this rumour; it's so old it has become true. In a minute, though, she
can turn those eyes on you with chilly hostility and hiss like a plump
white snake, 'This just will not do!' No lover would have dared woo
her then, let alone a trembling student appealing for mercy.

OK, on with the story. I just wanted to show you what we are dealing
with here. So, in higher, as it's called, we have this extra duty, and as
privileged young women in Uganda, a Third World country, don't
forget, because we are getting this excellent, government-subsidized
(white) education – we must represent all the impoverished throngs
who are not as lucky as we are, especially the women. We must be
graceful, hardworking and upright, disciplined enough to withstand
the hordes of lusty men at university, in offices or on the street who
will try to spoil us, unless of course they want to marry us. Then,
as educated, faithful wives, we will work alongside our Christian
husbands to bring progress to our modern homes (bedsheets folded

to make perfect hospital corners) and our country in a profession, and hopefully in public service. I won't forget Miss Straw at our first assembly in higher saying, 'You must not disgrace Gayaza, this great school that very few have the privilege of joining. The *privilege*,' she repeated sternly, as if saying 'punishment', as she slowly swept her glassy blue eyes over our sea of black heads. Like she was the Queen or something!

So now our uniform is a skirt and blouse – not those O-level dresses that billow out like parachutes unless held down by belts, cotton belts that had to be starched hard every week simply as a form of torture. And their colours! The brightest, most frightful blue, green, purple and yellow. You would not believe the Kiganda 'traditional' dress was designed at Gayaza; that's why it's called a *'bodingi'* for boarding school, or *'gomesi'* after an enterprising Goan tailor named Gomez. So much for tradition. But where was I? Oh, yes, we highers are now considered adults; we have to show the younger girls how to lead Uganda into its hopefully glorious future. We do this by walking with *digi* – i.e. dignity – slowly swaying from side to side, now that we have breasts and hips to carry, as well as huge black files full of notepaper that show we are clearly above and beyond the exercise books the senior ones to fours still use.

Another of Miss Straw's feature lectures is that the 'A' in 'A levels' does not stand for 'apathy'. That's her attempt at a joke. She even once slouched across the front of the assembly, showing us how our slow sway was a sign of lack of purpose in life. How we laughed that day. 'Shoulders back! Behind and stomach in! Walk like you mean it!' Someone should have told her to stick *her* non-existent butt out.

Enough of that. Here comes the juicy part. Have you heard the myth about safety pins and men? I didn't think so. Let's see, who first told me about it? It must have been Nassuna. We've shared dormitories since senior one up to now, so we've been through everything together. She's Muslim, but doesn't use her Muslim name, Halima; she prefers her Kiganda name. There we were, back in senior three, I believe, in Kennedy House, donated by the 'People of the United States of America', as was written on a little plaque stuck to one of the walls of the laundry room.

It was after lights out, which is the best time to gossip. Sometimes the teacher on night duty came round with a torch and gently opened the door to try and catch us talking or giggling in bed. In the dark you couldn't see who it was; all you saw was a glimmer of torch light, unless it was one of the *zungus*, Miss Hornbake or Miss Simpson. (Miss Straw wouldn't lower herself to stalking.) In that case you saw a ghostly-pale face, wrinkles and white hair gleaming, and that would shut you up with fright pretty fast. Whoever it was threatened us with entry into the Red Book, which usually meant standing under the Punishment Tree right in front of the staffroom. It sounds like a joke, but imagine the cutting words of all the teachers coming in and out of the staffroom, while you stood there exposed, looking foolish. As if you had asked their opinion. Of course, you were not allowed to sit down; it was a punishment, not an afternoon off. As the sun blazed away (it always did), two or three classes passed by on their way to the labs or the sports fields for PE. That meant about sixty girls gawked and giggled at you as they ambled past, as if they had never seen someone stand under a tree before. Ask me if I had been there. I preferred the afternoons at the farm digging or clearing up pig poo, however much more I sweated.

All this to explain that it was important not to get caught as we learned about *real life* from our roommates. In the dark, in bed, we stuffed our mouths with sheet and blanket to hide our laughter or gasps of fright, but as soon as the teacher left, we continued on in excited whispers. As voices and giggles streamed through the dark, you listened to stories about ghosts and powerful juju, and learned what's what about sex, imagining all the gory details. How men were strange, illogical in their cravings, so this is what you had to do to get them: never answer back, and have no less than three boyfriends – one for love, another for money and the third to marry. But what was best, looks, money or brains? These debates raged on night after night; they never lost their flavour.

'How many abortions did you say Miss Konkome had before she got saved? . . . Noooo!'

'It's true, I swear.'

'Konny, the one who acts like she's been in deep prayer since the day she was born? Ah-haaa! People get saved out of *despa'* – desperation – 'nothing else!'

My good friend Nassuna always had something to say. She's the one who brought up the story of men and safety pins, claiming that they made men 'react'.

We all went, 'What? How? What do you mean, react?'

'Well, you know, get excited.'

'Excited?'

'*Banange*, do you want me to . . . ? OK, they expand, swell . . . you know.'

We shrieked, then, remembering it was lights out, whispered, 'Ee-eeh, Nassuna, *naawe*! Stop lying. Safety pins?'

'Yes, I swear to God.' She licked her pointing finger, slashed it across her throat, then pointed up to heaven. God slice her dead if she was lying! 'This girl, Namata, remember her? She finished senior four last year. We both did housework in the classrooms together; that's when she told me. She said men have this problem of wanting women too much, and they can't control it, so we have this power over them.'

'What power?'

'Well, it's easy, actually,' she whispered confidently, as if she had done it. 'You secretly, *secretly*, mind you, rub a safety pin while looking *directly* at the man you like and you'll get him excited. Just like that. Then he will do anything for you.'

'*Choka*, Nassuna! Men aren't that weak or stupid!'

'I'm telling you.'

Another girl said, 'OK, they do what you want, but they also want something, am I wrong?'

We all squealed and shouted, 'Whaaaat? Something?'

'But of course!'

We laughed in shock and exhilaration. Oh my God, sex! That un-mentionable, dirty, shameful and most fascinating thing. Something men wanted from us that we could give out, or not, at will. Something to bargain with. Imagine that. Slowly, eventually, we calmed down. It was late, almost eleven. We had to get up at six-thirty for housework or PE before breakfast and class. Most of the girls may have forgotten this juicy bit of talk, but I hadn't. I stored it away, even as I thought, What rubbish!

Well, three years later, the idea popped into my head during English literature class one day. Guess who was teaching? The one and only Mr Mukwaya, the Walking Wodo. He is the hero of this tale, actually. The other hero, I mean. For those of you lucky enough not to have come to Gayaza, 'wodo' is short for 'wardrobe', which is what Mr Mukwaya looks like. He is tall, straight, stiff and thick.

Our teachers are picked out at circuses or museums, I swear. I could describe them all and you'd think I'm adding supu, or soup – i.e. exaggerating – but really, they are God's experiments at unique human shapes. God says, 'I am bored. Let me make a ball of a woman,' and Miss Okello appears, as short as she is wide, fat and dark, dark black, shiny black, a black so deep you dream of disappearing into it. You can't, though; she never keeps still long enough. She runs everywhere. If you see her far off down the path, you may think a huge wheel has escaped off a car and is careening off on its own wild way. Despite all her weight, she is so fast. 'Okello, duka! Okello, run,' girls call out and duck as she swivels round to chase after the mischief-maker, shooting pieces of chalk like bullets. As she runs, she throws sharp words at anyone in her path. All this, surprisingly, makes her a thrilling history teacher. Once you get used to the rapid tat-tat-tat as she spills out words, sentences, ideas, you enjoy how she spins tales out of the past while moving roly-poly round the room. Your eyes and mind blink and move just as rapidly to keep up with her. It's exhilarating. Exhausting, too, by the end.

Oh, sorry, sidetracked again. That's just one example, though. Another that's more to the point is the Walking Wodo. He teaches literature, which I love. Well, some of the books. No teacher can spoil novels for me; I soak them up like blotting paper. I wish I could say the same about plays and poetry. Don't make me read poems so clever and chock-full of words they mean nothing. I can make up something to say in class, though. Literature papers? Easy. Just write something about character and theme, whatever the teacher wants to hear. I seem to be good at making things up. Mr Mukwaya shares my delight in stories, but he is more extreme. He completely forgets about us, forgets *himself*. You should see him; he enters a trance. He gazes out of the window as if inspired by heaven itself, or turns to the blackboard, his back to us, and traces over what he has already written, looking like a huge insect trying to crawl up the board.

It's not Wodo's fault, though, that we're assigned books that bore most of us to tears. For example, we have to do one Shakespeare play for the A-level national exams in English literature. Ours is *King Lear*. But who wants to read the travails of a stupid old man who gives everything away? Serves him right, I say. And why in this ancient, unclear, so-called English? You wouldn't believe it, but the language sends Wodo into raptures, especially when Lear is running around naked in the rain abusing his daughters! '*Blow, wind, crack your cheeks! . . . Rumble thy belly full, spit fire, spout rain . . .*' Wodo quotes whole passages and then starts arguing, first with us, then with himself, getting more agitated by the minute. 'Could King Lear have acted any other way?' Wodo asks. 'Was Lear more "sinned against than sinning"?' We turn to each other, roll our eyes and sigh heavily.

That was the scenario the day the safety-pin idea came back to me. I was wondering whether anything at all could distract Wodo from his *King Lear* fantasy and bring him back to this world, right here to us. I wondered if he had a personal life apart from books. Was this a way to find out? And remember, I wanted my own proof for or against the power of juju. I giggled to myself at the thought of the experiment. It was ridiculous, so much so that it refused to leave my mind. I spent the rest of that class plotting ways and means.

Later that evening Nassuna, Harriet and I met for our study group. This is another good thing with higher: we don't have to go up to class for prep time any more; we can stay in the dorms and fool around or study, as we wish. We are supposedly mature enough to use our time properly. The pressure of preparing for national exams to enter the only university in the country is supposed to force us to be serious. It works for most of us. I confess I'm lazy, so I rely on study groups, where I can milk others while also enjoying the *kabozi*, good sweet talk, which is my specialty.

That evening I made *bushera* for the three of us. One of the advantages of coming from western Uganda is that we have a lot of millet, which we eat or make into a porridge called *bushera*, or *bush*, as we Gayaza girls call it. It is so filling, which always helps at school, what with starvé and all. All you do is add boiling water, but you've got to stir the mixture frantically or it will 'die'. Thank goodness in A levels starvé didn't hit us so badly because we were allowed to go home one weekend a month and bring back more supplies of sugar, groundnuts, *mberenge* and any other grub that wouldn't go bad. The suffering of O level was in the past, for the most part. I know, I keep getting sidetracked, but I'm trying to give you the whole picture, OK?

Anyway, there we were talking, our books neglected on our laps. We had heard that Maria, one of our classmates, had gone to Makerere University to see some guy instead of going home for her day off. To make things worse, she had stayed the night! The only way you could do that was if your parents, and *only* your parents, asked for permission in advance, *in writing*, or had really good reasons, like a death or something. And your parents, not anybody else, had to bring you back to school. It was serious.

Harriet asked, 'How could Maria do something so stupid? Now she'll get expelled.'

Nassuna answered in her usual, know-it-all way, '*Munange*, it's love. It makes you do crazy things. Her campus boy must have convinced her.'

Harriet, ever the strong-willed iron woman, scoffed, '*I* wouldn't do it just because some *campus boy* asked me to. Destroying my future just like that. I mean, what is she going to do now?'

'Finish her A levels somewhere else, Kampala SSS or someplace like that.'

'And fail.'

'Eee-hh, Harriet, are you saying all those in the city day schools fail? In fact, they probably have an advantage since their teachers cheat and get them the exams early.'

We laughed. 'Nassuna, stop lying,' I said. 'No, I think the real problem is we girls are weak. Anything a man says, we obey.'

'Aaa-ahh, not me!'

'Not you, of course, Harriet. You have never done anything you don't want to do, right?'

'Not with a boy: she hasn't had the chance.'

We laughed as Harriet made a mock-angry face and turned away.

I went on, 'Listen, women have power over men too. Remember, Nassuna, what you told us – was it in senior two or three? – about a trick some girl told you that makes men weak.'

'What?'

'Don't you remember? The safety-pin thing?'

'*Choka*, Rosa! Did you really believe that? And you stored that all these years?'

'Her head is empty. There's space for such!'

I waved down their laughter. 'No, seriously, think about it. We have physical power over men 'cos of sex, even though they are supposed to be stronger than us physically.'

'Ya, sure, if you believe in witchcraft!' More laughter.

'You laugh now, but wait till I try it.'

'What?' Nassuna and Harriet together.

'You heard. I'm going to test to see if it works or not. We're here at school to *study* and *observe* and draw conclusions, right?'

'And there'll be an exam afterwards, I suppose?' That was Harriet, Miss Comedian, or so she thinks.

'By the way, who will you test, here in this female-only zoo?'

'I know, I know men are as scarce as . . . as meat. No, worse, as snow! Really, they should hire at least a few more male teachers. Just for us to look at, at least.'

'You can count the men here on one hand, and even these few don't really count. Let's see – there's Mr Karugonjo, who is about what, fifty?'

'With grey steel wool for hair and a shuffle of an eighty-year-old. Thank God he is taken!'

'What about Mr Dawan?' We burst out laughing again.

'*Choka*, Nassuna, you're not serious. The poor Indian? Have you seen the way he walks? I mean, who cut off his bum?'

Harriet stood up to demonstrate, pushing her bum in and her hips forward and sliding across the floor. We almost died of laughter. Girls did that to poor Dawan as they walked behind him from class. They exaggerated his walk and then fell into giggling fits, hands over mouths, fingers pointing. *Bambi*, I pitied him, even though I laughed too. What was he doing here all alone? How come he didn't leave when Idi Amin kicked out all the Indians years ago? He must have been quite young in 1972, no more than a teenager. Was he a citizen or what? For us girls, he was just a laughing stock.

'Rosa, he would be great for your experiment: you could find out if African witchcraft works on Indians.'

Harriet followed, 'Next, you could try it on Miss Straw. A white *and* a woman.' We howled and rocked back and forth as if in pain.

'You people, please! Stop being silly. I'm serious. I don't think Dawan is a suitable candidate for my experiment on the honoured traditions of our ancestors that you have been taught to call "witchcraft", OK? Now control yourselves. Who's left?'

'How about the men on the farm and in the dining room?' Harriet suggested with a faint sneer.

'What if the experiment works? What would I do with one of them?'

'Oh, and what exactly are you planning to do with any other "suitable" man, may I ask?'

'At least it should be someone I can *talk* to.'

'Why are we wasting time?' Nassuna butted in. 'We know who you want: Mr Mukwaya, Wodo himself. You want us to say it for you, don't you?'

'What! Noooo, of course not. But yes, he's the only one left.'

'And your first choice, admit it.'

'The only logical choice. Haven't you seen how he is in class, completely taken by *King Lear* or *Devil on a Cross* or whatever we're reading? It's impossible to tear him away from his first love, literature.'

'Oh, I see, you're jealous of books!'

I ignored Nassuna. 'If the spell can distract someone like him, then it can work on anybody, don't you see? We would get husbands just like that.' I snapped my fingers.

Harriet was now utterly disgusted. 'Husbands! You've never even had a boyfriend and you're talking about husbands!'

Not Nassuna – the word 'husband' made her salivate. 'Hmm. But the power to excite a man is not the same as getting him to marry you.'

'This would be the first step. *Then* you simply refuse to give him what he wants, see? You make him suffer and plead until he is almost crazy and has nothing else to do but propose.' Wasn't I brilliant?

'This is the most stupid and . . . *pathetic* idea I have ever heard. Are we going to finish with the Songhai Empire tonight or not? We've wasted enough time.' Harriet was no longer amused. Her strict and sensible side was never far away and she always chose the best moment to ruin our fun.

Nassuna and I groaned. 'Songhai? It's too late to get back to books. Let's continue tomorrow, please?'

Harriet gathered up her books. 'You two just aren't serious,' and huffed out of the room, as if she hadn't been laughing with us just moments before. I swear she'll end up like one of these rock-hard spinster teachers here if we don't keep working on her.

I didn't wait; the very next day I was ready with my plan. Our heavy green A-level skirts have two big front pockets. I found a medium-sized safety pin that was actually keeping up the hem of another of my skirts and slipped it into my pocket. Our last class that Wednesday afternoon was literature. Afternoon is when time moves the slowest because the heat makes us sleepy, especially if we've had something starchy for lunch like cassava. Our classroom is nice, though, with large open windows on both sides that cool breezes sweep right through. The welcome distraction of bumblebees, flies, millipedes and such, which we make a big fuss about, pretending to be frightened, helps use up chunks of class time. Also, there are tall jacaranda trees with overhanging branches on either side of the building, so it's mostly in the shade. When in bloom, the trees throw perfumy mauve flowers into the class. I sit near the windows because it's almost like sitting outside right under the trees. A window creates space for the mind to wander; you can stare at the sky, the furthest thing ever, and think of nothing, especially during economics.

That day, if everything went as planned, I would save us all from *King Lear*. If the trick worked, that is. The spell, I mean. In class, before I sat down, I put my hand deep into my pocket and curled my palm over the safety pin. My pocket was beneath the desk; I could move my fingers without anyone noticing. As we waited for Mr Mukwaya, I wondered what I should think about as I concentrated on him. His nose or eyes? Love songs? When he walked in, my heart gave a little thump. Would I be able to go through with this? I had not told Nassuna or Harriet because I knew they would fidget and giggle and spoil the experiment. I didn't want to get caught, of course, but also, everything had to be as normal as possible so I could be sure that any change in Wodo was caused by the spell, nothing else. (I should have studied the sciences, chemistry perhaps, don't you think?)

My hand warmed up the thin piece of metal and then it got wet; my palms were sweating. I hoped Mukwaya wouldn't notice any difference in me. The best thing would be to start the spell study, or whatever it was, when he was deeply immersed in the play. We were at the point in *King Lear* when his two older daughters are spiralling deeper into evil. Act 3, Scene 7. We called Goneril 'Gonorrhoea', and Regan 'Reggae'. God, what evil women! Mukwaya says the best way to feel the poetry of Shakespeare's language is to read it out loud, so he picked three girls to take on different parts. They cleared their throats and began. Some of us followed, reading our copies, while others merely looked down, lost in their thoughts. This scene actually is interesting, horribly so. Goneril stamps her foot into one of Gloucester's eyes and Regan does the same to his other eye. As if this is not enough, one sister stabs a servant who tries to help Gloucester. Can you imagine? Some of us giggled; it was too much. After stumbling over mispronunciations, thees, thys and therefores, it was discussion time. I was ready.

Mukwaya asked, 'So, why were some of you laughing?' There were more low giggles, shifting in seats, then silence. Now, since everyone was looking up at Wodo, I too could stare directly at him. I realized it wouldn't be enough to concentrate on his wide, shiny nose, which took up most of his square face. I had to look directly into his eyes. Mukwaya pressed on, 'Come on, you can tell me what you think. With art, true art, there are many ways one can respond.' He kept going on about 'art, true art, real art!' No one was impressed. Well, maybe I was, sort of. The others exchanged bored looks and turned down their mouths. To help Wodo out, I started to put up my right arm, hesitated, then put up my left. I hoped no one noticed.

'Well, Rosa?'

'It's sort of funny. I mean, how can these two princesses act like this? It's . . . it's, well, not primitive, but . . . no, in fact *it is* primitive, and hard to believe.'

Harriet added, 'Imagine. They are in a castle, dressed up in fine clothes and all. Couldn't they take Gloucester to court or something—'

Another girl, Dorcas, interrupted, 'Or at least get their *servants* to hang him, shoot him, whatever.' We all laughed out loud. Wodo waved us down.

'Well, then, we have to ask ourselves why Shakespeare created such a bloody, graphic scene. Don't you think he knew what he was doing?'

After a pause a few hands went up. 'Yes, but—'

'Even Shakespeare can write badly.'

'Maybe he loved violence. Some people are like that.'

'People in power, mostly.' That was Nassuna. The others murmured agreement.

I rubbed the moist safety pin, softly at first, then harder. I looked into Wodo's eyes. No change. I kept on rubbing, but the mistake I made was not joining in the discussion. I am vocal by nature; those who know me know I cannot keep quiet, especially not in literature class. But I was concentrating deeply, repeating to myself, The eyes, the eyes only. I hadn't realized how often one blinked. But something was distracting me. I felt eyes on me on my left side. It was Nassuna. She sat next to me and had turned to me after her comment. She must have noticed that I hadn't reacted at all – no nod, no laughter. I refused to return her curious look. If I gave her even just a quick glance, she would read me and guess something was up. She knew me too well. Focus, Rosa, focus.

Wodo was now answering Dorcas. It was hard to keep staring into his eyes because he kept shifting his face. When he turned my way mid-sentence, I felt sweat break out. It tickled my armpits. I was dying to scratch, but it would be awkward with my left hand. I did anyway, quickly. Focus, Rosa. On what? I didn't know his face was so pimply. I wished I had a chant or something.

Nassuna nudged me. I ignored her. She nudged harder. I wanted to strangle her. There was no way I could continue. I turned and gave her the most irritated look I could. She frowned in question. Annoyed but resigned, I slipped my hand out of my pocket and showed her the safety pin in my open palm, below my desk. Nassuna breathed in sharply and widened her eyes. She gave me a shocked look, glanced up at Wodo, then back at me. Her face broke into a wide cheeky grin as I slipped the pin back into my pocket. Thankfully, she had the sense to hide her giggles in her copy of *King Lear*.

I mouthed, 'Leave me alone,' and turned back to Wodo. He was looking at me. Had he seen us? I wasn't going to give up so soon, but I knew I should say something about the play before he became too suspicious. 'A play is not real life; it's drama. It has to be dramatic.' OK, I admit, this wasn't my best idea ever.

Nassuna came to the rescue. 'I agree. The scene is exaggerated to create a strong reaction in the audience. Then they can feel pity for Gloucester even though he has acted like a fool. The same with Lear.'

Some girls protested, 'Eeeeeh, no!'

Wodo raised both hands, palms open, to shut us up. 'Please. One by one.'

Dorcas again. 'There are other, more believable ways to create pity. This action here is too extreme, too cruel for words!'

Wodo wrote 'catharsis' on the board and went on to define it. I knew he would go on for some minutes; it was time to try again. This time I would do it, I must. He talked; I stared. He talked; I stared even harder. My eyes seemed to glaze over. His face expanded, and his eyes became glowing black orbs. Still I rubbed the pin furiously. There was a soft giggle beside me. Nassuna again! God, why couldn't she control herself? Forget her. I decided to imagine Wodo . . . kissing, yes. Not me, of course, no way. Kissing Miss Bakunda. She had finished senior six last year and was back here teaching senior one until her university classes started in September. I could see her having an affair with Wodo. Like I said, there was no one else here.

OK, so Wodo and Bakunda were kissing. The more I concentrated, the wetter my armpits got. Sweat now trickled down. My blouse was damp. The staring, Wodo's deep drone of words, my own nervous heat, *something* was making me feel woozy, but I didn't dare shake my head to clear it. I felt the girls around me fidgeting. What was going on? Concentrate, ignore them, *concentrate*, I repeated desperately. Had Nassuna let the other girls know? Oh God, no! Focus, focus. I couldn't stop now. With my free hand I wiped drops of sweat from my forehead. I could see Wodo and Bakunda, mouth to mouth. He had her in his arms . . . He bent her over. Oh, what was he doing! I squealed.

Wodo stopped talking and looked at us, his eyes moving from face to face. I was transfixed. I couldn't stop staring at him, *at them*, mesmerized. The girls' shuffling and giggles ended in startled silence.

Wodo said, 'Do you find my explanation of cathartic action in *King Lear* funny?' and he scratched himself *right there*! A quick move, but one I had never seen him do before. OK, I had never watched him this keenly before either, but still. Strangely enough, I too wanted to scratch myself. Sweat was leaking out of me and yet the classroom wasn't that hot.

Nassuna, who I am going to kill one of these days, put up her hand. 'I have a question.'

'Go ahead.'

'Do you think Shakespeare had something against the female *sex*?' She stressed the word, knowing the effect it would have on everyone. 'You see, *sex*— Sorry, the female *sex* in this play acts like men, bad men.'

'You've moved on to another point, Nassuna, but let's talk about that. What about Cordelia?'

Wodo could usually handle tricky words like 'sex' in a classroom full of giggling girls; he was an expert at smoothing over uncomfortable moments. But this time, I swear, he was *physically* uncomfortable. He leaned his hips back against his desk and faced us with what was clearly a false air of ease. I was still rubbing my now hot secret, my eyes glued to his. Abruptly, Wodo stood up again, smoothed down *the front* of his trousers, then half sat back on the edge of the desk. Did I dare continue? Push him further? I confess I could not stop. My mind and body were an out-of-control machine manufacturing fantasies. I don't know how I managed to say, in a high, breaking voice, 'Cordelia really isn't a woman—'

Someone added, 'Yes, she is more of a child. Very innocent.'

Nassuna jumped in, 'You mean, she is not of the female *sex*?' Everyone gasped, fighting back hysterical laughter.

Wodo stood up again and shifted himself you know where! He contemplated his shoes for a second and then looked up directly at me. 'And you, Rosa, are you a child or a woman?'

Stunned silence. A bird outside yelped three notes repeatedly. Loudly. Wodo had never asked such a direct personal question before. He stared hard at me. I couldn't turn my eyes away. 'M-me?'

'Well, Cordelia might have been about your age, Rosa – seventeen, sixteen, maybe even younger.'

'I-I don't know.'

We waged a battle of the eyes, of stares, mine shocked. Had I been found out? His were questioning, insistent, mocking. A come-on? No! He wouldn't. But he kissed . . . No, he didn't. What was wrong with me? Suddenly he turned away, walked round the desk and said, 'One shouldn't say or do things one doesn't know about.' His tone was both kind and menacing, but I knew exactly what he meant. The trance broke.

Tears crept out of my eyes and I bowed my head. The hand in my pocket went limp. I was drenched in sweat, which was now cold. It was difficult to breathe. What had just happened? I needed to get out of there, out into the fresh air, take in gulps of it. Fading images of Wodo and Bakunda, their mouths still stuck together, swirled in my brain, then out, like dirty water disappearing down the drain. I pressed my eyes tightly shut.

The class seemed to let out a collective breath as it turned back to *King Lear*. Mukwaya chose three other girls to read the next scene aloud. Thank goodness, now I could hide my face in the book. I remained quiet until class was over; my mind wasn't working. Finally, much to my relief, the chapel bells rang out merrily and everyone sprang up to leave. It was over. As chairs scraped the floor and voices rose loud and free, Mr Mukwaya called out, 'Rosa, could I talk to you for a minute?'

Oh, no! I looked up at him, then back at my books. What would I say? Everyone else streamed out happily; class was over for the day.

Nassuna said to me, loud enough for Mukwaya to hear, 'I'll wait for you right outside, OK?' I nodded and walked warily up to Wodo.

He cleared up his notes slowly, thoughtfully, notes he hardly ever referred to anyway, until the last girl left. Then he leaned one hip casually on the desk, as casually as his stiff body could allow, and said, 'You know, Rosa, you are quite a good student.'

'Thank you, sir.' A 'sir' wouldn't hurt at this point.

'*Usually* a good student,' he amended. I kept silent. Praise was always a teacher's way to start criticism. But . . . He gazed out of the window thoughtfully for a few seconds, stroking his copy of *King Lear*. I felt my armpits tickle again. Goodness, what was happening to me? I must smell by now, I thought. Could he smell me?

'You know, literature requires passion. You have to get involved. You have to care.' He looked at me questioningly. 'And you do care. I've always thought you do. Your papers . . . yes, "passion" is the word.' He leaned his body earnestly towards me, then jerked it back in his stiff way, catching himself. He turned back to the window. Girls were streaming out of all the classrooms and down the cemented paths to the dorms to tea, to Ye Olde Shoppe for *kabs, mberenge*, bananas. They would spend the last daylight hours as they wished, before supper, prep time and then bed. I had been here four years already; the rhythm of the days was in my bones. I should have been outside with the others.

'Of course, you could end up a teacher like me.' What was Wodo talking about? He turned back to me suddenly. 'What was going on today?'

I took a step back and looked at my shoes. They were Bata boys' shoes, made in Jinja, the kind most of us wore. 'Today?'

'You know, the giggling, the shuffling and you acting . . . strange.'

'I-I don't know.'

'Rosa, I am not a fool.' I kept quiet, head still bowed. 'And neither are you.' He wagged a long finger at me. 'Don't become one.'

For one queasy moment I knew he knew everything. The safety pin burned in my pocket; could he see its shape? Had he or had he not felt it? Should I confess everything, just say—

'Passion, Rosa. Don't waste it.' He paused, then gestured at the laughing girls outside. 'You young women here, you are so protected from everything. Unlike Cordelia.' He smiled. 'But not for ever. You will be forced to grow.' He shrugged.

I was confused. Where was he heading? I looked out of the window, wondering if Nassuna could hear us. He wasn't mad at me; that I could tell. In fact he seemed to be taking me seriously, as a person, not just another student. 'Mr Mukwaya, I did not mean to do anything wrong.'

'No one means to make any mistakes, but they make enough of them,' and he laughed shortly.

'It was just a game.'

He shot me an almost angry look. 'A game?' Then, lowering his voice, he muttered, 'A game!'

'I'm sorry.' How small, how silly I felt. I wasn't even sure we were talking about the same thing. He kept his eyes on me grimly.

'My mother was already married at your age. My sisters—' He broke off abruptly and shook his head.

What could I say? 'I'm so sor—'

Wodo raised his hand to cut me off. 'Rosa, I think I've said what I can.' He stood up, a tall solid wall, a dam against the rushing river of the future. He moved to the other side of his desk, then paused and suddenly smiled down at me. 'You can go now.' He turned to his copy of the play, opened it and, without looking back at me, waved me out. 'Go on.'

'Thank you,' I gulped, and rushed out.

Just round the corner, I bumped into Nassuna, who had such a worried look I giggled and took her arm.

'What was that all about?' We took the steps together, almost leaping off them. *Digi* was completely forgotten.

'I don't know. How do I know?'

'Passion? You and Cordelia? His *mother*?'

'I know! I wanted to melt into the ground and disappear.'

'Do you think he's crazy? Seriously. Maybe he's read too many books.'

'And he's stuck here, poor him, with all that-'

'Passion!' we shouted together, and burst out laughing.

'You see, my spell worked.' I was so relieved I couldn't stop laughing.

'Of course it didn't, silly. He didn't stop thinking about *King Lear* for one second!'

'Yes, but didn't you see how he acted funny?'

'Because I said "sex" about ten times, you fool! And what about you? You should have seen yourself, your eyes as big as eggs. Why is your blouse damp?'

'Why were you messing up my experiment?'

'I was only trying to *help* you. To get you out of hot water! He obviously could tell something was up.'

'Oh, no, he felt me – I mean *it*. I'm convinced.'

'All this proves is that he's crazy. Or maybe you are. Experimenting on a crazy man!'

'He thinks I'll be a teacher, he said. Stuck in a place like this, just like him. He cares.'

'He said that? Oh God, Rosa, the Walking Wodo loooves you!' she sang out.

'Nassuna, please! Don't be silly.'

'And you looove him to-ooo!' She raised her voice even higher.

'Shut up! Stop it. Stop.'

'This secret romance! What are we going to do-ooo?' She flung her arms open dramatically, face raised to the sky, and then bent over laughing.

I slapped her arm, half angry, but she wouldn't stop. I just had to laugh too, but I knew she wouldn't let me forget this; she would milk it for weeks, months. We moved on down to the dorms, weaving our way through throngs of girl-women. They stared at two highers losing their *digi*, laughing like they were possessed. Later, no doubt this would swell into some dirty rumour: 'Wodo and who? . . . Nooo!' My hand crept into my pocket as Nassuna and I slowly calmed down and tried to become grown-ups again. I would leave the safety pin there. Why not? Not as a game, but to remind me of what he called passion. I was caught in its spell.

THE FUGITIVE

Alain Mabanckou

Translated from the French by Polly McLean

When I think back to it, seventeen years later, I'm always haunted by the same image. I'm dripping with sweat, out of breath, my mouth is open, and I'm running as fast as my legs will carry me through the endless corridor of Montparnasse-Bienvenüe Station in Paris. These memories are as dogged as the swamp leeches of the Lukula River, all the way back in my hometown of Pointe-Noire, Congo-Brazzaville. As I write these lines today, my heart starts pounding to the beat of those anguished strides – I had never run that fast at home, even on race days at school. I loathed PE, and especially running. At that stage it never occurred to me that one day in the French capital I would pay dearly for this aversion to sport. If I'd been a good runner in my youth, maybe I wouldn't have been rasping for breath, with my tongue hanging out and my muscles on fire, that day at Montparnasse-Bienvenüe.

But it wasn't really the moment for regrets over misspent youth. Not the moment for resenting my feeble legs. I had to run. Run from the threat drawing closer with every second. They say that fear gives you wings. To summon some extra speed, I thought of my classmate Ndomba, who could outrun his own shadow. He was our Lucky Luke of the racetrack. How did he do it? He explained that for him, the race took place entirely in his head, because the legs simply carry out the orders of the brain. So it's the brain that does the running. You just had to imagine the route in your mind, step, by step, by step. We were pretty sceptical – we'd never heard of anyone having legs attached to their brain – but in the end we realized Ndomba was right: by the time we reached the finish line, several minutes behind him, he would already be unlacing his trainers.

He loved to tease us, asking, 'Where was your brain?'

As I ran like the devil through the massive Paris station crammed with passengers, I murmured to myself that I was speedier than my shadow, that Ndomba was watching over me. And in fact I could see his face. I was channelling his legs. Channelling his brain. It was as if he was whispering, 'Run! Run! Fast! Fast! Follow the route in your head! Don't look back or they'll catch you!'

But the thing was, I didn't know the station. A real maze. How to imagine my route so I could shake off the men hot on my heels? All I could see in my mind was a wasteland. I had only been in France two months. I lived on the outskirts of the city, at Garges-lès-Gonesse, with my cousin Djoudjou. He was always telling me to avoid Montparnasse-Bienvenüe Station: 'I've had loads of mates sent back home from there. You should avoid it. It's a real rabbit warren. You'd have to be the architect's grandson or something to find your way out!'

And yet we'd been to Paris three or four times. I remembered that we often passed through Châtelet les Halles. In my mind, that was the only way to go, because it was there that we changed trains to go back to Djoudjou's place. We always came through Châtelet les Halles on our way into Paris, too. One day I took the train on my own. It would have been easy to get lost, but I had a landmark: the metro exit at Forum des Halles. You came out opposite the 1st arrondissement police station and Flunch restaurant. Then all you had to do was find Avenue de Strasbourg, walk along it and you'd be right in the heart of Château d'Eau, where all the Africans met. It was our capital, our stronghold, a kind of Africa in kit form. I'd already made the journey

several times when my cousin had asked me to go and buy metro
tickets on the black market at Château Rouge. I took the same route
to get my hair cut at the Afro 2000 barbershop.

But on that dark day of the longest marathon of my life, I had
accidentally taken a different route. I hadn't bought a ticket at
Garges-lès-Gonesse. Why should I, when I was on my way to get
a whole load of them on our black market at Château d'Eau? Also,
the ticket collectors hardly ever made it out to our town, which was
often caricatured in the press. People who'd never set foot in it were
convinced we lived in a war zone, with knives, submachine guns and
score-settling on every street corner.

On the train, I looked as if I were dozing. Actually, I was on the
alert. At every stop I would step over to the carriage door and scan
the platform for anyone in uniform. Then I would sit back down,
reassured. I wasn't the only one constantly on edge. Some passengers,
I noticed, were even jumpier than me. I was the pacesetter, the rabbit,
the watch. If I were to leave the carriage, they would all follow me. It
was a silent brotherhood. My gift to them, with nothing expected in
return. I was the most afraid, and so the perfect lookout. All they had
to do was watch my ears twitching.

When the train stopped at Châtelet les Halles, I decided to take
line 4 towards Porte de Clignancourt and get off at Château d'Eau,
but I accidentally boarded the train going in the opposite direction,
towards Porte d'Orléans. The names of the stations flashing by meant
nothing to me: Châtelet, Cité, Saint-Michel, Odéon . . .

When we got to Montparnasse-Bienvenüe, it felt like everyone was
getting off. A quick glance at the metro map and I realized I'd gone
the wrong way. I'd have to find out where to board the train back to
Porte de Clignancourt.

There I was, wandering down a long corridor like a blind man. All
the signposts just confused me further. I was a lemming, following the
others as if we were all going to the same place. When you're lost, it's
nice to be in a group. At least you're not alone in your confusion . . .

No, they mustn't catch me. I must not, cannot, be trapped like a rat. At a certain point I thought I was in bed, nice and warm under the covers, fast asleep. It seemed as if it was raining, and the sound of the rain on the roof was very soothing.

Yes, I must be dreaming. Chases like this only happen in dreams. You wake up in the middle of the night, with dogs barking in the nearby streets, and feel so relieved that it was all just a dream. You get up, go to the kitchen for a glass of cold water and return to bed for a less thrilling, less athletic dream.

But I wasn't dreaming. Otherwise I would have suddenly scaled the Great Wall of China. Or taken off and flown through the sky. Or run faster than my classmate Ndomba, reaching the finish line minutes before him and unlacing my trainers with a wry smile.

I was running for real, as if my life depended on the speed of my strides. And these were definitely my legs, stretching forward to swallow up the ground and shake off the pack behind me.

Yes, I was really running, and at this rate my muscles were going to give out. I should have chucked away the bag I was clutching, to shed excess weight. As if that tiny thing were crippling my escape. It only contained two books and a blank notepad, but in a race even a shirt becomes excess weight. And what about my leather shoes?

No, I wasn't about to take off my shoes and run barefoot like those Kenyan athletes I watched on TV!

I see myself on that day.

I'm being chased by three ticket inspectors. Two whites and a black man. They're after me because I took to my heels as soon as I saw them checking tickets a couple of hundred yards away. It's obvious to them that I don't have one. Or that I've something else to hide. How could such respectable inspectors *not* chase someone who was making them look stupid in front of the other passengers?

My mouth is open as I run. I push my way past outraged commuters, who swear and call me every name under the sun. I've one thing on my mind: finding the exit and melting into the crowd outside. My cousin is right: Montparnasse-Bienvenüe seems to be the most complicated station in the Paris metro system. I am not the grandson of the architect, so I take one-way passages the wrong way, leap up downwards escalators, run down stairs and come out on the platform for a train that could be going anywhere. The bell sounds just as I'm about to squeeze into a carriage, and the doors close. Time to start running again, heading for the end of the platform, where I can see a way out.

The three metro employees are still hot on my heels. I reach the end of the platform; it's not a way out, it's the start of a long corridor. I don't stop to think, just grit my teeth and go for it.

I hear a voice echoing from far away. It's one of the inspectors, shouting, 'Let the son of a bitch go, Joël! Just drop it. We don't have to kill ourselves for this.'

Looking back, I see that two of the officers have given up the chase. Only one is still desperate to catch me. He is black. Black like me, and he is making this his personal mission.

He's shouting himself hoarse: 'Catch him! Catch him! Catch him!!!'

The other passengers make no attempt to stop me. They aren't there to do someone else's work. At the most, they're amused to see two people of colour treating this metro corridor like an Olympic stadium . . .

I turn round again; the black man has disappeared at last. A great relief fills my lungs; at last I can breathe.

I am walking now, but fast. I need to find an actual exit. Not one of these long corridors.

After a few minutes I feel my left shoe starting to come loose. The laces are undone. I crouch down to tie them.

Done. As I straighten up, my blood runs cold. The black man is in front of me, less than 200 yards away. How did he manage that? Which way must he have gone to get there?

I turn round and start running back the way I came. Fearful of bumping into the two officers that gave up the chase, I take the first 'no entry' passage I see on my right. A corridor! A long corridor! The further I run, the darker and narrower the corridor becomes. The black man's footsteps ring out behind me like something out of a horror film.

I notice a faint light at the end of the corridor. That must be the exit. So there's no need to follow the 'no entry' sign I'm passing. I want to reach that light; it's the light of freedom, the end of a night that fell in the middle of the day.

I don't yet know that I've just been caught in a trap. This is a way out, but it's closed.

The black man is sniggering behind me.

'You bastard, thought you knew this station better than me, did you?'

I stop and don't even turn round. I've had enough.

The black man rugby-tackles me. Behind us, the two inspectors lumber up, heavy as elephants.

'Your papers!' yells the black man, yanking me up by my shirt collar.

I don't move a muscle, so he reaches inside my denim jacket, finds my wallet and starts rummaging through it.

'Right, you're a law student and you're cheating the metro! It's Africans like you giving blacks a bad name in this country. Did you know that? Eh?'

As I've 200 francs in my pocket – given to me by my cousin to buy the metro tickets – one of his colleagues suggests, 'Why doesn't he just pay the fine with this? Then we can let him go and that'll be the end of that.'

The black man doesn't agree: 'No, I know these Africans! Fines are no good for them – they need a beating. Let's take him down the police station.'

They put me in handcuffs. The black man keeps cursing these Africans in Paris. They've fucked everything up; the city used to be so peaceful; they should be sent back to where they came from. I recognize his West Indian accent – he speaks like Jacques from Martinique, who works with my cousin as a security guard in Goussainville. Jacques hates it when Djoudjou reminds him that we have the same ancestry, that West Indians originally came from Africa. Sometimes he gets so annoyed he slams the door on us and stops phoning. But he always comes back at the end of the month, because he needs the metro tickets from the black market at Château Rouge. He knows he can't buy them directly, because the vendors are convinced the police are using West Indians to spy on the Château Rouge blacks . . .

Yes, it's seventeen years later, and I'm remembering the day I was taken to a police station for the first time in my life. The day I realized that some of my writing would tackle the complexity of racism between people of the same colour. When I was writing my first novel, *Bleu-Blanc-Rouge*, I was haunted by that marathon sprint through the corridors of Montparnasse-Bienvenüe. I could still see the guys trading tickets at Château Rouge. I could feel the mood in the 'black areas'. I could see those natty *ambianceurs* selling off the European dream to the young Congolese guys who'd stayed back home.

And many years after that, as I was writing another novel, *Black Bazar*, I was haunted by the face of that black West Indian as he chased me. I could see him caricaturing me and complaining about the fraudulent activities of the 'African gangs' of Château Rouge. That West Indian who talked about Africans in the same tone used by the leaders of the far right, which was then at the pinnacle of its 'glory'.

Yes, that day I was sitting on a creaky chair. And as the policeman's fingers came down on the keys of the typewriter to record the West Indian's statement, I imagined it was my fingers coming down, writing. In my head I started writing a story – making one up, I was about to say.

I left the police station having paid a fine to the black inspector, who was probably hoping for the death penalty, which would have somehow returned a little dignity to his race. But what dignity? That was the question, and remains the question I feel sure I'll keep asking myself, in every book I write.

HAYWARDS HEATH

Aminatta Forna

The car radio issued a blast of sound so sudden and brutish that Attila nearly came to an emergency stop. It took a moment to gather himself. In his chest his heart beat wildly, and his scalp had shrunk against his skull, hair follicles tightened in alarm, altogether a sign he was more nervous than he let himself believe, though in every other way he was feeling pretty good about things. The weather, for one: a cool, clear spring day. The prospect of the drive on clean-surfaced, empty roads. An escape from the city, time to himself.

The youth at the car-hire desk must have turned on the radio when he brought the car round. The new generation could not tolerate the sound of silence. This was the second car, there having been little possibility of Attila's bulk being contained by the first. The desk clerk had failed to see what a fool could not have missed. Still, had it been otherwise, he wouldn't be driving a Jaguar XJ from the Prestige range for the same price. Attila fiddled with the radio until he found something pleasing. Gradually he felt his scalp withdraw its grip on his cranium.

At Crawley he left the M23. He thought he should eat and turned off the main road towards Haywards Heath. Haywards Heath. It had been a joke between himself and Rosie for a long time. The overseas students all had a hard time pronouncing it. *Ay-wads 'eat.* A sly tease, she would ask each new acquaintance to repeat the name of her hometown. After his turn she'd glanced at him over her sherry glass and he'd held her gaze until she'd turned away. He knew, from the way she stood, the way she walked, mostly from the way she refused to turn back in his direction, that she felt the mark of his gaze on her skin, like a touch on the back of her neck. Afterwards and perversely, many months into their affair, she denied she'd noticed him that evening. He wore a Malcolm X goatee and a suit to attend lectures. This made her feel sorry for him, she said. They were in their third year when they met, together for three more. By the time of their graduation ceremony he was already 6,000 miles away.

At the London hospital where he worked as a visiting consultant – visits that had occurred twice yearly for the last five years, because of his expertise in displaced populations, in trauma – he had exhaled all the breath in his lungs at the sound of her name. 'Early retirement,' his colleague replied in answer to Attila's careful enquiries. The idea for the trip came to him in a moment and had taken over. He had been consumed by the details: renting the car, planning the route, driving on the left-hand side of the road.

He thought again about food. At a pub he pulled over and parked. Inside he found a booth and ordered duck à l'orange, which arrived garnished with a rose of tomato peel, which he also consumed. He drew no stares. He opened the atlas out on the table. He reckoned he was less than five miles away. After he had eaten, he carried the map to the publican, who jerked his head at the Jaguar and said, 'What, no satnav? Where you headed?'

'Haywards Heath,' pronounced Attila, perfectly.

Next to Attila in the passenger seat, the publican pushed the buttons of the device and rubbed the tips of his fingers along the wood of the dashboard. Then, guided by the patient, electronic voice, Attila passed through one village after another. When he missed a turning, the voice redirected him in the same even tone. Attila found himself unaccountably irked by the smoothness of her voice. He took another wrong turn, quite deliberately. She proved unflappable.

Now he knew how his patients felt. He analysed his own behaviour. Prevarication. He drove steadily for ten minutes following the voice's orders.

'You have arrived at your destination.'

What had he imagined? A bungalow. Shelves of books and papers. A quiet, ordered existence writing for professional journals. Some vanity constrained his imagination before it could reach the point of giving her a husband.

Rosie hadn't published in years.

At the desk he asked for her by her maiden name.

'Are you a relative?' asked the woman, unblinkingly.

Attila hesitated. The woman was black herself. A young African man in a white nurse's uniform moved noiselessly across the hall carpet. 'A friend,' Attila said finally.

'In the day room.'

The air was overheated, filled with static and the smells of cooked food and talcum powder. Nobody minded him as he moved heavily through the building. In the day room residents slept in the pale sunlight. Others were gathered in a semicircle round a radio. He found her by the window, a newspaper on her lap. She hadn't noticed him. In that moment he was aware of the possibility of turning back, and also of all he had to say, all that had happened, the foreseen and the unforeseen. He wished now he had brought something, flowers or chocolates.

'Hello, Rosie.' When she didn't respond, he moved into the line of her vision.

Now she looked directly at him, 'Hello,' she said, and smiled.

'Hello, Rosie,' he repeated. He stood, his hands by his side. He smiled, too, and shook his head. 'How are you?'

'I'm very well,' she nodded.

'Your former colleagues helped me find you.' He moved to sit next to her.

'Did they?' She didn't turn to him and so he examined her offer-ed profile for a few moments. How much beauty there was still. Spontaneously he took her hand. His greatest fear had been that an excess of courtesy would surround their meeting. The last time they saw each other she had not wanted him to leave. He told her it was a condition of his scholarship. They'd argued for weeks, months. 'What about us?' she'd pleaded. But he went back to his country anyway, full of ideas of himself, of the future. Which one of them had been naïve?

They sat in silence and the silence felt comfortable already.

'Are you married?'

'I was,' replied Attila. 'She died.'

'Ah, I'm sorry.' She tutted and shook her head. 'That must have been difficult for you.'

He said nothing. The events had unfolded on news programmes around the world; he'd wondered then why she never made contact.

Outside, an elderly resident on a bench threw crumbs for a lone blackbird. Next to her a young woman turned away to speak into a mobile phone, her free hand thrust deep into the pocket of her coat. Where to begin?

In the end he said simply, 'I'm sorry. I'm sorry I didn't stay, *that* I didn't stay.' He waited for her response in silence. She must know exactly what he meant. It's what he came here to say, though he had not, until this moment, admitted it to himself.

She patted him on the arm with her free hand and the action brought him comfort. 'It's all right.' They sat once more in silence. When she spoke, she said, 'I'm afraid you'll have to tell me your name again, dear.'

He closed his eyes and breathed deeply. 'Attila.'

She smiled. 'I have a friend with the same name. What a coincidence! He's coming to see me anytime soon. I'm waiting for him. Maybe you two will meet.'

'Excuse me.' He rose and went in search of the men's room. Inside he leaned his back against the cubicle door until he gained some control of his breathing. The temperature in the place had brought him out in a sweat. He washed his hands and loosened the collar of his shirt. After he left the lavatory he didn't return immediately to the day room, but roamed the ground floor of the building. Through a porthole in a door he saw the young African helper spooning food into the mouth of an elderly woman. Something about the scene stopped Attila: the hand at her back, which prevented her from slumping, the infinite care in the way the young man wiped her slackened mouth with a napkin. At one point the careworker looked up, straight at Attila. Their eyes met. The young man said nothing but bent once more to his task. Attila turned away.

To Rosie he suggested a walk in the grounds and was relieved when she accepted.

'How long have you lived here?'

She misunderstood and replied, 'Since I was a girl. In Haywards Heath. What about you?'

'I went to university near here. It was a long time ago.'

But she was already distracted: 'People say you can't have two robins in the same garden, but there's no truth in it. Look!' And then, 'A wren. I do believe there are more of them than there were twenty years ago.'

She held on to his arm, seemingly awash with the wonder of it all. She reached out to touch the drops of rain on the leaves, tilted her head, gazed at the sky and closed her eyes. He waited and watched her. She stretched out her arms. He had a memory of a photograph of her in the exact same pose. Where was it now? She let her arms drop back to her sides. They completed a first tour of the garden.

Rosie said, 'Shall we do another turn, Attlia? Another turn?' It was a phrase she had used often in the past: at the funfair, boating on a lake, on a dance floor. She teased him for being too serious.

Attila felt light-headed and – somewhat bizarrely – youthful. It was the effect of Rosie's mood, her enthusiasm for this unremarkable, chrysanthemum-bordered square of lawn, also the fact of being the youngest in the place by twenty years, excepting the staff. Fewer silver strands in Rosie's dark hair than in his own. He remembered she had no brothers or sisters.

They passed for the second time the woman on the bench, her daughter still speaking on the telephone. Rosie bent forward, plucked a sweet from the box on the old woman's lap and popped it into her mouth. Rosie gave an impish giggle. The sweet bulged in her cheek. 'She won't miss one. They're my favourite.' She gripped his arm and leaned her head against his shoulder. He inclined his head to hers and smelled the faint brackish odour of her hair, resisted the urge to kiss it. Behind them the old woman sat staring into the middle distance, her hands curled limply around the box of sweets. Attila could hear the daughter finish her call.

'Promise you'll come and visit me again, won't you?' Rosie said suddenly, raising her head. 'It's deathly dull in here.'

He gave his promise and meant it. Perhaps if he kept coming, she would eventually remember him, as she almost had today. On this slender hope he hung his heart.

Two months later he returned carrying a box of Newbury Fruits. The sweets had not been especially easy to find, and the packaging had changed, as might be expected after forty years. Along the way he had stopped at the same pub, where the publican remembered him, or, more accurately, the Jaguar, which had been replaced by a Vauxhall for this trip.

Rosie wasn't in the day room, or in the garden, though the weather was fine enough to permit it. Attila retraced his steps back towards reception. The woman, a different one to before, angled her head in the direction of a corridor. Attila advanced down it, bearing the box of sweets clamped in his huge hand.

In the dining room he found an afternoon dance underway; a dozen people moved slowly to the sound of 'The Blue Danube'.

Mostly residents danced with members of staff. Around the room elders dozed and snored, made soporific as flies by music and heat.

There, in the centre, Rosie, cradled in the arms of the young African worker Attila had noticed during his last visit. Her forehead was pressed against his chest, her hand in his, eyes closed. The careworker had his head bent towards her. He had young, smooth skin and, Attila noticed for the first time, a small beard.

For some minutes Attila stood and watched. Then he placed the box of sweets down on a table and reached for a chair. As he did so, the music ground to a halt; people began to shuffle from the floor. He bent to pick up the box of sweets, heard Rosie say his name and looked up. The smile was already on his face.

But she was not looking his way, seemed not to be aware of his presence in the room. Rather she was looking up at the young careworker, who still held her in his arms. 'Shall we do another turn, Attila? Another turn. What do you say?'

And the young man replied, 'Whatever makes you happy, Rosie.'

Rosie nodded. The music began again. Attila replaced the box of Newbury Fruits on the table. He sat down and watched.

MISSING OUT

Leila Aboulela

In his first term at college in London, Majdy wrote letters home announcing that he would not make it, threatening that he would give up and return. To call him on the phone, his mother made several trips to the Central Post Office in Khartoum, sat for hours on the low wooden bench, fanning her face with the edge of her *tobe* in the stifling heat, shooing away the barefooted children who passed by with loaded trays trying to sell her chewing gum, hairpins and matches. 'Get away from my face,' she snapped at the girl who had edged by her side and was almost leaning on her lap. 'Didn't I just tell you I don't want your stuff?' On the third day she got through, wedged herself into a cubicle but did not close the glass door behind her.

Majdy's throat tightened when he heard her voice. In the cool corridor of the hostel he held the receiver and leaned his head against the wall, hiding his face in the crook of his arm. The students who passed him walked a little bit quicker, felt a little bit awkward hearing his voice heavy with tears, unnaturally loud, foreign words they could not understand echoing and hanging around the walls.

There in Khartoum, she also, in her own way, could not understand what he was saying. All this talk about the work being difficult was, of course, nonsense. Her son was brilliant. Her son always came top of his class. She had a newspaper photograph of him at sixteen when he got one of the highest marks in the secondary-school certificate, shaking the now-deposed president's hand. His father had slain a sheep in celebration and distributed the meat among the beggars that slept outside the nearby mosque. His sisters had thrown a party for him, heady with singing and dancing. And she had circled the pot of burning incense over his head, made him step over it, back and forth, to ward off the envy and malice that were surely cloaking him. 'Ninety-nine per cent in the maths paper,' she had ecstatically repeated to friends and relations. 'Ninety-nine per cent, and mind you, they took that extra mark from him from sheer miserliness, just so as not to give him the full marks.

'Put this thought of giving up out of your mind,' she said to him on the long-distance line.

'Can't you understand I've failed my qualifying exam?' The word 'failed' was heavy on his tongue. 'The exam I need to be able to register for a PhD.'

'So sit it again,' she insisted. 'You will pass, inshallah, and then come home for the summer. I myself will pay for the ticket. Don't worry.' She had independent means, that woman, and when she put the phone down, a project started brewing in her mind. She dawdled on her way home, plotting and wishing. A few hours later, refreshed from her siesta and the cup of tea with milk she always had at sunset, she gathered the family and launched a new campaign: 'My Poor Son All Alone in London Needs a Wife.' That was how Majdy came to marry Samra. After banging his head against books, working the proofs again and again, copying curvaceous lambdas, gammas and sigmas from the blackboard and into the whirling mass of his dreams, he was ready to sit for his qualifying exam. In June he flew to Khartoum. In July he received the good news that he had passed, and by the end of summer he was returning to London accompanied by his new bride.

All his life Majdy had known Samra, as a cousin of his sister's best friend, as the daughter of so-and-so. There was no sudden meeting between them, no adolescent romance. He had detached memories of her: a black-and-white photograph of a child squinting her eyes in the sun; standing with his sister and others in front of the giraffes' cage at the zoo; a teenager in a blue dress with her hair in a single braid, holding a tray of Pepsi bottles at a friend's engagement party. And the horrific story that had fascinated him in his childhood – Samra getting bitten by a stray dog and having to have thirty rabies injections in her stomach.

In 1985 he had seen her through grapevines, behind a carport over which the leaves climbed and weaved a crisscross maze. He was pressing the doorbell of a house near the university, on one of the smaller side roads that housed the university's staff. On the main road the students were demonstrating against the proposed execution of an opposition-party leader. While they were marching for justice, Majdy was searching for Professor Singh, lecturer in topology, to beg for a reference letter. It was for one of those numerous grants to do postgraduate research that he was always chasing. From where he was, he could hear the shouting. It came to him in waves, rising and falling, rhythmic and melodious. He could not make out the exact words.

They never let the students get very far; they never let them reach the marketplace, where they would swell in number and cause a riot, where other grievances and older pains would join the cry against the injustice of that one death. Deprivation might shake off its hypnotic slumber and lash out in the monotonous heat of the day. Down University Road until the first roundabout and then the tear gas would blind them, send them running back, tumbling through the dust and the fallen banners on the ground.

She was crying when she and her friend came running and stood underneath the carport of the house adjacent to the professor's. Crying from the gas and laughing. 'I tore my sandal. It's ruined,' he heard her say. She held it in her hand, the tears running in parentheses down her dust-coated face. Her *tobe* had fallen down, collapsed round her waist and knees, and her hair had escaped the one braid it was tied into and stuck out from her head in triangular spikes. At the nape of her neck, tight little ringlets glistened with sweat, dark and sleek. Laden with moisture, they lay undisturbed and appeared detached from everything else, the tear gas and the dust, her torn sandal, her fallen *tobe*. There was a *zeer* in front of the house and he watched her lift the wooden cover, fill the tin mug with water and begin to wash her face. She smoothed her hair with water, searched through it for hairpins, which she prised open with her teeth and use to lock the wayward strands.

And all the time she was laughing, crying, sniffing, chatting to her friend as they both pulled the ends of their *tobes* over their left shoulders, wrapped the material neatly in place and over their hair.

'This sandal is so ruined you can't even wear it as a slipper!' her friend said.

He felt cynical watching them, especially when, now that the demonstration was disbanded, other students passed by, cursing and spitting, with torn shirts and the pathetic remnants of their banners. He did not have the anger to demonstrate; he did not have the ability to enjoy the thrill of rebellion. And the next day, as he predicted, the futility of their action was exposed. Mahmoud Muhammad Taha was hanged on a Friday morning.

Later, or perhaps at the time he was looking at her through the vines, he thought, I could talk to her now. She would be approachable now, not formal or shy. She would yield to me now. And over the years we will talk of this day again and again and claim it was the start. But he let her go, rang the professor's bell and soon heard footsteps coming towards him from inside.

It is pointless to resist fate, impossible to escape its meanderings, but who knows how to distinguish fate's pattern from amid white noise? Years later, when his mother led her campaign, the name Samra cropped up. His older sister was despatched to test the waters. The reception was good. Prospective bridegrooms living abroad (it didn't matter where) were in great demand.

When they walked into his room in London, they quarrelled, but this was not because the room was small and designed for one student. He had applied for married students' accommodation, but the university had yet to allocate them a flat. The tension started up as soon as she stepped out of the bathroom. There were droplets of water on her hair and her arms, the sleeves of her blouse rolled up.

'Where is your prayer mat?' she asked.

'I don't have one,' Majdy said. He was lying in bed enjoying his return to the particular quiet of London, the patch of moving grey sky he could see from the window, the swish of cars on wet roads. It was as if Khartoum had been grinding around him in a perpetual hum and now that humming sound was pleasantly absent.

'Well, what do you use instead?' She was already holding a towel. 'Where's the *qibla*?'

He would need to figure out the direction of the *Ka'ba*. From Britain, Mecca was south-east of course, because Saudi Arabia was south-east. So in this particular room, which direction should she face? Where exactly was the south-east?

'I can't believe it,' she said. 'You've been here a whole year without praying?'

Yes, he had.

'And Fridays? What about the Friday prayers?'

'I have classes that day.'

'Miss them.'

He sat up. 'Don't be stupid. Where do you think you are?' The quick hurt look on her face made him regret that he had called her stupid. He took her in his arms and said, 'It's not as if I'm finding the course so easy that I can play truant.'

She smiled and was keen to brush away her disappointment. He suggested an outing and they went by bus to the Central Mosque. There he bought her a red prayer mat and a compass that pointed to the direction of Mecca. She also picked up a booklet that listed the times of the prayers. Each month was on a page, the days in rows and the different prayers in columns.

Sitting next to him on the bus, she studied the booklet. 'The times change so much throughout the year!'

'Because of the seasons,' he explained. 'In the winter the day is very short, and in the summer it is very long.'

'So in winter I will be rushing to pray one prayer after the other, and in the summer there will be hours and hours between afternoon and sunset.' She said 'I', not 'we', and that seemed to him proper and respectful. She would forge ahead on her own whether he joined her or not. He was relieved that this outing to the mosque had satisfied her. Cheap and hassle-free. On a student budget, he could scarcely afford expensive restaurants or luxurious shopping trips. It was good that she was a simple Khartoum girl, neither demanding nor materialistic.

Still, she said that she wanted him to promise to change, to try harder and commit to the compulsory prayers. She was intent on influencing him, but he was shy of the intimacy conversations about faith and practice evoked. After all, they did not know each other well and these were heady days of physical discovery, the smallness of the room making them bump and rub against each other. He was, naturally, the first man in her life, and she was swayed between discomfort and pleasure, between lack of sleep and the feeling that all her girlhood and all her beauty had led to this. A honeymoon in London, her wedding henna still bright on her palms and feet. Majdy was, he had to admit to himself, captivated by the comforts and delights she offered, charmed by her looks and laughter. Then she would spoil it all by talking about religion, by reminding him that without these five daily contacts one was likely to drift off without protection or grace or guidance. Was he not a believer? Yes, in a half-hearted way he was, but he was also lazy and disinterested. Here in London, Majdy argued, praying was a distraction, an interruption and, most of all, because of the changing times that followed the movement of the sun rather than the hands of the clock, praying was inconvenient. 'Don't talk to me about this again,' he finally said, drawing her towards him. 'Don't nag.'

In the days to come, when he became engrossed in his work again, he sensed her by his side, sympathetic, aware of his moods, sensitive to his needs, gentle and generous. Then she would move away to splash in the bathroom and come out to pray. She held the day up with pegs. Five prayers, five pegs. The movement of the sun was marked, the day was mapped, and Majdy felt his life become more structured, his time more blessed. In their cramped room Samra's prayer mat took up a large portion of the floor, the old *tobe* she covered herself with dropped over it in a coiled heap. Sometimes she reproached with a look or a word, sometimes she looked sad and worried on his behalf, but she continued to follow her own course, her own obligations, keen to preserve this practice even though she was away from home.

He wanted her to enjoy lively, civilized London. He wanted her to be grateful to him for rescuing her from the backwardness of Khartoum. He thought that, like him, she would find it difficult at first and then settle down, but the opposite happened. During the first months she showed the enthusiastic approval of the tourist. Enjoyed looking at the shops, was thrilled at how easy all the housework was. She could buy meat already cut up for her. There were all these biscuits and sweets to choose from, and they were not expensive at all. Even the pharmacies were stocked so full of medicine in so many different colours and flavours that she almost longed to be ill. Every object she touched was perfect; quality radiated from every little thing. The colour of hairpins did not chip under her nails like it had always done; chewing gum was not the brittle stick that often dissolved in her mouth at the first bite. Empty jam jars were a thing of beauty; she would wash them and dry them and not be able to throw them away. Biscuit tins, those she wanted to collect to take back home, her mother would use them to store flour or sugar, or put her own baked cakes in them and send a tin proudly to the neighbour, and days later the neighbour would return the tin with her own gift inside.

She put on weight. She wrote happy letters home. Majdy showed her the university's library – so many floors that there were lifts inside and even toilets! They toured the shining computer rooms and she was impressed. She made him feel that he was brilliant, which deep down he knew he was all along. Then the days shortened, became monotonous. She was like the holidaymaker who was getting a little bit tired of her exotic surroundings. Everything around her began to feel temporary, detached from normal life. This happened when Majdy began to talk of getting a work permit once his student visa expired, of not going back after he got his PhD.

It was the continuity that she found most alien. It rained and people lifted up umbrellas and went their way; the shelves in the supermarket would empty and fill again. The postman delivered the mail every day.

'Don't your lectures ever get cancelled? Don't your lecturers get ill? Don't their wives give birth? When the Queen dies, will they give everyone a holiday?'

'She'll die on a Sunday,' he would say, laughing at her questions. 'This is what civilization is, the security to build your life, to make something out of it. Not to be hindered all the time by coups and new laws, by sitting all day in a petrol queue, by not being able to get your ill child to a doctor because they are on strike.'

She listened carefully to everything he said, would nod in agreement, though her eyes remained wary. When she spoke of the future, however, she would imagine they were going back, as if his hopes of staying in London were only dreams, or as if his hopes were an inevitability she wished to deny. 'I imagine you coming home early,' she would say. 'There would not be this endlessly long working day like here.

'We would sleep in the afternoon under the fan, its blades a grey blur, the sun so hard and bright that it would still be with us through the closed shutters. I would tease you about your students – are the girls pretty? Do they come to your office after lectures and sweetly say, "Ustaz, I can't understand this. I can't understand that"? "Ustaz, don't be so hard on us when you're marking our exams." And you would laugh at me and shake your head, say I'm talking rubbish, but I would know from your eyes how much my possessiveness pleased you. The children playing on the roof would wake us up, their footsteps thudding over the hum of the fan. They are not allowed up there. It is not safe among the jagged green pieces of glass that ward off thieves. And you are furious with them; you go outside and throw your slipper at your son as he drops himself down from the tree, one foot balanced on the windowsill. He is the eldest, the instigator. But he is mischievous and ducks; you miss him and have to shout, "Bring the slipper back!" From inside I hear his laugh like cool tumbling water. You once bought a whip for this boy. You got it from the souk in Umdurman where they sell good whips, and you were quite pleased with yourself that day. You lashed it through the air to frighten the children with its snake-like power. But you did not have much of a chance to use it because he took it and threw it on top of the neighbour's roof and so it remained there among the fluffs of dust, razor blades and other things the wind carried to that roof.

'I would make tea with mint. By now the sun would have nearly set. It would be the hottest part of the day, no breeze, no movement, as if the whole world was holding its breath for the departure of the sun. Our neighbour comes over and you drink the tea together. He brings with him the latest gossip, another political fiasco, and you are amused. Your good mood is restored. Your son behaves well in front of guests; he leaves his play, comes and shakes the man's hand. The sound of grief cuts the stillness of the evening, like a flock of birds howling, circling and yapping with their throats. We guess it must be the elderly neighbour across the square; he has been in and out of hospital for some time. I grab my *tobe* and run, run in my slippers to mourn with them.'

'You are hallucinating, woman.' This was Majdy's answer. He had proof. 'Number one, I will never, with the salary the university pays its lecturers, be able to afford us a house or a flat of our own. Unless I steal or accept bribes, and there is not much opportunity for either in my kind of work. We would probably live with my parents; my mother would get on your nerves sooner or later. You will complain about her day and night, and you will be angry with me because you expect me to take your side and I don't. Number two, how will I ever get to the souk of Umdurman with no petrol? And there is unlikely to be any electricity for your fan. The last thing, why do you assume that nothing pleases me better than drinking tea and gossiping with the neighbour? This is exactly the kind of waste of time that I want to get away from. That whole atmosphere where so-called intellectuals spend their time arguing about politics. Every lecturer defined by his political beliefs, every promotion depending on one's political inclination and not the amount of research he's done or the papers he's published. My colleagues would be imagining that it is their responsibility to run the country. Debating every little thing from every abstract angle. The British gave it up, packed and left without putting up a fight, and somehow the Sudanese carry this air of pride, of belief that their large, crazy country will one day rise gracefully from its backwardness and yield something good!'

She sometimes argued back when he spoke like that, accused him of disloyalty, a lack of feeling. Sometimes she would be silent for days, control herself and not mention either the future or the past. Then, like one breaking a fast, she would speak, offer him memories and stories, and wait for him to take them. Wait with the same patience, the same serene insistence with which the little girls at the Central Post Office had offered pins and gum to his mother.

'I am not making this up,' she said one night as they walked on a side street sleek with rain and yellow lamplight. 'This really happened. After your mother phoned you at the Central Post Office she stood for an hour waiting for a bus or a taxi. None came; transport was bad that day because of the petrol shortage. The sun burned her head and she became exhausted from standing. So she walked onto the road, stood right in the middle of the road and raised her hand, palm upwards. She stopped the first car, opened the front door and got in. "My son," she said to the driver, "I am fed up of waiting for transport and I can't move another step. For Allah's sake, drive me home. I'll show you the way." And he did drive her home, even though it wasn't on his way. And as they chatted, he called her "aunt".'

And in July rain that made silver puddles. The sun disappearing for a day, the new smell of the earth. And there would be no work that day, no school. The cars stranded islands in the flooded streets.

'Because there are no proper gutters,' he would tell her. 'No drainage system and all those potholes. Remember the stink of the stagnant water days later. Remember the mosquitoes that would descend, spreading disease.'

'Silver puddles,' she would say, 'under a sky strange with blue clouds.'

Another memory. She offered it like a flower pressed into his hands. The week before the wedding, they had gone to visit his uncle. The electricity cut and the air cooler's roar turned to a purr, its fan flapped, and then all the sound died down. The sudden darkness, the sudden silence. They sat and listened to the gentle drip, drop of the water on the air cooler's fresh straw, then opened the windows to let in the faint night air and the scents from the jasmine bushes. Moonlight filled the room with blue-grey shadows. Outlines rose of the coloured sweets on the table, the ice melting in their glasses of lemon juice. While their hosts stumbled around in search of candles and lights, Majdy had leaned over and kissed her for the first time.

'But, Samra, do you want a power cut in London? Think of that – elevators, traffic lights, the trains. Chaos and fear. They would write about it in the newspapers, talk about it on TV. And in Khartoum it is an everyday event, another inconvenience, part of the misery of life. Defrosted fridges become cupboards with the food all soggy and rotting inside.'

Sometimes he looked at her and felt compassion. Felt that, yes, she did not belong here. Looked at the little curls at the nape of her neck, dry now and light, not moist with sweat, and thought that she was meant for brilliant sunsets and thin cotton dresses. Her small teeth were made to strip the hard husk of sugar cane, her dimples for friends and neighbours. He could see her in idle conversation, weaving the strands of gossip with a friend. Passing the time in the shade of palm trees and bougainvilleas, in a place where the hours were long.

Most times, though, he could not understand how she was not excited by the opportunities their new life held, how she could not admire the civilized way that people went about their business here, their efficiency and decency, ambulances and fire engines that never let anyone down. The way a debit card could slide through a wedge on the wall and crisp cash emerge. These things impressed her, but not for long. She exclaimed at how the pigeons and ducks in the parks were left unmolested. No one captured them to eat them. But instead of enjoying their beauty, she brooded over how poor her own people were.

He began to think of her homesickness as perverse. Her reluctance wholeheartedly to embrace their new life, an intransigence. He began to feel bored by her nostalgia, her inability to change or to initiate a new life for herself. Homesickness was blocking her progress, blinding her to all the benefits she could gain. There were so many choices, so many new doors, and yet she was stuck in the past, adoring Sudan and missing out on the present. He had, in the time he had spent in London, met Sudanese women who blossomed in their new surroundings. He had seen them in tight trousers they would not dare wear back home, playing with lighted cigarettes in their hands. And though he did not expect or really want her to do exactly these things, he was disappointed that she did not capture that same spirit and instead seemed shyer, more reserved than she ever was in Khartoum. She wanted to wear her *tobe*, to cover her hair, and he would say, 'No, no, not here. I do not want us to be associated with fanatics and backwardness.'

It is frightening to come home at the end of the day and find your wife sitting, just sitting, in her dressing gown and her hair uncombed just as you have left her in the morning. She who checks her reflection in every mirror, who for you scents her hair with sandalwood, dips steel in kohl to wipe the rims of her eyes. You find her sitting and the whole place is untouched – no smells of cooking, the bed unmade, mugs stained with tea, the remaining few flakes of cereal swollen in their bowl. She is silent, looks at you as if you don't exist, does not yield or soften under your touch. Stroke her hair and rub her hands and probe for the right words, the words she wants to hear. Talk of jasmine-scented gardens, of a wedding dance, of the high Nile breaking its banks. Until she can cry.

For days afterwards, as Majdy put his key in the lock, as he turned it, he would brace himself for that same scene; he would fear a reoccurrence. He had been happy that day. While she sat at home with a frozen heart, he had glimpsed a modest success, a slight breakthrough in his work. A paper he had been looking for, a paper written five years ago in his same area of work, was located in another library. And he had gone there, to that college on the other side of London, an event in itself, for he was always at the library or using the mainframe computers. He had found it, photocopied it, warmed to its familiar notation and travelled back, full of appreciation for that meticulous body of knowledge, the technology that enabled one to locate written material. 'We are centuries behind,' he would tell her later, 'in things like that we are too far behind ever to catch up.' And while she had sat in her dressing gown, immobile, ignoring hunger and thirst, he had entered the mind of that other mathematician, followed his logic and when finding an error (the subscript for lambda should have been 't-1' and not 't'), a typing error or a more serious slip from the writer, he had been infused with a sense of pleasure. So that even while he knelt next to her and asked, 'What is wrong? What has happened?' the formulae with their phis and gammas and lambdas still frolicked in his brain and the idea occurred to him that her name, if he ignored its real Arabic meaning, sounded just like these Greek letters, these enigmatic variables with their soft shapes and gentle curves. Alpha, lambda, sigma, beta, *samra*.

He proposed a practical solution to her problem. She must do something with herself, she was too idle, and as she was not allowed to work without a permit, then she must study. Already her English was good, so word processing would be ideal; she could type his thesis for him. He was enthusiastic about the idea; a word-processing course of a few weeks, and through it perhaps she would meet others like herself from all over the world, make friends and keep busy. So she, who had once braved tear gas, the crush of running feet, now faced a middle-aged teacher, a jolly woman who had recently travelled to Tunisia for her holidays and come back encased in caftans and shawls. The teacher gushed at Samra, 'You must be so relieved that you are here, all that war and famine back home. You must be relieved that you are not there now.' From such a woman Samra recoiled and like a spoiled, stubborn child refused to continue with the course.

Out of exasperation, Majdy suggested that she should go home for a few months. He winced as he saw her try to hide the eagerness from her voice when she said, 'Yes, that would be nice.' And the polite questions: wouldn't the ticket be too expensive? Would he be all right on his own? Then she left, easily, so easily, as if she had never truly arrived, never laid down roots that needed pulling out.

Without her, it suddenly started to feel like the year he had spent alone in London before they got married. The days drifting together, no reason to come home in the evening, all around him too much quietude. Without her he was not sure how to organize his day, to work at home or at the library, to work late at night or wake up early in the morning. He knew it did not matter either way, but that early sparkle of liberty that had characterized the first days of her absence, that feeling of relief, of a responsibility shed, soon faded away and freedom hung around him, stale and heavy.

While Samra was away, London became more familiar to him. He thought of it as his new home and it was as if the city responded. He could feel it softening around him, becoming genial in its old age, the summers getting hotter and hotter. A new humid heat, sticky, unlike the dry burning of the desert in Sudan. People filled the streets, the parks, a population explosion or as if a season of imprisonment was over and they were now let loose. They lay immobile on towels spread on the grass, drove in cars without roofs, spilled out of cafés onto the pavements.

Beggars squatted around the stations, Third World style. The sight of the beggars jarred him; he could not look them in the face; he could not give them money. It did not look right or feel right that white people should be poor. It was shameful that they were homeless and begging. It was unnatural that he was better off than them. He had a faint memory of discovering that in Europe begging was illegal. The information, incredible to him and awe-inspiring, had been in his mind part of the magic of the Western world, a place where everyone's livelihood was so guaranteed that begging could be considered a crime.

He had once told Samra that this country chips away one's faith, but he began to see that it chipped away indiscriminately at all faith, even faith in itself. And as it accepted him, his admiration for it stabilized, his faith in it wavered. It was no longer enough, as it once had been, that he was here, that he was privileged to walk London's streets, smell the books of its libraries, feast his eyes on its new, shining cars. He would walk on wet roads that never flooded and realize that he would never know what it would be like to say, 'My ancestors built this,' or, 'My grandfather borrowed a book from this library.' London held something that could never be his, that was impossible to aspire to.

His mother phoned him, her voice loud over the bustle of the Central Post Office. 'Why did you send Samra back for a holiday so soon? Is anything wrong between you?'

He was taken aback. 'No, of course not.' Marrying Samra had helped him feel settled and comfortable, well fed and looked after. He had liked working late into the night, kept company by her presence, the click of the spoon as she stirred sugar in tea, the chiming of her bangles, her movements when she stood up to pray in that early summer dawn. 'Did she complain about anything?'

'No.' His mother's voice was casual. 'She just mentioned that you don't pray.'

'Oh.' He could not think of a reply. The corridor of the hostel was empty. He stared at the vending machine, which sold chocolates and drinks. Samra had been fascinated by this machine. She had tried to get it to work with Sudanese coins. He missed her.

'Is it true that you want to stay on in London after you get your degree?' This was why she had telephoned. The nip of anxiety.

'Yes, it would be better for me.' His PhD was now within reach. He had been invited to a conference in Bath. He was stepping through the door, and after all this hard work he intended to stay and reap what he had sown.

His mother gasped down the line, 'How can you leave me all alone in my old age?'

He smiled because he had brothers and sisters living in Khartoum. There was no need for her melodramatic response. 'Don't you want the best for me? You are the one who is always complaining that Sudan is going from bad to worse.'

His mother sighed. First he had threatened to abandon his studies and return without a degree; now he was threatening the opposite! She had married him off so that he would not drift away, so that he would stay close. 'But what if things improve here, son? If they strike oil or make lasting peace, would you not be missing out?'

'I can't decide my future based on speculations.' Simulate a system over time, build a model, play around with a set of variables, observe what happens when you introduce a shock – this was his work.

Back in his room, Majdy noticed the silence. The floor looked strangely larger. Samra had folded her prayer mat and put it away in her side of the cupboard. She had not needed to take it with her. In Khartoum there were plenty of other mats, mats with worn, faded patches in those places where people pressed their foreheads and stood with wet feet. Majdy opened the cupboard and touched the smooth, velvet material. It stirred in him a childish sense of exclusion, of being left out, like a pleasure he had denied himself and now forgotten the reasons why. She had held the day up with pegs – not only her day but his too. Five pegs. And now morning billowed into afternoon, into night, unmarked.

WHY DON'T YOU CARVE OTHER ANIMALS

Yvonne Vera

He sits outside the gates of the Africans-Only hospital, making models out of wood. The finished products are on old newspapers on the ground around him. A painter sits to his right, his finished work leaning against the hospital fence behind them. In the dense township, cars screech, crowds flow by, voices rise, and ambulances speed into the emergency unit of the hospital, their flashing orange light giving fair warning to oncoming traffic. Through the elephants he carves, and also the giraffes, with oddly slanting necks, the sculptor brings the jungle to the city. His animals walk on the printed newspaper sheets, but he mourns that they have no life in them. Sometimes in a fit of anger he collects his animals and throws them frenziedly into his cardboard box, desiring not to see their lifeless forms against the chaotic movement of traffic which flows through the hospital gates.

'Do you want that crocodile? It's a good crocodile. Do you want it?' A mother coaxes a little boy who has been crying after his hospital visit. A white bandage is wrapped tight around his right arm. The boy holds his arm with his other hand, aware of the mother's attention, which makes him draw attention to his temporary deformity. She kneels beside him and looks into his eyes, pleading.

'He had an injection. You know how the children fear the needle,' the mother informs the man. She buys the crocodile, and hands it to the boy. The man watches one of his animals go, carried between the little boy's tiny fingers. His animals have no life in them, and the man is tempted to put them back in the box. He wonders if the child will ever see a moving crocodile, surrounded as he is by the barren city, where the only rivers are the tarred roads.

A man in a white coat stands looking at the elephants, and at the man who continues carving. He picks a red elephant, whose tusk is carved along its body, so that it cannot raise it. A red elephant? The stranger is perplexed, and amused, and decides to buy the elephant, though it is poorly carved and cannot lift its tusk. He will place it beside the window in his office, where it can look out at the patients in the queue. Why are there no eyes carved on the elephant? Perhaps the paint has covered them up.

The carver suddenly curses.

'What is wrong?' the painter asks.

'Look at the neck of this giraffe.'

The painter looks at the giraffe, and the two men explode into uneasy laughter. It is not easy to laugh when one sits so close to the sick. The carver wonders if he has not carved some image of himself, or of some afflicted person who stopped and looked at his breathless animals. He looks at the cardboard box beside him, and decides to place it in the shade, away from view.

'Why don't you carve other animals. Like lions and chimpanzees?' the painter asks. 'You are always carving giraffes and your only crocodile has been bought!' The painter has had some influence on the work of the carver, lending him the paints to colour his animals. The red elephant was his idea.

'The elephant has ruled the forest for a long time, he is older than the forest, but the giraffe extends his neck and struts above the trees, as though the forest belonged to him. He eats the topmost leaves, while the elephant spends the day rolling in the mud. Do you not find it interesting? This struggle between the elephant and the giraffe, to eat the topmost leaves in the forest?' The ambulances whiz past, into the emergency unit of the Africans-Only hospital.

The painter thinks briefly, while he puts the final touches on an image of the Victoria Falls which he paints from a memory gathered from newspapers and magazines. He has never seen the Falls. The water must be blue, to give emotion to the picture, he thinks. He has been told that when the water is shown on a map, it has to be blue, and that indeed when there is a lot of it, as in the sea, the water looks like the sky. So he is generous in his depiction, and shocking blue waves cascade unnaturally over the rocky precipice.

'The giraffe walks proudly, majestically, because of the beautiful tapestry that he carries on his back. That is what the struggle is about. Otherwise they are equals, the elephant has his long tusk to reach the leaves and the giraffe has his long neck.'

He inserts two lovers at the corner of the picture, their arms around each other as they stare their love into the blue water. He wants to make the water sing to them. So he paints a bird at the top of the painting, hovering over the falls, its beak open in song. He wishes he had painted a dove, instead of this black bird which looks like a crow.

The carver borrows some paint and puts yellow and black spots on the giraffe with the short neck. He has long accepted that he cannot carve perfect animals, but will not throw them away. Maybe someone, walking out of the Africans-Only hospital, will seek some cheer in his piece. But when he has finished applying the dots, the paint runs down the sides of the animal, and it looks a little like a zebra.

'Why do you never carve a dog or a cat? Something that city people have seen. Even a rat would be good, there are lots of rats in the township!' There is much laughter. The painter realizes that a lot of spray from the falls must be reaching the lovers, so he paints off their heads with a red umbrella. He notices suddenly that something is missing in the picture, so he extends the lovers' free hands, and gives them some yellow ice cream. The picture is now full of life.

'What is the point of carving a dog? Why do you not paint dogs and cats and mice?' The carver has never seen the elephant or the giraffe that he carves so ardently. He picks up a piece of unformed wood.

Will it be a giraffe or an elephant? His carving is also his dreaming.

THE CENTRE OF THE WORLD

George Makana Clark

For dinner I warmed an opened tin of meat paste in the convection oven, a massive appliance that in times past accommodated a prison loaf large enough to feed thirty-nine boys. The cooking smells rose with the heat into the rafters of the empty mess hall.

Days come to an abrupt end in the eastern highlands, and by the time I rose from the table, the view of the glen had already been replaced by my reflection on the windowpanes. I switched off the transistor radio, silencing the Christmas carols and war bulletins. Insurgents had crossed the Zambezi to fire up the faraway north country in these, the closing weeks of 1972.

As the last and sole ward of the Outreach Mission for Troubled Boys, it fell upon me to put out the lights and lock up. A framed map hung above the exit, paper continents arranged against a sea of blue felt. Africa rode too high on the Equator, Rhodesia slightly left of middle, locating the mission dead centre of the world.

Outside, a man was unhitching a dented horse trailer from the Very Reverend's Range Rover. Mrs Philips stood on the verandah of the rectory, arms folded, making certain the man left the blankets and tackle, which were not part of the purchase agreement. The Very Reverend had already retired for the night. Since the Prisons Department cancelled its contract with the mission, he slept more than he was awake, leaving his wife to supervise the dissolution of his life's work.

'Where are you off to?' she asked me.

I shrugged. The stables no longer needed mucking. Earlier in the week a representative from the Rhodesian Security Forces had collected all the mission horses, excepting the mare that drowned in the river.

Mrs Philips turned back to the rectory wherein her husband lay, the windows shuttered against his failure. 'Go on, then,' she muttered.

I watched the man drive away with the battered trailer. Once, when the trailer was filled with horses, a green mamba had crawled inside and got itself stamped to a pulp. This was how the dents had been made. The mission cook told me this in the days before he ran away to join the war of liberation. He used to say that I collected stories like other boys collect dead insects.

In my pocket was the typed notice I'd retrieved from the morning rubbish:

NOTICE OF CREMATION AND DISPOSITION
H. Takafakare Crematory
'Pay your last respects, not your lifetime earnings'
This is to respectfully inform concerned persons that the burning and disposal of all remains correlative to the deceased will be conducted by end of removal day.

I started along the dirt track that cut across the compound. Each morning women from the trust land raised their yokes and tramped down the mountain path through the mission to fetch water from the river. In their stories they referred to the track as Three Man Road.

Before their relocation to the trust land, the water drawers had inhabited a village on the river near a sacred kopje where heaven joined with earth. Always they beat the ground with their walking sticks as they followed the track that took them back to the river of their youth. Their descent into the glen took less than an hour; the laden climb back to the trust land consumed the balance of their lives.

As they walked, the women took turns reciting a communal narrative that began in a time when God and animals still spoke to people. On the occasions when I accompanied them, the women spoke English, happy to have an audience. Always the cadence of their voices rose and fell with the beat of the walking sticks. And when the final words were uttered – 'That is all' – and the women found themselves stranded in the present day, someone would cry out, 'A story!' evoking a chorus from the others: 'Bring it!' and the water drawers would begin again, reaching back into the days of creation.

I followed the track past the quiet stables, the abandoned out-buildings, the darkened dormitory that had once housed the criminal youth of our nation. These days Rhodesia needed her troubled boys for the war, and any interest in their redemption had evaporated. A soft tremor ran through the ground, making the soles of my feet itch. The glen lay on the southernmost boundary of a tectonic plate that stretched the length of Africa. It was a shifting, unsettled place and such quakes had become increasingly common, though nothing ever came of them.

The track crooked round the mission chapel, then traced the river bank half a mile to the foot of a kopje that rose up from the bottom of the glen. Some ancient cataclysm had sheared away the summit, giving it the appearance of a colossal altar. A pillar of smoke spiralled up from the kopje into the gloaming.

I began my climb, stepping along one of the twin ruts that angled across the steep face, my footprints superimposed over the imprint of a balding tyre. Snow fell against my face as I neared the top, the flakes warm on my cheeks. I brushed at them and my fingers came away grey and greasy.

The ground grew level beneath my feet as I reached the broad, flat-tened crest. In the darkness I could make out a brick oven that bulged and billowed amid a field of ash. A concrete-block house stood at the oven's mouth, illuminated by its flames. Chimes hung from the caves, hollow bones that twisted and came together in dull, yet musical clacks.

The owner of the field was named Mr Takafakare, a failed sweet-potato farmer given to great fits of coughing. He stood over a charred husk that had once been the neck and shoulder of the drowned mare. A lorry had been backed up to the oven, a chainsaw in its empty bed.

'Come to see the horse-burning,' Mr Takafakare said.

I blinked through the pong of charred hair and fat. Mr Takafakare gave a short bark of laughter that trailed into a phlegmy burr. 'You almost missed it, young sir.' He produced a perfectly white hand-kerchief, cleared his throat and spat. The wind lifted flakes of burnt bone and tissue into a swirl of carbon waste that rose and fell from the field.

Mr Takafakare had bought the field to grow sweet potatoes, and later added the kiln as a side business. He came upon the idea after listening to an African Service radio broadcast in which an agricul-turalist from the Ministry of Lands touted carbon as an excellent source for fertilizer. Mr Takafakare quickly discovered there was no market for sweet potatoes grown in human ash, and the path of his life turned away from farming and towards burning. For twenty years the oven exhaled the marrow of blackened bones into his face, forcing him to retreat each night into his house, where he buried his nose and mouth in freshly laundered linen handkerchiefs. Therein he spat and blew the corporeal residue of landless Shona, low-caste Indians, vagrants of mixed race and diseased livestock.

Mr Takafakare broke the mare's cremains in half with the edge of the spade and they reared up in a flurry of sparks and ash that made me step back and cover my nose and mouth with my sleeve. My gaze fell upon a girl who stood atop a ladder against the roof of the house. She held a laundry basket on her hip, the tip of her nose barely visible beyond the line of her cheek. Moses-in-the-boat grew in a windowbox next to her, pointed tongues of purple and green wagging in the blasted air. The girl's skin and hair were a uniform grey, save for the brown of her forearms, which looked as though they had been recently immersed in water. I watched her spread her father's handkerchiefs to wind-dry on the asbestos roof.

The cremator followed my gaze to his daughter. He might have told me to go home, but he knew I'd come from the mission and he didn't want any trouble. Ash rose in devils that swirled through the lower rungs as the girl descended the ladder with her empty basket.

Mr Takafakare buried his face in his handkerchief, blew noisily, then presented her to me. 'This is my child, Madota.' It is a custom to give children names that reflect a family problem at the time of the birth and so Mr Takafakare called his daughter Madota, which in the Shona language means 'ashes'. She stood before me in the light of the oven, enveloped in an aura of silence.

'A demon lives inside her,' Mr Takafakare told me. 'She cannot speak.' He shifted uneasily. 'Come inside and eat something,' he said finally.

Madota guided me into the house, her fingers exerting subtle pressures on my elbow. The furnishings inside were spare: a cooking pot and three metal bowls; a cardboard box containing groceries for the week; the typewriter and thesaurus that had produced the notice in my pocket; a sprung mattress, dark and shiny in the place where Mr Takafakare lay alone each night in his own sweat; a bucket of river water; a neatly made doss where his daughter slept; and four grey volumes, Winston Churchill's *The History of the English-speaking Peoples*, each with a facsimile signature of the former British prime minister scrawled across its cover in cramped, golden script, the handwriting of a megalomaniac. Their former owner was a teacher at the trust-land school who died intestate. Mr Takafakare had taken the books with the corpse as payment for the latter's removal, and now kept the volumes stacked on the floor for use as a stool.

An unframed picture of Mr Takafakare's dead wife was affixed to the wall, her wedding ring suspended from a tack. Mrs Takafakare's constitution had been defeated by the fine layer of human ash that covered every surface and utensil of that unclean house. It was said she left behind a corpse so diminished that when her husband folded and fed it into his oven, the flames only licked at the shroud before subsiding. In desperation Mr Takafakare doused his wife with petrol and she went up in a bituminous cloud that filled the sky until a cleansing rain erased it two days later.

Madota wiped the ash from the kitchen table before seating me in front of a large bowl of peanut-butter soup. It tasted faintly of carbon and I realized she had heated it atop the brick kiln. Her almond eyes followed each spoonful of soup to my mouth. I stared back, suddenly aware that I was eating her dinner.

I poured the unfinished soup into the sink and sat atop *The History of the English-speaking Peoples*. Madota squatted on her haunches beside me and the earth trembled lightly as we looked out of the window into a galaxy of stars that wavered in the heat of the brick oven. Her fingers were corded with muscle and tendon from a lifetime of wringing handkerchiefs. They squeezed my hand with a silent request. *Talk to me.*

I'd never spoken at length to a girl before, and as the warmth of her hand seeped into mine, I began to recite the stories I'd collected from the water drawers, braiding one into the next. 'This happened in a time,' I began, 'when people still listened to God and animals.'

As I spoke, Mr Takafakare looked up at me from his mattress across the room, distressed with the way things were turning in these, the last months of his life. I had seen blood mixed with ash and mucous in his handkerchiefs and knew that soon Mr Takafakare would be fed into his own oven.

The night wind rolled off the mountains, carrying away the heat from the oven, and the mare's remains cooled and fell to join the rest of the forgotten animals and ancestors that blanketed the flat summit of the kopje. Outside, hyenas, lured by the smell of charred meat, ploughed the field with their noses, breaking bones with their jaws and filling their bellies with ashes.

Four streams flowed down from the mountains that walled the glen. They came together to form the river, a topographical feature that, coupled with the abundance and variety of fruit trees, convinced the Very Reverend that he had found the location of Eden. He lobbied the Ministry of Lands and National Resources to bulldoze a Shona village and shift its inhabitants to the trust land on the mountainous periphery of the glen, so that he might establish the mission upon the geographical origins of his faith.

The Very Reverend no longer rose for breakfast. Mrs Philips and I ate fried eggs at opposite ends of the mess, the tink of our cutlery sounding unnaturally loud against the china plate in that cavernous place. When the mission's funding got the axe, the older boys were offered commuted sentences to join the Rhodesian Security Forces, while the younger ones were sent to industrial schools to serve out the remainder of their time. The boys had come to the mission with no place in the world, and many cried as they were taken away. With only a month left in my sentence, I'd been allowed to stay while Mrs Philips disposed of its assets.

I could hear the voices of the water drawers outside as they went down to the river with clay urns suspended from their yokes, always following the dirt track across the mission grounds. Half crippled by age, they refused the convenience of the communal tap in the trust land, preferring instead to fetch their water and gossip from the river.

In the early days of the mission the Very Reverend had ordered an end to this trespass, but his servants refused to interfere with the women. I sometimes followed them as far as the banks, where shards of sunlight floated on the dark currents, forcing me to avert my eyes as I listened to the words that streamed from their mouths.

Mrs Philips surprised me by speaking. 'I need you to help me dress the Very Reverend and bring him out onto the verandah.'

'I've got things to do,' I said. The Very Reverend's passion for discipline had faded with his spirits, and I no longer tried to invent excuses.

Mrs Philips pushed her eggs around on the plate for a few moments. 'When I was your age,' she said finally, 'I also believed the world revolved round me.'

I rose and quit the table, vaguely disappointed that she didn't ask where I was going.

Outside, two men struggled to push a pump organ through the double doors of the chapel, an uphill battle. The chapel had been built too close to the river and the altar end was sunk deep into the vlei.

The kopje was a short ride from the mission, but all the horses were gone and so I began the interminable walk to Madota's house. Red locusts crunched beneath my feet, spilling their eggs into the dirt, a sign, according to the water drawers, that the rains were coming. The women had warned me away from the kopje. They believed cremation was the worst form of desecration, that without the body, the spirits of the burned would become homeless and unpredictable.

I arrived to find Mr Takafakare forcing a corpse into a crouching position. The brick kiln was only four feet square.

'Back again, young sir. I'm afraid my daughter must go into the mountain to collect camphor basil to help with my coughing.' He shook his head regretfully. 'Perhaps you can come back next week.'

Madota's fingers settled lightly on the ball of my shoulder. *Come.*

And so I accompanied Madota down the kopje, her father staring after us. We walked along the river bank. My feet sank in the black vlei and I felt as if I were moving in a dream. 'Here is where the mare drowned,' I said. 'The one your father was burning when I first came to your house.' Already it had faded into a brief anecdote to associate with the moment of our meeting.

The track turned up at the chapel, and Mrs Philips watched in silence as we crossed the mission compound. A panel van was parked by the dining-facility entrance, a sandwich board affixed to its roof:

CONVERT YOUR USED APPLIANCES TO CASH. WE BUY IT ALL!!

The track climbed out of the glen and into the mountains that rose above the curve of the earth. Far above the mission, we passed by the foundations of a coriander plantation abandoned by Franciscan monks – Manicaland is littered with the ruins of forgotten missions – and I told Madota how, in olden times, the friars would move naked through the groves at night, fertilizing the rows of coriander with their semen. Her bare feet registered no sound as she stepped over the dead branches and leaves that littered our path.

The ground shuddered softly beneath us and we held hands for balance. Three Man Road crossed the mountain highway where market vendors choked on the dust and diesel that filled the mouth of the trust land.

My calves ached as I struggled to match Madota's pace, her form seeming always to hover ahead of and above me, ringed in light, a sign that the air was thinning and my mind was starved for oxygen. My words became lost in the roar that filled my ears.

Three Man Road came to an end in a profane place where God moulded Past, Present and Future into a single creature that chased itself in circles. All this I had learned from the women as they drew their water from the river. Deadfall blew across the clearing. 'South-blown leaves,' I said, parroting the water drawers. 'Rain to follow.'

Madota turned back to me, and her fingers found the base of my skull. *Kiss me.* I leaned towards her face, and her mouth swallowed my words before I could give them voice. Above, the sun moved unnoticed in its sky, the mountain air collected the moisture it had dispensed at dawn, and clouds erased the glen below us.

The river, straightened by age, bisected the glen into perfect halves. Each morning I walked its banks towards Madota's house, past the place where the drowned mare had lain for two days undiscovered, its stomach bloating with combustible gases until it produced a corpse that burned with such intense heat that the oven bricks began to melt. In order to prevent further damage to his livelihood, Mr Takafakare took to crouching by the mouth of the warped oven, its door open wide, as he tried to gauge the heat by the intensity of the blast that struck him full in the face. He endured this awful proximity for almost a month before finally resolving to travel across the mountains to Umtali, where he could purchase a pyrometer.

Mr Takafakare had never left the glen and so he asked me to come with him. The low clouds hung motionless in the surrounding air as the lorry struggled up the mountain face. Mr Takafakare stuffed camphor basil into his mouth while he drove, grinding it into a leafy bolus that filled all the gaps in his teeth. I spread a Survey Unit Reserve map across my lap, ready to call out directions once we reached unfamiliar territory. Rhodesia had been featureless before the English-speaking peoples came to chart and name it, one of Churchill's 'empty places of the globe'.

'Why do the water drawers think the kopje is sacred?' I asked.

The lorry whirred and lurched up the steep grade in low gear, while Mr Takafakare chewed on the camphor basil and my question. 'In the beginning of the world,' he said, finally, 'God tore apart the mountains, and the village was buried in ash. Some ran away. When they returned, the kopje had been cut in half.' Three Man Road floated before us on the clouds. 'Our ancestors took this as a sign that it was a sacred place and they began to bury their dead here, in a crouching position, shoulder to shoulder, generations upon generations, until the ground was filled. This is why I was allowed to buy the field. Even the Europeans refuse to live in this place.' He wanted to say more, but he fell into a coughing fit that peppered the windscreen with festive flecks of green and red.

We followed Three Man Road to a highway that ran through the mountains, but the lorry rolled to a stop before we could crest the first peak. Mr Takafakare turned in his seat and looked down on the glen. Perhaps he was afraid if we continued, we would drive off the face of the earth. He remained that way for several minutes, twisted in his seat, staring back on the road he had taken, the unmuffled engine idling and backfiring.

'You all right?' I asked.

He straightened in his seat and executed a three-point turn on the horizon of the world and we returned to the kopje without the pyrometer.

That night at the mission I dreamed Mr Takafakare was pushing me into his oven. I awoke crouching beneath my blanket, flames lapping at the wallpaper. The Very Reverend had splashed diesel fuel over the dormitory floorboards and lighted it.

I wrapped myself in my bedclothes and crawled through the smoke towards a gauzy rectangle of starlight framed by flaming curtains. Once outside, I threw off the burning blankets and rolled in the dirt, my lungs heaving.

The building was a lost cause by the time I reached the water hose, so I soaked the ground to keep the fire from spreading to the rectory. The Very Reverend quoted scripture as Mrs Philips led him away from the collapsing structure, the sparks catching and dying in her hair. 'Take heed to thyself,' he shouted at me, 'that thou offer not thy burnt offerings in every place that thou seest.'

Mr Takafakare was an outcast among the people who engaged his services, and he did not object when I offered to ride with him as he conducted his final removals. On these occasions he recited accounts, punctuated by coughs and throat-clearings, of the first ancestors who founded the bulldozed village. Mr Takafakare brought along the power saw when the removal was something large, a bull for instance that had succumbed to foot and mouth, its four stomachs heaving with gases. A dolly was required for medium-size removals such as a fighting dog, usually a ridge-back or a wild cape dog, its teeth sharpened with metal files, blood spattered waist high on the walls of the pit, wounds daubed with leopard's bane in a last-ditch effort to prevent blood loss and rouse the animal from shock. In the case of something small, say an infant dead of tuberculosis, Mr Takafakare would conduct the removal in a dignified manner with gloved hand.

Once, we removed one of the water drawers who had died in the trust land. We took her from a single-room house, its concrete-block walls cracked and seamed from seismic stress. A communal patch of stunted mealie struggled to survive in the granite and rime soil.

Madota travelled in the back with the corpse while I rode in the cab next to Mr Takafakare, his head tilted back to keep blood from streaming out of his nose. He downshifted the lorry as we passed through the mission, slowing almost to a stop. 'Here is the place where the dead woman was born. She was my cousin.' Mr Takafakare chuckled, then fell to coughing. 'Don't look so surprised,' he said. 'It was my village as well.' As he laughed, a thin trickle of blood stretched from his nostril to his lip. He nodded towards his daughter. 'She also knows all the stories of our village, stupid girl.' I looked over my shoulder to the lorry bed, where Madota lay across the blanket to keep it from blowing off the corpse. She was mouthing words to the bundle, stories, perhaps, of a village she never knew.

Mr Takafakare stared at his surd daughter in the rear-view mirror. 'Small matter, young sir,' he said. 'We have lost our place in the world, and our stories mean nothing any more.'

The rains, summoned by the spawning locusts, came to the eastern highlands, filling the glen. The river burst its banks and swollen currents swept away the mission chapel, leaving only naked pillars that canted in the vlei, indistinguishable from the handful of concrete headstones that marked the graves of boys and servants who'd died at the mission since its founding. There was rain enough to overfill the urns, but still the women came down to the river for their water. They shrugged when I told them that Mr Takafakare could recite a story for everything within the horizons of the glen. 'How would you know if he was lying?' one of them asked.

In the grey days that followed, the field atop the kopje became a lake of char. While Mr Takafakare struggled through the sheeting rain to fire his oven, I remained indoors with Madota, reading to her the stories of the English-speaking peoples that Churchill had taken and bound in volumes, his masterwork organized into chapters, books and volumes – divisions, regiments and battalions of words that advanced inexorably until they overwhelmed his audience.

My court sentence expired amid a series of unsubtle omens. The earth quaked and shook the glass panes from the window over the cot I'd set up in the stables, and I woke beneath a blanket of broken glass. Crows flew in through the empty frame and nested in the rafters, from which they would spatter my pillow and bedclothes with their white faeces.

The same day, Mrs Philips put her luggage and husband out on the verandah and locked the rectory. Disnested, the Very Reverend peered out at the compound through the grey lens of rain. His boys, horses and servants had been taken away to fight on different sides of the war, and the mission had the look of a razed military barracks.

I held an umbrella over Mrs Philips's head while she loaded the detritus of her life into the back of the Range Rover. The Very Reverend had located his faith in the centre of a map, but as he looked back through the rear window, he seemed not to know where he was. They drove away, leaving the buildings to collapse upon themselves and the land to become as it was in the beginning, a profane, uncreated place without form and void.

The absence of the Very Reverend and Mrs Philips left my routine unaltered. I rose from the spattered cot each morning to help Madota pick camphor basil for her dying father and search the ash for hollow ear and finger bones suitable for chimes. At sunset I lay beside her on the roof with the drying handkerchiefs, making shapes out of the clouds in the red sky, while below us Mr Takafakare fed his oven with scrub mahogany and fighting dogs. The oven flames continued to burn ungoverned without the pyrometer, and he kept the door agape, judging the heat by the force with which it struck his face and blistered his lungs. The sweat evaporated before it left his pores, and his skin became indistinguishable from the oven's brick. I reckoned he would die before the rains came again, leaving all his stories sealed within his voiceless daughter.

I sat up on the roof and pointed to a cloud. 'There. A horse,' I said to Madota, but already the wind had pulled the image apart and it looked as though flames were coming from its back.

We descended from the roof with the gloaming to take our places amid the volumes of *The History of the English-speaking Peoples*. Madota listened, as she had done all her life, while I spun out a filament of lore to drape across our sliver of world, my words clacking together over our heads like the dull music of her bone-chimes. Whereas Churchill was driven to account for all the English-speaking peoples across the globe, I recounted the meagre lore that fell within my circumscribed horizon. We differed, he and I, only in the scope of our compulsions.

I talked myself to sleep, my head cradled in Madota's lap, and dreamed of us alone in the valley as it had been in the beginning. *An unbroken canopy of ancient forest flanks a winding river. Granite mountains spill out fire and magma, the ground undulant and volatile beneath our feet. Madota leads me into a grove of young fruit trees, her fingers speaking with pressures against my arm.* I woke to the sound of phlegmy throat-clearing, my hand on Madota's breast, Mr Takafakare standing over us.

'Perhaps you should go now, young sir.'

The sun burned away the mist and sparked against quartz deposits that shot through the jet granite mountains, forcing me to squint out over the glen as I stood in the splintered threshold of the mess. Winds rippled through the forest canopy, turning each leaf in light and shadow. The previous night someone had prized open the door, ransacked the pantry and stolen the cutlery, dishes, food, tables and chairs, as well as the frame and the blue-felt backing for the Very Reverend's map. The paper continents swirled like leaves at my feet.

The water drawers stumped hopelessly along the track that ran through the mission compound. They numbered fewer than when I had arrived at the mission a year earlier. As young brides, their husbands had been press-ganged to improve the glen with grass buffers, dip tanks, drain strips, galley dams and a highway to bring the bulldozers that would push over their village. Now the women lived as widows amid concrete-block houses and dusty fields pegged out in grids, and their granddaughters drew water from a tap.

Above, I could see the brightly coloured umbrellas of the vendors who lined the entrance to the trust land. A column of armoured cars raced past them along the mountain highway, reducing its graded surface to scree beneath their solid rubber tyres and plated steel. The mission boys and servants would return to the glen in the coming years to fight each other in a war of repression and liberation, and the soft ground tremors would be replaced by a concussion of rockets and mortar shells that would shake the sacred kopje apart, spilling out the crouching bones of the village ancestors.

Once, mid-sermon, the Very Reverend had led his congregation of servants and troubled boys from the chapel out onto the bank of the lambent current. 'Look,' he commanded us. 'Fix this place in your hearts, so you can return in the dark times to come.'

The mountain shadows had retreated by the time I reached Madota's house, leaving the valley bathed in sunlight. The rains had just ended. Newly hatched locusts swarmed over the highlands to devour the tongues of Moses-in-the-boat that filled the windowbox.

Mr Takafakare stood over a sectioned cow that was dead of black-leg disease. I went over to help him clean the chainsaw, but he waved me away. 'Why do you always come sniffing about with all your talk! Leave us alone or I will take Madota far away from you.'

I laughed at this. 'You can't even leave the glen.'

Madota's chimes shook, though there was no wind, and I realized the ground was elastic with tremors. Mr Takatakare tried to menace me with the bloody chainsaw, but it would not start and so he tore through his own house in a fit of temper, kicking the cooking pot, overturning the water bucket, upending the cardboard box and strewing groceries across the room. He filled the box with Churchill's volumes and dropped them at my feet.

'Take them and go.' He wanted to say more, but a racking cough seized him. He stood before me, waiting for his lungs to quiet, wishing me away. Soon his chest would grow still altogether, as the earth would one day cease to shudder and sound Madota's bone-chimes.

Madota watched me from the threshold of the disordered house as I descended the kopje shouldering the burden of *The History of the English-speaking Peoples*. There came to me the cracked, halting voices of the water drawers as they returned from the river, laden, and I set down my books and listened to the broken rhythm of their gait, the thud of their walking sticks, the telluric drone of shifting plates of granite. Always, they had bound the glen together with their lore. Without them to remark on the connection, the red locusts would no longer lay the eggs that brought the rains to the mountains, the river would run dry, and the glen would become a furnace where sacred places warped and rifted, the world unmade.

PROPAGANDA BY MONUMENTS

Ivan Vladislavić

I
Grekov

Pavel Grekov paused for a moment in the overheated lobby of the apartment block to turn up his coat collar and smooth down his hair. He glanced sceptically at his watch – five to two – and then at the pinched face of the city behind the glass. He would have to hurry, which he was not in the habit of doing, but at least a brisk walk would get the circulation going. He pulled on his gloves, jammed his fists into his pockets and shouldered through the door.

He walked with his head pulled down into his collar and his eyes fixed on the toes of his boots. He saw from above the tentative splay-footed gait foisted on him by an icy pavement, and was not amused by it. The streets were almost deserted. Did it get this cold in the Transvaal? he wondered. Did it snow? Probably not; it was too close to the Tropic of Capricorn. Then he pulled his right hand out of his pocket and pressed three fingers to his chest, where a letter from those unimaginable latitudes was stored in an inside pocket. He might have been taking the letter's temperature through the thick cloth, or trying to feel the patter of its heart above the pounding of his own. Get more exercise, Grekov! he lectured himself. Out from behind that desk!

Grekov was a junior translator in the Administration for Everyday Services, an English specialist. Slowly but surely over the years he had established an interdepartmental reputation for his command of a fractious and somewhat eccentric English vocabulary. In recent months he had discovered his forte: rendering broken English in indestructible Russian. In the departmental estimation this was a highly desirable skill, and there were rumours, none of which had made an impression on Grekov himself, that he would soon be transferred to Foreign Affairs. He would have leaped at the opportunity.

The fact is that Grekov was bored. In the course of nearly five years in the same position no more than a handful of interesting documents had crossed his desk, precious messages in bottles carried to him on a tide of mundane communiqués and news clippings. It goes without saying that these rarities never originated in Everyday Services, but rather in the Ministry of Culture, or Foreign Affairs, or even Sport and Recreation, and they were so scarce that he was able to remember them all without effort.

He remembered them now, in chronological order, as he hurried through the snow-struck city. His career had started auspiciously with an exchange of telegrams about an inheritance and an itinerary issued by a travel agent in Kingston, which he could have sworn was in code – although this notion may have been put into his head by the security restriction stamped on the docket. In any event, this scoop had been followed by a dry spell of several years, until at last he was called upon by Culture to translate a menu for an official function. How many people could there be in Moscow who knew what a madumbi casserole was? Then another drought. More recently the tempo had started picking up: he'd done several love letters full of double entendres and a set of instructions for assembling a Japanese exercise bicycle. There had also been poems by a Malawian dissident and the lyrics of a song by a band called the Dead Kennedys. But nothing had gripped his imagination like the letter he now carried over his heart.

It had washed up in his in-tray a week ago, and its contents struck him as so unlikely that at first he thought someone higher up was pulling his leg – probably that Kulyabin character in Housing. Just the day before, Kulyabin had made faces at him in the men's room and told him to keep his pecker up.

But the letter proved to be genuine. The chief confirmed it: the translation had been requisitioned by Foreign Economic Relations. Still Grekov wasn't convinced. He phoned the Ministry himself, on the pretext of finding out how urgently the translation was required, and got hold of a certain Christov, the aide whose signature was on a covering note pinned to the envelope. Christov was adamant: the letter had come all the way from the Republic of South Africa, signed, sealed and delivered. He hadn't actually opened it with his own two hands, but he had seen it done with his own two eyes. Grekov knew where South Africa was, of course? Of course.

As he neared the river, Grekov became anxious that he had somehow lost the letter, or left it at home, and he had to lean against the parapet and fumble it out of his pocket. The envelope was green and edged around with blue and orange chevrons, and it was grubby, as if it had been dropped on a dusty floor. In the top left-hand corner was a pale blue rectangle containing the phrases '*Per lugpos*', 'By airmail' and '*Par avion*' in a tidy stack, and beside it, in a smaller orange window, some sort of winged mythological creature, a crude representation of Pegasus, perhaps, or a griffin with a human face. In the right-hand corner were three stamps, crookedly affixed: the largest, apparently the most valuable, depicted a pastoral scene, with herds of fatted sheep and cattle grazing on fertile steppes; the smallest symbolized energy and industrial progress in a collage of cooling towers, dynamos and pylons; the other was a portrait of a man – a politician, he assumed, or a king. All three were shackled together by a postmark that read, *Pretoria – 6.01.92.*

The address was in blue ballpoint pen, in a hand that had something childishly precise about it. The letters were all flat-footed, as if the writer had ruled lines in pencil to guide him and rubbed them out afterwards. The wording itself suggested a touching faith in the reliability of the postal service. It read:

The Ministir of Foreign Affairs
PO Kremlin
Moscow
Russia ('USSR')

If he hadn't been wearing gloves, Grekov would probably have taken out the letter and read it for the hundredth time. Instead he held the envelope up to the light to see the rectangular silhouette of folded paper inside. He turned the envelope over. On the back, in pencil, he had jotted down Christov's telephone number. He had also taken down some directions given to him by an acquaintance in Roads and Pavements. He studied them now, plotting his course to the monument, and suddenly regretted that he had spoiled the envelope by scribbling on it. He put the letter away with a sigh and went along the embankment towards Borovitskaya Square.

The people he passed were like himself, bundled up in their own thoughts, and he saw nothing out of the ordinary until he reached the end of Prospekt Marksa, where a dozen middle-aged men – tourists, to judge by the primary colours of their anoraks – were standing together in a frozen clump gazing at the outside of the Lenin Library. He was struck firstly by the fact that they were all men, and then by the more remarkable fact that every last one of them wore spectacles.

He went up Prospekt Kalinina, looking out for the park that was his landmark, and when he found it turned left into a side street. He became aware of a high-pitched buzzing in the distance, like a dentist's drill, and felt reassured that he was going in the right direction. In the middle of the next block he came to an even narrower street, a cul-de-sac called Bulkin, and at the end of that was the nameless square that was his destination.

The square at the dead end of Bulkin Street was surrounded by apartment blocks. In the middle of the cobbled space, on an imposing pedestal, was a large stone head. Not just any old head – a head of Lenin. And not just any old head of Lenin either. According to Roads and Pavements it was the largest head of Lenin in the city of Moscow. If Roads and Pavements were correct on that score, Grekov speculated, why should this not be the largest head of Lenin in Russia, or the broken-down Union, or even the whole out-of-order world?

The eyes in the head of Lenin looked straight at Grekov.

On this particular afternoon, as expected, two workers in overalls were standing on Lenin's bald pate, one wielding a noisy pneumatic drill and the other a gigantic iron clamp. A ladder rested against the cliff of a cheek, and at its foot a third worker was lounging against the pedestal. A lorry surmounted by a crane, and braced at each corner by a huge hydraulic leg with an orthopaedic boot on the end of it, stood to one side. Grekov judged that he was in good time, and so he crossed to the opposite pavement, which had been shovelled more recently, slowed his steps and strolled on at a leisurely pace, his usual one, enjoying the progressive revelation of detail.

Naturally, the stone head loomed larger the closer he got. The features, at first indistinct, now clarified themselves. The eyes were still looking straight at him, even though he had changed pavements. On a smaller scale this phenomenon might have qualified as a miracle; on this scale it was undoubtedly a question of perspective. They were kindly eyes, if not quite grandfatherly, then more than avuncular; but as the mouth came into focus, beneath the sculpted wings of the moustache, the whole face changed; it became severe and irritable; it took on the cross expression of a bachelor uncle who didn't like children. And then, quite unaccountably, as he came closer still, the face foreshortened into friendliness again.

The workers clambering about up there made the monument seem even more colossal than it was, and Grekov couldn't help but admire their gleeful daring and lack of decorum. The one with the drill was skating round on the great man's icy dome like a seasoned performer, and even as Grekov watched, the skater's companion, the one with the clamp, slid audaciously down the curvature of the skull, unloosing a shower of scurfy snow from the fringe of hair, and found a foothold on one of the ears.

Along one side of the square stood a row of empty benches, five in all, and Grekov made his way there. With a characteristic sense of symmetry he chose the one in the middle, wiped the slush off it with his cuff and sat down, tucking his coat-tails underneath him. He gazed about the square. Two little boys had climbed up on the lorry and were using the crane as a jungle gym, dodging the snowballs thrown by their earthbound companions. The yells of the children clanked like chains against the frozen facades overlooking the square. There were a few smudged faces at peepholes in the misty windows, but apart from the workers, who presumably had no option, Grekov was the only grown-up who had ventured out to watch this monumental lump of history toppled from its pedestal. The workers themselves, in their oversized mufflers and mittens and boots, looked to him like children dressed up in their parents' cast-offs.

How soon people become bored with the making and unmaking of history, Grekov thought, remembering the hundreds of thousands who had taken to the streets to watch the first monuments fall. Looking about at the empty square, becoming conscious of his singularity, he felt an uncomfortable sense of complicity with the overalled figures and their vandalizing equipment.

The driller finished his trepanation and called for an eye. This turned out to be a huge metal loop with a threaded shaft. It was toted up the ladder by the lounger from below, and the same man brought down the drill. The man balancing on the ear secured the eye with the clamp and screwed it into place. Three similar eyes already protruded from the skull, and the fourth completed the all-seeing square. The man with the clamp now climbed down, leaving the driller alone on the summit with his hands on his hips and his nose in the air, like a hunter dwarfed by his trophy.

The clamp, lobbed carelessly onto the back of the lorry, woke up the crane operator, who had been dozing unseen in his cubicle. Under the clamper's directions the operator began to move the boom of the crane so that its dangling chains and hooks could be secured to the eyes.

The lounger, still carrying the drill, shooed the children away to the other side of the square and then came and sat on the bench next to Grekov, who at once tried to strike up a conversation.

'Another one bites the dust,' he said cheerfully.

'Seven this month,' came the gruff reply.

'You don't say! Where do you put them all?'

'Scrap heap . . . of history.'

'No, seriously,' Grekov insisted, and demonstrated his good faith by taking off one glove and offering a cigarette, which was gladly accepted. 'What happens to them? I'm a student, you see. I'm making a study of monuments.'

'A man after my own heart,' said the worker, adopting a tone that was ingratiatingly earnest. 'Let's see now. First, the bronze ones. The bronze ones are melted down and reshaped into useful objects like door knockers and railings. Then the ones of stone: those are crushed into gravel and scattered on the paths in our public parks so that the citizens don't come a cropper. Now for the marble ones – not too many of those – and the ones of display-quality granite: the beautiful ones are sliced up for tombstones and carved into monuments of the new heroes – only smaller, of course, to accommodate the new noses and ears. But the ugly ones, like this one, have to be kept, or rather *preserved*, because they were made by famous artists long ago, whose names escape me for the moment, and they have to be cleaned up and put in museums. There's a heap of them at Vnukovo, behind the bus terminus.'

'At Vnukovo, you say.'

At that moment the crane's engines began to roar and drowned out the conversation.

The head wouldn't budge. The chains sang like rubber bands and the lorry rocked on its hydraulic legs, but the bone and sinew of that stubborn neck held fast. The pedestal shivered. Then there was a crack like a whiplash, a ruff of white dust burst from under the jawbone, and the head tore loose and bobbed wildly at the end of the chains. It was so startling to see this gigantic object bouncing playfully on the air, like a child's ball, while the lorry swayed perilously on its legs, that Grekov recoiled in fright.

The head was lowered onto the lorry and secured with a multitude of cables. It was made to look backwards, but whether by accident or design Grekov could not tell. A fifth worker, who had been sleeping in the cab, now came to life and drove the lorry away down Bulkin Street. His comrades posed on the rigging around the head like revellers on a Mardi Gras float. One of them had his foot propped in a dilated nostril; another scratched his back on the tip of a moustache. But despite all these little distractions, these buzzing flies, the eyes gazed back unflinchingly, and there was such a forbidding set to the bottom lip that Grekov took his hands out of his pockets and stood up. The lorry turned right at the end of the street and at last the stony gaze was broken.

The children had gone indoors, the watchers had withdrawn from the windows, and the peepholes had misted over again. Grekov was alone. He went to the pedestal and walked round it in both directions. There was no inscription. A single thread of iron, a severed spine twisting from the concrete, marked the spot where the head had stood. The head of Lenin. It was hard to imagine something else in its place. But that's the one certainty we have, he thought. There will be something in its place.

He sat down with his back against the pedestal and took the letter out of his pocket. He examined the winged beast again and failed to identify it. Then he took off his gloves, opened the envelope and spread flat the sheet of white paper it contained. Although Grekov had almost forgotten the fact, this was not the original letter, but a version of it twice removed. He had dared to keep the envelope, but keeping the letter itself had been impossible. Instead he had made a copy of the letter in his own hand, and this was a carbon copy of that. The original English was there, word for word, but there were also notes of his own, in parentheses and footnotes – guesses at meanings, useful turns of phrase culled from memory and the dictionary, corrections of spelling mistakes. This was a translation method he had devised himself, in the absence of tape recorders and word processors, and although it was primitive, he was proud of it.

There were also speculations – contained in a series of marginal notes and questions – that exceeded the bounds of his responsibilities as a translator and partly explained why the seat of his trousers was stuck to the plinth of an empty pedestal in a public square on a Sunday afternoon: who is this man Khumalo? Is he serious? What does he really want? Will he get it? Who will help him? Me (of all people)?

Grekov read the letter through again, although he practically knew it by heart. In a dimple in the middle of the sheet his eye came to a tight spring of black hair. It was in fact a hair from Boniface Khumalo's head, which Grekov's brisk walk had dislodged from a corner of the envelope and shaken into the folded sheet. But Grekov, understandably, failed to recognize it. He blew it into space in a cloud of steam.

II

Khumalo to the Ministir

(with selected notes by P. Grekov)

'Boniface Tavern'
PO Box 7350
Atteridgeville 0008
Tvl [Transvaal – peruse map]
5th Jan[uary] 1992

TO WHO[M] IT MAY CONCERN

Re: SURPLUS STATUES [in the matter of/concerning]

I am greeting you in the name of struggling masses of South Africa, comrades, freedom fighters, former journeymen to Moscow – you may know some . . . [Never met a military trainee, but believe they existed.] Also in the name of boergious countrymen known up and down [business 'contacts'? class alliances?] here at home. I myself am very much struggle [struggling – infamous Apartheid].

My particular personality is illustrious. I am doing many things well: initially gardening assistance, packer O.K. Bazaars [so-called 'baas'], garage attendance, petroljoggie [prob. brand-name cf. Texaco], currently taverner and taxi-owner, 1 X Toyota Hi-Ace 2.2 GLX (1989) [Japanese motor vehicle] so far – 'See me now, see me no more'. But especially now I am going on as Proprietor (Limited) Boniface Tavern, address above-mentioned, soon revamped as V.I. Lenin Bar & Grill. This is my very serious plan. You must believe it!

Hence it is I am taking up space to search out whether spare statues of V.I. Lenin are made available to donate me or if necessary I would be obliged to purchase on the most favourable terms (lay-by). [In a nutshell: his overweening desire is to buy a statue of Lenin. One can't help but bravo.] Please state prefference [one f], down payment, interest rates, postage, etc. etc.

Apartheid is crumpling as you know. Recently you visited a New South Africa to espy trade opportunities. [Trade Missionary to SA – check w. Grigoriev.] Here is one! I mean business! Fantastical benefits may amount to all of us. V.I. Lenin Bar & Grill is opening (1 May for publicity stunts) with unheard parties and festivities, free booze, braaid sheep [barbecued mutton], cows [beef], chipniks [prostitutes], members of the medias (TV 2 and 3, Mnet [!]), Lucky Dube [sweepstake?], Small Business Development Corporation (SDBC) [Grig.?], wide-scale representatives from organizations (SACP, ANC, PAC, ACA, FAWU, MAWU, BAWU, etc. etc.). [Check.] It will be a big splash [make a splash – attract much attention] for tourism and international relations.

As far as I'm concerned nothing can prevent my request to pass. I have pedestals galore and many other statues to compliment my favourite V.I. Lenin. Also recognition to be attached viz. [videlicet: namely] 'This Beautiful Monument was donated to Working People of Atteridgeville by Kind Masses of Russia, unveiled 1 May 1992 (is there time?) by Jay Naidoo (for example).'

After three weeks and no reply has forthcome I'll write again, not meaning to plead to you.

Amandla! [*Interj.* Power! Usually *A. ngawetu*]

Yours faithfully,

Boniface Khumalo
Proprietor (Ltd)

PS If you are not the right person please forward this letter to the same. Thank you.
PSS Toyota 10-seater is blood-red. MVM325T. Thanks.

III

Lunacharski and Lenin

(an offcut)

and in 1918 *Proletkult* declared that the proletariat should assimilate existing bourgeois culture and 'recast the material in the crucible of its own class-consciousness'.[6] Lunacharski himself argued against gimmicky experimentation: 'The independence of proletarian art does not consist in artificial originality but presupposes an acquaintance with all the fruits of the preceding culture.'[7] We may assume that as Commissar of Enlightenment – he had become head of the People's Commissariat for Education and the Arts (NARKOMPROS) in 1917 – Lunacharski knew only too well that experimental work would be incomprehensible to the illiterate masses. In the coming years Lunacharski and Lenin would clash over the position of *Proletkult*, with Lenin trying to subordinate it to NARKOMPROS and the Party, and Lunacharski arguing for a measure of independence.

These differences notwithstanding, Lunacharski looked back on the immediate post-revolutionary years with some nostalgia. In 1933, the year of his death, he recalled Lenin's scheme for 'Propaganda by Monuments' and sought to revive it. His reminiscences tell us something about the complex relationship between the two men and the vexed question of the role of art in the revolution.

Lenin's taste in art was conventional; he was fiercely opposed to the avant-garde, especially to futurism. Lunacharski recalled an episode during the 1905 revolution when Lenin passed the night in the house of Comrade D.I. Leshenko. Here he came across a set of Hermann Knackfuss's books on great artists and spent the night paging through them. The next morning he told Lunacharski how sorry he was that he had never had time to occupy himself with art. 'What an attractive field the history of art is. How much work there for a communist.'[8]

How did 'Propaganda by Monuments' come about? According to
Lunacharski, the idea was sparked off by the frescos in Campanella's
La Città del Sole (_The City of the Sun_). In the Utopian state depicted in
this work, frescos were used to educate the young. Lenin, mindful of
the straitened circumstances in which many of the artists of Moscow
and Petrograd found themselves (the latter would be renamed
Leningrad only in 1924), but mindful too that frescos would hardly
suit the Russian climate, proposed that artists be commissioned to
sculpt 'concise, trenchant inscriptions showing the more lasting,
fundamental principles and slogans of Marxism'[9] on the city walls
and on specially erected pediments, in place of advertisements and
posters.

'Please don't think I have my heart set on marble, granite and gold
lettering,' Lenin went on (in Lunacharski's reconstruction of their
dialogue). 'We must be modest for the present. Let it be concrete with
clear, legible inscriptions. I am not at the moment thinking of anything
permanent or even long-lasting. Let it even be of a temporary nature.'

'It's a wonderful idea,' Lunacharski said, 'but surely what you
propose is work for a monumental mason. Our artists will become
bored if they have to spend their days carving inscriptions. You know
how they lust after novelty.'

'Well, it happens that I consider monuments even more important
than inscriptions: I mean busts, full-length figures, perhaps – what do
you call them? – bas-reliefs, groups. And let's not forget heads.'

Lenin proposed that a list of the forerunners of Socialism, revolu-
tionists and other heroes of culture be drawn up, from which suitable
works in plaster and concrete could be commissioned.

It is important that these works should be intelligible to the masses,
that they should catch the eye. It is also important that they should
be designed to withstand our climate, at least to some extent, that
they should not be easily marred by wind, rain and frost. Of course,

inscriptions on the pedestals of monuments could be made – if such trifles are beneath your artists, perhaps the stonemasons will oblige us – explaining who the man was and so forth.

Particular attention should be paid to the ceremonies of unveiling such monuments. In this we ourselves and other Party members could help; perhaps also prominent specialists could be invited to speak on such occasions. Every such unveiling ceremony should be a little holiday and an occasion for propaganda. On anniversary dates mention of the given great man could be repeated, always, of course, showing his connection with our revolution and its problems.[10]

Lunacharski was consumed with the idea and immediately set about putting it into practice. Some inscriptions were set up on buildings, and quite a few monuments by sculptors in Moscow and Petrograd were erected. Not all the monuments were successful. Some of them broke. Perhaps the artists had misjudged the climate after all. A full figure of Marx by Matveyev cracked in half and was replaced by a less impressive bronze head. Other monuments were simply too ugly, and here the artists were definitely at fault. Moscow's statue of Marx and Lenin in 'some sort of basin'[11] was the most notorious failure. The citizens dubbed it 'the whiskered bathers' or 'Cyril and Methodius', because it made Marx and Lenin look like a pair of brotherly saints emerging from a bathtub.

The modernists and futurists ran amok. Korolev's statue of Bakunin was so hideous that horses shied when they passed it, even though it was hidden behind boards. It proved to be 'of a temporary nature'. No sooner had the statue been unveiled than the anarchists, incensed by its depiction of their hero, smashed it to pieces.

But although the manufacture of monuments left much to be desired, 'the unveiling of monuments went on much better'.[12] Taking to heart Lenin's suggestion that 'we ourselves could help', Lunacharski himself unveiled a string of monuments.

A contest was organized to choose a design for a statue of Marx, and both Lunacharski and Lenin participated enthusiastically in the judging. A well-known sculptor proposed a statue of Marx standing somewhat acrobatically on four elephants, but it was rejected – after personal adjudication by Lenin – as inappropriate. In the end a rather splendid design by a collective, working under the guidance of Aleshin, was chosen. It showed Marx with his feet firmly on the ground and his hands behind his back. The group built a small model of the statue in Sverdlov Square in time for that year's May Day celebrations, and Lenin approved of it although he did not think it a good likeness. The hair in particular was not very well done, and Lunacharski was asked to tell the artist to 'make the hair more nearly right'.[13] The torso was also too stout: Marx seemed about to burst the buttons of his coat, and some subtle tailoring was called for. Later Lenin officiated at a ceremony in the square to 'place the podium'[14] and made a remarkable speech on Marx and his 'flaming spirit'[15] – but the statue was never erected.

Lenin was disappointed by the quality of the monuments erected in Moscow, and not reassured to hear from Lunacharski that those in Petrograd were better. 'Anatoli Vassilievich,' he said sadly, shaking his head, 'have the gifted ones all gathered in Petrograd and the hacks remained here with us?'

And so 'Propaganda by Monuments' petered out.

A decade later, when Lunacharski tried to revive the scheme, he used Lenin's own words (although he closed his ears to the echo):

For the time being, I do not expect marble and granite, gold letter-ing and bronze – so appropriate to socialist style and culture. It is too early as yet for this – but, it seems to me, a second wave of propaganda by monuments, more lasting and more mature, also more effective for being enriched by the vital human element of sculpture, understood in the broadest terms could be instituted by

IV

Christov to Khumalo

(translated and annotated by P. Grekov)

> Ministry of Foreign
> Economic Relations
> 32/34 Smolenskaya Sennaya
> Moscow 121200
> 28 January 1992

My dear Mr B. Khumalo,

It is with rather a great deal of pleasure that I pen this missive, reactionary to yours of the 5th inst.

Some weeks may have passed, indeed, as your request flew from subtropical Pretoria, administrative capital of the Republic of South Africa, to our correspondent temperate urbanity, and henceforward overland to various ministries and departments, videlicet Foreign Affairs – to whom it had been addressed on the bottom line, so to speak – Trade, Tourism, Defence and Foreign Economic Relations, where it still resides and from whence this missive now therefore emanates. I am a member of the same ministry, sad to say in a somewhat subsidiary position (Protocol Department), but nevertheless by good fortune required to acknowledge the landing of your letter of the 5th inst. [I, contrarily, am a respected colleague of Everyday Services Department, City of Moscow, which we write 'Mockba'. – Tr.]

I am instructed to inform you that your letter is receiving considerate attention at many and various levels, local and national/ international. Soon we will pen additional missives to impart the final decision-making process and details.

[Feeling overwhelmingly cocksure that your request re: SURPLUS STATUE will meet with a big okey-dokey fairly forthwith, I make bold to expand the range and scope of the instructions by informing, firstly, that the surplus statue videlicet 'Head of V.I. Lenin' that is in mind for despatch to you is somewhat a national treasure. Materially it is stone. Proportionally it is large, without laying it on thick one says 'colossal', being by estimation 7 (seven) metres high, chin to crown, and 17 (seventeen) metres in circumference, at hat-brim level (but has no hat). Imperial equivalences for convenience: 23 feet by 56 feet approx. Will this serve? It will necessitate Herculean efforts in the transportation, but well worth it.

On a new thread. What is doing in the Transvaal? Do the cows and sheep graze on the veldt nearby free from harm? Much has been said and supposed vis-à-vis socio-political machinations of reformism in your motherland of which I am always an amateur or eager beaver as they say. But the horse's mouth is what you are. Your tidings have captivated me boots and all. Please correspond. – Tr.]

We look forward to hearing from you in the near future. [And who knows how long ago hence we may eat beefsteaks and drink vodkas – our patriotic highball – in V.I. Lenin Bar & Grill of Atteridgeville! – Tr. Tr. is for 'Translator', being me, Pavel Grekov, same as below.]

Yours faithfully,

A. Christov
Tr: P. Grekov

Postscript: please correspond to me personally at 63–20 Tischenko Str., Apt #93, Moscow 109172. No doubt it will suffice. Conclusively, do you question why the monuments, large and small, have no hats? The head of Lenin in history was fond of hats, precisely caps.

V
Khumalo

Boniface Khumalo put the letter in the cubbyhole along with the tub of Wet Ones. On second thoughts he took it out again and slipped it under the rubber mat on the passenger side. Then he caught his own furtive eye in the rear-view mirror and asked himself why he was playing postman's knock. There was nothing compromising about the letter. The Total Onslaught was over, even if a stale scent of danger still wafted from the exotic landscapes of postage stamps and the unexpected angles of mirror-script print. He retrieved the envelope again and put it in the pocket of his jacket, which hung from a hook on the door pillar behind his seat.

That everyday action dispelled the threat and left nothing in the air but the caramel tang of new imitation leather and the cloying lavender of the Wet Ones with which he had just wiped his hands. He checked that his fly was buttoned. He checked that his door was locked. Then he looked out of the window at the drab veld of the valley dipping away from the road, straddled by electricity pylons with their stubby arms akimbo, and dotted with huge, floppy-leaved aloes like extravagant bows of green ribbon. On the far slope of the valley was a sub-economic housing complex, a Monopoly-board arrangement of small, plastered houses with corrugated-iron roofs, all of them built to exactly the same design. The planners of Van Riebeecksvlei had sought to introduce some variety into the suburb by rotating the plan of each successive house through ninety degrees, with the result that there were now four basic elevations that repeated themselves in an unvarying sequence down the long, straight streets.

Khumalo had driven past Van Riebeecksvlei on his way to Pretoria a thousand times. But he was struck now, for the first time, by the fact that he could tell at a glance it was a white suburb, even though there wasn't a white face in sight. Was it because the walls of the houses were pastel plaster rather than raw face-brick? Or precisely because there was no one to be seen? Even at this distance it looked like a ghost town. Where was everybody? He thought of the stream of people that flowed up 5th Street from the taxi rank and cast his regulars up on his doorstep.

Khumalo buckled his seat belt. He tweaked the ignition key and the engine sprang to life. He goaded all six cylinders with petrol and then let them idle. The advertising was getting to him: he could almost hear the engine panting.

He gentled the car over the ruts at the edge of the tar and accelerated, watching the rev-counter. It was a Sunday afternoon and there was not much traffic. He flew past a bakkie laden with crates of vegetables and a minibus called 'Many Rivers to Cross', one of Mazibuko's. The car practically drove itself, as he liked to tell his envious friends, just the way the tavern ran itself and the taxi paid for itself. One of these days I'll retire, he said, because there won't be anything left for me to do. Made redundant by progress.

The Boniface Tavern was Khumalo's pride and joy. He had started the shebeen ten years earlier in his garage, adding on a room here and a room there until it was larger than the house itself. The 'tavern' of the title had been prompted by the medieval ring of his own first name – his late mother had named him for St Boniface, English missionary among the Germans, martyred in 755 at the ripe old age of eighty.

The Boniface Tavern had certainly been unusual in its day, but lately all licensed shebeens were being called taverns. 'I was ten years ahead of my time,' he would boast to his patrons. 'I was a taverner long before the Taverners' Association came along.' Secretly, the change made him unhappy. Now that every Tom, Dick and Harry had a tavern, the Boniface Tavern lost its special flavour. He began casting around for an alternative.

A new decade dawned. On the day Nelson Mandela walked from the shadows into the glare of daily news, Khumalo decided that his establishment needed more than a change of name to face the future in; it needed a change of clothes. It happened that the taxi he'd acquired a few months before was proving to be lucrative, and he was confident that he would soon be in a position to finance the new wardrobe.

The style he settled on had a touch of the 'taverna' about it: he wanted red plush, wrought iron, vine leaves, lashings of white plaster and crowds of venerable statuary. He saw the very thing in Nero's Palace, a coffee shop in the Union Hotel, and that became the model. He made a few enquiries about Nero's decor, and one Saturday afternoon went out to Hyperplant in Benoni, a nursery that specialized in garden statues. It was expensive – a common-or-garden gnome would set you back forty-four rand – but he came away with two disarmed goddesses, several cement amphorae with cherubim and seraphim in relief upon them, sufficient numbers of caryatids and atlantes to prop up a canvas awning over the courtyard, and a bench with mermaid armrests. He stockpiled his purchases in the backyard, where the elements could age them while his funds recuperated.

So far so good, except that the new name continued to elude him. He thought of exploiting the obvious political angle by honouring a popular leader. But in this capricious epoch how could you tell who would be popular in the new year? In any case, the old guard was getting on. The way of all flesh was fleeting, whereas decor had to last. He looked further afield: the Richelieu? Never mind the Napoleon! He was still undecided when a new possibility bobbed up unexpectedly in the pages of the *Pretoria News*.

One evening he read on page two that the Moscow City Council, in concrete expression of their commitment to the reforms sweeping through the Soviet Union, had decided to take down sixty-two of the sixty-eight statues and other memorial structures in the capital devoted to V.I. Lenin. 'All Lenin memorials in schools and other institutions for children also will be removed,' the report concluded. What other institutions for children are there? he wondered. Orphanages?

Hospitals? Reformatories? And then he thought further: what will become of all those statues? I could make good use of a couple myself, to string some coloured lights from.

That's probably as far as the fancy would have gone, had there not been a comment on the statues in the editorial column of that same newspaper. Although the tone was mocking – the simple act of giving 'Vladimir Illyich' in full was a sure sign of satirical intent – the idea struck a chord with Khumalo.

SURPLUS STATUES

Calling all enterprising businessmen! The import opportunity of a lifetime presents itself. The Moscow City Council has decided to dismantle the hundreds of monuments to Vladimir Illyich Lenin that grace its crowded public buildings and empty marketplaces. Cities throughout the crumbling Soviet Union will follow suit. We ask you: where else in the world is there a ready market for statues of Lenin but in South Africa? Jump right in before the local comrades snap them up for nothing.

Khumalo parked his car next to a building site in Prinsloo Street. An entire city block was being demolished, and all that remained of the high-rise buildings that had occupied the spot was one ruined single-storey facade with an incongruously shiny plate-glass window in it. It had once been Salon Chantelle, according to the sign. The departed proprietor had written a farewell message to her clients on the glass in shoe-white: *We apologize to all our ladies for the inconvenience caused by demolition. Please phone 646-4224 for our new location. Thank you for your continued support. XXXXX. C.*

Khumalo got out of the car. The building site looked as if it had been bombed, and the impression of a city under siege was borne out by the empty streets. He suddenly felt concerned for the welfare of his car. It only had 12,000 k's on the clock. Then he heard a metallic clang and traced it to an old man with a wheelbarrow scrounging among the collapsed walls. Perfect. He could keep an eye on the car. Khumalo called out to him, in several languages, but was ignored. In the end he had to go closer himself, through the gaping doorway of Salon Chantelle, stepping carefully over the broken masonry in his brown loafers.

The old man was salvaging unbroken bricks and tiles from the rubble.

'Greetings, Father,' Khumalo said.

The man glared at him suspiciously.

'What are you collecting there?'

It was obvious. The old man spat with surprising vehemence and accuracy in the dust at Khumalo's feet, picked up a brick with three round holes through it, knocked a scab of cement off it against the side of the barrow and dropped it on the pile.

'Are you building your own place?'

Another brick fell.

'Do you sell these things? I may have need of some building materials myself one of these days. Are you a builder?'

'This rubbish belongs to no one,' the old man finally said in a broken voice. 'It is just lying here. You can see it yourself.'

Khumalo gave him a one-rand coin and asked him to watch the car. He pocketed the money noncommittally, spat again with conviction and went back to work. Feeling as if he had been dismissed, Khumalo walked up Prinsloo Street towards the State Theatre.

At the Church Street intersection he waited for the robot to change even though there was no traffic. He looked right, and left, and right again towards Strijdom Square, and caught a glimpse of the dome like a swollen canvas sail over the head of J. G. Strijdom.

When the Strijdom monument was first unveiled, a story had gone round that its unconventional dome defied the laws of architecture, and therefore of nature. A group of city architects – the rivals whose tender had been rejected? – were so intrigued by it that they built a scale model in perfect detail out of chicken wire and plaster of Paris.

The model fell over. No matter how much they tinkered with it, it fell over.

The lights changed and Khumalo crossed the street with the same jaunty stride as the little green man.

J. G. Strijdom had been leader of the National Party in the 1950s and prime minister of the Union from 1954 to 1958. He was one of the great builders of apartheid. The details were on the pedestal. But though he had passed the monument often, Khumalo had never bothered to read what was written there. All he knew about Strijdom he had gleaned from the words of a popular political song. 'Sutha sutha wena Strijdom!' the song said. 'Give way, Strijdom! If you don't, this car, this car that has no wheels, will ride over you!' In Khumalo's mind Strijdom's face had never borne the serene, far-sighted expression he saw on it now, as the bronze head came into view over islands of greenery. Rather, it had a look of stupefied terror. It was the face of a slow-footed pedestrian, a moment away from impact and extinction, gaping at the juggernaut of history bearing down on him. *This* Strijdom is *that* Strijdom, Khumalo thought with a smile. As secure on his pedestal as a head on its shoulders.

In front of the monument, where one corner of the billowing dome was tacked to the ground, was a fountain: a thick white column rose from the middle of a pond and on top of it were four galloping horses, their hooves striking sparks from the air, their manes and tails flying. Usually jets of water spurted up from the pond and played against the column, but today they were still. Some crooked scaffolding leaned against the yellowed stone, and the stench of stagnant water rose from the slimy moat at the column's base. Khumalo sat on the dry lip of the fountain and looked at the limp agapanthuses and the grey river stones embedded in cement on the bottom of the pond.

Then he looked at the head. His heart sank. According to his calculations, the head of V.I. Lenin promised to him in the letter from Grekov was at least three times larger than the head of J. G. Strijdom! The pedestal would hardly fit in his yard. Perhaps if he knocked down the outside toilet and the Zozo . . . but surely it would cost a fortune just to build a pedestal that size. And who would pay for the installation? What if he approached the SACP, or the Civic, or a consortium of local businessmen? Atteridgeville needs a tourist attraction, after all, something with historical value. I'll donate it to the community, he thought; they can put it up on that empty plot by the police station. My name can go on the plaque. I'll unveil the bloody thing myself!

Still, it would be a pity to give it away, when *I've* gone to the effort to get hold of it. Has he promised it to me? I think he has . . . But who is this Grekov anyway? Can he be trusted? On whose behalf is he speaking? He doesn't sound like a very important person. Although he seems to know more than Christov, at any rate.

Khumalo shrugged off his jacket and took out Grekov's letter. He didn't think of it as Christov's letter, it had been so ruthlessly invaded and occupied by the translator. The fingerprint in ink from the typewriter ribbon, which was clearly visible in the top left-hand corner of the page, may have settled the question of authorship once and for all, had Khumalo been able to check it against flesh and blood.

He read the letter again. It had been typed on an old typewriter and all the loops of the letters were closed, like winking eyes. There were things he didn't understand. 'Colossal'? 'Please correspond'? He put the letter back in the envelope. The Cyrillic postmark read, *Mockba.*

For a reason he couldn't put his finger on, Khumalo felt better. He jumped up and paced out the dimensions of the pedestal. He multiplied them by three in his head and had to chuckle: the pedestal alone would be the size of a double garage! He studied the poetic verse inscribed on the salt-and-pepper stone but could not make head or tail of it. His Afrikaans had always been weak. He walked round the pedestal and at the back discovered two more inscriptions, twins, one in English and one in Afrikaans. He read the English version out loud in a cracked impersonation of the old scavenger.

The monument had been unveiled by Mrs Susan Strijdom on

Republic Day, 31 May 1972. The Honourable B. J. Vorster, then prime minister, had made a speech at the unveiling ceremony. The sculptor of the head of Strijdom was Coert Steynberg. The sculptor of the Freedom Symbol (the bolted horses) was Danie de Jager. With an admirable concern for fair play, the inscription went on to record the names of the architects of the unnatural dome (Hans Botha and Roelf Botha), the quantity surveyors (Grothaus and Du Plessis), the engineers (W. J. S. van Heerden and Partners, viz. Bruinette, Kruger, Stoffberg and Hugo), the electrical engineers (A. du Toit and Partners) and, with disappointing anonymity, the building contractors (Nasionale Groepsbou Korp.).

The sun was shining through the finely veined bronze ears of Johannes Gerhardus Strijdom.

Khumalo went and stood at a distance, upwind of the stinking Freedom Symbol, with his eyes half closed, squinting. And after a while he began to see how, but not necessarily why, the impossible came to pass.

MME ZITTA MENDÈS,
A LAST IMAGE

Alaa Al Aswany

Translated from the Arabic by Humphrey Davies

1961

On Sundays my father would take me with him to her house. The building, which was immensely tall, was situated halfway down Adly Street. The moment we went through the main door a waft of cool air would meet us. The lobby was of marble and spacious, the columns huge and round, and the giant Nubian doorkeeper would hurry ahead of us to call the lift, retiring, after my father had pressed a banknote into his hand, with fervent thanks. From that point on my father would wear a different face from the one I knew at home. At Tante Zitta's house, my father became gentle, courteous, playful, soft-spoken, tender, afire with emotion.

Written in French on the small brass plaque at the door of the apartment were the words *Mme Zitta Mendès*, and she would open the door to us herself, looking radiant with her limpid, fresh, white face, her petite nose, her full lips made up with crimson lipstick, her blue, wide and seemingly astonished eyes with their long, curling lashes, her smooth black hair that flowed over her shoulders, and the décolleté dress that revealed her ample chest and plump, creamy arms. Even her finger- and toenails were clean, elegant, carefully outlined and painted in shiny red.

I shall long retain in my memory the image of Zitta as she opened the door – the image of the 'other woman' enhanced by the aroma of sin, the svelte mistress who draws you into her secret, velvety world tinged with pleasure and temptation. Tante Zitta would receive me with warm kisses and hugs, saying over and over again in French, 'Welcome, young man!' while behind her would appear Antoine, her son, who was two years older than me – a slim, tall youth whose black hair covered the upper part of his brow and the freckles on whose face made him look like the boy in the French reading book we used at school.

Antoine rarely spoke or smiled. He would observe us – me and my father – with an anxious look and purse his lips, then make a sudden move, standing or going to his room. He always seemed to have something important on his mind that he was on the verge of declaring but which he'd shy away from at the last minute. Even when I was playing with him in his room, he would apply himself to the game in silence, as though performing a duty. (Just once, he stopped in the middle of the game and asked me all of a sudden, 'What does your father do?' I said, 'He's a lawyer,' and he responded quickly, 'My father's a big doctor in America, and when I'm older, I'm going to go there.' When I asked him disbelievingly, 'And leave your mum?' he gave me an odd look and said nothing.) Antoine's disconcerting, difficult nature made my father and I treat him with caution.

So there we would sit, all together in the parlour. My father and Tante Zitta would be trying to hold an intense conversation and Antoine would be his usual aloof self, but I'd be giving it all I had: I'd flirt with Tante Zitta and surrender to her kisses, her strong, titillating perfume, and the feel of her warm, smooth skin. I'd tell her about my school and make up fabulous heroic deeds that I'd performed with my fellow students and she'd pretend that she believed me and make a show of astonishment and fear that I might get hurt in the course of one of these amazing 'feats'.

I was very fond of Tante Zitta and colluded totally with my father when each time on the way back he'd impress on me that I shouldn't tell my mother. I'd nod my head like a real man who could be relied on, and when my mother, with her apprehensive, reluctant, alarming eyes, would ask me, I'd say, 'Father and I went to the cinema,' lying without either fear or the slightest sense of guilt or betrayal.

Zitta's magic world captivated me. I keep it in my heart. Even her apartment I can summon up in detail now as a model of ancient European elegance – the large mirror in the entrance and the curly wooden stand on which we would hang our coats, the round polished brass pots decorated with a lion's head on either side for the plants, the heavy, drawn curtains through which the subdued daylight filtered, the light-coloured patterned wallpaper and set of dark brown armchairs with olive-green slip covers, and, in the corner, the large black piano. (Zitta worked as a dancer at a nightclub on Elfi Street, which is where, I suppose, my father must have met her.)

Tante Zitta would go into the kitchen to get the food ready and my father would draw Antoine and me close and put his hands on us and talk to us like an affectionate father chatting with his sons during a moment of rest. From time to time he would shout out in mock complaint about how long the food was taking and Zitta would answer laughingly from the kitchen. (I now take these touches of domesticity as evidence that my father was thinking of marrying her.)

The luncheon table was a work of art – the shining white tablecloth, the napkins ironed and folded with offhand elegance, the polished white plates with the knives, forks and spoons laid round them in the same order. There would be a vase of roses, a jug of water, sparking glasses and a tall bottle lying on its side in a metal vessel filled with ice cubes. Tante Zitta's food was delicious and resembled that at the luxurious restaurants to which my father would occasionally take my mother and me. I would eat carefully and pretend to be full quickly, the way they'd taught me at home, so that no one might criticize me, but my father and Tante Zitta would be oblivious to everything, sitting next to one another, eating, drinking, whispering and constantly laughing. Then my father would urge her to sing. At first she would

refuse. Then she'd give in and sit down at the piano. Gradually
the smile would disappear and her face would take on a serious
expression as she ran her fingers over the keys and scattered, halting
tunes rose from the keyboard. At a certain point Zitta would bow her
head and close her eyes as though trying to capture a particular idea.
Then she would start to play. She would sing the songs of Edith Piaf
– 'Non, je ne regrette rien' and 'La vie en rose'.

She had a melodious voice with a melancholy duskiness to it, and
when she got to the end, she would remain for a few moments with
her head bowed and her eyes closed, pressing on the keys with her
fingers. I would clap enthusiastically and Antoine would remain
silent, but my father's excitement would know no bounds. By this
time he would have taken off his jacket and loosened his tie, and he
would clap and shout, 'Bravo!' – hurrying to her side and planting
a kiss on her forehead, or taking her hands in his and kissing them.
Experience had taught us that this was a signal for me and Antoine
to leave. Antoine would get up first, saying as he moved towards the
door of the apartment, 'Mama, we'll go outside and play.' I can see
now – with understanding and a smile – the face of my father, flushed
with drink, alight with desire, as he searched impatiently through
his pockets, then presented me and Antoine with two whole pounds,
saying, as he waved us towards the door, 'Tell you what, how about
some ice cream at New Kursaal after you've finished playing?'

1996

The foreigners' table at Groppi's. All of them are old – Armenians
and Greeks who have spent their lives in Egypt and kept going until
they are completely alone. Their weekly date is at seven on Sunday
mornings, and when they cross empty Talaat Harb Street, walking
with slow, feeble steps, either propping one another up or supporting
themselves on their walking sticks, they look as though they had just
risen from the dead, brushed off the grave dust and come.

In Groppi's they sit at one table, which never changes, next to the window. There they eat breakfast, converse and read the French newspapers until the time comes for Sunday Mass, when they set off together for church.

That morning they were all in their best get-up. The old men had shaved carefully, polished their two-tone English shoes and put on their three-piece suits and old ties, though the latter were crumpled and crooked. They were wrapped in ancient, heavy overcoats whose colours had faded and which they removed the moment they entered the restaurant, as convention required.

The old women, those once skittish charmers, were wearing clothes that had been in fashion thirty years ago and had powdered their wrinkled faces, but the old men without exception were careful to observe the rules of etiquette, standing back to allow them to go first, helping them to remove their coats and to fold them neatly and carefully, and pulling out chairs so that they could sit down, after which they would compete at telling them curious and amusing anecdotes. Nor had the women forgotten how to let out oohs and aahs of astonishment and gentle, delicate laughs.

For these old people, the Sunday table is a moment of happiness, after which they surrender once more to their total and terrifying solitude. All they have left is likely to be a large apartment in the middle of the city, coveted by the landlord and the neighbours. The rooms are spacious, the ceilings high and the furniture ancient and neglected, with worn upholstery; the paint on the walls is peeling and the bathroom, of old-fashioned design, is in need of renovation, the budget for which remains for ever out of reach; and memories – and only memories – inhabit every corner, in the form of beloved black-and-white photographs of children (Jack, Elena) laughing charmingly, children who are now old men and mature women who have emigrated to America, speak on the telephone at Christmas and send tasteful coloured postcards, as well as monthly money orders, which the old people spend a whole day standing in long, slow queues to collect, counting the banknotes twice, just to be sure, once they have finally cashed them, and folding them and shoving them well down into their inside pockets.

Despite their age, their minds retain an amazing capacity to recall the past with total clarity, while inside themselves they harbour the certainty of an impending end, always accompanied by the questions 'When?' and 'How?' They hope that the journey will end calmly and respectably, but terrifying apprehensions of being murdered during a robbery, of a long, painful illness or of a sudden death on the street or in a café haunt them.

That particular morning I noticed something familiar about the face of one of the old ladies. She was sitting among the old people, her face embellished with a heavy coating of powder, and on her head was a green felt hat decorated with a rose made of red cloth. I went on watching her and when I heard her voice, I was sure. It must have looked strange – a staid man in his forties rushing forward and bending over her table. I addressed her impatiently. 'Tante Zitta?'

Slowly she raised her head towards me. Her eyes were old now and clouded with cataracts, and the cheap glasses she wore were slightly askew, giving the impression that she was looking at something behind me. I reminded her who I was, spoke to her warmly of the old days and asked after Antoine. She listened to me in silence with a slight, neutral smile on her old face and for so long that I thought I might have made a mistake, or that she had completely lost her wits. A moment passed and then I found her pushing herself up with her hands on the table, rising slowly until she was upright and stretching out her arms, from which the sleeves of her dress fell back to reveal their extreme emaciation. Then Tante Zitta drew my head towards her and reached up to plant on it a kiss.

AN UNEXPECTED DEATH

Ungulani Ba Ka Khosa

Translated from the Portugese by Stefan Tobler

They shook him so insistently that his beer sloshed and rose up in a wave that bubbled and spilled over the rim of his glass. Before he turned his head, the watchman could see the beer slide over his black hand like the waters of the sea flowing over a black promontory whose rugged outcrops had long ago been worn away, and drip down the bar, streaming in various directions, like water that spreads over flat lands.

'What happened?' the watchman asked.

'A man died in the building,' the two boys who had been shaking him said at the same time, still gasping for breath.

'And what's it to me?'

'His head got jammed under the service lift.'

'Fuck!'

He put down his beer and walked away from the bar. He wiped his lips and straightened his old jacket, a gift from an elderly lady desperate to forget the husband still robbing her of sleep, who in death threatened her as gravely as he had when he pronounced his macabre sentence on the point of dying, so long ago now, shot by a capricious bullet that had been hiding away in the gun he decided to clean after years of neglect, recalling as he did the beautiful campaigns to pacify the blacks, who in despair threw their bows, arrows and skin shields into the air in outlandish and sometimes phantasmagorical arcs as they, incredulous that this death was striking them, scattered over the plain and made unintelligible guttural sounds.

The bullet had gone through the jacket between the lower right pocket and the buttonholes, penetrated his stomach, torn through his guts and exited his body, embedding itself in the tree he had been leaning on, while watching the river water lose itself in the bluish-green sea. His wife, her blonde hair a mess and her face bathed in tears, could only approach him slowly; his red bug eyes forcing her to do so. His lips gradually opened and she heard him say, in a voice as dry and hard as stone, the most macabre words that a man can say on the point of death: 'Note what I'm saying, woman. The day you dare to welcome another man between your thighs, I will strangle you with the same force I would use to crush a cockroach. You're mine, and you will be mine after my death!'

That was at the start of the century and she was eighteen. She was beautiful. Years later, after the menopause, when wrinkles covered her body like the larvae that dig into a putrefying body, and still afflicted by his evil prophecy, she resolved to give the jacket to the first person who passed in the street.

The watchman took the jacket and at night in his boxroom he repaired it, erasing for ever the curse, for that very same night the ill-omened old lady, who wanted to celebrate the end of her in-somnia, died in the middle of a meal, struck down by a heart attack, the wine spilling across the table, the chairs, the floor, climbing the walls in a pattern of non-existent weaving. The morsels of meat, bread and fruit floated on the rising wine and, like pestilential reptiles streaming from stagnant water, left the house by its doors and windows, as misshapen and soggy morsels. In the street, people's eyes popped out of their sockets and their mouths opened in astonishment at the sight of the remains of the lavish meal filling the front garden.

At that moment the watchman was enjoying the jacket, which was still in remarkably good condition, walking up and down in his little room and posing in front of an imaginary mirror.

Almost at the door, the watchman remembered that his glass was still half full. He went back and downed it in one.

'This time I'll lose my job,' he said, running his right hand through his hair.

'They've been looking for you for over half an hour.'

'But where the hell did that son of a bitch get the idea of putting his head through that little glassless window?'

'He's already dead.'

'You're right. Should speak well of the dead. Who is it?'

'Simbine.'

'Simbine?'

'Yes.'

'They used black magic on him,' he added, and quickened his step.

Little thinking that the lift was not coming because her son's head was jammed under it, an old lady started to climb the stairs, cursing under her breath the world and the men who made evil and unreliable machines. Reaching the third floor, she needed to rest. Her legs could not take the troublesome, painful climb. She cursed her son, who dared to live up in the sky, and sat down, only to get up again hurriedly; people were flooding down, talking and screaming like the cawing crows when they settled in the tops of the pine trees at the close of the day.

'What happened?'

'A man died.'

'On what floor?'

'On the tenth, lady,' and the two boys disappeared. And then others came, and there was more screaming. The old woman tried to launch herself upstairs, but her body was not willing. Instead of worrying where the tragedy had occurred, she had the sense to ask after her son, in the clear hope of not hearing his name. Reaching the fifth floor, after innumerable questions, someone told her, without the faintest idea that she was his mother. She could only sit down and cry. Her tears gushed from her hollow and tired eyes with such force that they reached her flaccid breasts within seconds and descended in continuous streams down her dress, soaking it until it stuck to her body.

A few minutes later, acting on the unfounded feeling that death had knocked at someone else's door, she set off up the stairs. However, like all mothers in shock at the misfortune of losing a child still in the prime of life, she remembered the day when she had dropped her hoe and on all fours had rushed home down the path, feeling her son moving inside her. The women chased after her and led her to the main hut. It was the start of a week of intense suffering. In terror and fear the old women had abandoned her after the first day, aware that the demon she was carrying would not be born, for after having been present at so many gruesome scenes, they had never experienced anything like this, with a woman who had started to howl like the dogs whose barking echoes ominously inside locked houses each night. The witchdoctor, called for the job, confessed after three days and three nights of intense work that he was unable to deliver her from the evil spirits that had taken possession of her. And her howls filled the days and nights until, on the seventh day, Simbine appeared between the thighs of his mother, who fainted the very moment she finished a scream that was so piercing that everyone around the house buried their hands and faces in the white sand, while others, who were further off, threw themselves into the mango trees in the yard.

'You'll die a terrible death, son,' she told her son years later, when he was already a teenager and refused to go to school, giving the same reasons his grandfather had given by a fire whose sparks shot up into a night sky full of stars, stating that black people had lived for centuries without quinine and books, that their vitality was passed down the generations and their history was alive in the fertile memory of the old people who had lived in these lands before men the colour of a skinned goat had come with the noise of their weapons, their tongue and their books.

'Times have changed, son.'

'The roots are still in the earth, Mum. Didn't you once teach me that the elephant doesn't forget its resting place?'

'You're right, but I also said that the only thing that doesn't end is a miracle. You have to go to school.'

'I'm not going, Mum. And don't forget that you only get a chicken from a chicken.'

'A drumhead has to be stretched, son.'

'Don't worry, Mum.'

He preferred to run through the green and endless bushes every morning and afternoon like a gazelle, scattering branches and twigs across the humid and dry ground, and to go deep into the high, green grasses, breathing in the clear air and listening to the unstaved sonatas played by the multicoloured birds who warbled away at the end of the afternoon, when the red sun burned the green crowns of the trees, which, whether tall or low, spread out as far as the eye could see. Or, with the frenzy of an animal, he would pull down the women who came back clean from the river, their breasts like green monkey oranges stuck to their little wet blouses, which did not reach over their navels, and would quickly pull off their kangas, revealing their naked bodies and the entrancing scent coming from their pubis. Then the snapping of branches and the death rattles from their bodies mingled with the birds' trilling to form an unheard harmony in the immense space. Shattered, their bodies still laid out on the grass, they felt night fall with its different rhythms and deeper music, which seemed to rise out of the entrails of the earth. It was the hour when souls awaken and roam between the houses, raising their malign and benign voices.

'This wild land is my world, Mum,' he said. 'It's my school.'

If Simbine had been clairvoyant, he would never have broken

his adolescent promise, because it was school, with its teachers and books, that brought about his death.

After saying goodbye to his three wives and the children, he left the flat at ten past six in the evening, holding his books at his side. Calling the lift, he realized that, as always, it was taking its time coming. He peered through the little round window, something he had never done before, and stuck his head through. The lift was coming down from the fifteenth floor at a sluggish pace. He called one of his sons. He gave him his books and, grasping the metal door firmly with his hands, tried to get his head out. Without success. The lift was still coming down. He tried to pull open the door. He had no luck. Death found him with his veins bulging in his hands and his arms tensed. He died in silence.

. Minutes later, when his wives saw him – standing up stiffly, his hands on the door and one of his sons tugging on his trousers, asking him to buy a toy that he had seen and dreamed of – they immediately fell into convulsive crying. Thinking that he was still alive, they pulled at his legs. They felt the cold skin of a corpse. They let go of his legs and embraced him, asking him to take them with him.

While they cried and the lift alarm rang out like the church bell on ill-fated days, astonished neighbours appeared like cockroaches from hidden corners. The hallway filled with voices and shouting. They called for the watchman. They looked for him. They did not find him. In the middle of the shouting and crying, one of the boys said, 'He must be drinking in one of those bars. I'll go and look,' he added, and off he went down the stairs, accompanied by a friend. Some floors further down they passed Simbine's mother, without knowing it was her.

The more the people screamed, the more the man in the lift pressed the alarm. The screams scared him so much that he imagined his own death, little thinking there was a corpse below his feet. When they rescued him hours later, he swore he would never set foot in the building again. His oath was unnecessary: he went mad after interminable nights of insomnia in which he was hounded by the sound of the alarm and the screams of men and women who, on the other side of metal walls, were shouting unintelligibly.

And all on account of the damn cigarette that he had wanted to buy from a friend of his, after a day at work when the idea of a cigarette had been so impossible to shake off that it had even entered his mouth and filled his lungs, exploding his thoracic cavity and blurring his sight, which was tired after searching the deaths pages in the paper, whose words had leaped and danced in front of his eyes like acrobats in full swing.

He was still smoking his first cigarette of the day when the lift ground to a halt on the tenth floor. He pressed the alarm. He pushed all the buttons. The lift did not budge. He put out his cigarette with his foot to free up both his hands. He started to shout. Fear had taken root deep in his flesh.

The watchman climbed the stairs, listening to the invective of the residents going the other way. His eyes were as red as they always had been since he started drinking to excess twenty-five years ago. He had hit the bottle when it was clear he would never marry, after the day he dared to insult a great-aunt in public, calling her a witch, and had then been unable to have sex. The jacket reached down to his knees. He kept the sleeves turned up so that his hands poked out. He did not say much when he was drunk, and as he was inebriated every day, he was a man of few words.

From the moment he left the bar, he was only thinking about his immediate dismissal. He had made the unpardonable mistake of not providing some relief to Simbine in his death. In his view, APIE was to blame, because he had told them long ago that they should put glass in the windows. And as for Simbine, no question about it – it was witchcraft. You couldn't live with three wives nowadays, he thought to himself. The three women had got fed up with their husband. It's impossible for three women like Simbine's wives to get on like friendly sisters. It was witchcraft. Something similar had happened to his cousin. His two wives had got on so well that one day the man, who was only twenty-five, had woken up with white hair and his skin all wrinkled, as if he were a man much older than fifty.

'It's witchcraft,' he murmured.

'It's not witchcraft; it's your negligence,' asserted a resident who was going down, unable to cope with seeing the death. The watchman looked at him but did not say anything.

Entering the hallway full of people and screams and whispering and crying, he had to move people aside to get through.

'We need to call the ambulance,' the watchman said, looking coldly at the corpse.

'You're right,' agreed some people.

Hounded by the alarm, which would not stop sounding, but filled the stairs and flats and the night dotted with stars, the watchman started to walk with his chameleon's gait up to the top floor, followed by a few of the men.

When the lift started its slow ascent, the corpse fell with a crash, like an old sack, onto its back in the hallway. His arms were folded and ended in hands whose fingers were curved like a raven's claws. The lower jaw jutted out, showing teeth covered in dried and drying blood, which ran in rivulets down the gaps between the teeth and flowed onto his lips like a river that flows to the sea down a number of branches. His face was taut and the eyes protruded enormously, hiding his eyelids. His pupils were covered in blood, which spilled over in threads that covered his face like some scarification carried out by a sadist.

The people surrounding the corpse were silent for some seconds, which turned into centuries, as they contemplated the death and the horror of it, until the wives' crying again filled the hallway. They were taken into the flat. The watchman asked for a kanga to cover the body. The paramedics appeared with their equipment. The wrinkled face, the popping-out eyes and the dried blood disappeared under the blue and black kanga. And elsewhere in this mass of cement, life flowed on, carrying death, and the moon rose, fragmented and luminous.

THE HOMECOMING

Milly Jafta

The bus came to a standstill and all the passengers spilled out as soon as they could. It was Friday, end of the week, end of the month, end of the year, and the trip from Windhoek to the north was hot and unending. Unlike previous times, I remained in my seat until the bus was empty. Then I gathered my belongings and moved to the door. Through the window I could see Maria scrambling to claim my two suitcases.

The heat of the late afternoon sun hit me as I alighted from the bus. The warmth outside was different from the human heat that I felt inside the bus. Now the smell of sweat and over-spiced fast food seemed like a distant memory. The welcome smell of meat overexposed to the sun filled my nostrils. I could even hear the buzzing of the metallic-green-coloured flies as they circled and landed on the meat hanging from the tree branches and the makeshift stalls. Circled and landed, circled and landed . . . Hawkers and buyers were busy closing the last deals of the day. The air was filled with expectancy.

Maria bent down and kissed me on the lips – a dry and unemotive gesture. She smiled, picked up the larger of the two suitcases and placed it on her head. Then she started walking ahead of me. I picked up the other case, placed it on my head and put both my hands in the small of my back to steady myself. Then I followed her. I looked at Maria's straight back, the proud way she held her head and the determination with which she walked. How beautiful is the unbroken human spirit. I tried desperately to think of something to say, but could not find the words. Thoughts were spinning in my head, but my mouth remained closed and empty. So we continued in silence, this stranger – my daughter – and I.

So this was it. My homecoming. What did I expect? The village to come out in celebration of a long-lost daughter who had come home? How long had it been? Forty years? It must have been about forty years. How I have lost track of the time. How could I be expected to keep track of the time, when I could only measure it against myself in a foreign land? When I planted seeds but never had the chance to see them grow, bore children but never watched them grow . . . when I had to make myself understood in a foreign tongue . . . had to learn how an electric kettle works, how and when to put the stove off, that doors are not opened to strangers, and that you do not greet everyone you meet with a handshake.

I tried not to look at the long, dusty road ahead of us. In any case there was nothing in particular to look at. Everything seemed barren and empty. No trees, no grass, just the sprawling brown and orange ground all around us. The last rays of the sun seemed to lighten it to a golden glow. I am sure this would make a beautiful colour picture: the two of us walking behind each other in the narrow path with my luggage on our heads, silhouetted against the setting sun. One December I saw a large picture like that, only it was of giraffe. I remember standing there, looking at it and for a moment longing to smell the fields after the rain. But I was in Swakopmund with my *miesies*[1] and her family as she needed the rest. It was holiday time, family time, but I was without my own family, just as I was for the rest of the year and for most of my adult life.

Now all that has changed. I am on my way home. I am walking the

---

[1] Mistress of a household.

same path as I walked many years ago. Only then I was seventeen and my eyes looked forward. A young girl has left and now – after forty years, three children and a couple of visits to the village – an old woman is on her way back home. An old woman who has her eyes fixed on the ground.

My daughter, the stranger, stopped suddenly, turned round and looked enquiringly at me. I realized that she must have been waiting for an answer or a reaction of some sort. I was so lost in my thoughts that I had no idea what she was waiting for. But then, I never had any idea what my children's actual needs were. In her calm voice she repeated the question, asking whether she was walking too fast for me. Oh dear God, what kindness. Someone was actually asking me whether I could keep up, not telling me to walk faster, to have no males in my room, to get up earlier, to pay more attention, to wash the dog . . . I was overcome. Tears filled my eyes. My throat tightened, but my spirit soared. The stranger, my daughter, took the case from her head and put it on the ground next to her. Then she helped me to take my case down from my head and placed it next to hers.

'Let us rest for a while,' she said gently. After we sat down on the cases next to each other, she said, 'It is so good to have you home.'

We sat there in complete silence, with only the sound of some crickets filling the air. I never felt more content, more at peace. I looked at the stranger and saw my daughter. Then I knew I had come home. I did matter. I was together with the fruit of my womb. I had grown fruit. I looked down at my wasted, abused body and thought of the earth from which such beautiful flowers burst forth.

'We must go now. Everybody is waiting for you,' Maria said, standing up. 'You walk in front. You set the pace; I will follow you.'

I walked ahead of Maria on the narrow path, my back straight and my eyes looking forward. I was in a hurry to reach home.

OXFORD, BLACK OXFORD

Dambudzo Marechera

A few rusty spears of sunlight had pierced through the overhead drizzling clouds. Behind the gloom of rain and mist, I could see a wizened but fearfully bloodshot sun. And everywhere, the sweet clangour of bells pushed in clear tones what secret rites had evolved with this city. Narrow cobbled streets, the ancient warren of diverse architecture all backed up into itself, with here, there and everywhere the massive masonry of college after college. Sudden and thrifty avenues winding past close-packed little shops. And the Bodleian, which American Margaret portrayed as an upside-down artichoke. The Cornmarket with its crowded pavements, its rebelliously glossy and supermarket look: did Zuleika Dobson ride past, her carriage horses striking up sparks from the flint of the road? Myth, illusion, reality were all consumed by the dull gold inwardness, narrowness, the sheer and brilliant impossibility of all as the raindrops splashed and the castanets of stray sunlight beams clapped against the slate roofs, walls and doorways. I walked slowly towards All Souls. My mind an essay to itself.

Drawing apart the curtains, opening the windows, to let in not the driving snow but the hail of memories. The reek and ruin of heat and mud huts through which a people of gnarled and knotty face could not even dream of education, good food, even dignity. Their lifetime was one long day of grim and degrading toil, unappeasable hunger whose child's eyes unflinchingly accused the adults of some gross betrayal. The foul smells of the pit latrines and the evil-sweet fumes of the ever-open beer halls, these infiltrated everything, from the smarter whitewashed hovels of the aspirant middle class to the wretched squalor of the tin and mud huts that slimily coiled and uncoiled together like hideous worms in a bottomless hell. And here I was in Oxford thinking of the castanets of stray sunlight, calmly going to my tutorial in All Souls.

A sudden downpour made me run the last few yards into All Souls. The bloodshot mind up there was now completely shrouded by the heavy clouds coming in from the east. Stephen was already waiting outside the tutorial room. I was shaking and brushing the rain from my clothes, stamping my feet on the faded mat. He smiled.

'Wretched weather,' he said.

'Stinking rain.'

'I hear you were sozzled last night. Had a brush with the porter.'

'As usual,' I said. 'But what brush? I can't remember a thing.'

'Thought you wouldn't, actually.' He leaned back against the wall, hands in his pockets, ankle over ankle. 'He caught you climbing back in. He's got a black eye to show for it.'

Shit. I had forgotten to check my mail. There was probably a summons to the dean in it. Not again, for Chrissake. But I said in an offhand way, 'Bloody uppity these porters, if you ask me. When a bloke is quietly sneaking back into his rooms, they make a fuss.'

'You weren't quietly sneaking back to your rooms. Apparently you were howling the "Hallelujah Chorus" and cursing some unfortunate called Margaret.'

He blinked, asked, 'Is she *the* Margaret in St Hilda's? Rumour, you know, about you and her whatsit.'

'Can't say, old man. I haven't the foggiest about last night,' I said ruefully. 'I managed to finish the bloody essay this morning. With a little help from Scotch, that funny malt we got at Smiley's.'

'Lethal concoction, that.'

I could see he still wanted to drive home his point. He did.

'I heard it's not the dean this time. It's the walrus himself who wants to see you. I'm wondering what you're doing here, actually.'

The warden. Damn it.

'The damn walrus can bloody sing while waiting.'

'Language, dear boy. Language.'

The language of power.

'Sod it. And sod Old English too,' I said briskly. Changing the subject. 'Have you done yours?'

'Yes and no. It's still under "Unfinished business".'

The white-hot bitch. He had never produced a single essay for all the tutorials we had had together. Nobody seemed to care. Certainly he himself did not give a fig. I sighed.

'So I'll still have to read mine yet again.'

'You'll have to do the honours, I'm afraid.'

'Yeah, honky. Sure. Why not?'

'West Indian lingo, isn't it?'

'No. I'm just dying for a drink.'

He produced his hip flask, a silver and leather thing. We drank.

'Rather good, what?'

'Quite, O shit, quite.'

'Always wanted to ask where you learned your English, old boy. Excellent. Even better than most of the natives in my own hedge. You know, Wales.'

'It's the national lingo in my country.'

'It is not bambazonka like Uganda?'

'Actually yes, your distant cousins are butchering the whole lot of us.'

'Mercenaries, eh. Sorry, old man. Money. Nothing personal.'

Before I could say anything, he went on casually, 'Here he comes.'

Dr Martins-Botha, in jeans and anorak, was stamping his boots on the mat and shaking the rain from his person, from his umbrella.

'Sorry I'm late. The traffic. Come in, come in.'

The book-lined shelves. The desk in the corner at the end. With nothing on it but a glass paperweight. And the three chairs close to the single-bar electric fire, which Dr Martins-Botha switched on as we sat down – 'Anywhere' – and began to arrange ourselves and our papers.

'Brr,' he said. 'Brr,' he repeated. And SNEEZED.

As he blew his nose and wiped his spectacles, he turned to Stephen.

'I got your note. It's all right. Hand it in sometime. Brr.' He turned to me. 'And how are you?'

I nodded as he had already turned back to Stephen.

'Had a good shoot?'

Stephen actually blushed with pride as he said, 'I bagged seven. Two are on the way to your house right now.'

'Ah, decent meal for once.'

He stared at the papers in his lap. As he did so, the telephone rang. 'Yes, speaking,' he said. He listened. Glanced at me. Frowned. 'Yes, he is here. I've just begun my tutorial.' He listened again, staring gas-fire eyes at me. 'Yes, I'll tell him.'

'Were you supposed to see your warden at nine o'clock?'

'First I've heard of it. You see, I did not check my mail. Survival instinct, I suppose.'

But the lame joke fell flat on its face. Its monkey face.

He blew, 'Brr, brr.' He said, 'You are to present yourself at his office as soon as this tutorial is over. It sounds very serious to me.'

'I honestly do not know what I am supposed to have done. I was drunk.'

Dr Martins-Botha whistled through his teeth.

'I have heard about your drinking. Have you tried the AA?'

'I do not think they are the answer.'

'They could be a step towards it.'

'Perhaps.'

He opened his mouth to shout something but stopped and shook out his papers. I was thinking how All Souls' Day is also Walpurgisnacht.

Just a fancy, but it made me shiver. Stephen was smiling behind a cupped hand. He suddenly winked. When I did not wink back, he exploded with laughter. The doctor, startled, looked up, stared hard at Stephen and grunted what to me sounded like a bad version of an ingratiating chuckle.

'Quite, ah quite. These things happen,' he said. Abruptly he turned to me. 'Begin.'

I picked up my essay from the floor and began to read. I was halfway through it when Dr Martins-Botha laughed quite scornfully. I stopped. I did not look up. I waited until he had finished. I was about to resume when he suddenly – or was it Stephen's voice? – said, 'Nothing personal, you know.'

That is when I looked up. Dr Martins-Botha's right hand was between Stephen's thighs. They were both looking at me. I will always remember their eyes.

'Shall I go on?' I asked.

The doctor nodded. Once more I began to read. I know my face was quite impassive, but behind it I knew my brains had been touched by a thin, slimy secret. It was as if an earwig was eating its way through my head. I finished reading. I felt very tired, very thirsty.

'That's it,' I said, and sank back into my chair.

'Well,' the doctor began, 'that's the best essay I've heard for years on the Gawain Poet. Have you any questions, Stephen?'

'It was brilliant. It quite settles everything,' Stephen said, smiling. Christ. They were actually mocking me.

I gathered up my papers, stuffed them into my battered briefcase and stood up.

'Yes,' the doctor said, 'there is nothing else to be said. That's all for this week, then. Ah, Stephen. I want your advice about something. Will you stay for a few minutes?'

'Of course.'

I do not know how I got there, but I suddenly found myself standing in front of a triple whisky in the Monk's Bar at the Mitre. I drank two of those before I began to feel who I was waiting for in there. Margaret. She came in about ten minutes later. Her left hand was in plaster. Something that had always been intact in my mind suddenly tore at the sight of the plaster. Soon she saw me; she blew a kiss and was almost running as she made her way towards my table.

At last something – not much – but something intensely personal was flying towards me like the flight of a burning sparrow.

YOU CAN'T GET LOST IN CAPE TOWN

Zoë Wicomb

In my right hand, resting on the base of my handbag, I clutch a brown leather purse. My knuckles ride to and fro, rubbing against the lining . . . surely cardboard . . . and I am surprised that the material has not revealed itself to me before. I have worn this bag for months. I would have said with a dismissive wave of the hand, 'Felt, that is what the base of this bag is lined with.'

Then Michael had said, 'It looks cheap, unsightly,' and lowering his voice to my look of surprise, 'Can't you tell?' But he was speaking of the exterior, the way it looks.

The purse fits neatly into the palm of my hand. A man's purse. The handbag gapes. With my elbow I press it against my hip, but that will not avert suspicion. The bus is moving fast, too fast, surely exceeding the speed limit, so that I bob on my seat and my grip on the purse tightens as the springs suck at my womb, slurping it down through the plush of the red upholstery. I press my buttocks into the seat to ease the discomfort.

I should count out the fare for the conductor. Perhaps not; he is still at the front of the bus. We are now travelling through Ronde-bosch, so that he will be fully occupied with white passengers at the front. Women with blue-rinsed heads tilted will go on telling their stories while fishing leisurely for their coins and just lengthen a vowel to tide over the moment of paying their fares.

'Don't be so anxious,' Michael said. 'It will be all right.' I withdrew the hand he tried to pat.

I have always been anxious and things are not all right; things may never be all right again. I must not cry. My eyes travel to and fro along the grooves of the floor. I do not look at the faces that surround me, but I believe that they are lifted speculatively at me. Is someone constructing a history for this hand resting foolishly in a gaping handbag? Do these faces expect me to whip out an amputated stump dripping with blood? Do they wince at the thought of a hand, cold and waxen, left on the pavement where it was severed? I draw my hand out of the bag and shake my fingers ostentatiously. No point in inviting conjecture, in attracting attention. The bus brakes loudly to conceal the sound of breath drawn in sharply at the exhibited hand.

Two women pant like dogs as they swing themselves onto the bus. The conductor has already pressed the bell and they propel their bodies expertly along the swaying aisle. They fall into seats opposite me – one fat, the other thin – and simultaneously pull off the starched servants' caps, which they scrunch into their laps. They light cigarettes and I bite my lip. Would I have to vomit into this bag with its cardboard lining? I wish I had brought a plastic bag; this bag is empty save for the purse. I breathe deeply to stem the nausea that rises to meet the curling bands of smoke and fix on the bulging bags they grip between their feet. They make no attempt to get their fares ready; they surely misjudge the intentions of the conductor. He knows that they will get off at Mowbray to catch the Golden Arrow buses to the townships. He will not allow them to avoid paying, not he who presses the button with such promptness.

I watch him at the front of the bus. His right thumb strums an impatient jingle on the silver levers; the leather bag is cradled in the hand into which the coins tumble. He chants a barely audible accompaniment to the clatter of coins, a recitation of the newly decimalized currency – like times tables at school, and I see the fingers grow soft, bending boyish as they strum an ink-stained abacus; the boy learning to count, leaning earnestly with propped elbows over a desk. And I find the image unaccountably sad and tears are about to well up when I hear an impatient empty clatter of thumb-play on the coin dispenser as he demands, 'All fares, please,' from a sleepy white youth. My hand flies into my handbag once again and I take out the purse. A man's leather purse.

Michael too is boyish. His hair falls in a straight blond fringe into his eyes. When he considers a reply, he wipes it away impatiently, as if the hair impedes thought. I cannot imagine this purse ever having belonged to him. It is small, U-shaped and devoid of ornament, therefore a man's purse. It has an extending tongue that could be tucked into the mouth or be threaded through the narrow band across the base of the U. I take out the smallest note stuffed into this plump purse, a five-rand note. Why had I not thought about the bus fare? The conductor will be angry if my note should exhaust his supply of coins, although the leather bag would have a concealed pouch for notes. But this thought does not comfort me. I feel angry with Michael. He has probably never travelled by bus. How would he know of the fear of missing the unfamiliar stop, the fear of keeping an impatient conductor waiting, the fear of saying fluently, 'Seventeen cents, please,' when you are not sure of the fare and produce a five-rand note? But this is my journey and I must not expect Michael to take responsibility for everything. Or rather, I cannot expect Michael to take responsibility for more than half the things. Michael is scrupulous about this division; I am not always sure of how to arrive at half. I was never good at arithmetic, especially this instant mental arithmetic that is sprung on me.

How foolish I must look sitting here clutching my five-rand note. I slip it back into the purse and turn to the solidity of the smoking women. They have still made no attempt to find their fares. The bus is going fast and I am surprised that we have not yet reached Mowbray.

Perhaps I am mistaken; perhaps we have already passed Mowbray and the women are going to Sea Point to serve a nightshift at the Pavilion.

Marge, Aunt Trudie's eldest daughter, works as a waitress at the Pavilion, but she is rarely mentioned in our family. 'A disgrace,' they say. 'She should know better than to go with white men.'

'Poor whites,' Aunt Trudie hisses. 'She can't even find a nice rich man to go steady with. Such a pretty girl too. I won't have her back in this house. There's no place in this house for a girl who's been used by white trash.'

Her eyes flash as she spits out a cherished vision of a blond young man sitting on her new vinyl sofa to whom she serves ginger beer and koeksisters, because it is not against the law to have a respectable drink in a coloured home. 'Mrs Holman,' he would say, 'Mrs Holman, this is the best ginger beer I've had for years.'

The family do not know of Michael, even though he is a steady young man who would sit out such a Sunday afternoon with infinite grace. I wince at the thought of Father creaking in a suit and the unconcealed pleasure in Michael's successful academic career.

Perhaps this is Mowbray after all. The building that zooms past on the right seems familiar. I ought to know it, but I am lost, hopelessly lost, and as my mind gropes for recognition, I feel a feathery flutter in my womb, so slight I cannot be sure, and again, so soft, the brush of a butterfly, and under cover of my handbag I spread my left hand to hold my belly. The shaft of light falling across my shoulder, travelling this route with me, is the eye of God. God will never forgive me.

I must anchor my mind to the words of the women on the long seat opposite me, but they fall silent as if to protect their secrets from me. One of them bends down heavily, holding on to the jaws of her shopping bag as if to relieve pressure on her spine, and I submit to the ache of my own by swaying gently while I protect my belly with both hands. But having eyed the contents of her full bag carefully, her hand becomes the beak of a bird dipping purposefully into the left-hand corner and rises triumphantly with a brown paper bag on which grease has oozed light-sucking patterns. She opens the bag and her friend looks on in silence. Three chunks of cooked chicken lie on a piece of greaseproof paper. She deftly halves a piece and passes it to her thin friend. The women munch in silence, their mouths glossy with pleasure.

'These are for the children,' she says, her mouth still full as she wraps the rest up and places them carelessly at the top of the bag.

'It's the spiced chicken recipe you told me about.' She nudges her friend. 'Lekker, hey!'

The friend frowns and says, 'I like to taste a bit more cardamom. It's nice to find a whole cardamom in the food and crush it between your teeth. A cardamom seed will never give up all its flavour to the pot. You'll still find it there in the chewing.'

I note the gaps in her teeth and fear for the slipping through of cardamom seeds. The girls at school who had their two top incisors extracted in a fashion that raged through Cape Town said that it was better for kissing. Then I, fat and innocent, nodded. How would I have known the demands of kissing?

The large woman refuses to be thwarted by criticism of her cooking. The chicken stimulates a story so that she twitches with an irrepressible desire to tell.

'To think,' she finally bursts out, 'that I cook them this nice surprise and say what you like, spiced chicken can make any mouth water. Just think, it was yesterday when I say to that one as she stands with her hands on her hips against the stove saying, "I don't know what to give them today. I've just got too much organizing to do to bother with food." And I say, feeling sorry for her, I say, "Don't you worry about a thing, Marram. Just leave it all in cook's hands" – wouldn't it be nice to work for really grand people where you cook and do nothing else? No bladdy scrubbing and shopping and all that – "... in cook's hands," I said,' and she crows merrily before reciting, 'And I'll dish up a surprise / For Master Georgie's blue eyes.

'That's Miss Lucy's young man. He was coming last night. Engaged, you know. Well, there I was on my feet all day starching linen, making roeties and spiced lentils and sweet potato and all the lekker things you must mos' have with cardamom chicken. And what do you think she says?'

She pauses and lifts her face as if expecting a reply, but the other stares grimly ahead. Undefeated, she continues, 'She says to me, "Tiena," because she can't keep out of my pots, you know, always opening my lids and sniffing like a brakhond, she says, "Tiena," and waits for me to say, "Yes, Marram," so I know she has a wicked plan up her sleeve and I look her straight in the eye. She smile that one, always smile to put me off the track, and she say, looking into the fridge, "You can have this nice bean soup for your dinner so I can have the remains of the chicken tomorrow when you're off." So I say to her, "That's what I had for lunch today," and she say to me, "Yes, I know, but me and Miss Lucy will be on our own for dinner tomorrow," and she pull a face. "Ugh, how I hate reheated food." Then she draws up her shoulders as if to say, *That's that.*

'Cheek, hey! And it was a great big fowl.' She nudges her friend. 'You know for yourself how much better food tastes the next day, when the spices are drawn right into the meat, and anyway, you just switch on the electric and there's no chopping and crying over onions; you just wait for the pot to dance on the stove. Of course, she wouldn't know about that. Anyway, a cheek, that's what I call it, so before I even dished up the chicken for the table, I took this' – and she points triumphantly to her bag – 'and to hell with them.'

The thin one opens her mouth, once, twice, winding herself up to speak.

'They never notice anyway. There's so much food in their pantries, in the fridge and on the tables; they don't know what's there and what isn't.' The other looks pityingly at her.

'Don't you believe that. My marram was as cross as a bear by the time I brought in the pudding, a very nice apricot ice it was, but she didn't even look at it. She know it was a healthy grown fowl and she count one leg, and she know what's going on. She know right away. Didn't even say, "Thank you, Tiena." She won't speak to me for days, but what can she do?' Her voice softens into genuine sympathy for her madam's dilemma.

'She'll just have to speak to me.' And she mimics, putting on a stern horse face. '"We'll want dinner by seven tonight," then, "Tiena, the curtains need washing," then, "Please, Tiena, will you fix this zip for me. I've got absolutely nothing else to wear today." And so on the third day she'll smile and think she's smiling forgiveness at me.'

She straightens her face. 'No,' she sighs, 'the more you have, the more you have to keep your head and count and check up because you know you won't notice or remember. No, if you got a lot, you must keep snaps in your mind of the insides of all the cupboards. And every day, click, click, new snaps of the larder. That's why that one is so tired, always thinking, always reciting to herself the lists of what's in the cupboards. I never know what's in my cupboard at home, but I know my Sammie's a thieving bastard – can't keep his hands in his pockets.'

The thin woman stares out of the window as if she has heard it all before. She has finished her chicken, while the other, with all the talking, still holds a half-eaten drumstick daintily in her right hand. Her eyes rove over the shopping bag and she licks her fingers abstractedly as she stares out of the window.

'Lekker, hey!' the large one repeats. 'The children will have such a party.'

'Did Master George enjoy it?' the other asks.

'Oh, he's a gentleman all right. Shouted after me, "Well done, Tiena. When we're married, we'll have to steal you from Madam." Dressed to kill he was, such a smart young man, you know. Mind you, so's Miss Lucy. Not a prettier girl in our avenue and the best-dressed too. But then she has mos' to be smart to keep her man. Been on the pill for nearly a year now; I shouldn't wonder if he don't feel funny about the white wedding. Ooh, you must see her blush over the pictures of the wedding gowns, so pure and innocent she think I can't read the packet. "Get me my headache pills out of that drawer, Tiena," she say sometimes when I take her cup of cocoa at night. But she play her cards right with Master George; she have to 'cause who'd have what another man has pushed to the side of his plate. A bay leaf and a bone!' Moved by the alliteration, the image materializes in her hand. "Like this bone," and she waves it under the nose of the other, who starts. I wonder whether with guilt, fear or a debilitating desire for more chicken.

'This bone,' she repeats grimly, 'picked bare and only wanted by a dog.'

Her friend recovers and deliberately misunderstands, 'Or like yesterday's bean soup, but we women mos' know that food put aside and left to stand till tomorrow always has a better flavour. Men don't know that, hey. They should get down to some cooking and find out a thing or two.'

But the other is not deterred. 'A bone,' she insists, waving her visual aid, 'a bone.'

It is true that her bone is a matt grey that betrays no trace of the meat or fat that only a minute ago adhered to it. Master George's bone would certainly look nothing like that when he pushes it aside. With his fork he would coax off the fibres ready to fall from the bone. Then he would turn over the whole, deftly, using a knife, and frown at the sinewy meat clinging to the joint before pushing it aside towards the discarded bits of skin.

This bone, it is true, will not tempt anyone. A dog might want to bury it only for a silly game of hide-and-seek.

The large woman waves the bone as if it would burst into prophecy. My eyes follow the movement until the bone blurs and emerges as the Cross where the head of Jesus lolls sadly, his lovely feet anointed by sad hands, folded together under the driven nail. Look, Mamma says, look at those eyes molten with love and pain, the body curved with suffering for our sins, and together we weep for the beauty and sadness of Jesus in his white loincloth. The Roman soldiers stand grimly erect in their tunics, their spears gleam in the light, their dark beards are clipped, and their lips curl. At midday Judas turns his face to the fading sun and bays, howls like a dog for its return as the darkness grows around him and swallows him whole with the money still jingling in the folds of his saffron robes. In a concealed leather purse, a pouch devoid of ornament.

The buildings on this side of the road grow taller, but oh, I do not know where I am and I think of asking the woman, the thin one, but when I look up, the stern one's eyes already rest on me while the bone in her hand points idly at the advertisement just above my head. My hands, still cradling my belly, slide guiltily down my thighs and fall on my knees. But the foetus betrays me with another flutter, a sigh. I have heard of books flying off the laps of gentle mothers-to-be as their foetuses lash out. I will not be bullied. I jump up and press the bell.

There are voices behind me. The large woman's 'Oi, I say' thunders over the conductor's cross 'Tickets, please.' I will not speak to anyone. Shall I throw myself on the grooved floor of this bus and, with knees drawn up, hands over my head, wait for my demise? I do not in any case expect to be alive tomorrow. But I must resist; I must harden my heart against the sad, complaining eyes of Jesus.

'I say, miss,' she shouts, and her tone sounds familiar. Her voice compels like the insistence of Father's guttural commands. But the conductor's hand falls on my shoulder, the barrel of his ticket dispenser digs into my ribs, the buttons of his uniform gleam as I dip into my bag for my purse. Then the large woman spills out of her seat as she leans forward. Her friend, reconciled, holds the bar of an arm across her as she leans forward shouting, 'Here, I say, your purse.' I try to look grateful. Her eyes blaze with scorn as she proclaims to the bus, 'Stupid, these young people. Dressed to kill maybe, but still so stupid.'

She is right. Not about my clothes, of course, and I check to see what I am wearing. I have not been alerted to my own stupidity before. No doubt I will sail through my final examinations at the end of this year and still not know how I dared to pluck a fluttering foetus out of my womb. That is if I survive tonight.

I sit on the steps of this large building and squint up at the marble facade. My elbows rest on my knees flung comfortably apart. I ought to know where I am; it is clearly a public building of some importance. For the first time I long for the veld of my childhood. There the red sand rolls for miles, and if you stand on the koppie behind the house, the landmarks blaze their permanence: the river points downward, runs its dry course from north to south; the geelbos crowds its banks in near-straight lines. On either side of the path winding westward plump little buttocks of cacti squat as if lifting the skirts to pee, and the swollen fingers of vygies burst in clusters out of the stone, pointing the way. In the veld you can always find your way home.

I am anxious about meeting Michael. We have planned this so carefully for the rush hour, when people storming home crossly will not notice us together in the crush.

'It's simple,' Michael said. 'The bus carries along the main roads through the suburbs to the City, and as you reach the post office, you get off and I'll be there to meet you. At five.'

A look at my anxious face compelled him to say, 'You can't get lost in Cape Town. There' – and he pointed over his shoulder – 'is Table Mountain, and there is Devil's Peak, and there Lion's Head, so how in heaven's name could you get lost?' The words shot out unexpectedly, like the fine arc of brown spittle from between the teeth of an old man who no longer savours the tobacco he has been chewing all day. There are, I suppose, things that even a loved one cannot overlook.

Am I a loved one?

I ought to rise from these steps and walk towards the City. Fortunately I always take the precaution of setting out early, so that I should still be in time to meet Michael, who will drive me along de

Waal Drive into the slopes of Table Mountain, where Mrs Coetzee waits with her tongs.

Am I a loved one? No. I am dull, ugly and bad-tempered. My hair has grown greasy, I am forgetful, and I have no sense of direction. Michael, he has long since stopped loving me. He watched me hugging the lavatory bowl, retching, and recoiled at my first display of bad temper. There is a faraway look in his eyes as he plans his retreat. But he is well brought up, honourable. When the first doubts gripped the corners of his mouth, he grinned madly and said, 'We must marry,' showing a row of perfect teeth.

'There are laws against that,' I said unnecessarily.

But gripped by the idyll of an English landscape of painted greens, he saw my head once more held high, my lettuce-luscious skirts crisp on a camomile lawn and the willow drooping over the red mouth of a suckling infant.

'Come on,' he urged. 'Don't do it. We'll get to England and marry. It will work out all right,' and betraying the source of his vision, 'and we'll be happy for ever, thousands of miles from all this mess.'

I would have explained if I could, but I could not account for this vision: the slow shower of ashes over yards of diaphanous tulle, the moth wings tucked back with delight as their tongues whisked the froth of white lace. For two years I have loved Michael, have wanted to marry him. Duped by a dream, I merely shook my head.

'But you love babies, you want babies sometime or other, so why not accept God's holy plan? Anyway, you're a Christian and you believe it's a sin, don't you?'

God is not a good listener. Like Father, He expects obedience and withdraws peevishly if His demands are not met. Explanations of my point of view infuriate Him so that He quivers with silent rage. For once I do not plead and capitulate; I find it quite easy to ignore these men.

'You're not even listening,' Michael accused. 'I don't know how you can do it.' There is revulsion in his voice.

For two short years I have adored Michael.

Once, perched perilously on the rocks, we laughed fondly at the thought of a child. At Cape Point where the oceans meet and part. The Indian and the Atlantic, fighting for their separate identities, roared and thrashed fiercely so that we huddled together, his hand on my belly. It is said that if you shut one eye and focus the other carefully, the line separating the two oceans may rear drunkenly but remains ever clear and hair-fine. But I did not look. In the mischievous wind I struggled with the flapping ends of a scarf I tried to wrap round my hair. Later that day on the silver sands of a deserted beach he wrote solemnly, *Will you marry me?* and my trembling fingers traced a huge heart around the words. Ahead the sun danced on the waves, flecking them with gold.

I wrote a poem about that day and showed Michael. 'Surely that was not what Logiesbaai was about,' he frowned, and read aloud the lines about warriors charging out of the sea, assegais gleaming in the sun, the beat of tom-toms riding the waters, the throb in the carious cavities of rocks.

'It's good,' he said, nodding thoughtfully. 'I like the title, "Love at Logiesbaai (Whites Only)," though I expect much of the subtlety escapes me. Sounds good,' he encouraged. 'You should write more often.'

I flushed. I wrote poems all the time. And he was wrong; it was not a good poem. It was puzzling, and I wondered why I had shown him this poem that did not even make sense to me. I tore it into little bits.

Love, love, love, I sigh as I shake each ankle in turn and examine the swelling.

Michael's hair falls boyishly over his eyes. His eyes narrow merrily when he smiles and the left corner of his mouth shoots up so that the row of teeth forms a queer diagonal line above his chin. He flicks his head so that the fringe of hair lifts from his eyes for a second, then falls, so fast, like the tongue of a lizard retracted at the very moment of exposure.

'We'll find somewhere,' he would say, 'a place where we'd be quite alone.' This country is vast and he has an instinctive sense of direction. He discovers the armpits of valleys that invite us into their shadows. Dangerous climbs led by the roar of the sea take us to blue bays into which we drop from impossible cliffs. The sun lowers herself on to us. We do not fear the police with their torches. They come only by night in search of offenders. We have the immunity of love. They cannot find us because they do not know we exist. One day they will find out about lovers who steal whole days, round as globes.

There has always been a terrible thrill in that thought.

I ease my feet back into my shoes and the tears splash on to my dress with such wanton abandon that I cannot believe they are mine. From the punctured globes of stolen days these fragments sag and squint. I hold, hold these pictures I have summoned. I will not recognize them for much longer.

With tilted head I watch the shoes and sawn-off legs ascend and descend the marble steps, altering course to avoid me. Perhaps someone will ask the police to remove me.

Love, love, love, I sigh. Another flutter in my womb. I think of moth wings struggling against a windowpane and I rise.

The smell of sea unfurls towards me as I approach Adderley Street. There is no wind, but the brine hangs in an atomized mist, silver over a thwarted sun. In answer to my hunger, Wellingtons looms on my left, the dried-fruit palace that I cannot resist. The artificial light dries my tears, makes me blink, and the trays of fruit, of Cape sunlight twice trapped, shimmer and threaten to burst out of their forms. Rows of pineapple are the infinite divisions of the sun, the cores lost in the amber discs of mebos arranged in arcs. Prunes are the wrinkled backs of aged goggas beside the bloodshot eyes of cherries. Dark green figs sit pertly on their bottoms peeping over trays. And I too am not myself, hoping for refuge in a metaphor that will contain it all. I buy the figs and mebos. Desire is a Tsafendas tapeworm in my belly that cannot be satisfied, and as I pop the first fig into my mouth, I feel the danger fountain with the jets of saliva. Will I stop at one death?

I have walked too far along this road and must turn back to the post office. I break into a trot as I see Michael in the distance, drumming with his nails on the side of the car. His sunburnt elbow juts out of the window. He taps with anxiety or impatience and I grow cold with fear as I jump into the passenger seat and say merrily, 'Let's go,' as if we are setting off for a picnic.

Michael will wait in the car on the next street. She had said that it would take only ten minutes. He takes my hand and so prevents me from getting out. Perhaps he thinks that I will bolt, run off into the mountain, revert to savagery. His hand is heavy on my forearm, and his eyes are those of a wounded dog, pale with pain.

'It will be all right.' I try to comfort and wonder whether he hears his own voice in mine. My voice is thin, a tinsel thread that springs out of my mouth and flutters straight out of the window.

'I must go.' I lift the heavy hand off my forearm and it falls inertly across the gearstick.

The room is dark. The curtains are drawn and a lace-shaded electric light casts shadows in the corners of the rectangle. The doorway in which I stand divides the room into sleeping and eating quarters. On the left there is a table against which a servant girl leans, her eyes fixed on the blank wall ahead. On the right a middle-aged white woman rises with a hostess smile from a divan that serves as sofa, and pats the single pink-flowered cushion to assert homeliness. There is a narrow dark wardrobe in the corner.

I say haltingly, 'You are expecting me. I spoke to you on the telephone yesterday. Sally Smit.' I can see no telephone in the room. She frowns.

'You're not coloured, are you?' It is an absurd question. I look at my brown arms, which I have kept folded across my chest, and watch the gooseflesh sprout. Her eyes are fixed on me. Is she blind? How will she perform the operation with such defective sight? Then I realize: the educated voice, the accent has blinded her. I have drunk deeply of Michael, swallowed his voice as I drank from his tongue. Has he swallowed mine? I do not think so.

I say, 'No,' and wait for all the cockerels in Cape Town to crow simultaneously. Instead the servant starts from her trance and stares at me with undisguised admiration.

'Good.' The woman smiles, showing yellow teeth. 'One must check nowadays. These coloured girls, you know, are very forward, terrible types. What do they think of me, as if I would do every Tom, Dick and Harry. Not me, you know; this is a respectable concern and I try to help decent women, educated, you know. No, you can trust me. No coloured girl's ever been on this sofa.'

The girl coughs, winks at me and turns to stir a pot simmering on a primus stove on the table. The smell of offal escapes from the pot and nausea rises in my throat, feeding the fear. I would like to run, but my feet are lashed with fear to the linoleum. Only my eyes move, across the room, where she pulls a newspaper from a wad wedged between the wall and the wardrobe. She spreads the paper on the divan and smooths with her hand while the girl shuts the door and turns the key. A cat crawls lazily from under the table and stares at me until the green jewels of its eyes shrink to crystal points.

She points me to the sofa. From behind the wardrobe she pulls her instrument and holds it against the baby-pink crimplene of her skirt.

'Down, shut your eyes now,' she says as I raise my head to look. Their movements are carefully orchestrated, the manoeuvres practised. Their eyes signal and they move. The girl stations herself by my head, and her mistress moves to my feet. She pushes my knees apart and whips out her instrument from a pocket. A piece of plastic tubing dangles for a second. My knees jerk and my mouth opens wide, but they are in control. A brown hand falls on my mouth and smothers the cry; the white hands wrench the knees apart and she hisses, 'Don't you dare. Do you want the bladdy police here? I'll kill you if you scream.'

The brown hand over my mouth relaxes. She looks into my face and says, 'She won't.' I am a child who needs reassurance. I am surprised by the softness of her voice. The brown hand moves along the side of my face and pushes back my hair. I long to hold the other hand; I do not care what happens below. A black line of terror separates it from my torso. Blood spurts from between my legs and for a second the two halves of my body make contact through the pain.

So it is done. Deflowered by yellow hands wielding a catheter. Fear and hypocrisy, mine, my deserts spread in a dark stain on the newspaper.

'OK,' she says, 'get yourself decent.' I dress and wait for her to explain. 'You go home now and wait for the birth. Do you have a pad?'

I shake my head uncomprehendingly. Her face tightens for a moment, but then she smiles and pulls a sanitary towel out of the wardrobe.

'Won't cost you anything, lovey.' She does not try to conceal the glow of her generosity. She holds out her hand and I place the purse in her palm. She counts, satisfied, but I wave away the purse, which she reluctantly puts on the table.

'You're a good girl,' she says, and puts both hands on my shoulders. I hold my breath; I will not inhale the foetid air from the mouth of this my grotesque bridegroom with yellow teeth. She plants the kiss of complicity on my cheek and I turn to go, repelled by her touch. But have I the right to be fastidious? I cannot deny feeling grateful, so that I turn back to claim the purse after all. The girl winks at me. The purse fits snugly in my hand; there would be no point in giving it back to Michael.

Michael's face is drawn with fear. He is as ignorant of the process as I am. I am brisk, efficient and rattle off the plan. 'It'll happen tonight, so I'll go home and wait and call you in the morning. By then it will be all over.' He looks relieved.

He drives me right to the door and my landlady waves merrily from the stoep, where she sits with her embroidery among the potted ferns.

'Don't look,' she says anxiously. 'It's a present for you, for your trousseau,' and smiling slyly, 'I can tell when a couple just can't wait any longer. There's no catching me out, you know.'

Tonight in her room next to mine she will turn in her chaste bed, tracing the tendrils from pink and orange flowers, searching for the needle lost in endless folds of white linen.

Semi-detached houses with red-polished stoeps line the west side of Trevelyan Road. On the east is the Cape Flats line, where electric trains rattle reliably according to timetable. Trevelyan Road runs into the elbow of a severely curved Main Road, which nevertheless has all the amenities one would expect: butcher, baker, hairdresser, chemist, library, off-licence. There is a fish-and-chip shop on that corner, on the funny bone of that elbow, and by the side, strictly speaking in Trevelyan Road, a dustbin leans against the trunk of a young palm tree. A newspaper parcel dropped into this dustbin would absorb the vinegary smell of discarded fish-and-chip wrappings in no time.

The wrapped parcel settles in the bin. I do not know what has happened to God. He is fastidious. He fled at the moment that I smoothed the wet black hair before wrapping it up. I do not think he will come back. It is 6 a.m. Light pricks at the shroud of Table Mountain. The streets are deserted and, relieved, I remember that the next train will pass at precisely six twenty-two.

CAGES

Abdulrazak Gurnah

There were times when it felt to Hamid as if he had been in the shop always, and that his life would end there. He no longer felt discomfort, nor did he hear the secret mutterings at the dead hours of night that had once emptied his heart in dread. He knew now that they came from the seasonal swamp that divided the city from the townships, and which teemed with life. The shop was in a good position, at a major crossroads from the city's suburbs. He opened it at first light when the earliest workers were shuffling by, and did not shut it again until all but the last stragglers had trailed home. He liked to say that at his station he saw all of life pass him by. At peak hours he would be on his feet all the time, talking and bantering with the customers, courting them and taking pleasure in the skill with which he handled himself and his merchandise. Later he would sink exhausted onto the boxed seat that served as his till.

The girl appeared at the shop late one evening, just as he was thinking it was time to close. He had caught himself nodding off twice, a dangerous trick in such desperate times. The second time he had woken up with a start, thinking a large hand was clutching his throat and lifting him off the ground. She was standing in front of him, waiting with a look of disgust on her face.

'Ghee,' she said after waiting for a long, insolent minute. 'One shilling.' As she spoke, she half turned away, as if the sight of him was irritating. A piece of cloth was wrapped round her body and tucked in under the armpits. The soft cotton clung to her, marking the outline of her graceful shape. Her shoulders were bare and glistened in the gloom. He took the bowl from her and bent down to the tin of ghee. He was filled with longing and a sudden ache. When he gave the bowl back to her, she looked vaguely at him, her eyes distant and glazed with tiredness. He saw that she was young, with a small round face and slim neck. Without a word, she turned and went back into the darkness, taking a huge stride to leap over the concrete ditch that divided the kerb from the road. Hamid watched her retreating form and wanted to cry out a warning for her to take care. How did she know that there wasn't something there in the dark? Only a feeble croak came out as he choked the impulse to call to her. He waited, half expecting to hear her cry out, but only heard the retreating slap of her sandals as she moved further into the night.

She was an attractive girl, and for some reason as he stood thinking about her and watched the hole in the night into which she had disappeared, he began to feel disgust for himself. She had been right to look at him with disdain. His body and his mouth felt stale. There was little cause to wash more than once every other day. The journey from bed to shop took a minute or so, and he never went anywhere else. What was there to wash for? His legs were misshapen from lack of proper exercise. He had spent the day in bondage; months and years had passed like that, a fool stuck in a pen all his life. He shut up the shop wearily, knowing that during the night he would indulge the squalor of his nature.

The following evening the girl came to the shop again. Hamid was talking to one of his regular customers, a man much older than him called Mansur who lived nearby and on some evenings came to the shop to talk. He was half blind with cataracts, and people teased him about his affliction, playing cruel tricks on him. Some of them said of Mansur that he was going blind because his eyes were full of shit.

He could not keep away from boys. Hamid sometimes wondered if
Mansur hung around the shop after something, after him, but perhaps
it was just malice and gossip. Mansur stopped talking when the girl
approached, then squinted hard as he tried to make her out in the
poor light.

'Do you have shoe polish? Black?' she asked.

'Yes,' Hamid said. His voice sounded congealed, so he cleared his
throat and repeated, 'Yes.' The girl smiled.

'Welcome, my love. How are you today?' Mansur asked. His
accent was so pronounced, thick with a rolling flourish, that Hamid
wondered if it was intended as a joke. 'What a beautiful smell you
have, such perfume! A voice like *zuwarde* and a body like a gazelle.
Tell me, *msichana*, what time are you free tonight? I need someone to
massage my back.'

The girl ignored him. With his back to them, Hamid heard Mansur
continue to chat to the girl, singing wild praises to her while he tried to
fix a time. In his confusion Hamid could not find a tin of polish. When
he turned round with it at last, he thought she had been watching him
all the time and was amused that he had been so flustered. He smiled,
but she frowned and then paid him. Mansur was talking beside her,
cajoling and flattering, rattling the coins in his jacket pocket, but she
turned and left without a word.

'Look at her, as if the sun itself wouldn't dare shine on her. So
proud! But the truth is, she's easy meat,' Mansur said, his body gently
rocking with suppressed laughter. 'I'll be having that one before long.
How much do you think she'll take? They always do that, these
women, all these airs and disgusted looks . . . but once you've got
them into bed, and you've got inside them, then they know who's the
master.'

Hamid found himself laughing, keeping the peace among men,
but he did not think she was a girl to be purchased. She was so certain
and comfortable in every action that he could not believe her abject
enough for Mansur's designs. Again and again his mind returned to

the girl, and when he was alone, he imagined himself intimate with her. At night after he had shut up the shop, he went to sit for a few minutes with the old man Fajir, who owned the shop and lived in the back. He could no longer see to himself and very rarely asked to leave his bed. A woman who lived nearby came to see to him during the day and took free groceries from the shop in return, but at night the ailing old man liked to have Hamid sit with him for a little while. The smell of the dying man perfumed the room while they talked. There was not usually much to say, a ritual of complaints about poor business and plaintive prayers for the return of health. Sometimes, when his spirits were low, Fajir talked tearfully of death and the life that awaited him there. Then Hamid would take the old man to the toilet, make sure his chamberpot was clean and empty, and leave him. Late into the night Fajir would talk to himself, sometimes his voice rising softly to call out Hamid's name.

Hamid slept outside in the inner yard. During the rains he cleared a space in the tiny store and slept there. He spent his nights alone and never went out. It was well over a year since he had even left the shop, and before then he had only gone out with Fajir, before the old man was bedridden. Fajir had taken him to the mosque, every Friday, and Hamid remembered the throngs of people and the cracked pavements steaming in the rain. On the way home they went to the market, and the old man named the luscious fruit and the brightly coloured vegetables for him, picking up some of them to make him smell or touch. Since his teens, when he first came to live in this town, Hamid had worked for the old man. Fajir gave him his board and he worked in the shop. At the end of every day he spent his nights alone and often thought of his father and his mother, and the town of his birth. Even though he was no longer a boy, the memories made him weep and he was degraded by the feelings that would not leave him be.

When the girl came to the shop again, to buy beans and sugar, Hamid was generous with the measures. She noticed and smiled at him. He beamed with pleasure, even though he knew that her smile was laced with derision. The next time she actually said something to him, only a greeting, but spoken pleasantly. Later she told him that her name was Rukiya and that she had recently moved into the area to live with relatives.

'Where's your home?' he asked.

'Mwembemaringo,' she said, flinging an arm out to indicate that it was a long way away. 'But you have to go on backroads and over hills.'

He could see from the blue cotton dress she wore during the day that she worked as a domestic. When he asked her where she worked, she snorted softly first, as if to say that the question was unimportant. Then she told him that until she could find something better, she was a maid at one of the new hotels in the city.

'The best one, the Equator,' she said. 'There's a swimming pool and carpets everywhere. Almost everyone staying there is a *mzungu*, a European. We have a few Indians too, but none of these people from the bush who make the sheets smell.'

He took to standing at the doorway of his backyard bedchamber after he had shut the shop at night. The streets were empty and silent at that hour, not the teeming, dangerous places of the day. He thought of Rukiya often, and sometimes spoke her name, but thinking of her only made him more conscious of his isolation and squalor. He remembered how she had looked to him the first time, moving away in the late evening shadow. He wanted to touch her . . . Years in darkened places had done this to him, he thought, so that now he looked out on the streets of the foreign town and imagined that the touch of an unknown girl would be his salvation.

One night he stepped out into the street and latched the door behind him. He walked slowly towards the nearest streetlamp, then to the one after that. To his surprise he did not feel frightened. He heard something move, but he did not look. If he did not know where he was going, there was no need to fear, since anything could happen. There was comfort in that.

He turned a corner into a street lined with shops, one or two of which were lit, then turned another corner to escape the lights. He had not seen anyone, neither a policeman nor a night watchman. On the edge of a square he sat for a few minutes on a wooden bench, wondering that everything should seem so familiar. In one corner was a clock tower, clicking softly in the silent night. Metal posts lined the sides of the square, impassive and correct. Buses were parked in rows at one end, and in the distance he could hear the sound of the sea.

He made for the sound and discovered that he was not far from the waterfront. The smell of the water suddenly made him think of his father's home. That town too had been by the sea, and once he had played on the beaches and in the shallows like all the other children. He no longer thought of it as somewhere he belonged to, somewhere that was his home. The water lapped gently at the foot of the sea wall, and he stopped to peer at it breaking into white froth against the concrete. Lights were still shining brightly on one of the jetties and there was a hum of mechanical activity. It did not seem possible that anyone could be working at that hour of the night.

There were lights on across the bay, single isolated dots that were strung across a backdrop of darkness. Who lived there? he wondered. A shiver of fear ran through him. He tried to picture people living in that dark corner of the city. His mind gave him images of strong men with cruel faces, who peered at him and laughed. He saw dimly lit clearings where shadows lurked in wait for the stranger, and where later men and women crowded over the body. He heard the sound of their feet pounding in an old ritual and heard their cries of triumph as the blood of their enemies flowed into the pressed earth. But it was not only for the physical threat they posed that he feared the people who lived in the dark across the bay. It was because they knew where they were, and he was in the middle of nowhere.

He turned back towards the shop, unable to resist, despite every-thing, a feeling that he had dared something. It became a habit that after he had shut up the shop at night and had seen to Fajir, he went for a stroll to the waterfront. Fajir did not like it and complained about being left alone, but Hamid ignored his grumbles. Now and then he saw people, but they hurried past without a glance. During the day he kept an eye out for the girl who now so filled his hours. At night he imagined himself with her. As he strolled the silent streets, he tried to think she was there with him, talking and smiling, and sometimes putting the palm of her hand on his neck. When she came to the shop, he always put in something extra and waited for her to smile. Often they spoke, a few words of greeting and friendship. When there were shortages, he served her from the secret reserves he kept for special customers. Whenever he dared he complimented her on her appearance, and squirmed with longing and confusion when she rewarded him with radiant smiles. Hamid laughed to himself as he remembered Mansur's boast about the girl. She was no girl to be bought with a few shillings, but one to be sung to, to be won with display and courage. And neither Mansur, half blind with shit as he was, nor Hamid had the words or the voice for such a feat.

Late one evening Rukiya came to the shop to buy sugar. She was still in her blue workdress, which was stained under the arms with sweat. There were no other customers, and she did not seem in a hurry. She began to tease him gently, saying something about how hard he worked.

'You must be very rich after all the hours you spend in the shop. Have you got a hole in the yard where you hide your money? Everyone knows shopkeepers have secret hoards . . . Are you saving to return to your town?'

'I don't have anything,' he protested. 'Nothing here belongs to me.'

She chuckled disbelievingly. 'But you work too hard, anyway,' she said. 'You don't have enough fun.' Then she smiled as he put in an additional scoopful of sugar.

'Thank you,' she said, leaning forward to take the package from him. She stayed that way for a moment longer than necessary; then she moved back slowly. 'You're always giving me things. I know you'll want something in return. When you do, you'll have to give me more than these little gifts.'

Hamid did not reply, overwhelmed with shame. The girl laughed lightly and moved away. She glanced round once, grinning at him before she plunged into the darkness.

THE LAST BORDELLO

Manuel Rui

Translated from the Portugese by Ronald W. Sousa

They came in the back way. And, as was their custom, the one in the lead gave a greeting in Portuguese: 'Good evening, "sister".'

Silence in return. Mana Domingas pretended that she hadn't noticed them and went right on, her chubby face engrossed in the piece of plain-coloured crocheting that she had all but finished.

'You have that doily just about finished, Mana Domingas,' one of the younger women said, by way of praise. She was seated beside the small table on which sat the record player and also the oil lamp with the shade on it, which illuminated the room with a yellowish glow.

The proprietress sighed, still not raising her eyes from her work, indeed quickening a bit the speed with which she twisted the threads. 'Yes, my daughter, it is just about finished.'

The man who had come in first had his hands on his hips, his legs apart in military posture. The other four stayed back against the wall, all of them impeccably dressed in uniforms, green, with new boots and Uzi automatic pistols across their chests.

'It's all sad in here tonight. Why?'

None of the women answered. From different parts of the room pairs of eyes focused complicitly on the heavy figure of the aged madam as she went impassively on with the rhythmic movement of her crochet hook.

He turned his head and stammered something in French to the other four. Mana Domingas paused surreptitiously in her crocheting. She peeked out of the corner of her eye, saw one of them step out from the wall, stick his thumbs inside his sagging belt and answer in a highly irritated tone of voice. The old woman did not know French, but she gathered that the group suspected there was some sort of plot behind the silence. And they weren't liking it.

'We're not going to have any music?' the man in the lead started in again, openly scowling towards the table with the record player on it.

Again silence fell upon the room, to be broken by the proprietress's voice: 'Milú, a glass of water, please.'

The young woman got to her feet and walked with her eyes glued to the floor. The man who spoke Portuguese tried to caress her neck with his hand. She drew back, responding, 'Hey, take your hand off me; you can stick it you-know-where.'

Mana Domingas pretended that she hadn't seen, and paused only to pull back apart a piece of her work in which she had made a mistake.

'So there's not even any music?' he asked again, now with a greedy look devouring the prominent breasts filling out the low-cut top worn by the girl sitting beside the record player. With one of her hands she smoothed out the doily that adorned the little table, and with the index finger of her other hand she began to trace sensuously its crocheted pattern.

'Beautiful crocheting, Mana Domingas. A wonderful job. But that new one you're working on, it could grace a wedding.'

The madam profiled a smile of superiority, raised the water to her lips, took a swallow without showing any pleasure and then sat the glass on the floor.

It was the only whorehouse left in the *bairro*. The one that had survived. When the Movement arrived, the populace had organized an offensive against prostitution. And, as if by a miracle, almost all the houses on the outskirts of Luanda disappeared. There remained only the fancy houses in the Baixa, which, under the cover of functioning as bars and nightclubs, went right on as in times past. It was in the neighbourhoods that they had vanished. And some of the more unyielding of the prostitutes had not comprehended the change. They found the whole thing very strange. Men who knew their nightlife, from bordello to bordello, now passed them by with disdain, wrapped up in what they called 'people power' and 'neighbourhood committees'. There were others who even spat on the ground in disgust, and, among the women, the greengrocers who had their stalls in the area started refusing to sell tomatoes or onions to any female who, by her dress, walk or perfume, signalled that she made her living by selling her body.

But Mana Domingas's establishment had held on! It had been the most expensive, and most frequented, in the area – in fact, in competition with the best in all of Luanda. A truly elite house! With carefully picked girls, well kept, dressed in provocative miniskirts, high heels, blouses with less cloth than the skin they revealed, and they were always engaging, active in serving drinks, changing records, going back and forth to the rooms. The house had gained its notoriety through its high prices and distinguished clientele of important people from that part of the city where the streets were paved: captains and majors in the *tuga* military, doctors, engineers and even a doctor of law, head of the judiciary, who, in his passion for one of the prostitutes, had lived there in scandal with that woman whose name in fact appeared on the police register.

A house of repute, with Mana Domingas in charge.

Then the MPLA Delegação[1] arrived, and the various houses of assignation began their almost natural decline.

At the same time the puppet forces began locating military bases all over Luanda. They dug in in this neighbourhood, convinced

---

[1] The reference is to the organized presence of the MPLA. The Delegação, located in Vila Alice, was one of its headquarters buildings.

that since the majority of the inhabitants here came from the north, they could transform it into a kind of headquarters for terrorism. Then they discovered Mana Domingas's house, which, increasingly estranged from the neighbourhood people and deprived of its accustomed revenues, took in these new clients with open arms. And they protected the house. They even set up security, impressing upon the girls' minds the notion that they were indispensable, since one of these days 'people power' might come in and ruin everything.

Then began the repression of the neighbourhood people. Mainly of anyone suspected of being an MPLA militant or sympathizer. People Mana Domingas had known from birth on. Now she would hear that they had been found with their bodies riddled with bullets, limbs cut off. There were even stories of 'serious' girls, only twelve or thirteen years old, being raped under threat of violence.

But they came. They brought money. They kept the bar stocked. And Mana Domingas tolerated them. With the result that neither madam nor any of her girls dared walk through the area, so great were the rejection and the hostility they encountered on the faces of each and every person. The clients themselves ended up having to bring in the food. The food that was so scarce in this Luanda at war.

So Mana Domingas, after the phase of receiving them as grand clients had passed, now tolerated them with a mixture of fear, hatred and resignation.

The one who spoke for them all insisted, now with authority in his voice, 'Music, "Sister" Domingas!'

The old woman raised her magisterial head, hands folded, the crocheting spread out in her lap. 'We can't: the needle broke.' And, lowering her head back down like a dead weight, almost to the point where she touched the hook and thread with her eyes, she started in on her work even faster than before.

He went back to speaking French. The other men responded with

a raucous laugh, and one of them pulled a pack of cigarettes out of
his pocket.

First he held out the cigarettes to the girl next to the record player.
She didn't want one. Then he started making the rounds of the room.
There were eight girls in all. One by one they turned him down.
They shook their heads and either thanked him or simply said no.
He finally walked across the room and held the cigarettes out to
Mana Domingas. The old woman didn't even thank him. She very
convincingly pretended she didn't even see him. The soldier put
on a forced smile to compensate for his lack of success and droned
something in French.

'Mana Domingas, when are you going to finish that piece? You
started it a long time ago,' asked one of the girls, who wore a tall wig
and whose lips were heavily painted with brown lipstick.

'I'll finish when God wills it.'

'And if He doesn't will it?' kidded another one, tongue-tied.

'God always wills, my child,' aphorized Mana Domingas, sweat
beading on her face. 'God always wills . . .' And she let out a deep
sigh, her breasts rising almost high enough to touch the fat of her
chin.

The soldier who spoke Portuguese sat down in one of the easy
chairs upholstered in blue imitation leather. He placed his weapon
on the floor. The others remained standing, in a constant, patient
surveillance of the girls.

There was something strange, free-floating in their look. The
bordello was different today. Quiet. No music, no laughter. The
madam's attitude and the girls' behaviour, too, were totally different
from normal.

They hadn't accepted business for almost three days now. It was a
time when war was raging in the neighbourhood between the FNLA
and the people. Three days in a row. Shells shaking the ground,
landing on top of houses. Weapon fire pouring out from anywhere
and everywhere. During that period the proprietress ordered the

doors kept closed, the curtains tightly drawn, and only occasionally would she send one of her employees out to take a careful look around. People running in all directions. Individuals passing by outside the door in tears and with cries of anguish. Some had saved small possessions and were carrying them on their heads, the women always cursing the disaster of not at least being able to recover the bodies of family members or look for the missing.

Today, at nightfall, the conflict had abated. An occasional shot or volley could still be heard, but that alone didn't frighten anyone. Because that was the way the *bairro* had been since the puppet soldiers had set up their installation here.

'Who's running the larder today? Give us some beer to celebrate. Let's toast!'

No response. So he spoke louder, clapping his hands together: '"Sister" Domingas, beer!'

The madam stopped her crocheting for an instant, answering without even altering the position of her head, 'There is no beer.' And she went on wielding her hook as if nothing had happened.

Flashes of fear shone on the girls' faces because of the boldness of Mana Domingas's response.

'That is right, isn't it, Mana Domingas? No more beer comes into this house.'

'Yes, it is, my child,' said the proprietress, this time raising her head to give a look of gratitude for the girl's attempt to help her out of this awkward situation.

He stood up and went back to jabbering with the other men in French. They spoke loudly, gesticulating with their arms. Mana Domingas could not hide an air of concern, convinced that they were discussing what was taking place, the strange and unusual manner of their reception. She stopped her crocheting and started to move her lips in a silent prayer.

But just as she began, the soldier who spoke for them all walked across the room with long strides, shoved aside the prostitute who happened to be in his way by pushing her shoulder, and banged open the pantry door. The other men burst into laughter.

Mana Domingas and the eight girls stiffened in a silence of frozen dread as they heard the noise of the refrigerator opening and counted, one after another, the tinkling of the bottles. Then the man came back to the door and beckoned to the others to come in. The girl seated near the door pushed her chair further away, to avoid more collisions.

Every man brought out beers, three in each hand, holding their necks between their fingers. Then the leader came back out of the pantry with an entire case, which he held vertically and then dropped onto the floor beside the chair he had been sitting in. He spoke in French, and one by one the others went back into the small room.

When they heard the noise of the refrigerator crashing flat on the floor, Mana Domingas took her hands off her crochet work and raised her head, her trembling eyes fixed on the open door. The girls remained silent. They focused their gaze on the madam's eyes, to see if they could discover from her a means of putting an end to this calamity. None of them was attentive to the goings-on in the pantry: the sounds of kicks and hammering pistol butts falling on the refrigerator, glass being shattered, shelves being pulled out, tins and bottles falling to the floor in pandemonium. They heard it all quite distantly.

When she saw the first soldier come back into the room, the proprietress automatically lowered her head and took up her crocheting again. But she couldn't concentrate; she merely went through the motions. The hook in her right hand did not engage the linen thread, nor did the other hand feed it in. She was constructing a kind of imaginary crochet work with an agitated trembling of her jowels, chin and arms.

The soldier opened a beer with his sabre. Three of the men did the same after him. The last one chose to use his teeth.

The girls kept their eyes glued to the floor.

The soldier gulped the beer down in a single swallow, raised the empty bottle high in his right hand and turned to the others to get their attention. Then he aimed a smile towards the madam of the house as though he were about to offer a toast: 'You old whore! Catch!'

Mana Domingas barely had time to duck as the bottle whistled over her head and flew through the glass window before shattering on the ground outside. Even after that Mana Domingas went on engaging in her threadless crocheting with her hands, tears welling out of her eyes.

'Common whore!' and with his left hand he gestured towards the metal point of his sabre. 'Only respect for the "sisters" here keeps me from running this up your ass!'

The madam couldn't control herself any longer and broke down in grotesque sobbing, the crochet work, the hook and her hands over her semi-toothless mouth.

'So you whores are hiding beer now, huh?' and he launched another empty bottle, this time against the ceiling, and the girls ran terrified out of the way to avoid the shower of falling glass.

Then there began what was for the men the high point of this entertainment. They drank beer after beer, throwing the empty bottles against the walls in a game in which they watched and laughed as the prostitutes ducked the flying glass. The man who spoke Portuguese was the only one who didn't join in on the breakage. He remained lost in thought, looking at Mana Domingas, who, once in a while, glimpsed with her eyes an occasional spark in his. She experienced there moments of short-lived but profound victory. None of her employees had given in and done what these men expected: get up and sue for peace with arms of flesh, passionate smiles and sex.

'If it wasn't for the girls, I'd run this up your ass, you rotten old bitch. You can bet I would!' and he belched as he repeated in French what he had just said, for the benefit of the other men.

The proprietress took up her crocheting once more, the hook re-engaging the thread. The parade of bottles against the wall had ended, and the madam was inciting the visitors' ire with her haughtiness. She organized herself as she had been at the outset: pretending that she was alone and absorbed in her crochet work.

Then the one who had been acting as interpreter threw himself in a fury against the semicircular piece of furniture that served as the bar. The glasses made a clinking noise as they broke against the concrete. He grabbed hold of one of the giraffe-foot benches and, with infuriated pounding, tore apart the piece of furniture from which the prostitutes usually served drinks to their clients.

Suddenly there came from outside the sound of a shell exploding. Then another one – and single-shot weapon fire.

The group of men exchanged looks. They traded more words in French. Mana Domingas gleaned, with satisfaction, from their tone of voice that they were now in a hurry to leave. She hadn't learned much in the way of French, but from the rhythm and intonation of their utterances she could guess the sense of the conversations. They were now hurrying to divide up the girls.

'Hey, Sophia! You go into the room with this *frère* . . . this "brother",' and he pointed with his right index finger to the prostitute wearing the brick-coloured *bubu* in a mask print. He was now thoroughly drunk and he gave orders like a general at a military parade: 'With . . . this . . . *frère!*' he slowly repeated, emphasizing each word.

'But I cannot,' answered the girl, pasting a falsely sweet, experienced smile on her face.

'Why?'

'I just got it today.' And she proclaimed moralistically, 'It's fate.'

The leader turned back with a sidelong glance to the other man involved. Mana Domingas understanding that he was explaining things to the other man, who at the same time was nodding his head and searching over the room with his eyes, until he fixed his lust upon the big girl with the huge eyes who wore green bell-bottom trousers and a miniblouse that covered just a bit of the lower part of her breasts.

'Guida, you go into the room with the "brother".'

She stood up slowly, theatrically, having first glanced over to authority in the figure of Mana Domingas. Swaying her hips with practised provocativeness, with her left hand she let down erotically her long, loose, smooth hair, holding her chins with her right.

'You're going to have to leave me out, pal. When the fighting's over, I'm going to have this tooth pulled. I have what you call an "abscess". Say, maybe your army pharmacy has some *milongo* herb you can get me for it.'

The madam travelled through her almost-forgotten crocheting with a splendid calm painted on her face for the girls to see. There was no further sound until the visitors began to dialogue in French again.

Mana Domingas paid even greater attention to the tones of voice. There was no doubt: they were arguing and, in the midst of a serious difference of opinion, were looking for the most practical solution. At that point the man who spoke Portuguese, staggering in his drunkenness, went over to the slender girl in the jeans who had her elbows resting on the small table with the record player on it.

'You go.'

The young woman remained absolutely still, the soldier staring at her with a domineering look. He walked over to her and shook her by the shoulders: 'Let's go; do what I say. Into the room – now!'

'I won't go,' and with a twist she pulled herself back out of his grip.

'Who says you won't go?'

'I'm the one who gets to say, and I won't.'

And she kept on, her elbows pressed to the tabletop, her head hanging suspended between her hands.

She was the newest prostitute in the house, aspired to by all the clients but the hardest to get, because Mana Domingas would set the price very high. And she would hold firm. Without vacillating.

The spokesman now began walking about the room, kicking the bottle shards, trying to intimidate the girls, who, in contrast, continued to manifest a sublime indifference.

The refrigerator had been completely destroyed and now was good for nothing more than scrap metal. The pantry had been torn apart, cans and jars of macaroni, rice, salt and other condiments all heaped together on the floor along with fragments of glass from the jars, and beer soaking it all. The semicircular bar and high stools had been reduced to kindling. These objects of food, drink and ornament were what was of greatest value to these women who earned their livelihood by selling themselves. He could not, therefore, understand the girls' behaviour. Tonight an atmosphere of tension floated through the room. They seemed to be at a wake for someone they had hated in life. Neither bottles thrown over their heads nor falling glass nor any of those other things had moved them.

In the midst of such thoughts, standing in the middle of the room, under the careful scrutiny of Mana Domingas, he fixed his eyes again on the young girl. The table, the record player covered by a doily crocheted by the proprietress's own hand. In a sudden burst of rage he pulled off its glass cover and threw it against the wall.

'Today we're going to end up torching all this crap!' and he ripped the arm off the record player.

The girl remained impassive. She seemed to be half asleep.

The men exchanged more words in French. Their rage was obvious; they spoke very loudly, evidencing a certain clash of opinion. Mana Domingas raised her head up with greater calm. The experience of year after year in the whorehouses had instilled in her an inner hope: these men, drunk, the alcohol going to their heads, might end up cancelling each other out in their confusion.

Not a shot was to be heard. The night seemed about to yield a miraculous calm after the last three days of conflict. Three days of terror during which Mana Domingas had prayed like she had never prayed before. But at this moment, seeing the house torn apart, its contents all smashed, the madam found herself praying for the war to come back. With whole volleys of bullets. And mortar rounds. Yes, that was the salvation. She knew these men well. If the firing came again in earnest, they would leave on the run, each in a different direction. So Mana Domingas, eyeing the figure of the leader as he weaved back and forth on his feet, went on meticulously forming the stitches in her crocheting.

He coughed, sucking in the spit, almost choking. He wiped his mouth on the back of his hand and then pulled a wad of crumpled banknotes out of a hip pocket, growling, 'It's money, isn't it? With you whores it's always money. Well, there it is!'

He became exasperated. He expected to see one of the prostitutes leap up and grab at the money – especially the young girl – but none of the women even so much as looked at the notes scattered on the floor.

Desperate, he threw himself upon the young girl. He stuck his hands down inside her blouse to grab her breasts. She rose up like a spring, flung out her arms, screamed and, struggling to free herself from the hands that were squeezing her breasts, defended herself by sinking her teeth into the aggressor's arm until he released her.

'I'm not going into that room!'

'Why?' he asked, his drunken eyes staring at the wrist pitted with wounds from the prostitute's teeth. 'Why?' I asked. And he hit her, hard.

'I'm not going to bed with any French speakers!' the girl said, now somewhere between tears and sobs.

It was as though the roof had fallen in. Mana Domingas almost stopped breathing. He took his hands off the girl and stopped for a lucid instant, thinking, his head down in shock. This time he didn't translate for the others.

'But then you'll go to bed with *me*. If you don't, you're going to see what an ELNA soldier is made of. An ELNA soldier!'

'I'm not going to bed with anybody; I've left the business. Get away from me!'

'But I speak Portuguese,' and saying that he grabbed her by the arms and tried to pull her with him. 'Let's go. Pick up the money. All of it! All the money.'

'I'm not going. Leave me alone.'

'But I do speak Portuguese,' he insisted. He made an effort to pull the girl with him. He got her up and with one hand ripped off her blouse. Her breasts were left bare, taut and adolescent. The prostitute, in a virginal gesture aimed at preserving her integrity, covered herself with her arms, leaned back with every iota of strength she had and burst out with the sobbing words. 'I'm not going to bed with . . . murderers!'

Mana Domingas stopped her work and remained motionless, the hook suspended in her right hand, seeking a thread in the air. The crocheting fell to the floor. There was a brief glimpse of the sabre blade gleaming within the sculptural brilliance of the young woman's breasts in the yellow light of the lamp with the shade, her cry as she fell over on top of the table, the crash of the lamp to the floor and then darkness everywhere. The madam leaped up and with sure fingers felt for the door latch.

Once outside, she ran, panting crazily, until she reached the start of the asphalt pavement.

There was no other safe route to use in fleeing. Behind were only enemies. Either random shooting – never, at night, aimed at any intended victim – or the well-known rampant rapes on the part of the ELNA soldiers, or shame and deprecation before the neighbourhood people. No, this was the right path: into the great anonymity of the city.

There, before her in the dark, at the entrance to the avenue, Mana Domingas glimpsed some familiar figures. She went another hundred metres forward, the superfluous crochet hook still clutched nervously in her right hand. She hadn't even shed a tear.

Three of the girls were there. Silent. At this, the only practicable point of meeting and of flight.

The proprietress looked back again to where they had come from, but when she heard the echoes of automatic-weapon fire followed by the explosion of a grenade, she took a definitive step onto the pavement.

There was no doubt. The sounds were coming from the bordello.

They then began walking, single file, hurriedly. They walked along the right side of the street. Without saying a word.

At one point they saw a group of people on the other side of the street walking in the same direction. Four women were carrying bundles on their heads. An old man with a child on his shoulders. Two men. And a young man in front, with a weapon in his hand.

Mana Domingas started across the road diagonally, followed by the three girls. The people on the other side stopped their progress.

When the madam got close to the young man at the head of the line, she asked, 'Where are you going, Comrades?'

The militiaman came up close to the old woman. He studied that face so widely known and talked about in the *bairro*. And after being sure, he spat in repugnance, 'Aha! So now you are comrades? Since when?'

'Yes, we are, Comrade.'

Mana Domingas was trembling. Two thick tears now rolled down from her eyes, but she stifled her sobs by squeezing the superfluous crochet hook deep into her right hand.

Two more grenade bursts were heard and they all turned their heads towards the source of the sound. It was Mana Domingas's house.

The young man's eyes remained fixed indecisively on the old woman's fat face until the tall flames began to lick up into the night. Another house on fire. The house that had belonged to Mana Domingas. The last bordello.

The old woman smiled. She touched with her fleshy hand the hot face of the young man whom she had known since he was an infant, measuring in her memory the time gone by during which he had grown, and she asked, 'Where are you comrades going?'

'We're going to Vila Alice, to try to get weapons.'

'Then we'll go too.'

And as no one in the group raised an objection or made a comment, the young militiaman gave with a gesture a sign to recommence the march.

The single line had grown. One of the girls carried her yellow high-heeled shoes in one hand. Mana Domingas was walking along barefoot. And when she instinctively raised her hand to her throat and felt the gold choker that another Zairian commander had given her when the fighting had first moved into the city, she undid the cord, weighed it in her hand, walked along a few more paces with the gold clutched in her right hand and then, without anyone seeing, let it fall into the grass that grew along the edge of the street.

The night was enveloped by the usual freshness of the sea breeze, and, in the sky, some stars shone, while the silence seemed to promise a hiatus in these disastrous times. But a few tracers painted the space between Avenida Brasil and Vila Alice. A space of life or of death. With Mana Domingas walking along, her superfluous crochet hook still tightly clutched in her hand.

THE EYES OF THE STATUE

Camara Laye

Translated from the French by Una MacLean

She stopped walking for a moment – ever since she had set out, she had been feeling as though she had earned a moment's rest – and she took stock of her surroundings. From the top of the hill on which she stood, she saw spread out before her a great expanse of country.

Far away in the distance was a town, or rather the remains of a town, for there was no trace of movement to be seen near it, none of the signs of activity that would suggest the presence of a town. Perhaps it was merely distance that hid from her sight all the comings and goings, and possibly once within the town, she would be borne along on the urgent flood of activity. Perhaps . . .

'From this distance anything is possible,' she was surprised to hear herself say aloud.

She mused on how, from such a vast distance, it seemed still as though anything could happen, and she fervently believed that if any changes were to take place, they would occur in the intervals when the town was hidden by the trees and undergrowth.

There had been many of these intervals and they were nearly always such very long intervals, so long that it was now by no means certain that she was approaching the town by the most direct route, for there was absolutely nothing to guide her and she had to struggle continually against the intertwining branches and tangled thorns and pick her way around a maze of swamps. She had tried very hard to cross the swamps, but all she had succeeded in doing was getting her shoes and the hem of her skirt soaking wet and she had been obliged to retrace her steps hurriedly, so treacherous was the surface of the ground.

She couldn't really see the town and she wasn't going straight towards it except for the rare moments when she topped a rise. There the ground was sparsely planted with broom and heath and she was far above the thickly wooded depths of the valleys. But no sooner had she finished scrambling up the hills than she had to plunge once more into the bushes and try to force her way through the impenetrable undergrowth where everything was in her way, cutting off her view and making her walk painful and dangerous again.

Perhaps I really ought to go back, she said to herself, and certainly that would have been the most sensible thing to do. But in fact she didn't slacken her pace in the least, as though something away over there was calling to her, as though the distant town were calling. But how could an empty town summon her? A silent, deserted town!

For the closer she came to it, the more she felt that it must really be a deserted city, a ruined city in fact. The height of the bushes and the dense tangled undergrowth about her feet convinced her. If the town had still been inhabited, even by a few people, its surroundings would never have fallen into the confusion through which she had been wandering for hours; surely she would have found, instead of this tangled jungle, the orderly outskirts of which other towns could boast. But here there were neither roads nor paths; everything betokened disorder and decay.

Yet once more she wondered whatever forced her to continue her walk, but she could find no reply. She was following an irresistible urge. She would have been hard put to it to say how this impulse had arisen or indeed to decide just how long she had been obeying it. And perhaps it was the case that if only she followed the impulse for long enough, she would no longer be capable of defying it, although there was no denying that it was grossly irrational. At any rate the urge must have been there for a very long time, as she could tell from the tiredness of her limbs and moreover it was still very close. Couldn't she feel it brimming up within her, pressing on her breast with each eager breath she drew? Then all of a sudden she realized that she was face to face with it.

'The urge is me,' she cried.

She proclaimed it defiantly, but without knowing what she was defying, and triumphantly, although unaware of her opponent. Whom had she defied, and what could she be triumphing over? It was not simply that she was identifying herself with the strange compulsion in order to get to know more of it and of herself. She was obliged to admit that the urge was indefinable, as her own being for ever escaped definition.

After one final struggle with the branches and obstacles, and after skirting one more morass, she suddenly emerged in front of the city, or what remained of it. It was really only the traces of a town, no more than the traces, and in fact just what she had feared to find ever since she set out, but so sad, so desolate, she could never have imagined such desolation. Scarcely anything but rough heaps of walls remained. The porticoes were crumbling and most of the roofs had collapsed; only a column here or a fragment of a wall there proclaimed the former splendour of the peristyles. As for the remaining buildings, they seemed to waver uncertainly, as though on the very point of tumbling. Trees had thrust their branches through broken windows; great tufts of weeds pushed the blocks and the marble slabs upwards; the statues had fallen from their niches; all was ruined and burst asunder.

I wonder why these remains seem so different from the forests and bush I have come through already? she said to herself. There was no difference except for the desolation and loss, rendered all the more poignant by the contrast with what had once been. What am I searching for here? she asked herself once more. I ought never to have come.

'Many people used to come here once,' said an old man who appeared out of the ruins.

'Many people?' she said. 'I have not seen a single soul.'

'Nobody has been here for a very long time,' said the old man. 'But there was a time when crowds of people visited the ruins. Is that what you have come for?'

'I was coming towards the city.'

'It certainly was a great city once, but you have arrived too late. Surely you must have been delayed on the road.'

'I should not have been so late but for my battles with the trees and undergrowth and all my detours around the swamps. If only they hadn't held me back . . .'

'You should have come by the direct route.'

'The direct route?' she exclaimed. 'You cannot have any idea of the wilderness round this place.'

'All right, all right,' he said. 'I do have some idea of it. As a matter of fact when I saw that people had stopped coming, I guessed how it was. Perhaps there isn't any road left?'

'There isn't even a bush path!'

'What a pity,' he said. 'It was such a fine town, the most beautiful city in all the continent.'

'And now what is it?' she said.

'What is it?' he replied dismally.

With his stick he began to mow down the nettles that rose thick and menacing about them.

'Look at this,' he said.

She saw, in the midst of the nettles, a fallen statue, green with moss, a humiliated statue. It cast upon her a dead, grey glance. Presently she became aware that the look was not really dead, only blind, as the eyes were without pupils, and it was in fact a living gaze, as alive as a look could be. A cry came from it, an appealing cry. Was the statue bewailing its loneliness and neglect? The lips drooped pitiably.

'Who is it?' she asked.

'He was the ruler who lived in this place. His rooms can still be seen.'

'Why don't you set up the statue over there?' she said. 'It would be better there than among all these nettles.'

'That is what I wanted to do. As soon as the statue fell from its alcove I wanted to put it back, but I simply hadn't the strength. These stone sculptures are terribly heavy.'

'I know,' she replied, 'and after all it is merely a stone sculpture.'

But was it merely carved stone? Could sculptured stone have cast upon her such a piercing glance? Perhaps, then, it wasn't mere stone. And even if it were nothing more than mere stone, the fact remained that for all the nettles and moss and the vagaries of fortune that it had endured, this stone would still outlast man's life. No, it could not be mere stone. And with this sort of distress in its look, this cry of distress . . .

'Would you care to visit his rooms?' asked the old man.

'Yes, take me there,' she answered.

'Pay particular attention to the columns,' he told her. 'No doubt there is only one hall left here now, but when you consider the number of broken and fallen columns it does look as though there used to be at least ten halls.'

With the end of his stick he pointed out the marble stumps and debris of broken slabs buried in the grass.

'This gateway must have been exceedingly high,' he said, gazing upwards.

'It can't have been higher than the palace, surely,' she said.

'How can we tell? I haven't seen it any more than you have. By the time I arrived here it had already fallen into the grass; but those who were here before my time declared that it was an astonishing entrance. If you could put all this debris together again, I dare say you would get a surprise. But who could tackle such a task?'

He shrugged his shoulders and continued, 'You would need to be a giant, to have the hands and the strength of a giant.'

'Do you really believe that a giant . . . ?'

'No,' he replied. 'Only the ruler himself, who had it erected, could do it. He could certainly manage it.'

She gazed at the niches where great tufts of grass had been bold enough to replace the statues. There was one space, larger than all the rest, where the weeds grew particularly ostentatiously, like a flaming torch.

'That is the niche, over there, where he used to stand before his fall among the nettles,' he remarked.

'I see,' she said. 'But now there is nothing left but wild grass and the memory of his agony.'

'He used to find this city and his palace trying enough. He personally supervised the building of the entire place. He intended his town to be the biggest and this palace the highest. He wanted them built to his own scale. Now he is dead, his heart utterly broken.'

'But could he have died any other way?'

'No, I suppose he carried his own death within him, like us all. But he had to carry the fate of a felled Goliath.'

By this time they had reached the foot of a staircase and he pointed out a little door at the end of the corridor on the left.

'That is where I live,' he told her. 'It is the old porter's lodge. I suppose I could have found somewhere a little more spacious and less damp, but after all, I am not much more than a caretaker. In fact, a guide is only a caretaker.'

So saying, he began to make his way painfully up the steps. He was a decrepit old man.

'You are looking at me? I know I'm not much better than the palace! All this will crumble down one day. Soon all this will crumble down on my head and it won't be a great loss! But perhaps I shall crumble before the palace.'

'The palace is older,' she said.

'Yes, but it is more robust. They don't build like that nowadays.'

'What have you been saying?' she demanded. 'You are not stone! Why compare your body to a palace?'

'Did I compare myself to a palace? I don't think so. My body is certainly no palace, not even a ruined one. Perhaps it is like the porter's lodge where I live, and perhaps I was wrong to call it damp and dark, perhaps I should have said nothing about it. But I must pause for breath. These stairs. At my age no one likes climbing stairs.'

And he wheezed noisily, pressing his hand over his heart as though to subdue its frantic beating.

'Let us go,' he said at last, 'up the few remaining steps.'

They climbed a little higher and reached a landing with a great door opening off it, a door half wrenched from its hinges.

'Here are the rooms,' he said.

She saw an immense apartment, frightfully dilapidated. The roof had partly collapsed, leaving the rafters open to the sky. Daylight streamed in upon the debris of tiles and rubbish strewn upon the floor. But nothing could take from the chamber its harmonious proportions, with its marble panel, its tapestry and paintings, the bold surge of its columns, and the deep alcoves between them. It was still beautiful, in spite of being three-quarters ruined. The torn and rotten tapestries and the peeling paintings were still beautiful; so were the cracked stained-glass windows. And although the panelling was practically torn away, the grandeur of the original conception remained.

'Why have you let everything deteriorate so far?' she asked.

'Why indeed? But now it is too late to do anything about it.'

'Is it really too late?'

'Now that the master is no longer here . . .' He tapped the panels with his stick.

'I don't know how the walls are still standing,' he said. 'They may last a fair time yet. But the rain floods through the roof and windows and loosens the stones. And then when the winter storms come! It is those violent storms that destroy everything.'

He dislodged a scrap of mortar.

'Just look, it's no more than a bit of grey dust. I can't think why the blocks don't fall apart. The damp has destroyed everything.'

'Was this the only room the master had?' she asked.

'He had hundreds of them and all of them richly furnished. I've pushed the movable stuff into one of the smaller rooms, which was less damaged.'

He opened a door concealed in the panelling.

'Here is some of it,' he said.

She beheld a jumble of carved furniture, ornaments, carpets and crockery.

'Gold dishes, please note. The master would eat off nothing but gold. And look at this. Here he is in his robes of state.' He pointed to a canvas where the face of the statue was portrayed.

The eyes were marvellously expressive. They were so even in the statue, although the sculptor had given them no pupils, but here they were infinitely more expressive and the look that they gave was one of anguish. 'Is no one left near me?' they seemed to ask. And the droop of the mouth replied, 'No one.' The man had known they would all forsake him; he had long foreseen it. Nevertheless she, she had come! She had fought through the bush and she had wandered around the swamps, she had felt fatigue and despair overwhelming her, but she had triumphed over all these obstacles and she had come, she had come at last. Had he not guessed she would come? Yet possibly this very foresight had but accentuated the bitter line of his set lips. 'Yes,' said those lips, 'someone will come, when all the world has ceased to call. But someone who will be unable to soothe my distress.'

She swung round. This reproach was becoming unbearable, and not only this reproach, which made all her goodwill seem useless, but the cry of abandonment, the wild lonely appeal in his look.

'We can do nothing, nothing at all for him,' the old man declared.

And she replied, 'Is there ever anything we can do?' She sighed. In her innermost being she felt the anguish of this look; one might have thought it was she who cried, that the cry of loneliness welled up from her own lonely heart.

'Perhaps you can do something,' he said. 'You are still young.

Although you may not be able to do anything for yourself, you might perhaps help others.'

'You know very well that I cannot even do that,' she said.

She seemed overwhelmed, as though she bore the ruins on her own shoulders.

'Are there still more rooms?' she asked him.

'Lots of them, but it is getting late; the sun is sinking.'

Daylight was fading fast. The light had become a soft, rosy glow, a light that was kinder to details, and in it the great room took on a new aspect. The paintings and panels regained a freshness that was far from theirs by right. This sudden glow was the gentlest of lights. But not even this light could calm a tormented heart.

'Come along,' called the old man.

'Yes,' she answered.

She imagined that once she went out of this hall and its adjoining storeroom, her heart would perhaps calm down. She thought that perhaps she might forget the great cry coming from the storeroom. Yes, if only she could get away from this palace, leave these ruins, surely she could forget it. But was not the cry inside herself?

'The cry is within me,' she exclaimed.

'Stop thinking about it,' advised the old man. 'If you hear anything, it's because the silence has got on your nerves. Tomorrow you will hear nothing.'

'But it is a terrible cry.'

'The swans have an awful cry too,' he remarked.

'Swans?'

'Yes, the swans. To look at them gliding over the water you might never believe it. Have you ever happened to hear them cry? But of course not; you are scarcely more than a child, and, with less sense than one, you probably imagine that they sing. Listen, formerly there were lots of swans here; they were at the very gate of the palace. Sometimes the lake was covered with them like white blossoms. Visitors used to throw scraps to them. Once the tourists stopped coming, the swans died. No doubt they had lost the habit of searching for food themselves and so they died. Very well, never, do you hear me, never, did I hear a single song coming from the pond.'

'Why do you have to tell me all this? Have I ever told you that I believe swans sing? You didn't need to speak to me like that.'

'No, maybe I shouldn't have said it, or I should have said it less suddenly at least. I'm sorry. I even believed that swans sing myself once. You know how it is – I am old and lonely and I have got into the habit of talking to myself. I was talking to myself then. I once believed that the lord of this palace, before he died, sang a swan-song. But no, he cried out. He cried so loudly that—'

'Please tell me no more,' she begged.

'All right. I suppose we shouldn't think about all that. But let's go.'

He carefully closed the storeroom door and they made their way towards the exit.

'Did you mean to leave the door of the big room open?' she asked once they had reached the landing.

'It hasn't been shut for a long time,' he replied. 'Besides, there is nothing to fear. No one comes here now.'

'But I came.'

He glanced at her.

'I keep wondering why you came,' he said. 'Why did you?'

'How can I tell?' she said.

Her visit was futile. She had crossed a desert of trees, and bush and swamps. And why? Had she come at the summoning of that anguished cry from the depth of the statue's and the picture's eyes? What way was there of finding out? And moreover it was an appeal to which she could not respond, an appeal beyond her power to satisfy. No, this impulse that had moved her to hasten towards the town had been mad from the start.

'I don't know why I came,' she repeated.

'You shouldn't take things to heart like that. These painters and carvers are so crafty, you know, they can make you work out the portrait, for instance. Have you noticed the look in the eyes? We begin by wondering where they found such a look and eventually we realize they have taken it from ourselves, and these are the paradoxes they would be the first to laugh at. You should laugh too.'

'But these paradoxes, as you call them, which come from the depth of our being, what if we cannot find them there?'

'What do you find within yourself?' he answered her.

'I have already told you: unbearable loneliness.'

'Yes,' he said, 'there is something of that in each one of us.'

'But in me . . .'

'No, not more than in anyone else,' he insisted. 'Don't imagine that others are any less alone. But who wants to admit that? All the same, it is not an unendurable state of affairs. It is quite bearable in fact. Solitude! Listen, solitude isn't what you imagine. I don't want to run away from my solitude. It is the last desirable thing left me; it is my only wealth, a great treasure, an ultimate good.'

Is he just saying that to comfort me? she wondered. But it is not consolation, a shared solitude can be no consolation. The sharing only makes the solitude doubly lonely.

Aloud she said, 'That doesn't console me in the least.'

'I didn't think it would,' he replied. They had by now reached the foot of the staircase and the old man showed her the little corridor leading to his room.

'My lodge is here.'

'Yes, I know,' she said. 'You've told me already.'

'But I haven't told you everything: I didn't say that my room is right beneath the staircase. When visitors used to climb up there in throngs, they were walking over my lodge. Do you understand?'

'Yes.'

'No, you don't understand at all; you don't realize that they were marching on my head, wiping their feet on my hair. I had plenty of hair in those days.'

'But they weren't really wiping their feet,' she said. 'They—'

'Don't you think it was humiliating enough anyway?'

She did not know how to reply. The old man seemed slightly crazy: some of what he said was very sensible, but a lot of it was sheer nonsense. That solitude has gone to his head, she told herself, and she looked at him afresh. He was certainly very old. There must be times when age and loneliness together . . . Aloud she remarked, 'I don't know,' and then, all of a sudden, 'What made you say that solitude is an ultimate good?'

'How very young you are,' was his only reply. 'You should never have come here.' He made off towards his lodge, saying, 'I'm going to prepare a meal.'

'I shall rest here awhile,' she said as she climbed the steps.

'Yes, do have a rest. You've certainly earned one. I shall call you when the food is ready.'

She sat down and gazed at the evil weeds. The nettles were by far the most numerous and reminded her of the ocean. They were like a great green sea that surged around the palace trying to drown it, and ultimately they would completely engulf it. What could mere stones do against such a powerful wave? A wave with the deceptive smoothness of velvety leaves, a wave that hid its poisons and its sorcery beneath a velvet touch. It seemed to her fevered imagination that the wave was already rising. Or was it simply the darkness? Was it night, which was burying the lowest steps? No, it was really the wave of nettles, imperceptibly advancing in its assault upon the palace. A transient attack, no doubt. Probably this sea of nettles had tides like the ocean. And perhaps it wasn't merely a simple tide. Perhaps . . .

She leaped to her feet. The tide was about her ankles. She climbed several steps and the tide rose as quickly.

'Caretaker!' she screamed.

But she could no longer see the porter's lodge. Perhaps the sea had already entered the room while she was sitting down. She couldn't be certain now whether it had a door that shut. Even suppose it did have, how could a door stop such a wave?

What is to become of me? she asked herself. She climbed a few more steps, but the tide continued to pursue her; it really was following her. She paused; perhaps if she stopped, the tide in its turn might stop rising. But instead it flowed right up to her, covering her shoes. Feverishly she resumed her upward flight and gained the landing opposite the doorway of the main hall. But to her horror she realized that the wave was there almost as soon. It was inches away. Must she drown in those horrible weeds?

She rushed to open the storeroom door, only to find that the sea had beaten her and had borne everything away, literally washed off the face of the earth. There was no longer any storeroom left! It had been engulfed beneath the flood of nettles, with its furniture and tapestries and dishes, and the portrait as well. Only the cry, the great cry of anguish remained, and it had become vaster and louder, more piercing and heart-rending than ever. It swelled to fill the whole earth! It seemed to her as though nothing could silence it any more and that whatever she did she could never escape. Her heart could never escape again. Yet at the same time she tried to bolt the door upon it as though in spite of all she knew she might evade it yet. But what could she escape to? There was no way of escape left open; it was either the cry or the flood. She was a prey to this cry and in no time she would be the victim of the flood. She was trapped between two floods, the one that swallowed up the storeroom and was lying in wait menacingly on its threshold, and the other one, which had pursued her step by step up the stairs and across the great hall. She had no choice but to cast herself into one of these two floods which were soon to merge. Placed as she was, she could neither advance nor retreat.

'Caretaker!' she cried.

But did she actually shriek? No sound came from her lips. Terror was throttling her. It had her by the throat. She only imagined she had shouted.

At the second attempt she could not even pretend to herself that she had shouted. She no longer even had the will to cry out. She realized that her terror was so extreme that she could never shout again. Nevertheless she continued to struggle hopelessly; she fought and struggled silently and in vain.

And meanwhile the flood was steadily rising beyond her ankles and up her legs. Confident of its power, it rose more rapidly than ever.

Then, while she was struggling and trying desperately to regain her voice, she suddenly caught sight of the statue. The sea of weeds had lifted it and was tossing it on its waves.

She stopped struggling to watch it and at once she could see that its eyes were looking at her just as they had done when the old man had first thrust aside the nettles. It was the same look, the same cry of distress and bitter loneliness.

She longed to awake from her nightmare and she tried once more to call for help, but in vain. Must she really die alone beneath the flood of weeds, all alone? She hid her face in her arms.

A little later she felt a blow on her forehead and she felt as if her skull were bursting.

SLIPPER SATIN

Alex La Guma

The street couldn't have changed much in four months. The same two rows of houses were there, with their fenced stoeps and verandahs; the same Indian grocery shop, and the back of the warehouse that had a big sign painted across the whole expanse of wall. There were the same grey pavements, cracked in places. Perhaps the paint and colour-wash on the houses had faded and peeled somewhat during the four months, and there were wide streaks down the wall of the warehouse, damaging the big black lettering.

And the people were there too. The little knots of twos and threes at the gates of some of the houses, the row of idle men against the warehouse wall, and the children playing in the gutters. Nothing had really changed in the street.

She stared straight ahead as she came into the street, but sensed the wave of interest that stirred the people. Recognition tapped them on the shoulder, and she felt the faces turning towards her. There was a little flurry among the group at one gate, or at a fence, and then it ran on quickly and mysteriously to the next, and the next, down the street, so that the women peered slyly at first, murmuring among themselves, watching her approach, and then breaking into loud chatter when she had passed.

'That is she . . . That's she . . .'

'Got four months, mos', for immorality . . .'

'Come home again, hey? We don't want damn whores on this street.'

And the needle-sharp eyes followed her all the way, suspicious, angry and secretly happy, too, that there was another victim for the altars of their gossiping.

With the men it was different. They watched her come, some openly, some from under the rims of their lowered eyelids, watching her and smiling gently at the thought of her conquest. Who the hell cared if it had been a white boy? He had been lucky enough, hadn't he? A man didn't begrudge another that kind of victory, even if it had been across the line. A man was a man, and a girl a girl. She was still around, anyway, so maybe there was a chance for one of them.

They were amused at the stupid malice of the womenfolk, and they showed their defiance by saying, 'Hello, Myra. How you, Myra? Nice to see you again, Myra. How you keeping, Myra?' And they felt the stares of the women, too, and grinned at the girl to show that it was OK with them.

She smiled gently, hearing their voices, but kept her head up and her eyes forward. But she felt the bitterness inside her like a new part of her being. She had finished with crying, and crying had left the bitterness behind like the layer of salt found in a pan after the water had evaporated. So that even as she smiled there was a scornful twist to her mouth.

She was tall and brown and good-looking, with the fullness of lips, the width of cheekbone, the straight nose and firm chin, and the blue eyes that she had inherited from the intermarriage of her ancestors generations past. Her body was firm, a little hardened from hard work for four months, but still beautiful; the breasts full and wide at the bases, the belly flat, and the thighs and legs long and shapely.

She reached the house at last and climbed the steps onto the verandah. When she opened the front door, the smell of cooking came to her from the kitchen at the end of the passageway. The old smell of frying onions and oil.

She walked down the passage and there was the elderly woman, her mother, standing over the pots on the black iron stove, short and stout, with thinning hair tied in a knot at the back of her head.

Myra leaned against the jamb of the kitchen door, a small panic struggling suddenly inside her. But she fought it off and said, casually, 'Hello, Ma.'

Her mother looked round with a jerk, a big stirring spoon, poised over a saucepan, in the thick, scrubbed hand that shook a little. Myra looked into the decaying, middle-aged eyes and saw the surprise replaced slowly by hardness, the twist of the elderly mouth, the deep lines in the throat and neck, and the network of wrinkles.

'Oh. So you're back. Back with your shame and disgrace, hey?'

'I'm back, Ma,' Myra said.

'You brought disgrace on us,' her mother said harshly, the spoon waving in the girl's face. 'We all good and decent people, but you brought us shame.' The face crumbled suddenly and tears seeped out of the eyes. 'You brought us shame. You couldn't go and pick a boy of your own kind, but you had to go sleep with some white loafer. You brought us shame, after how I worked and slaved to bring you up. Nobody ever been to jail in our family, and you a girl too. It's enough to give an old woman a stroke, that's what it is.'

Myra gazed at her mother and pity edged its way forward at the sight of a work-heavy body, the ruined face, the tears, but something else thrust pity aside and she said steadily, 'It wasn't any disgrace, Ma. It's no disgrace to love a man, no matter what colour he is or where he comes from. He was nice and he wasn't what you call a white loafer. He would have married me if he could. He always said so.'

'What's the matter with your own kind of people? What's the matter with a nice coloured boy?' The quavering voice sobbed and hiccoughed and the girl felt a pang of revulsion.

'There's nothing wrong with coloured boys,' she said, more in irritation than anger. 'Nobody said there was anything wrong with coloured boys. I happened to fall for a white boy, that's all.'

'It's no better than being a whore,' the old woman sobbed. 'No better than that.'

'All right,' the girl said bitterly. 'I'm no better than a whore. All right. Leave it like that. I'm a whore and I brought you disgrace. Now then.'

'Don't you talk to your own ma like that!' The old woman began to shout angrily, waving the spoon about. 'You got a cheek to talk to your poor ma like that, after all I done for you. You haven't got respek, that's what. Got no respek for your betters. There's your sister, Adie, getting married soon. To a nice boy of her own land. Not like you. Getting married and a fine example you are for her. You. You. Yes, you.'

'I'm glad Adie's getting married,' Myra said with forced dryness. 'I hope to God her husband takes her away to go and live on their own.'

'You haven't got no respek, talking to your mother that way. Just shows what kind you are. Adie at least been supporting me while you been in that disgrace, in that jail for four months. And now you just come to bring bad luck into the house. You bad luck, that's what you are.'

Myra smiled a little scornfully and said, 'All right, I'm a whore and a disgrace and bad luck. All right, Ma. But don't worry. You won't starve with me around.'

'If you get a job,' the mother snapped. 'And if I was a boss, I wouldn't give no damn whore a job.'

'Oh, stop it, Ma. You'll make yourself sick.'

'Ja. And whose fault will that be?'

Myra looked at the hysterical old woman for a second and then turned away. She felt like crying, but she was determined not to. She'd had enough of crying. She left the old woman and turned into the room off the passageway.

It was still the same room, with the wardrobe against one wall and the dressing table between the two single beds where she and her sister, Ada, slept. She lay down on her bed in her clothes and stared at the ceiling.

Ada getting married. She was genuinely glad about that. She and Ada had always been very close. She thought, No Mixed Marriages Act and no Immorality Act and maybe I'd be getting married too, but you got four months in jail instead of a wedding. Poor old Tommy.

She began to wonder whether Tommy really had been serious about loving her. No, he must have been. He really had been. He had loved her, but it must have proved too much for him. But what did he have to go and do that for? If he had loved her that bad, he would have stuck it out, no matter what. Maybe Tommy just couldn't see any other way. So that night when the police had come in on them, he'd gone from the bedroom into the living room and to his desk, and before they knew anything about it he had the little automatic pistol out of the drawer and had shot himself.

So that was that. Poor Tommy. Maybe he thought it was a disgrace too. Maybe he thought that, in spite of all his love. But she didn't care any more.

She lay on the bed and tried not to think about it. She thought about Ada instead. She would like to give Ada a nice wedding present. She wouldn't go to the wedding ceremony, of course. She'd save the dear old family the embarrassment. But she'd have to give Ada a nice wedding present.

And then in the middle of her thoughts the front door banged, feet hurried along the passageway, and the door opened and there was Ada.

'Myra. Myra, ou pal. You're back.'

Her younger sister was there, flinging bag and jacket aside and hugging her. 'I heard those damn old hens up the street cackling about my sister and I just ran all the way.'

'Hello, Adie. Good to see you again. Give me a kiss. Yes, I think they'll be cackling a long time still.' She added bitterly, 'The old woman feels the same.'

'Don't you worry, bokkie. Hell, I'm glad you're back for the wedding.'

'How's the boyfriend?'

'OK.' Ada grinned at her sister. 'He doesn't give a damn. His family had things to say, of course. But I've got him like that.' She showed a fist, laughing. 'He'll listen to Adie, family or no family.'

'You got everything ready?'

'Oh, yes. The wedding dress will be ready the end of the week, on time for Saturday. I managed to save and bought some stuff for the house. Joe put in for one of those council cottages and they said we can move in.'

'I'll miss you.'

'Garn. You can mos' come and visit us anytime. Listen, if you like, I could talk to Joe about you coming to stay with us. What do you say?'

'No. You go off on your own and be happy. I'll stay on here. Me and Ma will maybe fight all the time, but I'll manage.'

'What you going to do, Myra?'

'Don't know,' Myra told her. 'The old lady will need looking after. Say, have you really got everything?'

'Oh, yes. Except maybe the frock to change into next Saturday night. I'll have to wear the wedding dress right through the whole business. I did see the damn nicest party frock at the Paris Fashions, but I suppose I'll have to do without a change on Saturday night. It's so lousy having to wear the wedding dress at the party too. Things and stuff might spill onto it. The bride ought to change for the evening celebrations. We're having a party at Joe's place. I thought it'd be grand to have a dress to change into, though. But I worked out every penny, so I won't be able to afford eight guineas. Such nice darn slipper satin too. Real smart.'

Ada got up from the edge of the bed and started removing her work clothes. 'Tell me, Myra, was it bad up there?'

'Not too bad. I did washing most of the time. But I don't want to talk about it, man.'

'We won't,' Ada smiled, struggling into black stovepipe jeans.

'That's all finished and done with. Now, you just take it easy and I'll call you when supper's ready. You like some tea?'

'Thanks.'

Ada grinned and ducked out of the room, leaving Myra alone again on the single bedstead. Dear old Ada, with a whore for a sister. The old woman would probably say it would be bad luck to have me coming visiting them. She felt sorry for her mother, for Ada, for all those women up the street, for Tommy. Poor old Tommy. Tommy couldn't stand up to it. Him and his love. Him and his 'I love you.' She had died too, she thought, the instant Tommy pulled the trigger. Poor old Tommy. She felt sorry for all of them.

She thought, Adie is going to be happy. She wanted Adie to be happy and she told herself that Adie would have that slipper-satin dress she wanted, as a present from her. She could earn eight guineas easily.

CONTRIBUTORS

Authors

Leila Aboulela (b. 1964)

Leila Aboulela is the author of four books: *Lyrics Alley*, which has been longlisted for the 2011 Orange Prize; *The Translator*, a novel published to critical acclaim in 1999 and longlisted for the Orange Prize and the International IMPAC Dublin Literary Award; *Minaret*, a novel longlisted for the 2006 Orange Prize; and a book of short stories, *Coloured Lights*, published in 2001, which contained her story 'The Museum', which made her the first winner of the Caine Prize for African Writing.

Chimamanda Ngozi Adichie (b. 1977)

Chimamanda Ngozi Adichie was born in Nigeria. She is the author of two novels, *Half of a Yellow Sun*, which won the 2007 Orange Prize and was a finalist for the National Book Critics Circle Award, and *Purple Hibiscus*, which won the Commonwealth Writers' Prize and the Hurston/Wright Legacy Award. She is the recipient of a 2008 MacArthur Foundation Fellowship. She was named one of the twenty most important fiction writers today under forty years old by the *New Yorker*.

Uwem Akpan (b. 1971)

Uwem Akpan was born in Ikot Akpan Eda in Nigeria. After attending Creighton and Gonzaga universities in the US and the Catholic University of Eastern Africa in Kenya, he was ordained a Catholic priest in 2003. He received his MFA from the University of Michigan (2004–6), and his first book, *Say You're One of Them* (Little, Brown), came out in 2008. Among other awards, it won the Commonwealth Writers' Prize and was Oprah's bookclub pick in 2009. Last year Uwem was a Tom and Mary Gallagher Fellow at the Black Mountain Institute of the University of Nevada, Las Vegas, and he is currently the Norman Freehling visiting professor at the University of Michigan.

Alaa Al Aswany (b. 1957)

Alaa Al Aswany originally trained as a dentist and still has his own practice in Cairo. He worked for many years in the Yacoubian Building, which lent its name to his bestselling novel. *The Yacoubian Building* was longlisted for the International IMPAC Dublin Literary Award in 2006, has sold over a million copies worldwide and was the bestselling novel in the Arab world for over five years. Alaa Al Aswany is also the author of *Chicago* (named by *Newsday* as the best translated novel of 2006), *Friendly Fire* and *On the State of Egypt*. His work has been translated into more than thirty languages and published in over a hundred countries. He speaks Arabic, English, French and Spanish. He was recently named by *The Times* as one of the best fifty authors to have been translated into English over the last fifty years.

Ungulani Ba Ka Khosa (b. 1957)

Ungulani Ba Ka Khosa is a Mozambican writer born in Inhaminga, Sofala Province. After university he worked as a school teacher and in the Ministry of Education. He was one of the founders of the magazine *Charrua* of the Mozambican Writers' Association (AEMO). In 2002 his first novel, *Ualalapi*, was announced by a panel of judges in Accra,

Ghana, as one of Africa's 100 best novels of the twentieth century. His books include *Orgia dos Loucos*, *Sobreviventes da Noite*, *Choriro* and *Histórias de Amor e Espanto*.

Doreen Baingana (b. 1966)

Doreen Baingana is a Ugandan writer and author of *Tropical Fish: Stories out of Entebbe*, which won an AWP (Association of Writers & Writing Programs) Prize for Short Fiction (2003) and a Commonwealth Prize for Debut Fiction, Africa Region (2005). She has also won the Washington Independent Writers Fiction Prize and been nominated twice for the Caine Prize for African Writing. She has also published two children's books: *Gamba the Gecko wants to Drum* and *My Fingers are Stuck*, and has a law degree from Makerere University and an MFA from the University of Maryland.

Brian Chikwava (b. 1972)

Brian Chikwava won the Caine Prize for African Writing in 2004 for his short story 'Seventh Street Alchemy'. He was born in Victoria Falls in 1972, but later moved to the UK in order to study engineering at the University of Bristol. In 2004 he was awarded a Charles Pick Fellowship in creative writing at the University of East Anglia. His first novel, *Harare North*, was published in 2009 to critical acclaim. He is also a singer-songwriter and has released a blues album entitled *Jacaranda Skits*.

Fatou Diome (b. 1968)

Fatou Diome is a Senegalese writer who now lives in France. She is the presenter of a cultural programme on the French television station FR3 and also teaches at the University of Strasbourg, where she previously studied. Fatou Diome is the author of two novels, *The Belly of the Atlantic* and *Ketala*, in which she explores the relationship between France and Africa. She has also written a collection of short stories entitled *La Préférence Nationale*.

Rachida el-Charni (b. 1967)

Rachida el-Charni was born in Tunis and studied law. She has published two collections of short stories in Arabic, *The Life* (1997) and *The Neighing of the Questions* (2000). Both collections won Arabic literary prizes in Tunis and Sharja. She has just finished her first novel. Rachida still lives in Tunis, where she works as an inspector of primary schools.

George Makana Clark (b. 1957)

George Makana Clark was raised in Rhodesia. He is the author of a novel, *The Raw Man* (Jonathan Cape), and a short-story collection, *The Small Bees' Honey* (White Pine Press). His work has appeared in the *Georgia Review, Glimmer Train*, the *Massachusetts Review, The O. Henry Prize Stories, Southern Review, Transition, Tin House, Witness, Zoetrope: All Story* and elsewhere. Clark was awarded a National Endowment of the Arts Fellowship and named a finalist for the Caine Prize for African Writing. He teaches fiction writing and African literature at the University of Wisconsin-Milwaukee.

Mansoura Ez-Eldin (b. 1976)

Mansoura Ez-Eldin is an Egyptian novelist and journalist. She was born in the Delta, Egypt. She studied journalism at Cairo University. She published her first collection of short stories, *Shaken Light*, in 2001. This was followed by two novels, *Maryam's Maze*, in 2004, and *Beyond Paradise*, in 2009. Her work has been translated into a number of languages, including an English translation of *Maryam's Maze* by the American University in Cairo (AUC) Press, which came out in 2007. In 2009 she was selected for the Beirut39, as one of the thirty-nine best Arab authors below the age of forty. Her second novel, *Beyond Paradise*, was shortlisted for the prestigious Arabic Booker Prize in 2010 and is being translated into Italian, German and Dutch. Ez-Eldin has worked for *Akhbar al-Adab* literary magazine since 1998 and became the book-review editor for the magazine in 2003.

Aminatta Forna (b. 1964)

Aminatta Forna's most recently published novel, *The Memory of Love*, won the Commonwealth Writers' Prize (Africa) and has been nominated for the Orange Prize. 'Haywards Heath' was shortlisted for the 2010 BBC Short Story Award. Aminatta has homes in south-east London and Rogbonko Village, Kholifa Rowallah, Sierra Leone.

Abdulrazak Gurnah (b. 1948)

Abdulrazak Gurnah was born in Zanzibar in 1948. He moved to Britain as a student in 1968 and now lives in Brighton. He is the author of seven novels, including *Memory of Departure* (1987), *Paradise* (1994), for which he was shortlisted for both the Booker Prize and the Whitbread Award, and *Desertion*, which was shortlisted for the 2006 Commonwealth Writers' Prize. Gurnah is also associate editor of the journal *Wasafiri* and teaches at the University of Kent.

Milly Jafta

Milly Jafta was born in Port Elizabeth, Republic of South Africa, in the mid-1950s. She wrote for her university and hostel magazines, and worked as a public servant before penning 'The Homecoming', her first published work. 'The Homecoming' has since been translated into German and Spanish. Jafta has also written a short film, *The Homecoming*, which told a different story. She has also published a poem, 'Unclosing Eyes', in the anthology *Different Horizons*, compiled by the Poetry Institute of Africa. Since its independence in 1990 she has been a citizen of the Republic of Namibia, where she lives and works in the capital, Windhoek.

Alex La Guma (1925–85)

Alex La Guma was born in Cape Town, South Africa. A decisive political figure in his home country, he led the South African Coloured People's Organisation (SACPO) and was the chief representative of the African National Congress. He is the author of several novels, including *A Walk in the Night* and *Fog of the Season's End*, and in 1969 he was awarded the Lotus Prize for Literature by the Afro-Asian Writers' Conference. He died in South Africa in 1985.

Laila Lalami (b. 1968)

Laila Lalami was born and raised in Morocco. She attended Université Mohammed-V in Rabat, University College London and the University of Southern California, where she earned a PhD in linguistics. Her work has appeared in the *Boston Globe*, the *Los Angeles Times*, the *Nation*, the *New York Times*, the *Washington Post* and elsewhere. She is the recipient of a British Council Fellowship and a Fulbright Fellowship. She was shortlisted for the Caine Prize for African Writing in 2006 and for the National Book Critics Circle Nona Balakian Award in 2009. She is the author of the short-story collection *Hope and Other Dangerous Pursuits* and the novel *Secret Son*. Her work has been translated into ten languages. She is currently associate professor of creative writing at the University of California at Riverside.

Camara Laye (1928–80)

Camara Laye was born in Guinea. In 1947 he won a scholarship to study in France, and his first novel, *L'Enfant noir* (*The Dark Child*), was published there in 1953. The novel received critical acclaim and he was awarded the Prix Charles Veillon. Camara Laye returned to Guinea on its independence in 1958 and held a series of prominent positions, including director of the Department of Economic Agreements at the Ministry of Foreign Affairs. He died in Senegal in 1980.

Alain Mabanckou (b. 1966)

Alain Mabanckou is a Franco-Congolese novelist and a professor at the University of California, Los Angeles. He is mostly known for his novels, notably *Verre cassé* (*Broken Glass*), which received rave reviews and has since been the subject of several theatrical adaptations. In

2006 he published *Memoires de porc-épic* (*Memoirs of a Porcupine*), which garnered him the prestigious Prix Renaudot. *Broken Glass* was published in English translation in 2009. His works are published in many languages, including English, Hebrew, Korean, Spanish, Catalan and Norwegian. His books translated into English are *African Psycho* (Serpent's Tail, UK, 2007), *Broken Glass* (Serpent's Tail, UK, 2009) and *Memoirs of a Porcupine* (Serpent's Tail, UK, 2011).

Dambudzo Marechera (1952–87)
Dambudzo Marechera was a Zimbabwean writer and poet, born in Rusape (Rhodesia) in 1952. His first book, *The House of Hunger* (1978), for which he was awarded the Guardian Fiction Prize in 1979, set a landmark in African writing through its avant-garde narrative structure and the shocking images with which it captured the situation of oppression and violence in the settler state. It was followed by the experimental novel *Black Sunlight* (1980) and *Mindblast* (1984), a compilation of plays, prose and poetry. After the writer's early death of Aids in Harare in 1987, the Dambudzo Marechera Trust was founded with the aim of securing Marechera's literary estate. Under the scholar Flora Veit-Wild the trust published several of Marechera's works, including *The Black Insider* (1990), the poetry collection *Cemetery of Mind* (1992) and *Scrapiron Blues* (1994) as well as Veit-Wild's *Dambudzo Marechera: a Source Book on His Life and Work* (1992).

Maaza Mengiste (b. 1970)
Maaza Mengiste was born in Addis Ababa, Ethiopia, and lives in New York City. A Fulbright scholar, she has also received fellowships from Yaddo, the Virginia Center for the Creative Arts and the Emily Harvey Foundation. Her debut novel, *Beneath the Lion's Gaze*, was published by W. W. Norton in 2010 and has been translated into several languages.

Patrice Nganang (b. 1970)

Patrice Nganang is a Cameroonian writer. He is an associate professor of cultural and literary theory at the State University of New York, Stony Brook. His first volume of poems, *Elobi*, appeared in 1995. His most acclaimed novel, *Temps de chien*, was awarded the Prix Marguerite Yourcenar (for Francophone writers living in the US) in 2001 and the Grand Prix Littéraire de l'Afrique Noire (the leading literary award for African Francophone writers) in 2002. This novel has been translated into German, Italian and Spanish, and has been released in English as *Dog Days* by the University of Virginia Press. His latest novel, *Mont Plaisant*, was published in 2011.

E. C. Osondu (b. 1966)

E. C. Osondu was born in Nigeria. His writing has appeared in the *Atlantic Monthly*, *Fiction*, *Vice* and the *New Statesman*, among other publications. He won the 2009 Caine Prize for African Writing and holds an MFA from Syracuse University. He currently teaches at Providence College in Rhode Island. His short-story collection *Voice of America* was published by Granta Books in 2011.

Henrietta Rose-Innes (b. 1971)

Henrietta Rose-Innes is a South African writer based in Cape Town. Her novel *Nineveh* was published by Umuzi (Random House Struik) in August 2011. She has also published a collection of short stories, *Homing* (2010), and two earlier novels, *Shark's Egg* and *The Rock Alphabet*. In 2008 she won the Caine Prize for African Writing, for which she was shortlisted the previous year, and in 2007 she received the South African PEN Literary Award. Her work has appeared in various publications, including *Granta*, *AGNI* and *The Best American Nonrequired Reading 2011*.

Manuel Rui (b. 1941)

Manuel Rui has written poetry, short stories, novels and plays. He was

born in Angola in 1941 and studied law at the University of Coimbra
in Portugal. His collections of short stories include *Regresso Adiado*
(*Delayed Return*, 1973) and *Sim, Camarada!* (*Yes, Comrade!*, 1977), and
his most recent novel, *O Manequim e o Piano* (*The Mannequin and the
Piano*) was published in 2005. Manuel Rui has been strongly involved
in Angola's cultural life; he is a founder member of the Angolan
Writers' Untion, the Union of Angolan Artists and Composers and
the Society of Angolan Authors.

Olufemi Terry (b. 1973)

Olufemi Terry has published fiction, poetry and non-fiction in several
publications, among them *Chimurenga* and *Guernica.* 'Stickfighting
Days' won the 2010 Caine Prize for African Writing. He lives in south-
west Germany and is at work on a novel.

Yvonne Vera (1964–2005)

Yvonne Vera was born in Bulawayo, Zimbabwe, and attended
university in Canada. She wrote her first book, a collection of short
stories, while finishing her Master's thesis at York University in
Toronto. *Why Don't you Carve Other Animals* (1992) was published in
Toronto. After her first novel, *Nehanda*, was published in Zimbabwe a
year later, she returned to her home country in 1995 where she wrote
her subsequent books. *Under the Tongue* (1996) won the Commonwealth
Prize for Africa. Her other titles were *Butterfly Burning* (1998) and *The
Stone Virgins* (2002). She won the Swedish literary award, The Voice
of Africa, in 1999, the Macmillan Writers' Prize for Africa in 2002,
and the Tucholsky Prize from PEN (Sweden) in 2004. She returned to
Toronto in 2004 and died there the following year.

Ivan Vladislavić (b. 1957)

Ivan Vladislavić is the author of the novels *The Folly*, *The Restless
Supermarket*, *The Exploded View* and *Double Negative*. The latter first
appeared in *TJ/Double Negative*, a joint project with the photographer

David Goldblatt. Vladislavić has written extensively about Johannesburg, where he lives. *Portrait with Keys* (2006) is a sequence of documentary texts about the city. He has edited volumes on architecture and art, and published a monograph on the conceptual artist Willem Boshoff. His early stories were republished in the compendium volume *Flashback Hotel* in 2010. His work has won many awards, including the Sunday Times Fiction Prize and the Alan Paton Award for Non-fiction.

Binyavanga Wainaina (b. 1971)
Binyavanga Wainaina is the founding editor of *Kwani?*, a leading African literary magazine based in Kenya. He won the 2002 Caine Prize for African Writing and has written for *Vanity Fair*, *Granta* and the *New York Times*. He is the author of the memoir *One Day I Will Write About This Place*, published by Granta Books. Wainaina directs the Chinua Achebe Center for African Writers and Artists at Bard College, New York.

Zoë Wicomb (b. 1948)
Zoë Wicomb is a South African writer born in the Cape Province, now Namaqualand. Her first book, *You Can't Get Lost in Cape Town*, a collection of short stories, was published in 1987 and gained her an international reputation. She has since written a number of novels and short stories, including *David's Story* and *Playing in the Light*. Her work has been translated into Dutch, Swedish, French, Italian and German. Zoë Wicomb now lives in Glasgow and is a professor in the Department of English Studies at the University of Strathclyde.

Translators

Piers Amodia
Piers Amodia translates from Arabic, Spanish and Italian into English. He spent eight years in the merchant navy before going to Edinburgh University to study Arabic. He lived briefly in Cairo teaching Italian

before moving to Rome where he works as a translator for the Vatican.

Raphael Cohen
Raphael Cohen is a translator from the UK based in Cairo. His translation of the Egyptian novel *So You May See*, by Mona Prince, was published in spring 2011 by AUC Press.

Humphrey Davies
Humphrey Davies has translated more than fifteen works of modern fiction and literary non-fiction from Arabic, including *The Yacoubian Building* by Alaa Al Aswany, *Sunset Oasis* by Bahaa Taher and *Life is More Beautiful than Paradise* by Khaled Al-Berry, as well as the seventeenth-century *Brains Confounded by the Ode of Abu Shaduf Expounded* by Yusuf al-Shirbini. Davies has twice received the Banipal Prize for Arabic Literary Translation, first in 2006 for *Gate of the Sun* by Elias Khoury, and then in 2010 for his translation of the same author's *Yalo*. His translation of Mourid Barghouti's *I Was Born There, I Was Born Here* (the sequel to *I Saw Ramallah*) and his re-translation of Naguib Mahfouz's classic *Midaq Alley* are forthcoming in 2011. His translation of Khoury's *As Though She Were Sleeping* will be published imminently. Davies lives in Cairo and is presently at work on a translation of *al-Saq 'ala al-Saq (Leg upon Leg)* (1855) by Faris al-Shidyaq, a seminal figure of the nineteenth-century Arab renaissance.

Polly McLean
Polly McLean is a freelance translator born in South Africa and based in Oxford. She won the 2010 Scott Moncrieff Prize for her translation of *Gross Margin* by Laurent Quintreau. Recent translations include Atiq Rahimi's Goncourt-winning *The Patience Stone* and *This Is Not the End of the Book* by Umberto Eco and Jean-Claude Carrière.

Ronald W. Sousa

Ronald W. Sousa translates from Portuguese into English. His translations include Clarice Lispector's *The Passion According to G. H.* (1988), Manuel Rui's *Yes, Comrade!* (1993) and *The Watch*, and a joint-translation of Lidia Jorge's *The Murmuring Coast*. He is the author of *The Rediscoverers: Major Writers in the Portuguese Literature of National Regeneration*. He has been a faculty member at the University of Texas at Austin, University of Minnesota Twin Cities – where he founded the Department of Cultural Studies and Comparative Literature – and University of Illinois Urbana-Champaign. He has held grants from, among other agencies, the National Endowment for the Humanities, the American Philosophical Society and the Fundação Calouste Gulbenkian.

Stefan Tobler

Stefan Tobler is a literary translator from Portuguese and German, and a Translators Association committee member. He also founded the new literary publisher And Other Stories, which is supported and guided by circles of readers, writers and translators.

PERMISSIONS

'Missing Out' from *Granta 111: Going Back* by Leila Aboulela. Copyright © Leila Aboulela, 2010. Reproduced by kind permission of the Gernert Company.

'The Arrangers of Marriage' excerpted from *The Thing Around Your Neck* by Chimamanda Ngozi Adichie. Copyright © Chimamanda Ngozi Adichie, 2009. Reproduced in the UK by kind permission of HarperCollins Publishers Ltd. Reproduced in the US by kind permission of the Wylie Agency. Reproduced in Canada by kind permission of Knopf Canada. Reproduced in other territories by kind permission of Kachifo Ltd. All rights reserved.

'An Ex-mas Feast' from *Say You're One of Them* by Uwem Akpan. Copyright © Uwem Akpan, 2008. First published in Great Britain in 2008 by Abacus. Reproduced by kind permission of Little, Brown Book Group Ltd.

'Mme Zitta Mendès, a Last Image' from *Friendly Fire* by Alaa Al Aswany. Copyright © Alaa Al Aswany, 2004, 2008, 2009. Originally published in Arabic in 2004 under the title *Niran sadiqa*. First published in English in 2009 by the American University in Cairo

draws on A. Lunacharski, 'Lenin and Art', in *International Literature*, No. 5, 1935. Copyright © Ivan Vladislavić, 1992. Reproduced by kind permission of the author and of Blake Friedmann Literary, TV and Film Agency Ltd.

'Ships in High Transit' by Binyavanga Wainaina. Copyright © Binyavanga Wainaina, 2006. Reproduced by kind permission of the Wylie Agency. All rights reserved.

'You Can't Get Lost in Cape Town' from *You Can't Get Lost in Cape Town* by Zoë Wicomb. Copyright © Zoë Wicomb, 1987. Reproduced in the US with kind permission of the Feminist Press, www.feministpress. org. Reproduced in all other territories with kind permission of the author and Umuzi. All rights reserved.